LATINO RISING

AN ANTHOLOGY OF LATIN@ SCIENCE FICTION AND FANTASY

"El Muerto: Los Cosmos Azteca"
by Javier Hernandez

LATIN@ RISING

AN ANTHOLOGY OF LATIN@ SCIENCE FICTION AND FANTASY

EDITED BY

MATTHEW DAVID GOODWIN

WingsPress

San Antonio, Texas
2017

Latin@ Rising: An Anthology of Latin@ Science Fiction and Fantasy
© 2017 by Wings Press
All rights revert to the individual editors, authors, and artists.

Cover image: "Luz nocturna" © 2016 by Liliana Wilson.
Used by permission of the artist.

Frontispiece: "El Muerto: Los Cosmos Azteca" © 2016 by Javier Hernandez.
Used by permission of the artist.

ISBN: 978-1-60940-524-3 (Paperback original)

E-books:
ePub: 978-1-60940-525-0
Mobipocket/Kindle: 978-1-60940-526-7
Library PDF: 978-1-60940-527-4

Wings Press
627 E. Guenther
San Antonio, Texas 78210
Phone/fax: (210) 271-7805
On-line catalogue and ordering:
www.wingspress.com

Wings Press books are distributed to the trade by
Independent Publishers Group
www.ipgbook.com

Library of Congress Cataloging-in-Publication:

Names: Goodwin, Matthew David, editor.
Title: Latin@ rising : an anthology of Latin@ science fiction and fantasy /
  edited by Matthew David Goodwin.
Other titles: Latina rising | Latino rising
Description: San Antonio, Texas : Wings Press, 2016. | Includes
  bibliographical references.
Identifiers: LCCN 2016027239| ISBN 9781609405243 (pbk. : alk. paper) | ISBN
  9781609405267 (kindle/mobipocket ebook) | ISBN 9781609405250 (epub
ebook) | ISBN 9781609405274 (library pdf)
Subjects: LCSH: American literature--Hispanic American authors. | Science
  fiction, American. | Fantasy literature, American. | Hispanic American
  literature (Spanish)--Translations into English.
Classification: LCC PS508.H57 L36 2017 | DDC 810.8/01508968073--dc23
LC record available at https://lccn.loc.gov/2016027239

CONTENTS

✳

To Nahir, always.

Nahir and I dedicate this book to our daughter, Violet Mariluz,
who will be the one living in the futures imagined here.

FOREWORD

Matthew David Goodwin

Latin@ Rising is a collection of science fiction and fantasy stories written by U.S. Latinos and Latinas. While there have been numerous anthologies of Latin@ Literature, this one focuses specifically on the confluence of science fiction and fantasy. The collection works like an eclectic mixed tape (playlist) in which there is an ebb and flow as you move through the loud and brash, the quiet and thoughtful. The book contains writers you may recognize such as Daína Chaviano and Ana Castillo, and it contains authors who are relatively new on the scene such as Alejandra Sanchez and Richie Narvaez. There are comforting and familiar stories, strange tales that will disturb your dreams, and then of course, las sorpresas.

Like any good mixed tape, this anthology expresses the flavor of a cultural moment. There is a growing movement of scholars and fans who are recovering the history of Latin@ science fiction and fantasy, and promoting the many contemporary writers and artists who have turned to these genres. It is the bubbling up of curiosity about Latin@ science fiction and fantasy which we hope to uncork with this anthology. This energy is present in the fiction as well, and the stories that bookend the collection express this energy. Even when there is a rushing sense of urgency as in Kathleen Alcalá's "The Road to Nyer," and even when a techno-future comes crashing in as in "Traditions" by Marcos Santiago Gonsalez, the deep call of the past resounds. *Latin@ Rising* taps into this back-and-forth from the past to the future, and hopes to express the enthusiastic energy particular to the growth of the Latin@ community in the United States.

But why join science fiction and fantasy together? Beyond the simple fact that many readers of fantasy also like to read science fiction, and vice versa, the two genres are classically difficult to firmly pry apart and are often umbrelled under categories such as speculative fiction or imaginative literature. In that shared space, they move beyond the constraints of realist narrative, are generally judged by their capacity to imagine new worlds, and they often invite allegorical readings. As a rule of thumb, science fiction narratives remain tied to the laws of natural science while fantasy stories depict supernatural, magical, and unexplained events (Frederick Luis Aldama will be discussing further the signfiance of science fiction in his introduction). But in truth these two major genres have been in dialogue for quite a while, and like many of the stories included in this anthology, very often one story will draw on both traditions. In E.T.A. Hoffmann's 19th century short story "The Sandman," for example, it is exactly the confrontation between the fantastical and scientific explanations of strange events which move the narrative to its ultimate tragic ending. It is useful to think about the science fiction and fantasy traditions as distinct entities, but it is just as important to bring this rowdy family together.

The shadow of magical realism haunts any discussion of Latin@ science fiction and fantasy. This state of affairs rises from the popularity of Latin American magical realist works such as Gabriel García Márquez's *One Hundred Years of Solitude,* which first appeared in English in 1970. For better or worse, magical realism (in which fantastical elements are included in the narrative in such a way that they seem unsurprising) then formed the boundaries of Latin@ literature for the general reading public. My experience is that too many writers have been pushed (by academics, publishers, or financial reasons) to write in a magical realist style even though it was not exactly what they wanted to write. In addition, it has been common among readers to unthinkingly categorize a story written by a Latin@ as magical realist when there is just a hint of something strange or even when the story is flat out science fiction or fantasy. At its worst, this imposed magical realism is a way to relegate U.S. Latinos and Latinas to the realm of the irrational, the mythological, effectively cutting off the ability to engage science and technology. One or two of the stories in this anthology could be categorized as magical realist; however, the point is not that there is a problem with magical realism as such, since it is a wonderfully rich genre with great political potential, but that magical realist stories should be joined to their brothers and sisters of fantasy and science fiction.

In his essay "Racism and Science Fiction," Samuel R. Delany warns against the use of narrow categories like "African-American science fiction." The separateness which such categories enact is congruent with the separateness of racism, as he puts it clearly "... what racism as a system does is isolate and segregate the people of one race, or group, or ethnos from another" (393). This idea of Delany's is essential and it is not something that we should get away from or erase. Diversity very quickly can become multicultural segregation and Delany's idea should stand as a reminder. What we hope to do in this anthology is to counter the separateness of Latin@ science fiction and fantasy by presenting a thrilling multiplicity of writers and stories, and by demonstrating that these writers have been part of the genres all along. We hope to demonstrate the actual breadth of genres being used by Latin@ authors and so show that Latin@ literature is, and has been, wider than previously thought.

By way of Delany's warning, the authors included in this anthology come from a wide range of backgrounds, including Latin@ authors from both coasts and from eight different national traditions. Some of the writers have substantial connections to Latin America and the Caribbean and write primarily in Spanish, others were born and raised in the United States and write only in English. All of them are comfortable in multiple worlds. The literary backgrounds of the authors display the interweaving lines of the publishing worlds, some connected primarily to the category of Latin@ literature, others to science fiction or fantasy. In these ways, our assembly of authors mirrors the complexity of twenty-first century Latin@ communities.

Though the anthology uses the term "Latin@," this anthology is comprised of authors based in the United States, not Latin America. Fortunately, a number of anthologies of Latin American science fiction and fantasy in translation are now available: *Cosmos Latinos* and

Three Messages and a Warning are two examples. There is, nevertheless, something unique about the experience of those of Latin American origin, recent or distant, who are living in the United States such that a distinct anthology is merited. And while there is not one kind of U.S. Latin@ experience, there are historically some overlapping themes, such as migration, colonialism, conflict between Latin@ and Anglo groups, code-switching between Spanish and English, and an indigenous political heritage much different from indigenous groups in the United States. The way these concerns are expressed differs from story to story. In Alex Hernandez's "Caridad," which is centered on the second generation immigrant experience, American individuality is pitted against the collective Latin@ family, while in Ernest Hogan's "Flying under the Radar with Paco and Los Freetails" it is the Chicano individual who stands outside the trap of American imperialism. In Sabrina Vourvoulias' "Sin Embargo," the number of cultures in dialogue expands out into a multi-ethnic and very lively mix. The concerns may be similar, but these stories ultimately show that the configurations of what "Latin@" means is multiple, and ever growing.

Latin@ Rising certainly expresses some of my personal taste in its selection, in particular the number of works that deal with the experience of migration and dislocation. It is a topic I am personally interested in and it directs my creative endeavors. Science fiction and fantasy are uniquely able to deal with the experiences of migration in that they are generally dependent on the existence of at least two worlds, and it is migration that puts these worlds in contact. Science fiction theorist Darko Suvin observes that it is "a *voyage* to a new locus" that creates the novum (the new element) of a science fiction story (71). And while the relationship between migration and the genres is important in understanding what is going on in Latin@ science fiction and fantasy, readers will find a host of themes in this anthology. A number of the stories are politically oriented while some would be better described as psychological tales. Some focus on community-specific issues while some have nothing that could be identified as specifically Latin@. All are excellent stories that maintain the wonder and astonishment that only science fiction and fantasy can offer. Punto.

Works Cited

Delany, Samuel R. "Racism and Science Fiction." *Dark Matter: a century of speculative fiction from the African diaspora.* Ed. Sheree R. Thomas (New York: Warner Books, 2000), pp. 383-397.

Suvin, Darko. *Metamorphosis of Science Fiction* (Yale University Press, 1979).

Note: We have retained individual author's paragraph styles rather than imposing strict stylistic conformity.

INTRODUCTION

Confessions from a Latin@ Sojourner in *SciFilandia*

Frederick Luis Aldama

I have a confession to make. Science fiction in comic books, TV, and film got me into world literature — and not mainstays of a school curricula with its Austens, Twains, and Fitzgeralds. As a teen I did feast on these authors and others such as Borges, Cortázar, García Márquez, Rushdie, but only after I'd discovered the SciFi storyworlds of *Flash Gordon, Buck Rogers, Superman ... The Fantastic Four*, only after I'd put myself on a strict and steady diet of Mary Shelley, Jules Verne, Stanislaw Lem, Aldous Huxley, George Orwell, William Gibson, Frank Herbert, Ursula LeGuin, and Edwin Abbott, among others. And, while I became a big fan as a young man of Italian neo-realist and French New Wave cinema (enamored especially with Jean-Luc Godard's metafictional SciFi *Alphaville*) as well as alternative flicks from the Americas, it was films like *The Day the Earth Stood Still, Star Wars, Blade Runner,* and *Donnie Darko* that had the biggest influence on my choice of career: to teach, study, and write about narrative fiction in all its worldly guises.

Of course, with the veneer of seriousness that envelopes the academy and that generally considers SciFi lowbrow, it takes some *huevos* to admit that this was instrumental in my coming of age as a professor. While I was living the cultural studies revolution, with few exceptions like Octavia Butler and Samuel R. Delany, SciFi remained hidden within scholarly shadows. It continues to be the case today.

Yet, isn't it here that we see some of the most incredible storytelling innovation taking place? This is certainly the case with cultural phenomena created by and about Latinos and Latinas — the area of study that has kept me busy for the last couple of decades. I think of comic book author/artists, Los Bros Hernandez, whose first parachute drop into the comic book scene was with *Love & Rockets* — a series that intermixed UFOs and flying Latina superheroes with Latin American melodramas and civil uprisings. I think of what they were able to achieve in their SciFi infusion and remastering of Dean Motter's and Paul Rivoche's otherwise tellurian *Mister X*. I think of their use of the SciFi conceit in the making of their futuristic thriller, *Citizen Rex*, and its center-staging of civil rights struggles. I think of Jaime Hernandez's *God and Science: Return of the Ti-Girls* that takes us into uncharted physical, social, and behavioral spaces with the creation of superhero Latinas like Maggie, Angel, Alarma, and Xochitl. I think of Frank Espinosa's German Expressionist, Japanese fine-art inspired *Rocketo* that's set 2,000 years into the future where only Mappers exist with a memory of place to navigate a planet filled with Dogmen, Fishmen, and other hybrid ontologies. I think of Alex Rivera's film *Sleep Dealer* that immerses viewers within a U.S./Mexico borderland filled with Coyotecs and high-tech neural implants (or nodes) that allow for global capitalist exploitation of the Latin@ population as virtual *braceros* working as nannies, high-rise welders, and the like — till they die from cognitive and physical overloads. I think of other cinematic visionaries such as Robert Rodriguez (*Planet Terror*) and Guillermo del Toro (*Pacific Rim*) that create SciFi storyworlds to present rich and complex multiracial subjectivities. I think even of TV shows like *The Event* that features an Afrolatino President. I think of the reboot of *Battlestar Galactica* that stars Chicano actor Edward James Olmos as William Adama — leader and savior of the Capricans, progenitors of humankind.

Of course, storytelling innovation in Latin@ SciFi takes place also in those good old fashioned formats: the novels and short story. In addition to those wonderfully varied and rich short stories collected in *Latin@ Rising*, I think of novels such as *Rescue from Planet Pleasure* (Mario Acevedo), (*Cortez on Jupiter, High Aztech, Smoking Mirror Blues* (Ernest Hogan), *Ink* (Sabrina Vourvoulias), *Signal to Noise* (Silvia Moreno-García), *The Closet of Discarded Dreams* (Rudy Ch. Garcia), *The Hunted* (Matt de la Peña), *The Dinosaur Lords*

(Victor Milán), *Shadowshaper* (Daniel José Older), *The Smoking Mirror* (David Bowles), and *Atomik Aztex* (Sesshu Foster). All of these Latin@ inflected time-spacescapes open readers' senses, thoughts, and feelings, to new ways of being in the world.

Certainly, and my brief summary of my journey through *SciFi-landia* already makes this abundantly clear, this storytelling mode has been and continues to be considered unworthy of our study and teaching. Even though we have a Popular Cultural Studies minor at Ohio State University, when SciFi is taught, it's on the books as a special topics course. And, if graduate students were inclined to write on SciFi alone, faculty would likely encourage the student to mix up his or her dissertation with other storytelling modes — for job placement marketability. This doesn't mean, of course, that we should stop studying and trying to understand how SciFi narrative fiction is built and consumed. It's an object out there that we create and consume abundantly. It demands our scholarly attention.

With this in mind I ask: What *is* SciFi — Latin@ or otherwise? After all, isn't narrative fiction generally a carefully crafted and willful realization of our counterfactual capacity to create storyworlds that potentially open us to experiential newness?

I'm not the only one asking such questions. Indeed, much ink has been spilled trying to get at how SciFi narrative fiction is built — and usually how science and scientific knowledge (in varying degrees of hard and soft reference to science) inform how its storyworlds are built differently from, say, straightforward realism. For Darko Suvin, it is a "literature of cognitive estrangement" (*Metamorphosis of Science Fiction* 4) that jolts readers into action for social change. For Gerry Canavan and Priscilla Wald, it is the *what if?* question that characterizes SciFi and allows readers to *think* about our future and about Otherness and difference. It is, as they remark, the making of "a funhouse mirror on the present, a faded map of the future, a barely glimpsed vision of alterity, and the prepped and ready launchpad for theory today" (247).

Perhaps, however, it's all much more straightforward. Like all aesthetic artifacts, SciFi narrative fiction is the distillation then *recreation* of a chosen slice of reality to *make new* our perception, thought, and feeling. It is the making of a blueprint inclusive of mention of "scientific knowledge" (in bold scare quotes) that aims to create a new relational experience between the subject (reader/viewer) and object (novel, comic book, film). When Hal goes crazy in *2001,* all along the story we have a series of explanations given to the audience as to what is going on. We're given a "scientific explanation" all along. This differs from, say, Cortázar's short story "Axolotl," where the human protagonist transmogrifies into an Axolotl without scientific explanation. The interpenetration of different ontologies simply happens. In each case the pact established with the viewer and reader is very different. SciFi is all about how creators create relations (or pacts) with their readers through a "scientific" explanation.

I might add, that no matter how purposefully the SciFi author (Latin@ or otherwise) seeks to contradict his or her reader's expectations, they generally don't seek to override the legality of the universe; the laws that govern the physical and social universe as we know it today. Even in some of the most creatively envisioned fictions like Lem's *Solaris* with its sentient planet and *Flatland* with its 2D universe, there are referents to a law-like universe with its furnishings.

Within the constraints outlined above whereby an author chooses certain conceits to establish a pact with the reader, there is total freedom. Authors like Ernest Hogan, Sabrina Vourvoulias, Frank Espinosa, Los Bros Hernandez, and all those collected in this volume, do indicate — *reference* — the universe, its laws, and its furnishings, but within this they also imagine new technologies, objects, and ontologies. That is, within the indexical constraints that allow us readers to recognize inanimate things and living entities, anything can and does *go.*

✳

Creators of narrative fictions with a so-called scientific explanation (hard or soft) distill from, then reconstruct the building blocks of reality. Today, and yesterday, these building blocks of reality in the US have been increasingly made up of Latinos and Latinas. Today, as the majority minority in this country (and in many states the majority), our existence, actions, and products are undeniably visible. Yet, we're still oddly absent from mainstream SciFi narrative fictions. It doesn't help matters either that we are egregiously absent from SciFi scholarly histories, including most glaringly Brian Stableford's *The A to Z of Science Fiction Literature*. (Scholars like Christopher González, Catherine Ramírez, and Andrea L. Bell and Yolanda Molina-Gavilán are working to set the record straight here.) *Latin@ Rising* shows the world something different. That we are capable of creating (and consuming) storyworlds whereby we are the subjects of scientifically explained future-set worlds.

As seen with the great abundance of stories in this volume, Latin@ authors can and do imagine storyworlds that at once call attention to the past (colonial histories) and look forward to a future where there exist relations of equality between Latin@s and others—and where empathy and solidarity are the rule everywhere. They move beyond those SciFi stories created by non-Latin@s who often seem boxed in by capitalist modes of thinking. The white savior, Manifest Destiny mythos of James Cameron's *Avatar* is a case in point. Authors included here such as Kathleen Alcalá, Ana Castillo, Junot Díaz, Carlos Hernandez, Ernest Hogan, Adál Maldonado, Carmen Maria Machado, Daniel José Older, Edmundo Paz-Soldán, and Sabrina Vourvoulias, among others, throw us into the middle of hot zone apocalyptic plagues, shapeshifting robots, intergalactic skinwalkers, pre-Columbian holobooks, cyberpunkistas, banderos for hire, Crypto-Jews, transatlantic Latin@s, hybrid invertebrate/human mestizos, chino-cubano and Nipo-peruanos border crossers, Mars inhabiting Jewish Tejanos, Latina cyborgs born of recycled parts, and cybernetically-wired patron saints. They open our eyes, thoughts, and feelings to issues of colonialism, migration, racism, and totalitarian regimes. They offer alternative social structures that allow for the full realization of our potentialities.

To return where I began, I am a Latin@ whose intellectual journey was born from my encounter with SciFi. And if Latin@s are the future of this country, I dare end by saying that science fiction *is me*.

Works Cited

González, Christopher. "Intertextploitation and Post Post-Latinidad in *Planet Terror*". In *Critical Approaches to the Films of Robert Rodriguez*. Ed. Frederick Luis Aldama (Austin: University of Texas Press, 2015).

—. "Latino Sci-Fi: Cognition and Narrative Design in Alex Rivera's *Sleep Dealer*". In *Latinos and Narrative Media: Participation and Portrayal*. Ed. Frederick Luis Aldama (New York: Palgrave Macmillan, 2013).

Bell, Andrea L. and Yolanda Molina-Gavilán. Eds. *Cosmos Latinos: An Anthology of Science Fiction from Latin America and Spain* (Wesleyan University Press, 2003).

Suvin, Darko. *Metamorphosis of Science Fiction* (Yale University Press, 1979).

Canavan, Gerry and Priscilla Wald. "Preface," in *American Literature,* Vol. 83, no. 2 (June 2011).

LATIN@ RISING

THE ROAD TO NYER

(after Isak Dinesen's "The Roads Round Pisa")

Kathleen Alcalá

In a review of Alcalá's remarkable collection of short stories, *Mrs. Vargas and the Dead Naturalist* (1992), Ursula K. LeGuin points to the originality of Alcalá's vision: "The kingdom of Borges and García Marquez lie just over the horizon, but this landscape of desert towns and dreaming hearts ... is Alcalá-land. It lies just across the border between Mexico and California, across the border between the living and the dead, across all the borders — a true new world." Alcalá has a BA in Linguistics from Stanford, a MA in Creative Writing from the University of Washington, and a MFA from the University of New Orleans. She is the author of a trilogy of historical novels and a collection of essays, *The Desert Remembers My Name: On Family and Writing* (2007). A past alumnus and instructor at the Clarion West Science Fiction Workshop, her stories have appeared in magazines such as *Isaac Asimov's Magazine of Fantasy and Science Fiction* and in numerous anthologies including *Like Water for Quarks* (2011). Her forthcoming work of nonfiction is titled *The Deepest Roots: Finding Food and Community on a Pacific Northwest Island*. Although her writing very often hearkens back to 19th Century Mexico, in "The Road to Nyer," the narrator visits Catalonia and gains a new understanding of the ancient roots of her family heritage.

The road to Nyer hairpinned back on itself just past the turnoff, our first clue we were coming from the wrong direction. Otherwise, the approach was swathed in greenery, vigorous ferns punctuated by palm trees. Beyond the road sign indicating a town in two kilometers, it was impossible to deduce what lay ahead. An easy place to waylay travelers. Perfect country for bandits, I thought, the supposed occupation of my ancestors. Drop a rough log across a narrow road flanked by steep cliffs, and your victim, perhaps in a carriage, perhaps pulling a handcart, has nowhere to go but straight into your arms.

The road curved west and then swung south, now in the lee of houses clinging to the cliff above it. All at once the village lay before us, topped by a picture book castle at its highest point.

We parked and got out of the car. It was very quiet. All we could hear was the rushing water of an unseen river below. Perhaps the town was deserted, its use as a fortress having outlived its practicality. Yet everywhere was evidence of habitation, from live potted plants in the windows, to freshly patched and painted walls. The hand-painted portrait of a man in a cap grinned out at us from a small stained glass window that was bricked up from the back. Community water ran into a carefully maintained cistern.

A boy of around ten sat on the curb, as though waiting for someone, but he scampered off when we drew close. I doubt we could have talked to him anyway, this far north of Barcelona and any dialects I might venture into.

We trudged up a steep path to the castle, which appeared to have no entrance, and circled left around the base of the tower. Up close, we could see that the wall had been patched and re-patched numerous times over the centuries, brick replaced by stone and filled in with plaster. I ran my hand along the rough surface, wondering how many assaults it had withstood, or if this was a replica built to mimic a "real" castle. It certainly looked authentic — there was no gift shop at ground level, welcoming tourists across a faux drawbridge for a Disneyfied tour of the past. There was no Princess Room, although I could certainly use one after three hours in the car.

As we entered an alley skirting the east side of the turret, we could look up to a balcony far above. Standing back to examine the decoration, I could see a crest depicted in relief. It consisted of a rooster facing left above an oak tree, next to a pair of crossed quills. Oh joy! I thought. I've come to my vocation as a writer honestly. But who uses a pen on their shield? Is the pen really mightier than the sword? Above the shield itself hovered a crown, evidence of their protection by or allegiance to someone or another.

As we rounded another corner, a burst of noise erupted from a doorway just in front of us. This was followed by silence. Curious, we approached the modern glass door, incongruous with the rest of the building. Inside, we could see people moving about, but when we drew close, all was quiet again. The door was locked.

We retreated, confused. Cars began to arrive, and people began to enter the same doorway. Each time the door opened, a torrent of noise poured out. I walked up to the door, hoping to discern a friendly face. But the people going in looked neither interested nor menacing, as though we really did not exist. It is the survival instinct of those who live in small towns, I thought. No reason to cozy up to strangers.

Finally, I screwed up my resolve and approached the door for the third time. After all, I would probably never visit this place again. Let them throw me out. This time, I noticed a second glass door, and as I stared through it at the people milling about inside, a very small man leaning on two canes saw me and struggled with the unwieldy door to let me in.

I caught the door and entered. Inside was a place neither here nor there, not ancient, but not new, with stone floors and a stairway that curved up into the tower and out of sight. The man said something I could not understand.

I tried to say, "I'm here to see the castle. I am a Nyer" in my poor French. He looked confused. "Just a minute, let me get my husband." Sometimes men were more comfortable talking to him, although he could not speak any of the local languages. This usually led to an interesting game of charades: I spoke to the locals, they looked at my husband and spoke to him, he shrugged, and I answered. Repeat.

The man balanced precariously on his canes looked at me with incomprehension. He looked very old, and was wearing a beret. "Qu'est-ce que signifie mari?" he asked someone behind me.

I turned to see a girl in a patched grey dress carrying armloads of food from the kitchen to a commotion of people who filled a dining area I had not noticed before.

I said the same thing in Spanish, and she recoiled as though I had said something obscene. Right. Best stick to French.

A woman in a red dress came out, regarded me, then shrugged and pointed up the stairs. She knew what I wanted. She said something to an elderly woman cradling her purse as though it was her last possession on earth. The second woman started up the huge stairway, pausing to see if I would follow.

I looked outside for my mari, but he had wandered away.

What the heck, I thought. How often do I get to visit the family castle? Up I went.

The second floor (or the first, in Europe, since the ground floor does not count) was a long way up. As the spiral staircase finished its first turn, I could hear a clattering sound below. Lawn mowers? Serving platters? As we reached the second landing, rather than growing fainter, the noise from below grew louder. I could hear shouting now, and pounding feet. Maybe a spontaneous soccer game had broken out. The old woman redoubled her efforts and picked up the pace. She was pretty spry for her age, I thought, working to keep up.

As we reached the last floor, she turned left and, clutching her bundle against her chest, broke into a run. I did, too, but found that I had to lift my skirts to do so. Skirts? She, too, wore a long skirt, something I had not noticed before. When we came to an open doorway, she motioned for me to go inside. But she was clearly going somewhere else. I wasn't about to be left behind with that mob behind us.

"Nyer?" she said.

"Oui," I answered. "Je suis de la famille Nyer." I had decided by now that they were speaking some form of Languedoc, a close cousin to Catalan. My poor French would have to do. Again, she motioned for me to go inside, but I would have none of it. We ran around to the other side, and popped through double doors onto the balcony I had seen from below. The woman was now carrying a wriggling infant dressed in ribbons and velvet. I looked from it to her face in amazement, and saw that she was not so old after all, her hair pulled back from a youthful face into a white lace cap. She crouched down on the balcony. I pulled back my veils (veils?) and tried to peer over the balustrade. Something thonked against the wall above our heads and clattered to the floor between us. An arrow. Crouching behind the railing, I decided, was just fine. Most of the action seemed to be indoors anyway, and soon, the terrifying noise, people shouting, the clashing of metal on metal, was very near. My elbow bumped something hard at my waist, and I pulled a large, squarish knife out of its casing. Good for beating a weft or ... It would have to do.

A deafening explosion came from below, and fragments of masonry rained down on us. Pity, I thought. There goes that lovely crest. The baby, which had been fussing slightly, was now screaming. The woman spoke urgently to me now, in a panicked voice, but I still could not understand her.

The small man who had let me in now burst onto the balcony, dressed in yellow hose and a doublet striped in the bright red and yellow of the Catalan flag. With his bowed legs now exposed and a velvet cap on his large head, I could see that he was a dwarf. A twin, dressed identically, followed close behind.

In a crouch, I was level with the little men. The first looked at me, his eyes widening in recognition and his face turning red. His eyes focused on my throat, and reflexively, I covered it with my hand. My fingers touched an elaborate necklace I had been unaware of until that moment. Looking down, I could see the prominent diamond at its center. He shook one of his canes in my face. "Nyer!" the man bayed loudly. He turned so his voice would carry down the stairwell. "Nyer-r-r-r!"

I understood that.

"Why, you little traitor!" I yelled, kicking his other cane out. We skirmished briefly, cane to weftbeater, before I bolted past, sending both men tumbling. I could hear fighting on the stairs, women screaming. I caught a glimpse of a man in a long cape and a swoopy hat. He gave me an appraising look, then must have realized I did not pose a threat.

He didn't look very friendly. Serrallonga? He was supposed to be on our side. I ran the other way. Were we fighting for the Banyuls or the Hapsburgs? I forgot. Where was that room she kept trying to push me to into? Maybe I could barricade myself in. I pulled out the weftbeater and made a dash for it.

Skidding inside, I swung the heavy wooden door closed and threw the bolt, sliding the sword in on top to reinforce it. The room was still and bathed in half-light from small, high windows. The noise outside seemed far away. As my eyes adjusted to the light, I noticed with a start that a man and woman sat quietly behind a wooden table, facing the doorway. Dressed in medieval finery, they, too, like the little boy we had first spotted outside, appeared to be waiting for something, or someone, who had not yet arrived.

I introduced myself in some dreadful mixture of Spanish and French, and clasped each of their hands. The woman motioned to the wall on the far side of them, where a massive fireplace dominated the room. It too, looked original, but how could the carved wooden surround of a fireplace survive for seven hundred years? Things burned down a lot in the old days. I stepped closer to examine it.

The shield of Catalan, familiar now from our travels in northern Spain, was carved and painted prominently above the mantle. It consists of four red stripes on a field of yellow, from the once yellow flag that the Catalan national martyr, Count Guifré el Pilóss, stained with his bloody fingerprints in a dying attempt to raise the banner. Or so they say. It was flanked on either side by depictions of knightly armor. Over a bricked-up doorway to the right was painted more of the same — not the portrait of a knight, but a fresco of empty armor.

Finally I understood: The Nyers were not bandidos, but banderos. They were mercenaries — guns for hire. Or at least harquebusiers. You paid your money and they took their chances on your behalf. Their nemesis, the Cadells, were the same — available to whichever royalty had the money to hire them. Usually, the Nyerros and Cadells fought against each other, but sometimes they were on the same side, carving out the borders between Catalan and the Pyrénées-Orientales department of France, one stone fortification at a time. After all these years, there were no portraits of individuals — they were who you needed them to be. My ancestors must have used up the last of their luck before embarking for the Americas to start anew.

This would explain all the coats of arms I had seen over the years, from four six-pointed stars on a field of blue surrounding the castle, to the cock and the quills on the outside of the tower. The Nyers — or Narros, or Nyerros — were shape-shifters, evaders, Crypto-Jews, according to family legend. Once we lost the keys to our houses in Barcelona during The Plague, or the Inquisition or whatever other excuse was given for taking our properties, all the world was our temporary habitation. We saw each place through the eyes of the stranger seeking that pocket of refuge where we could set up shop until the next disaster turned people against us.

There were no relations left here, I realized, only ghosts. Like Serrallonga, my ancestors had vanished into the mists, only to appear a few years later in a different time and place. In 1348, the Jews were first ejected from Barcelona; ten years later, the castle at Nyer was completed. On September 27, 1791, Napoleon granted full citizenship to the Jewish inhabitants of France. Shortly after that, my ancestors showed up in Saltillo, Mexico, probably bearing papers that did not betray their open secret — that they had come to join an existing community of Jews and start yet again.

Outside, all had fallen quiet. I opened the door and listened for a moment. Then I ventured gingerly down the stairs, no longer tripping over a long skirt. Too bad I hadn't paid more attention to what the dress had looked like. I touched my throat, only to find it bare.

In the vestibule, the woman in red smiled slyly, as if we now shared a secret. She handed me a calling card with a picture of the castle on it, but nothing more.

Outside, the two small men struggled with their canes to climb into an equally diminutive, bright yellow car. I tried not to stare.

The woman who had led me up the stairs came running after me. "Will you drive me to Olette?" she asked.

That seemed like a reasonable request. Oddly I was starting to understand people. Olette was the next town, just on the other side of the highway. I looked hard at the bundle in her hands. It was definitely a purse.

When I pointed to where our car was parked, she hesitated and looked back over her shoulder. Maybe she did not want to walk that far. I stood and waited. After a few minutes, the woman in red ran out and took the woman by the arm. "She always tries to leave," she said, "but she belongs here."

"But I am not dead," the woman wailed as they turned to go inside, "I am not dead!" The woman in red smiled apologetically.

The whole town was quiet again. The other cars had vanished as mysteriously as they arrived, and no one was on the street, either by the castle, or on the road out of town. The man in the stained glass window wore a cap identical to the berets worn by the twins. He seemed to be winking now. The river ran on. Shadows began to gather as we drove out of the little valley, and the golden light reflected from the peaks of the Pyrenees began to fail.

There was something hard in my shoe. When I reached in and pulled it out, a nugget of coal sat in the palm of my hand.

How fitting, I thought. After all, what is the passing of time but a diamond turned to dust?

CODE 51

Pablo Brescia

In the stories of Pablo Brescia, books matter, and the reading and writing of literature is a dangerous activity. In his short story "The Last Hero," a ten-year-old boy is shot and killed in a duel with the fictional cowboy who appears in his comic books. In "Your Hour Has Arrived," an inveterate reader survives the end of the world, only to break his glasses just as he is about to crack open Aristotle's *Ethics*. The story presented here takes a new tack, drawing on science fiction film rather than literature, and set in a police station rather than a library. Though born in Buenos Aires, Argentina, Brescia has lived in the United States since 1986 and is now a professor at the University of South Florida. He is the author of three short story collections: *La apariencia de las cosas*, *Fuera de lugar*, and the retrospective *ESC*, and under the pseudonym Harry Bimer he published a hybrid text, *No hay tiempo para la poesía*. Brescia was the recipient of the prestigious Jamie Bishop Memorial Award given by the International Association for the Fantastic in the Arts.

A light flashed across the horizon.

Suddenly, the phone rang. *The telephone always rings "suddenly,"* he thought.

He picked it up. The voice sounded anxious on the other end. He nodded, cleared his throat, seemed concerned.

The police station was a clean, well-lighted place. Everything there served the truth.

"OK. We'll be by shortly," said sheriff Torres.

He hung up and grimaced.

Sergeant Wilson couldn't help himself:

"Boss, don't you think this would be a good scene from one of those detective movies from the 1940s? Picture it: It's midnight, somebody calls, we got a mystery! We're smoking of course, and you say: 'We'll be by shortly.' Don't you think?"

"Sh-ut-up Wilson," said Torres, fighting his asthma.

The call had come from inside Chupadero (pop. 351), to report an ominous light flying in the sky. *I can't believe these people use the word 'ominous,'* Torres said to himself in disbelief. Something had made a noise in the immediate vicinity of Susan Navajo's house. That was the story.

Torres did not usually pay much attention to the kind of people who called to report an unidentified flying object in the area. The police station of Chupadero, New Mexico, received around a hundred calls a year about flying saucers or extraterrestrials. More than thirty percent of the population living in Chupadero not only believed in extraterrestrial life but was absolutely certain that beings from another planet had naturally chosen their tiny town to make first contact with Earth.

So, it could have been just another call. But it wasn't.

Miss Navajo, divorced, mother of a six-year-old boy and a teenage girl, came from an eminent family in the Navajo community. Its members had occupied key political positions for years. And when sheriff Torres needed support to get re-elected for another four years, the Navajo were at his side at every political speech and town hall meeting. And so, when the story came in about the ominous light, Torres knew he could not ignore the call. Besides, there was another reason. It was a well-known fact that the sheriff's heart pounded faster when he would run into Susan at the town's market. *Sooner or later everybody here bumps into everybody*, thought Torres, who very much believed the old saying of his grandma: "Pueblo chico, infierno grande".

"Wilson, get your feet off the table. Haven't I told you a thousand times not to put your feet on the table? Let's go. We've got a Code 51," Torres announced.

The sergeant's eyes lit up.

"Code 51? This is it, boss, don't you think? We're always coming up empty handed.... Maybe this time we'll see a spaceship like in *Close Encounters of the Third Kind*! Don't you think? (♩♪) Daa-daa-daa-duuh-daaaaaaaaaa! (♩♪)"

"Sh-ut-up Wilson!"

The broken yellow lines that divided the highway absorbed the sheriff's attention while the sergeant moved his head softly back and forth humming Spielberg's movie score. The siren howled blue and red and many things passed through Torres' mind. He thought about the future that he had ruined by a single mistake in his youth. He thought about his shitty job in this dirty, God-forsaken corner of the world. He thought about poor Wilson and his autistic obsession with movies. He thought about the asthma that made him feel like he belonged to another species. He thought about how he was such a coward for not having talked to Susan yet. *Five years have gone by, what am I waiting for?*, he asked himself.

Almost without realizing it, they arrived.

The Navajos lived on the outskirts of Chupadero in an old mansion that had known better times and now looked like an abandoned gothic castle. Torres wished he were as far from this place as possible. Preferably in his bedroom reading books about ancient civilizations, his only hobby.

Strangely enough, the road was muddy even though it had not rained for weeks. Just getting up to the door was an ordeal.

The sheriff knocked, with Wilson behind him.

"Steve ... Is it you?" Susan said, as she opened the door for them.

Torres was happy to see her. He was always happy to see her.

"Miss Navajo, we are responding to a call from your house about an unidentified flying object in the area," said the sergeant.

Shut up Wilson, thought Torres.

Susan looked surprised but let them in anyway. They were now in the living room, bathed in dim light, their silhouettes performing a theatre of shadows.

Sheriff Torres matter-of-factly informed her about the situation and took pains to emphasize that the Chupadero police always took Code 51 calls seriously. Susan explained that she had not telephoned the police and that she didn't know anything about a light in the sky.

Wilson was quiet.

There was a moment in which each of them understood something different from what was actually happening, or, rather, what was going to happen.

Suddenly, Sergeant Wilson took Susan by the waist with a move that looked choreographed. He pointed his gun at Torres.

"Let's end this charade," he said.

Torres was frozen in place.

"You are an idiot, sheriff, you really are. Haven't you seen *Alien*? The enemy is *inside*. You always thought you were better than small town Chupadero, you insulted us, you thought we were beneath you. We couldn't stop the stupid old lady from defending you, who knows why, but we finally convinced her to call the station. Susan and I faked everything, the light, the Code 51 story. We knew you'd come, you always come, to do your duty ... like when you got that little girl killed, remember? At the end of the day, you're a fuckin' Mexican living on our land. You don't belong here, understand? As far as I'm concerned, Chupadero can be sucked into the desert! You're about to die and we're leaving. Susan, say goodbye to your boyfriend," shouted Wilson, twisting her even closer.

Susan didn't move.

"Let's go!" Wilson demanded. "What's wrong Susan?"

The lights flickered and a shot rang out. Sargent Wilson fell straight to the floor.

At the door, Grandma Navajo clutched an 1892 Winchester rifle. Susan's children stood next to her, still and quiet as stone.

"We have waited many cycles. The time for unification has arrived. Susan Navajo and Steve Torres, you who came from another time and place, are twin halves. You are our salvation. This land is diseased and must be purified. They, our own, have returned. The children of the gods have come back to take what is rightfully theirs," said the old woman, seemingly reciting a script.

Torres felt he was inside an absurd nightmare from which he did not want to wake. The woman was obviously crazy, but her madness might also mean his liberation. He thought he was going to die and that it didn't matter because he had been dead for many years.

"It is time," said Grandma Navajo.

Then, with a resolute gesture, she ordered Susan and the sheriff to approach the door.

As they stepped out they were momentarily blinded. Close to the stable, at the edge of the lot, the ominous light, in ovoid form, was emitting white noise. Torres turned around and saw that a dark luminosity shot through the eyes of Susan's children. They looked like lanterns.

The light is the ship. The ship is the light. Who would believe this crazy stuff?, thought Torres, and then he shrugged.

The sound intensified, and without warning, jets of water started to shoot from the ship. Potent, unstoppable, they flooded the farm quickly. The liquid, a water not of this earth, began to rise. Everything was so unbelievable that it made sense.

At that moment, the sheriff realized that sergeant Wilson would have known exactly which movie this scene belonged to. And Torres came to the conclusion (because after all his was a call of duty) that he should have taken all those Code 51s more seriously.

A halo of glowing water seized Susan and propelled her towards the spaceship. She extended her arms towards the fountain of light. She let go and began to scream in an unfamiliar language.

Torres felt something in his gut. Now under water, he breathed better. He was no longer afraid.

Susan, his dear Susan, swam back to him. When their bodies touched, he noticed the gills. And in the face of sheriff Steve Torres horror set in.

Illuminated by the flashing light, shining like a priestess from a time and place immemorial, Grandma Navajo watched it all and smiled with satisfaction. The truth, finally, was beginning to make way.

UNINFORMED

Pedro Zagitt

Born in Mexico City, Pedro Zagitt has a degree in Ciencias de la Comunicación (Media) from the Instituto Tecnológico y de Estudios Superiores de Occidente (ITESO) in Guadalajara, México. His two pieces included here "Uninformed" and "Circular Photography" were originally published in the fiction collection *Historias de Las Historias* edited by Mexican author Alberto Chimal. "Uninformed" introduces us to a feisty, and probably familiar to many readers, grandmother who is fortunately insistent with her home remedies. In "Circular Photography," Zagitt, who is also a well-established photographer, develops in Borgesian proportions his sense of the unexpected consequcnes of art.

October 30, 1938. The house of Doña Carmen. Queens, New York, USA. The subway lines are not running, the entire island is in chaos because of a radio broadcast. Doña Carmen can't go to the second of her three jobs and returns home walking, as well as she can, avoiding the crowd gripped with panic.

"This is getting worse, let's see if they don't run me over ..."

"..."

"Dios Mío! Poor thing, what are you doing up there? And look how green you are ..."

"..."

"Ah yeah no, with so many cars, sometimes I can't even breath."

"…"

"You must be malnourished, but I'll just give you some leftover lentils from yesterday. Hurry up and come over here."

"…"

"You'll forgive me if I can't give you some tortillas, but the market was closed. I don't understand what's happening with everyone today …"

"…"

"Are you making faces at my lentils? I know the food here is not the same as in Puebla but it's not so bad that you can't eat it, so go on."

"…"

"Could it be that you get all green like that from the dollars. No way … I'll just stay here one more year and then it's back to my farm. Eat up."

"…"

"It seems to me that you've got a hex on you, first thing tomorrow I'll take you to St. Patrick's to get the devil out of you."

"…"

"No, actually your tummy looks kind of bloated*. Let's see if I can fix that up."

"…"

"Wait a second child, I'm not done. Come here."

And without realizing it, Doña Carmen saved humanity from an intergalatic invasion.

_____

* Empachado

CIRCULAR PHOTOGRAPHY

Pedro Zagitt

Even though it was not entirely my idea, at the end of the project, they all saw me as the one responsible for the result. The idea, as well as all the work on the logistics and the production, was appropriated by the collective so that it is difficult to determine the principle author. But eventually they all decided that I was the one.

The project was nothing more than a photograph of a person taking a photograph of a person who in turn was taking a photograph and so on successively until we made an unbroken person-camera-person chain around the most important (and oldest) estate in the small town. With luck, the desired result would be an uninterrupted circle of simultaneous images in succession.

Technically, it was perfect, all fingers pressing the device with perfect synchronicity. But the glare of the flashes in unison castigated us, the arrogant photographers who played with the physical and the metaphysical, with total (and now I know permanent) blindness. We woke the snake that devours itself and us with it.

When they learned that they were blind, they began to curse me, swearing that the idea had been mine and that I should pay for it with my life. Feeling their way, they began to search for me, to make me suffer for their blindness. To save myself, I had to pretend to be my colleague opposite from me and I started beating him so that the enraged sightless masses would think that he was me.

In their outburst of anger, stirred by a hopeful and desperate attempt at redemption, the newly blind decided to set fire to the cameras, so that circular photography ended in a ring of fire. Only the photo I took survives, a memory of the day from which I must now dictate instead of write.

SIN EMBARGO

Sabrina Vourvoulias

Told through multiple narrators, Vourvouias' novel *Ink* (2012) takes on the contemporary immigration system, extrapolating out from its injustices, and showing how the system we have is a small step away from the future dystopias commonly depicted in fiction and film. In the short story presented here, "Sin Embargo," she turns to the continued impact of the Guatemalan dirty wars from the 1980s on Guatemalans now living in the United States. As becomes apparent in "Sin Embargo," every story has more than one interpretation and words can sometimes cross between languages in fascinating and complex ways. Vourvoulias studied writing and filmmaking at Sarah Lawrence College and now works as a journalist for the Spanish newspaper Al Dia in Philadelphia.

1.

Nevertheless.

That is the word that starts nearly every statement I make to my clients as I'm detailing what they can expect during treatment, or during a forensic evaluation should they ever be permitted to witness in court.

I say it in Spanish because though many of them have been here for decades and no longer speak first in Spanish, most of them still think first in it. Their children, when and if they accompany them to the First State Survivors Center, roll their eyes at me.

Nevertheless. Sin embargo.

Now say it with an English accent and an American reading of the interlingual homographs — sin embargo — and it becomes policy. Banned and barricaded, it says, because of transgression. Your transgression, your community's, your state's.

For the Guatemalans and Hondurans; the Salvadorans and Colombians; the Cubans and Venezuelans I work with, each originating transgressive circumstance may be as distinct as an owl is from a hummingbird. But the sin embargo falls on their head the same way, righteous as a curse.

Is your fear credible?

Do you (who got away with no more than the breath in your chest) have documentation?

And how is it, anyway, that you got away?

The First State Survivor Center is privately funded. We treat both immigrant and asylum-seeker, because immigration trauma can manifest in ways remarkably similar to survivor trauma. Also because the government's designation of which countries produce refugees and which produce immigrants is a lesson in politics, not psychology.

Anyway. You know (or if you don't know, you can guess) there is more than one way to translate "sin embargo" from Spanish to English. Sometimes instead of nevertheless, I go for this: the fact remains.

The fact of report; of U.N. statistics and special procedures; of federal applications, deferred action and memoranda.

There is fact of flesh, too. Here, by Istambul Protocols: thickened plantar fascia; perforated tympanic membrane; rectal tearing; keloids and hyperpigmentation; chronic lung problems. I know how to translate these flesh facts into words, even when the government claims it cannot: bastinado; teléfono; rape; necklacing; wet submarino and waterboarding.

Sin embargo, sin embargo, sin embargo — the fact remains. In Spanish, in English, in the hauntingly untranslated gulf between.

2.

Someone famous, I can't remember who, once said that when a language dies, so does memory.

I wonder about that whenever María José Manrique comes to the center and sits across the desk from me. She doesn't come regularly, and no longer makes the impression she once did. In the early days of her counseling, she not only wore her traditional blouse and skirt, she wound a bright, twenty-meter ribbon around her head in imitation of the sun.

The headdress is called a tocoyal in Tz'utijil, but it's been at least a decade since she's spoken it. And today, when I ask her why she doesn't wear the headpiece anymore, she refers to it by the Guatemalan Spanish word for all such ornamentation — tocado — then skillfully avoids answering my question.

Tocado, in case you were wondering, also means "touched." Touched has an odd set of meanings in English. Those seven letters convey the straightforward tactile, intangible compassion, and assumed mental illness or incompetence all at once. Survivors of torture, no matter how touching their testimony, are often written off as touched.

Last year's genocide trial in Guatemala is a good example. The Ixil women who stood and recounted gang rapes and massacres that wiped out full villages, were discredited with arguments of hysteria, of confabulation, of the childish inability to distinguish protective action from oppressive.

María José and I watched some of the live-stream of the trial together in my office while it was happening. My client sat dry-eyed and unmoving even when one of the testimonies — recounted in a different indigenous language and translated into Spanish — was remarkably similar to her own story.

The live-stream winked in and out, and each time it did, I studied la Marijoe (as she's come to be known after so many years in the United States).

"¿Qué buscas?" she had finally asked when she noticed my scrutiny. What are you looking for? As if that wasn't a question to be answered in a lifetime instead of a 50-minute session.

"I guess I'm looking for a reaction," I had said. "I want to know if this serves as proxy justice for you."

What you've got to understand about la Marijoe is that she smiles a lot. A wide rictus of a smile that you can never be sure is about something good. She hadn't answered my question that day, just smiled and smiled, and months later, after the genocide verdict was vacated and we all understood that no one was going to be serving a sentence for crimes against humanity, her only comment was that smile.

I can't remember if I smiled on that rescinded verdict day. Maybe later, at home, as I was carving a figure from an apple I had on hand. Maybe when I bored a hole through its chest with the tip of my paring knife. Maybe every time I hear that the tough, old ex-president and military man from Guatemala has started having some trouble breathing.

3.

I'll be having pie de pie.

Pronounce the first pie in that sentence in English, the second in Spanish.

It means I will be eating pie standing up. Although ... I could be telling you I'm going to be eating foot pie.

But, I'm not. I'm going to be telling you about my girlfriend, Daiana, who is a pastry chef and makes the best pie. Never foot pie, just so-good-I-can't-even-wait-to-sit-down-to-eat-it pie.

Right now she is flattening dough with an antique glass roller she fills with ice water. And raising her eyebrows at me. It's not the fact I'm talking into empty space (she believes in the paranormal, as do many of her fellow immigrants from San Mateo Ozolco) it's just this monologue-ish style that bothers her.

It sounds like I'm chiding, she tells me. Her convos with ghosts and ancestors and saints are always a back-and-forth, and as she tells me this, her words adopt the rhythm of the roller over dough, smooth but firm, perfecting everything beneath it.

After an hour, when the oven buzzer goes off, she looks at me before opening the door. Her eyes are what I first loved about her: letter Ds resting belly-up and barely containing the Abuelita-chocolate-discs of her irises.

"Magic," she says. "Pay." And hands me a perfect slice.

P-a-y is how we transcribe the English word "pie" so Spanish speakers know we don't mean foot. And so we create yet another homograph, thorny and confusing for the translator. Do we mean pay or pay?

"You can't get a loan to eat."

When I first met Daiana this was the way she explained her decision to immigrate. Now that she has her green card and works at the top boutique bakery in Philly, she and her cohorts ("The Bank of Puebla" they call themselves) leave sunken brioches and imperfect cannoli on the loading dock where those whose credit is hunger know to seek them out.

I'm not chiding now. Consider this a benediction instead. There are many innate, unschooled magicks — love, food, compassion, solidarity. May your mouth fill with them.

4.

My grandparents were Nipo-peruanos, which is how I come to speak some Japanese, and Spanish as well as I do. Not a native speaker, by any stretch, but good enough to confuse. Before you mistake this for boasting, know that in addition to French, my colleagues at the Survivors Center collectively speak Tigrinya, Amharic, Zigula, Khmer, Nepali, Arabic, Cantonese and Kreyòl. I am clearly the underachiever of the bunch.

My boss, a chino-cubano whose years as an imprisoned dissident have left him with limited movement in his shoulders, tells me that the fact I've just turned thirty but look eighteen, more than makes up for my unexceptional Spanish or contextually useless Japanese language skills.

Many of the survivors I work with are older — think the first wave of Central Americans fleeing torture and civil war in the 1970s and '80s — and the fact I look to be the same age as their grandchildren are (or would be) makes most of them warm quickly to me.

Most of them.

Today, la Marijoe comes in unscheduled, storms past the gatekeepers at registration, and upturns her handbag on my desk. A flood of scraps torn from matchbook covers, business cards, receipts and lined note-book paper streams out. No wallet, no sunglasses, nothing else.

I poke at one of the scraps, flip it over. There is a name written on it.

"What's this?" I ask.

"Each is a child detained at the border," she says. "The ones you want to deport."

"You know *I* don't want to repatriate them," I say. I play with the bits of paper; they all have different names written in pencil, in pen, in something that looks like it might be halfway between a crayon and brow pencil. "Anyway, how can you know their names?"

"People have names," she says. Then she turns her back and leaves before I can say anything else.

I sweep the paper bits into plastic baggies. I count some of them at the break room as I eat the empanadas Daiana has packed for my lunch. My colleagues help me count, even without an explanation. And later, at home, Daiana does the same.

There are 60,000 scraps of name.

Magic isn't instinctive, at least not for me. I have had to learn it as carefully as at one time I learned the alphabet and vowel sounds in Spanish. A-E-I-O-U.

And in English, A-E-I owe you.

Sale, as Daiana says.

It is slang, in Mexico, for "agreed." In other Spanish-speaking countries it means "to leave," and you already know its definition in English.

Which do I mean?

The translator's dilemma.

5.

I go get la Marijoe a full two hours before our appointment, because PTSD makes survivors unreliable about keeping time. Plus, we're taking public transit.

She comes out of her apartment wearing new plastic shoes and a fuschia-print dress. The mostly grey hair she usually pins high on her neck is loose and falls heavy past her shoulders. The smell of almond oil wafts up from it. Before almond oil hair treatments became hipster, they were old school. This I know from my own mother.

Today there is a creature riding la Marijoe's shoulders. It is a man-bird, ungainly despite the strong, wide wings it extends. Its long toenails puncture the skin just above la Marijoe's clavicles and sink straight through muscle to bone. The creature's ugly pin head turns to meet my gaze.

"Vamos, pues," la Marijoe says to me.

She knows I see the creature, have seen it from the first day she became my client. If I've earned any respect from her it is because I didn't run out of the office screaming that day.

Marijoe calls it her zope — after zopilote, vernacular for the vulture from which the creature takes its shape — and these days I only see it riding her when something has pushed her beyond survival and deep into her core, where fear still lives.

It is the appointment that's done it. The notice that perhaps they've located her brother living in a small town in Oaxaca these 30 plus years he's been disappeared and she's believed him dead. This is why I'm accompanying her. To help her through her first meeting with him, via internet hangout, at the State Department office.

That's why her zope comes too.

The past is carrion memory, and the three of us — client, shrink, the monster given vulture shape by survivor guilt — live by picking at it.

6.

Voice comes before image.

The community library in Juchitán has broadband, but the image of the librarian leaning into the computer keeps freezing with Rolando just a shadowed bit of background pixelation, even as the sound comes through. The librarian nods at me, then tries adjusting on that end, while the State Department functionary and I make strained conversation, and la Marijoe and her brother repeat each other's names in a circlet of syllable and breath.

Rolando's voice through the monitor is soft and sibilant; he still sounds like the youngster orphaned, then separated from his older sister and forced to find his way out of a place of fantastic, inconceivable violence alone, first by trailing after scavenger birds, then following migratory ones as he made his way north.

The internet coughs up a perfect image. The librarian seated at the computer is a muxe dressed in the huipil of the indigenous population of the town. Standing behind her, in western wear and twisting his hands in expectation, is Rolando. He looks much older than his voice, older even than la Marijoe. It is a quick impression, really, because our screen goes to black as the feed buffers, and this time the sound cuts out too.

The zope fans its huge wings, digs its claws deeper into la Marijoe's flesh. In fact, I see the wicked ends poking all the way through her back; dark, blackish blood caught in the tips. I wonder about the State Department guy — Frank — and whether he sees something because every time the zope moves its wings, he seems to flinch.

The computer screen in front of la Marijoe lightens again, then fills with smoke.

I can smell it. Wood smoke. Pine, resiny and hot. Frank grabs my shoulder, crushes it in his grip. The smoke on screen clears after a second, two, three … and then we stare at a stand of pinabetes — Christmasy, quick-growing trees prone to lightening strikes — rooted in a ground of charred bodies.

There is a child, maybe six, standing in front of the pile. His eyes dart from the corpses to whomever is holding the recording device from our point of view. La Marijoe puts her hand to the screen and the small one on the other side meets it. She says one word in that language she hasn't spoken in a decade, and even though the glottals are foreign to my ear, I understand the word means hide.

The child scoots toward the bodies. He picks his way gingerly among them, drops to his knees, then to his back. He grabs an arm to pull the body closer to him. The flesh comes off the bone as if it were a glove, but the torso doesn't budge. He drops the mass of charred skin and semi-liquid tissue, and starts inching his body closer to the body on his other side. He whimpers a bit as he pushes under it, and I wonder how long a burnt body holds the heat that killed it; and if the child, too, will be singed while hiding beneath it.

The child is completely hidden by the burnt corpses when we hear the crack of gunfire. The image shakes violently, dives, captures a minute of tilted ground then fades to black. The hangout site pops up a static image onscreen to indicate the connection has dropped.

"Rolando," la Marijoe says one last time, then goes silent as the zope's huge, dark wings curve forward to cover her eyes.

Frank lets go of my shoulder at the same time as the zope plunges its curved beak into the crown of la Marijoe's head. The monstrous creature pushes its ugly head so deep inside the old woman, its beak temporarily bulges out a spot on her neck.

"Marijoe?"

She turns to me. Zope feathers are coming through the skin beneath her eyebrows and behind her ears, but it's what's happening on her forehead, cheeks and chin that gets my attention. Fine particles of whatever powder or foundation makeup she's been wearing slough off from the pressure of feathers prodding at the skin from within. Under the flaking cover-up, la Marijoe's face is hyperpigmented, shiny, and her skin is too thick for even the big vulture quills to get through.

Like my girlfriend Daiana's wrist, where a third-degree burn from one of the bakery's commercial ovens has healed into a bracelet of contracted skin.

By Istambul Protocols ....

"We can try this again a different day," Frank says.

"No," la Marijoe answers. "I see Rolando is alive. That is enough."

Frank stops me on our way out. "I can't begin to understand what happened here today. But if you convince her to come back and try this again, make sure the appointment is with me."

I nod.

After a moment he adds, "Was the librarian with Rolando —" but I stop him before he can say anything else. "I've got to catch up with my client."

"You've been telling tales," I say to la Marijoe when we're on the bus. "All these years in treatment, you've been lying to me."

"No," she answers. "Everything I told you happened exactly as I recounted it."

"But not to you. Rolando's sister was shot dead if that digital translation of memory is to be believed."

She smiles. "You should know better than to trust a translation."

"If you are not Rolando's sister, who are you? Why search for him, to what purpose? And what's your real name anyway?"

She doesn't answer, doesn't speak, until her stop. "So, now that you know, will you still see me?" she asks as she gets to her feet after signaling the busdriver.

"Of course," I answer. "I've got an opening Tuesday, I'll pencil you in."

7.

She doesn't show that week. In fact, she doesn't show at the First State Survivors Center ever again.

A month into her absence, I set aside my injured professional pride, and go to her apartment to talk to her. After I knock, a young woman with three children clinging to her legs opens the door. I give her my name and ask about la Marijoe and she invites me in, offers me a lemonade.

"I've always wondered about her," Anabelle — that's the new tenant — says as she mixes tap water with the drink mix, then puts the can of mix back into a cupboard that holds just it and four tins of evaporated milk. "I found something of hers jammed up behind the pipe under the sink in the kitchen when I moved in. I thought she'd come back for it. I'll go fetch it."

She disappears into the next room and one of the toddlers trots after her, but the other two stay and watch me with big, wary eyes. It takes Anabelle a long time — long enough for me to notice that there isn't much furniture in the apartment, and that what is here has the look of hand-me-down or Goodwill.

She comes back with a cigar box which she hands to me. Inside is about $1,000 in crisply folded bills and a sealed envelope with my name on it. When I open it, a torn matchbook cover with the words "sin embargo" and a string of what look like library call numbers written in grease pencil flutters out, followed by the primary feather of a vulture.

"A mystery wrapped in an enigma," Anabelle says with a shrug when I look back at her. "But that's definitely a turkey buzzard feather."

Never underestimate people. Never figure that the young, or the poor, or the humble don't have something important to teach you about your own assumptions. I stay long enough to find out that the public library is Anabelle's favorite haunt, and that she can not only paraphrase Churchill and quote chapter and verse of the Stokes' Field Guide to North American Birds, but knows that if the numbers are Dewey call numbers, they are all over the place — from occult to salvation, psychology to philosophy.

I go back to my office, put the feather in my pencil cup and stare at it for a while. Then I dial Frank's number.

The hangout connection is much better this time.

"Where is my sister?" Rolando says when he sees only us onscreen.

"Let me ask you something, Rolando," I say. "So many years have passed, how can you be sure the woman sitting in front of the monitor last time we talked is really your sister?"

He looks confused for a few moments, then gives us a smile. It is so like la Marijoe's it lands a punch to my gut.

"I could never confuse her voice for another's," he says finally. "I still have dreams about being buried under bodies. It was my sister's voice that reminded me I wasn't dead. Then and now."

"All those years ago ... was she there when you ventured out from your hiding place?"

He shakes his head. "Nobody was there. Just the burnt bodies and the vultures feasting on them. But I knew my sister would find me. I knew that she would never stop looking for me."

He sounds just like the other survivors I treat, whose hopes — no matter how infinitesimal — cling like a burr. Just last week, when there was news that one of the Madres of the Plaza de Mayo in Argentina had been reunited with a grandson missing since the dirty war, all of my clients spoke again about their own disappeared loved ones, their own future reunification days. One spoke of that to me even though we both know her husband was pushed out of a helicopter over open sea.

"Are you sure all of the burnt bodies were dead?" I ask Rolando, picturing la Marijoe's contracted skin as I say it.

"Yes," Rolando says. "All of them."

Frank clears his throat. "Last time we tried the hangout, what did you see when the video part wasn't working?"

I translate the question into Spanish.

"What do you mean 'what did I see?' A dark screen. My own reflection, and la Tere, the librarian, reflected on it too. May I talk to my sister now?"

"She's disappeared," I say, before I can reconsider my word choice. "I don't know where."

"At least I know she is alive," he says after a moment. "That big empty space her disappearance left in my life can fill up now. I imagine it is the same for her." He starts to get up to leave.

"Wait," I say, fishing the scrap of paper out of my pocket. I hold it as close to the computer's camera as I can. "Do you have any idea what this number is?"

I hear him call the librarian closer to the computer, and then their quick consultation in a Zapotecan language quite different than the Tz'utijil he and la Marijoe spoke together. Not for the first time I feel dazed by the sheer number of languages in the world, the sheer number of opportunities for translation to leave out that one element that gives real meaning to what is being said.

"We don't have any idea. But we'll think about it some more," Rolando says as the librarian writes down the numbers in a spiral-bound pad.

"She hid some money away," I say then. "I figure she'd want you to have it. Tell me where we can wire it to you—"

He puts his hand up to stop me. "I don't want it. I have what I need," he says, then signs off so quickly I can't argue it with him.

"That's it, then," Frank says. He takes the scrap out of my hand, squints at what's written on it: b52:b122:b131:b211:b215:b501:d150:e234.

"Looks like an i-p-v-six number," he says. When I shake my head, he adds, "Internet protocol version six, which is what currently routes all the traffic over the web. Could be what you have is a location and i.d. number tied to some service provider. Is Marijoe tech savvy?"

I snort, which prompts a smile. "Well, I hope you figure it out," he says handing back the scrap.

I can tell he thinks it is an intellectual puzzle to be pieced together and solved, but it's not. It is another translation calling for memory, ear and soul to complete.

8.

Will you still see me?

Those were la Marijoe's last words to me, and I understand them differently now.

I try, I really try. She may not be who I thought she was, but she is la Marijoe, and she is someone. Someone tied — however tenuously or fantastically — to massacre victims from an ossuary that the Guatemalan Forensic Anthropology Foundation has probably already exhumed and catalogued.

So, that's my first step. I call the tech our Center has worked with before, and read him the numbers I want him to check against their registrar's catalogue. The quantity of pieces they've catalogued is huge — every bone chip, every piece of tooth — and includes not only the victims of the genocide and three decades of armed internal conflict, but the remains of the more than 6,000 migrants dead last year alone. Many of the old and the new don't have names, but some do, and maybe hope clings to me like a burr too.

The second step I take is to get Frank to ply his government muscle and find out if the numbers are, in fact, IPv6 numbers and, if so, which provider bills them, and to whom.

Third step: After I chance upon Anabelle in the stacks of the Ramonita de Rodriguez branch of the Free Library, I enlist her help in searching through all the books under the call numbers that coincide with la Marijoe's sequence. I pay her a bit of a stipend, so her lunch and bus fare doesn't tip her budget into deficit, and once a week she brings me what she finds stuck between the pages. A prayer card of St. Gall; the yellowed clipping from a newspaper from 1974; an Amtrak ticket stub, round-trip to New York City; a small feather from a cedar waxwing — a bird, Anabelle further informs me — she has never seen in the city.

The objects don't all — or any? — belong to la Marijoe, she knows it and I know it. But it is a catalogue anyway, and I treat the objects with the respect my friends at the Forensic Foundation accord their remains.

Anabelle comes to the apartment to deliver the items to me because if I went off to see another woman on a regular basis, Daiana would see red. Another homograph, by the way. In Spanish, red means net or web, and that is what is being woven every time Anabelle — kids in tow — stops by the apartment. Daiana has started baking special treats to coincide with the delivery of book findings.

The fourth step I take in trying to figure out la Marijoe and the clues she's left me, is actually taken for me not by me. The Juchitán librarian emails me an invitation to a private hangout — no Frank, no Rolando. She sends it to my work email because that's the one attached to my digital footprint. I'm actually not that easy to find, but she is a librarian, after all.

I don't respond right away, and not only because the Center's emails are automatically saved and archived for accountability and transparency. I think I know why Tere-the-librarian has contacted me privately, and it has nothing to do with my quest to find la Marijoe. I believe it is curiosity that has prompted it. The desire of a muxe in Juchitán to understand the life of a trans man in Philly; the desire to confirm that her small, indigenous community is — and always has been — less hesitant about the everydayness of trans folk than any U.S. metropolis.

I let Daiana know I'll be staying late at work, and she's fine with it, mostly because it's an evening Anabelle and her brood are scheduled to stop by. Daiana is making the kids the new cake she just introduced at the bakery, flavored with dragon fruit and iced in the fruit's distinctive dark pink hue. For the children's sake she's going to try baking it in shape of a flying dragon.

When the hangout window on the computer opens up, Tere looks around with interest. "So that's what the inside of a psychiatrist's office looks like," she says.

"I'm a clinical psychologist," I say, "but, yeah."

"You need more colorful artwork."

I smile a bit, wait.

"So I wanted to talk to you," she says, "about the numbers. I found something that if not significant is at least interesting. Have you ever heard of the Aarne-Thompson Index?"

"No."

"It categorizes folk and fairy tale types and motifs that recur in mostly Indo-European folktales," she says. "Though I think it has started including stories from other cultures as well. Anyway, most of them are two, three or four digit numbers preceded by an AT."

"Well that doesn't fit."

She makes an exasperated noise. "But some of them are instead sub-categorized with the letters A, B, C, and so forth, to indicate that they are tales that involve mythological motifs, or animals, or tabus."

"Okay," I say, "cut to the chase — which do our numbers coincide with?" I don't know if she knows that expression, but she does what I ask.

"B 52 is under the general bird-men category of tale, but is specifically about harpies, or bird-women."

So, I'll be honest, this seems an unlikely concordance for la Marijoe's numbers, but that doesn't keep me from feeling a weird sort of unease. I don't have much of a classical education, but I kind of remember that harpies chased one of the Greek heroes to his death.

"B 122 is code for tales of birds with magic, and B 131 is all truth-telling birds," Tere continues. "B 211 and 215 are both tied to animal languages and animals that can speak. B 501 is a category of tales where an animal gives part of its body to a human as a magical talisman."

"Jesus," I say. I tell her about la Marijoe then, including what we saw during the half-failed hangout, the bit about her sprouting feathers and even that she left me one of those feathers in a cigar box she could have no certainty I'd ever find. Of course I sound like a nutburger as I recount it. Tere doesn't say anything for a while, then drops her eyes to the spiral-bound notebook open in front of her.

"So, maybe I copied one of the other numbers down wrong," she says finally. "Is it really D 150 not D 152?"

I pull out la Marijoe's scrap of paper. "Yeah. 150. Why?"

"Because D 150 stories are about humans transforming into birds; D 152 tales are about birds transforming into humans," she says. "Given what all the other numbers are keyed to, I think the latter would better fit the narrative we're piecing together."

"You can't really mean to tell me you think that la Marijoe is a bird turned human."

She laughs at me. "Because a human turning into a bird is easier to accept?"

"I do deal with the most inventive forms of human denial at my job."

The laugh is genuine this time. Then she grows serious. "You don't think even a vulture can grow weary of the dead we leave for them to clean up? You don't think a great mother bird might adopt another's fledgling found living among the hundreds, the thousands of corpses?"

She sighs. "Is there a difference really? Whether one of the vultures at the massacre site took pity on Rolando and magically turned itself human for him, or his sister's dying spirit hopped into the body of one of the birds that was already there, it was to the same end. To protect him."

"Nice thought, bad job."

She shrugs. "He got out of there alive."

"Luck."

"Magic."

"Fairy tale magic," I say. "Not the kind I believe in."

She grins. "No? Me, I believe in every kind. I couldn't be a librarian otherwise."

When it's clear that's all she has for me, I thank her and sign off quickly, then sit in the quiet of the Survivors Center emptied of survivors and staff. I don't want to go home yet, I can't go home yet, and I'm not sure why. I wander out to the break room and let my eyes rest on the world map that takes up one full wall. There are pins color coded for each of our clients at their country of origin, and then at every country they've landed for a time on their journey here, to us. I find la Marijoe's pin in Guatemala and trace the unbroken line to the one in Delaware.

Thousands of miles as the crow — or vulture — flies.

There's another homograph for you. Miles means thousands in Spanish. I go back into my office and get back on the internet. I search for the Aarne-Thompson index and look for the last number on la Marijoe's string, the one Tere-the-librarian had forgotten to translate for me.

Am I surprised when I read the description of the motif that ties together the E 234 tales? Not really. Nations are built on bones, so is it any wonder there are so many stories that revolve around those who return from death to avenge it?

Guatemala, Syria, Bosnia, Cambodia, Rwanda, East Timor, Angola, Kurdistan and all the other genocides I know about from the Center's clients: there must be miles of E234 tales waiting to be found.

9.

The past is never as simple as we've been told it is. In some languages there is an admission of this in a verb aspect without any certainty of completion.

La Marijoe is my past imperfect.

My friend at the Forensic Foundation finds a match for the numbers I've given him, identifying an ossuary and the date of exhumation. It is one of several mass graves that have been tied to the massacre that left María José and Rolando orphaned and on the run, but barring further identification by the FAFG, we can never know if the specific numbers are keyed to the Manrique family members they lost.

Neither can I tell you if la Marijoe's numbers are what Frank believes they are, or what Tere-the-librarian does, or even what Anabelle thinks them, as she collects her evidence of life in books from every library branch in the city.

Perhaps the numbers are all of these, or none.

I mail the vulture feather to Rolando care of the Juchitán library. The $1,000 from the cigar box I give to Anabelle because I know she's hurting enough that even that little bit will seem a godsend, and hey, she's got fledglings too, so I think la Marijoe would have approved.

And one weekend when Daiana is working a double in preparation for the Fat Tuesday before Lent, I rent a car and drive about forty-five miles out of Philadelphia, to a little town — the internet is my informant — where there are four trees that hold near as many turkey vultures as leaves.

I watch the birds for hours, riding thermals, landing and hopping from branch to branch. They watch me too, and despite the sympathetic magic I attempt in their language of whines and gutteral hisses, I get no answer.

Because there are no answers in this tiempo, this time, this present tense. It is filled with infinitives instead — absolutes and constructs; marked and unmarked; active and elliptical.

Today, Jamila, who speaks the best Arabic at the Center, finagles shelter and the promise of a job for a Middle-Eastern client so her hand can heal from its session in a meat grinder.

Today, my boss brings the staff a coconut pound cake baked by a client who has finally set up the dessert shop he dreamed about during his years at a Cambodian refugee camp. When my boss sets the cake on the break room table, he tells us we're totally worth the two-hour drive to go get it.

Today, the DART train comes exactly three minutes late so I am able to catch it and get back to the apartment in Philly before Daiana comes home. I place some flowers in a vase so they are the first thing she sees when she opens the door.

Today, she tells me that although she is mexicana, someone assumes she's Asian while she's in line at Hai Street Kitchen and asks her to check the status of their order.

Today, I tell her I don't see it, that she'll never look like me, and we bicker about whether I'm Latino or sansei or both or none and I tell her that what I am is a trilingual homograph, and let's leave it at that.

Today, she rolls her eyes at my verbal conceit, and we lounge on the couch eating Hai Street's expensive sushi burritos and rub our feet together, watching reality TV neither of us can relate to because it has nothing to do with what's real.

Today, I remember that the word relate is another homograph.

Today, I weigh credible fears, burden of proof, deportation orders, detainers and directives against several plastic baggies filled with 60,000 scraps of paper.

Today, the names are an incantation as they leave my lips.

Today, I feel the feathers pushing their way through the walls of my heart.

Accursed Lineage

Daína Chaviano

Born in Havana, Chaviano came to Miami in 1991 to escape the restrictive atmosphere imposed on artists. In Cuba she was a significant figure in the development of Cuban science fiction, penning a number of novels herself, including *Los Mundos que Amo* (1980) (The Worlds I Love) and *Fábulas de una Abuela Extraterrestre* (1988) (Fables of an Extraterrestrial Grandmother). Since coming to the United States, she has focused primarily on the fantasy genre. In 1998 she received the prestigious Azorín Award from Spain for her mystical-political novel *El hombre, la hembra y el hambre* (Man, Woman and Hunger). Her only novel so far translated into English, *The Island of Eternal Love* (2008) *(La isla de los amores infinitos*, 2006), has been translated into over 25 languages making it the most translated Cuban novel in history. In *The Island of Eternal Love* (which Chaviano describes as "Caribbean Gothic") a mysterious house appears and disappears, as the meanings of family, home, and nation are in constant flux. "Accursed Lineage" follows similar lines of familial mystery.

It's close to midnight now and the noises will soon begin. From here I can observe everything: each movement inside the house, each whisper, each secret visitor. As always, I will be in my position until sunrise. And while the neighborhood sleeps, two households will remain awake: mine and *that one*.

We light the house up only slightly, as they do, to not draw attention. My parents and siblings move with stealth, so no noise slips out. Every so often mama or papa put down what they're doing to look around a bit. My siblings also leave their games to see what they can make out through the windows. Only I remain steady, not diverging one iota from what I consider to be my primary job: to discover what is happening in that house.

I don't know why I do it. I don't know where this obsession with perpetual surveillance comes from. It's a reflex, almost a sickness; something that I learned from the grown-ups. Papa and mama set the example, although without much conviction. They say that it's their obligation. Nevertheless, when my siblings ask about the origin of the vigil, no one can give a coherent answer. I don't get worked up about those things. I limit myself to completing my duties.

It has just turned twelve, and I stand on my tiptoes on the edge of the roof to see better. Now the commotion will start up. No doubt about it. They have already turned a light on at the top floor. It's the old lady. I can see her through a broken window. She moves through her room filled with junk and lights up a candle. She bends down next to what seems to be a trunk, tries to separate it from the wall, but can't succeed in moving it. Then she leaves the candle holder on the floor and pushes with all her might until it detaches from the corner. She leans over it, as if she were going to take out something ... at that precise moment someone bumps into me and I almost lose my balance. It's my little brother.

"What are you doing here, idiot?" I reproach in a whisper. "You scared me half to death."

"I came to play," he responds without noting my anger, and strews some bones on the eaves.

"And since when do you play on the roof?"

"It's hot in there."

He takes two finger bones and starts to hit them against each other as if they were tiny swords. I look at the house out of the corner of my eye, but the old lady has already disappeared with the candle and everything. I'm left not knowing what she was trying to take out of that corner.

"And those?" I ask without much interest, because I just now make out two figures that are quickly crossing the entrance and are immediately led into the interior of the house by someone who's opened the door for them. "Are they new?"

My brother looks at me a moment, uncomprehending.

"Oh! These?...They're from the Rizo baby."

"The one that they buried last week?"

"No. That was the grandson of Mrs. Cándida. This is a much older baby."

Slow music rises and falls in pitch until it's lost in a murmur: someone is operating the radio in the house next door. For some reason, I know that it is prohibited to listen to the voices and news that come from afar. I discern the eagerness of the listener to evade the interference which they use to jam any outside signal. We are isolated. Not only us, them as well ...

"Come on, coward!" says my brother, projecting his voice, making the bones collide in swordfight. "Don't run away, face my fury!"

"Get out of here." I push him a little to get my place back. "If you don't get down right now, I'll tell papa to not raise you up again."

He shrugs his shoulders.

"I don't have to go to the charnel house to get toys now. Mami always ..."

"If you don't go now, I'll drop you on your head. Don't you see that I'm busy?"

The front door of the house opens slowly. A man sticks his head out to inspect the surroundings. He goes back inside. Then he comes out again. He's carrying a knife in his hand. He stealthily approaches a corner of the garden and starts to dig a hole aided by that tool. He rapidly buries a medium sized packet that he has taken out of his clothes. In the silence of the morning, I hear him mumbling:

"I won't be able to use it, but neither will they."

He finishes his work and goes inside.

My brother shoves me to get more space.

"Stupid idiot!" I turn towards him, coiled and ready.

I jerk him by the neck and squeeze as hard as I can until he weakens from lack of air. He seems to have lost consciousness. Then my eyes go back to the house and on looking through the window on the top floor, I come across a rare spectacle: the diffuse light falls on a bed where a couple is getting undressed. I'm astonished. I let my brother go and three seconds later, I hear the dull thud from a body that has fallen on the pavement many meters below. I hardly pay attention to the flattened body, because I spy another silhouette that leaves the house and crosses the garden. At that moment, an enormous cloud covers the disc of the moon and I'm left without knowing if it's a man or a woman who is going down the walkway with a bundle in arm.

A gong from far away brings me back to reality. It's my mother calling us to dinner. I look for a second at the big house wrapped in darkness and reluctantly detach from the eaves.

When I come into the dining room, everyone is already seated at the table. Mama serves soup, red and thick like beet juice. I try a spoonful and almost burn my lips.

"It's boiling!" I protest.

"Be careful with the tablecloth," she warns me. "You know how much that stains."

"I don't like old blood!" one of my siblings complains.

"Well, you'll have to get used to it. Things are getting more difficult each day and I can't get it fresh like I could before."

"Where did you get it from?" asks my father devouring a bit of ear.

"Gertrudis sold it to me overpriced. I've had it in the freezer from six months ago because little Luis ..." She looks around — "Where is Junior?"

We all stop eating and fix upon my brother's empty seat.

Then I remember.

"I think that ..." A knot forms in my throat.

I'm terrified of the punishment.

All eyes turn to me in silence, waiting for an explanation. I decide to tell everything: my determined vigilance over the mansion, the suspicious behavior of the old lady, the secret burial of treasure, my brother's sudden interruption and our struggle on the roof, the couple in the room, the sound of a body falling on the cement, the mysterious person leaving the house.... I prepare for the worst.

"And you couldn't see what the guy was carrying?" mother asks.

"I don't even know if it was a man: it was really dark."

"Too bad!"

They eat in silence.

"So, what do we do about Junior?" says my father, leaving blood-stains on his napkin.

"Let's make the best of it — mama decides. How does brain stew sound for tomorrow?"

We scream enthusiastically.

Mama stands up and goes in search of dessert, but I can't wait. I go up to the balcony and climb once again onto the roof. The wind makes the loose floor boards of the attic creak. From there I hear the muffled uproar of my siblings who flood the dawn with howls, ignoring the oft-repeated prohibition.

In front of me, in the other house, a window opens. I attentively observe the faces that emerge: the old lady with the trunk and an unknown youth. They look with fear and concern towards our house.

"Be gone!"* — I hear the old lady say, who then crosses herself three times in a row. "The agitated spirits again."

"I'm calling the police."

"Yeah? And what are you going to tell them?" scolds the old lady who now takes on the voice of the youth: "*Listen, in the house next door there was a massacre many many years ago and now the dead walk about howling at all hours.* — That's what you're going to say? Well, I suggest that you leave them to their unrest. Anyway, that's the only thing the dead can do when they've been finished off."

Both women cross themselves again. They half-close the blinds after them, and I'm left open-mouthed, completely confused by what I just heard. What are they talking about? None of us have died ... except Junior, who I let fall by accident, the fault of an unfortunate mistake. And if one can die, it's because one is not dead. Or can the dead die again?

---

*Solavaya!

I try to see what's going on behind the curtains, but I can't stay. The light of the sun announces itself in a hazy clarity over the roofs of the city.

I should return to my refuge. I'll sleep all day until night falls, and when the stars begin to come out, I'll unfold my membranous wings and fly up to my usual position.

COCONAUTS IN SPACE

ADÁL

Roy Brown in his iconic song "Boricua en la Luna" (Puerto Rican on the Moon) proclaims that Puerto Rican culture will survive no matter where its people are dispersed — even somewhere as strange as the moon (or the United States). *Coconauts in Space*, created by Puerto Rican artist ADÁL, brings this image of Puerto Rican culture on the moon to life. In this photo narrative, ADÁL alters images from the 1969 NASA moon landing and integrates them into an alternate history which includes a 1963 moon landing by Puerto Rican astronauts. The work uses this fictional history to critique the fictional and incomplete history that has been told about Puerto Rico by the U.S. Though terrestrially born in Utuado, Puerto Rico in 1948, ADÁL spent much of his artistic career in New York, working in photography, theatre, installation art, and performance. After retiring from the New York Department of Transportation in 2010, he returned to Puerto Rico where he continues his artistic journeys into space. *Coconauts in Space* was first presented in 2004 at the *Taller Puertorriqueño* in Philadelphia, Pennsylvania.

COCONAUTS IN SPACE
[Pre-NASA Lunar Landings]

ADÁL

Made in El Spirit Republic de Puerto Rico

Cast / Acknowledgments

NASA Astronauts......................................NASA Astronauts

Los Coconautas...........Members of the Coconauts Space Team of El Spirit Republic de Puerto Rico

Face on moon surface...ADÁL

Photographs of moon voyage were appropriated from the NASA archives and digitally manipulated.

Lunar Module aka Domino1 is made possible courtesy of El Spirit Republic de Puerto Rico

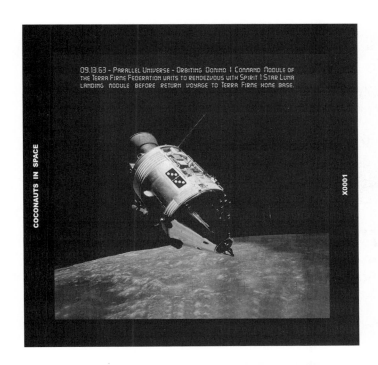

09.13.63 - Parallel Universe - Orbiting Domino 1 Command Module of the Terra Firme Federation waits to rendezvous with Spirit 1 Star Luna landing module before return voyage to Terra Firme home base.

COCONAUTS IN SPACE

X0001

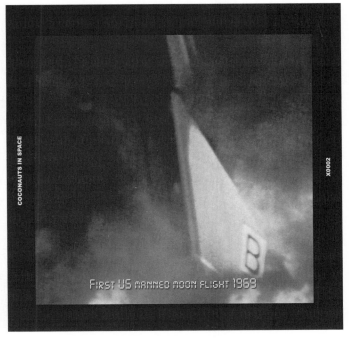

COCONAUTS IN SPACE

X0002

First US manned moon flight 1969

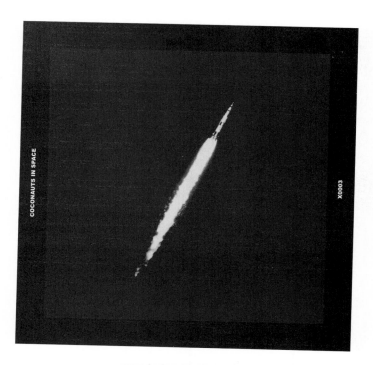

COCONAUTS IN SPACE

X0003

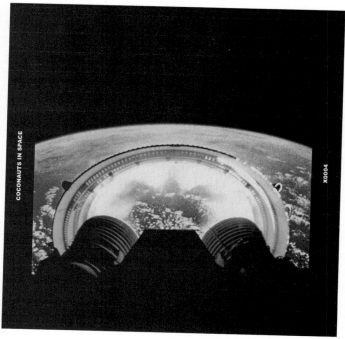

COCONAUTS IN SPACE

X0004

COCONAUTS IN SPACE

X0005

COCONAUTS IN SPACE

X0006

COCONAUTS IN SPACE

X0007

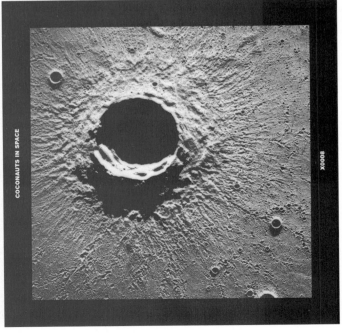

COCONAUTS IN SPACE

X0008

COCONAUTS IN SPACE

X0009

COCONAUTS IN SPACE

X0010

COCONAUTS IN SPACE

000012

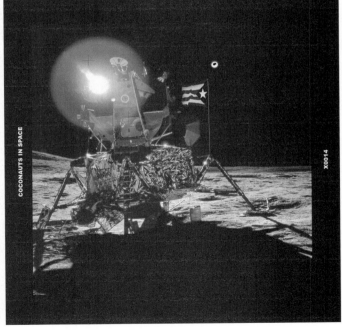

COCONAUTS IN SPACE

X0014

COCONAUTS IN SPACE

X0012

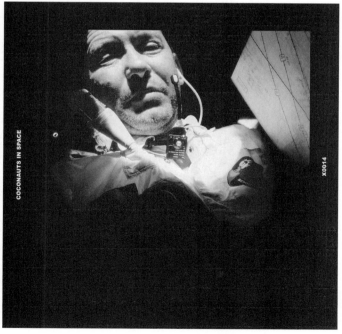

COCONAUTS IN SPACE

X0014

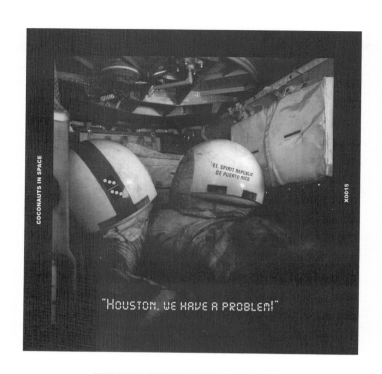

COCONAUTS IN SPACE

EL SPIRIT REPUBLIC
DE PUERTO RICO

X0015

"HOUSTON, WE HAVE A PROBLEM!"

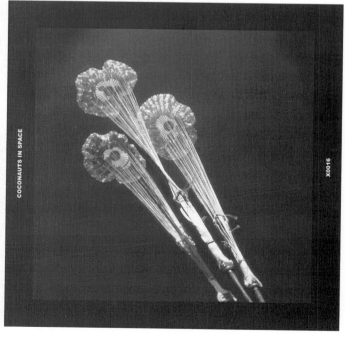

COCONAUTS IN SPACE

X0016

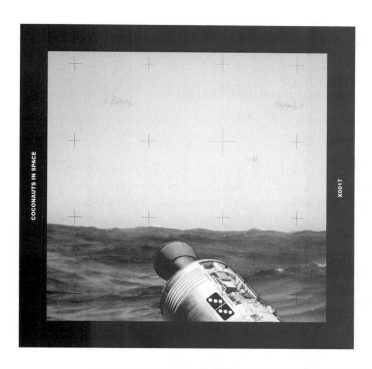

X0017

Comandante Adal Lucian del Planeta Maldonado

Captain: Space Craft Domino 1
Federation: Parallel Planeta Terra Frime
Citizen: El Spirit Republic de Puerto Rico
Date of Birth: 11.01.28
Graduate: Agapito Zpace Academy

Led first Coconaut Space Mission to Star Luna
from Terra Firme on 09.13.63. Left behind Domino Shuttle II Capsule with coconaut space
suits and helmets to mark the successful manned
exploration of Star Luna - moon of Terra Firme
- for other celestial explorers who follow.

COWBOY MEDIUM

Ana Castillo

Ana Castillo is a relentless activist for women and was a key figure in the development of xicanisma (Chicana feminism). She has been at the forefront of Latino letters since the 1980s and was the principle translator of the classic *This Bridge Called My Back* (1981). She is a multi-talented writer who continues to work in a variety of genres, the short list includes fiction, poetry, and translation. Her first novel *The Mixquiahuala Letters* (1986) is an experimental novel in tribute to Julio Cortázar's novel *Hopscotch* which traces the lives of two Chicanas, Teresa and Alicia. Her spectacular novel *So Far From God* (1993) tells of four sisters and their mother living in New Mexico who must face the large forces that confront them: patriarchy, government, corporations, and religion. Castillo received her a BA in art from Northwestern Illinois University, an MA in Latin American Studies from the University of Chicago, and her doctorate in American Studies from the University of Bremen, Germany. "Cowboy Medium," which features roommates Hawk and Gordo, is the opening chapter from her uncoming novel *The Last Goddess Standing*.

That evening when Gordo came home, on his way to take a shower he found Hawk playing with the Ouiji Board. His housemate frequently consulted the board game with life's difficult questions. For the old cowboy who had neither cow nor a horse, they were all difficult questions. Hawk believed in the spirits. It was just who he was. A spirit had given him the name Hawk, in fact, a long time ago. It was in a tee-pee meeting with Pueblo Indians up in Taos. Years later, after he'd gone on the wagon and attended a similar Native American ceremony Hawk started getting 'contacted.'

Gordo turned on the shower. He tried not to judge people. Being a lawyer for so long, however, made assessing people's character second nature. While the water warmed up the attorney carefully removed the new suit and hung it up on a hanger he'd left for that purpose on a hook behind the door. The rest of his clothes were shoved into the hamper. He was the only one who used it. On laundry day Gordo had to catch his housemate snoozing on the Laz-y-Boy recliner just to pull off stiff socks to get them in the wash.

Leaning over the sink Gordo examined his cherubic face in the mirror. He'd started shaving in eighth grade and had a full beard in high school. To shave again or not to shave. Why were genetics so unfair that a balding man had more hair on his face and every inch of his body (save the soles of his feet and the palms of his hands, like an orangutan) than he had on his head? Now, *that* really was a question for ancients and scientists alike.

Gordo snapped his fingers and ran out. Hawk looked up, clearly bored with the seànce. The spirits were slow in coming around that evening. "What've I said about you running around like that?" Hawk asked, reaching over for a cigarette. Blowing out a deep sigh, he added, "Don't you think I'm shell-shocked enough as it is?"

"I forgot my underwear in the dryer," Gordo replied half-apologetically. The other half was of the mind that if he hadn't traumatized a good part of the female population of the town of La Trinidad, males should surely fear no harm at the sight of his manliness.

On his way back from the dryer, which, with the washer was just outside the backdoor beneath the portal, and with fresh as a daisy tightie-whities in hand, it was Hawk who stopped him. "By the way, man, how'd the case with old man Soldaño go?"

"Not good," Gordo said, dashing off for an ashtray to put under Hawk's cigarette. "Eileen said they had nothing in writing, plus, being related, the old man *could* have once given the ranchería to his son, as the young Soldaño claimed — before his supposed father's dementia. Then there was the expired statute of limitations. He didn't have much of a case against his shiftless son. And so, one more family land grant wastes away. The son is selling. Judge Eileen and I both knew the old man was telling the truth but the law is the law."

Both Hawk and Gordo shook their heads. The case had been only one of many where traditional landholders were selling out to developers. The longtime residents couldn't afford the new housing and left town. In came new people and thus, La Trinidad was becoming a thing of the past. Some people liked change. Others didn't. You couldn't stop change, though.

"Eileen now, is it?" Hawk said, letting out a perfect ring of smoke. In the dim light of the lamp on the end table, kicking back and hat tipped forward on his noggin, Gordo thought his friend bore a faint resemblance to Clint Eastwood, specifically in *High Plains Drifter*. (It was in the squint.) He'd never say that to Hawk. It wasn't because his friend would be flattered or oddly insulted. The material world meant very little to Hawk.

"We've been on first name basis since the first happy hour we shared in her Honor's chambers," Gordo said. He lowered his eyes momentarily and then said, "Sorry, Hawk. I don't mean to talk about drinking...."

Hawk waved the hand with the cigarette as if to say, don't worry. "On the other hand, I do mind ..." he said, motioning with eyes and cigarette hand at the other man's bare everything. As Gordo slipped into his shorts, he said. "You know, I was remembering a case back in Chicago today ..."

"One you lost?"

"Yes, one of the first," Gordo said, "It was pro-bono — my uncle had worked in the Civil Rights Movement and all that — and I represented a young black — African-American youth. That morning when the judge found him guilty and after I apologized to him he said, 'What do you know about injustice, man? When your people have been slaves, that's something you never forget. It stays in your bones. You pass it on to your children.'"

"I don't doubt that's true," Hawk said although he had never contemplated the emphatic claim before.

"Listen," Gordo continued, "the boy goes ..."

"Boy?"

"He was scarcely eighteen ... I stand by my choice of words." Gordo smoothed back the ten hairs on each side of his head. To Hawk, the other man did not resemble any movie star, even in the growing dimness of the living room. Instead, he looked a little like a bad spirit. Or maybe a garden gnome. Hawk pushed the Ouiji Board away and concentrated on his cigarette instead, deep inhales, loud exhales. Gordo rolled his eyes but went on with his story, "The *youth* says something like, 'What're you, man? Celli? Is that Italian? Your people were Romans. They were the slave keepers of their time. They killed Jesus.'" Being from Chicago, Gordo had said yute not youth. It had taken Hawk a time to get used to the accent, which his housemate insisted he did not have.

"'Whoa, whoa, whoa! Stop right there,' I says," Gordo went on, now all-wound up. "'Yeah. My grandpa, one of the best people you'd ever want to meet, did not have no part in enslaving you,' I says. And you know what the kids says? He goes, 'Humph.'"

"Humph?"

"Humph," Gordo affirmed. His nose suddenly went up and he began to sniff. The faintest odor of the morning's chorizo and eggs was still in the house. "I think I'm hungry," he muttered.

"And you are telling me this, standing naked in my living room tonight — *¿Por qué?*" Hawk asked, putting out his cigarette. "And pray tell, why is it that you move your hands all over the place when you speak?" Hawk asked, "It's distracting as all hell."

"It's how we Italians express ourselves, O' Sir Hawky-Stick," Gordo laughed, with bunched fingers of both hands that motioned toward his own face like two birds wanting to peck out his eyes. He continued, "That claim, you know, that people who were descendents of the oppressed never forget ... and who weren't at some point in history, I might add ...? Well, it got me to thinking, especially since I moved down here to the Wild West of New Mexico. With all due respect to my family, the Celli (distantly related to the Medicis) in my blood must run some Indian blood, American Indian. I just feel it. Maybe Cherokee."

"Right. Like every other red-blooded American," Hawk muttered, unimpressed.

"Whoa, Hawkman," Gordo said, trying to look put off. "I was a foundling too, Hawk. Just like you," Gordo said bringing up the most painful part of his existence and that of his friend. Gordo was not a Celli. He didn't have a clue who his biological family had been. "Who knows?" He wondered, "I may even have some Apache blood, just like you. Just like you, my dear silent warrior." He went off to get ready for his date. Like the good or at least hard-edged attorney he was, he'd gotten in the last word.

Hawk shook his head. Now his orphaned housemate wanted to be an Indian. Just like those artsy-farties moving into La Trinidad, New Agers, whatever they called themselves, they claimed they were reincarnated from Indians—usually a chief or a chiefteness. Everybody wanted to be Sitting Bull. Well, good luck with that, Hawk concluded. For the time being, sober as the day he was born and whether Apache or not himself, Hawk was left to his brooding and the Ouiji board game that nevertheless was no game.

Somehow, he'd become the town medium. It was a whole lot better than being the town's scourge, like he'd felt he was all his days as a drunkard. Now, whenever someone had a need to communicate with a dearly departed one, Hawk was ready to serve as a conduit. Although he never would have asked for much needed compensation, satisfied customers always wanted to give him something. They'd offer a few dollars, homemade tamales or a maybe a pot of posole. A live goat. A roasted goat. One woman wanted to give him her defunct husband's sheepskin jacket. Hardly worn. She was sure the dead man would have wanted him to have it. When Hawk refused the gift, she said, "*Bueno,* then, let's ask him." That would have required another session. Being a conduit was draining. Hawk took the jacket. It hung in the back of the armoire. Draining and life changing, that's what these disembodied missives from the outside world were. Paralyzing, even, he thought, watching the Ouija start to spell something, Hawk's fingertips weren't even on the gadget.

Flying~ Under the Texas Radar
with Paco and Los Freetails

Ernest Hogan

Hogan's trail blazing novel, *Cortez on Jupiter* (1990), lives in the same neighborhood as Oscar Zeta Acosta's novel *The Revolt of the Cockroach People*, except for the fact that Hogan shoots his Chicano hero into outer space. In an interview with Rudy Ch. Garcia, Hogan reports: "When Norman Spinrad reviewed *Cortez on Jupiter* for *Asimov's*, he assumed I was an Anglo. I wrote the magazine declaring, 'I AM A CHICANO!'" Though it may seem an impossible error to make given the deep familiarity with Chicano life in the novel, the ethnic confusion shows the barriers and assumptions faced by Latinos wanting to write science fiction. In addition to a number of short stories, Hogan has written two novels *High Aztech* (1992) and *Smoking Mirror Blues* (2001), which while departing from the tradition, are very much in dialogue with the genre of cyberpunk. In the short story included here, Paco, who is currently residing on Mars, relates the adventures of the rock band he had back on Earth and how he ran into trouble with the CEO of Texas, Billy-Bob Paolozzi.

Why did I leave Texas, and come to Mars? Why does everybody ask me that? Haven't you ever been there? Or heard anything about it? Especially way-the-chingada back then, when they were worried about who was Texan, and the whole Great Texas Identity Crisis broke out.

In case you don't remember (nobody seems to remember anything these days, history becomes myth before you know it — I have a hard time convincing my daughter that I wasn't born on Mars) the whole Texas secession thing was largely the work of a billionaire/politician/entrepreneur named Billy-Bob Paolozzi who, quasi-legally, in the name of the Second Amendment, acquired some nuclear weapons. "If nukes were outlawed, only outlaws would have nukes. Besides, I'm just a concerned citizen looking out for the security of my proerty and/ or country!" Billy-Bob forced what used to be the United States of America to let Texas go and declared himself interim President/CEO.

It was a hell of a time to be a young man full of talent, hormones, and the urge to fuck and fight, scream and shout, and do something that would shake the world (or at least make for an exciting weekend).

Suddenly, everybody was making a big deal about Texas and how free it was — there was even some talk about officially changing the name of the country to Free Texas.

But, as Billy-Bob put it. "Texas ain't free — it's expensive!"

So there I was, a young Jewish Tejano, figuring that this was a real ¡REVOLUÇION! My chance to jump on the center stage to impress the world with my incredible talent, to send civilization off in a new direction, and to lasso me some babes while I was at it. It seemed so right.

Little did I know that the powers-that-be had other ideas. But then, don't they always, no matter who they are, or what planet they're raping?

It was my first taste of the cheap thrill of deluding myself that I was on top of the world — now, all these years later, I have a totally different idea of what it is to be on top, and of what a world is. Then I had a talent for music, and my parents kept exposing me to an eclectic mix of sounds. They actually encouraged me to go wild.

They were kind of wild themselves. Probably why dad died young, and Mom got sad and quiet.

My meshuguna antics made her smile. And that made me happy.

There was still some sadness in those smiles. As if she could see how it was going to end.

"Mijo, don't be yutz!" she would keep saying. "Why can't you make beautiful music?"

"I've got ambition. I'd like to do a symphony someday, but it's got to come out of the life I'm living and the world I live in. I can't just pretend I'm Zappa living back in the 20th century."

Then she started humming Dog Breath Variations and smiled.

I loved the way she smiled.

Anyway, I soon founded a band called Paco and Los Freetails.

And of course, you can't find any information on Los Freetails — the Texas government was working on wiping us out of all electronic memory just before the Big Kerblooie, and the shitstorm that had me hightailing it out off the Earth prompted the Texas' Bureau of Infomanagment to seek&destroy anything they could find about us.

It really is too bad. Some of those songs weren't bad.

By the way, I'm not calling Los Freetails by their real names.

Except for Tongoléléita — her folks actually made that her legal name, without a surname like a real mondoultramegasuperstar. Then she did become kinda famous.

The others sort of disappeared. Maybe they're dead. Maybe they escaped to somewhere better than Texas. If they did, I hope they're alive and well.

Tongoléléita had become a masterpiece of plastic surgery. Her family had so much faith in her voice that they went into serious debt making her face and body into something that could compete with other corporate sex idols of the era.

Her body was a bit too hard from all the implants to give her a fashionable superhero/bodybuilder-with-big-bubble-boobs&butt look. The unnatural dark chocolate skintone did make the mouth water. And those sculptured lips could do things pushing toward the supernatural.

I got distracted thinking about that, sorry. Where was I?

Why Los Freetails? It's like BúmBúmi, our drummer, said: "We're like the Mexican freetail bat. It revitalizes our desert environment by shitting on it."

She was a bit of a genius, and we came up with some fun songs together. If she hadn't preferred women we could have been a real item. As it was, we just got together a few times, because she thought she could get me in touch with my feminine side — talk about a disaster! She would have gone for more of a dikey look if the anti-homosexuality laws weren't so severe back then:

Or, as Billy-Bob put it: "Sex not according to God's laws in the Christian nation of Texas? I don't think so — we need to make it a capital offense! Or at least banish the perverts! Maybe we should just round them up and put them into the camps."

"Shitting on it," said El Muertonto. "I like that!"

Except for his darker-than-a-black-hole sense of humor, and the fact that he could turn his brain off and play a bass line forever, El Muertonto wasn't very likable. "Shit. Everything's shit," he would always say. He was totally death-absorbed. Skeletons and calaveras were tattooed all over his body — he even had skull features tatted onto his face. He liked groupies, but I think the babe he really wanted to bed was his beloved Santa Muerte. The image comes so naturally — him banging away at a skeleton in a wedding dress.

"Sounds more like you guys are expecting to get a lot of free tail," said Tongoléléita.

"That too," I said.

"What?" She pressed her perfectly spherical breasts against my arm. "I'm not enough for you."

"You? You're too much." El Muertonto slapped her buttocks, which weren't quite as spherical as her breasts.

"Too much for everybody." Búmbúmi blushed.

Tongoléléita made a pretense of being my girlfriend, but mostly because of her instinct to seek out alpha males and demand their attention. I knew damn well that once out of my vicinity, she'd go after whomever she figured was the nearest top dog.

I preferred my women soft and natural, but there was something about when Tongoléléita wanted you. When she focused those sapphire eyes on you, you were doomed.

She'd done the hotchachacha with El Muertonto, and Búmbúmi. The three of us discussed it behind her back. We let her think she had us all fooled. It would have broken her brittle heart if we didn't.

It was a gig at this place called Galaxia Tejana, one of those music places that was popping up all over the Earth back then the way nanohudu shrooms do on Mars in the spring. A Franketech fusion of an intimate joint where folks of assorted sexual identities could get together for high-decibel entertainment so they could do their own biological fusion later in private — though sometimes they did it right on the dance floor — hooked into the megawebs and satellite systems for live participation and monetary input from beyond the Texas borders. A lot of things that went on weren't exactly legal under the post-secession regime, but then when a lot of people start having a lot of serious fun, you gotta watch out for the authorities.

Mostly we were doing the download thing and private gatherings. By viral underground standards we were a success. This got us some breakout global corporate deals. Not to mention real money, rather than the peanuts they were throwing at us up to this point.

We were all excited.

"Do you think there are any corporati here?" Tongoléléita asked no one in particular as she scanned the smoky — it was legal to smoke government-approved tobacco everywhere in Texas then — room.

"Maybe even something better than that!" Búmbúmi's grin was more than natural — she had just amped herself with some of the cyberpsychedlics she couldn't seem to live without. "I feel a powerful presence. Something cosmic."

"I just hope I can get me one of those gals out there before we get some kind of police action coming down on us." El Muertonto was his usual morbid self. "Some of the gadgets I see out there aren't just for sharing entertainment."

The crowd was well-peppered with flashing and twittering gizmos. Most the usual, fashionable, wearable electrosocial hardware, but some exotic, custom-jobs that could be some renegade connoisseur's playthings, or the tools of law enforcement.

"I can feel something out there," said Tongoléléita. "We are going to be discovered."

"Yeah," said El Muertonto, but by what?"

Búmbúmi closed her dilated eyes. "I feel something ... beyond ... human...."

"Whatever it is," I said, "we better get ready to play."

"Yeah." El Muertonto squinted through the lights, trying to see the crowd. "Let's get these zombies dancing."

"Maybe we could de-zombify them!" Búmbúmi grinned too hard.

"How do I look?" asked Tongoléléita as she did that peculiar tip-toe spinaround that she did when trying to see her own body.

"You look great," I slapped her implant-stretched ass, and almost hurt my hand.

"I'm gaining fat and losing muscle! If only I was rich enough to afford a tech to make surgical adjustments on me before every performance."

"Mija, you look great," Búmbúmi said with a flirtatious wink.

"Delicioso!" El Muertonto did something obscene with his tongue.

The owner drooled onto the jutting lapels of his cornball zoot suit at the sight. El Muertonto actually did the casting couch boogie with him to get us booked. "He was almost as good as this guy I did in jail once."

I was all decked out in a Huichol shaman's hat, a guayabera shirt, made-in-Vietnam Levi 501s, and my prize Virgin of Guadalupe cowboy boots. I tucked the 501s into the boots to expose the Virgins. My mother always liked it I when showed an interest in religious imagery.

El Muertonto was all in black as usual, his shirt cut to show off his skeletoid tats.

Búmbúmi was in a strobing cyberpyschedlic suit that left multiple after-images on your retinas when you looked at her.

Tongoléléita was dressed in a lacy film that clung to her implant-festooned form like a second skin. Male and female eyes locked onto her like bugs.

Bugs were different back then. Bigger, louder, less subtle. Not like the ones these days that either look like real insects, or you can't tell they're there. That reminds me — l should do a sweep with the sniffer, just to make sure.

There were probably bugs watching us at those Austin gigs. We were too busy — and too distracted — to notice. Lately, here on Mars, I'm on the lookout for such things — you can't be too careful with all those rumors of new-improved killer ninja bugs. It's possible — the technology exists.

They say I'm paranoid. But the older I get, I get more convinced that I've been watched my entire life. Like everybody else.

We're probably being watched right now.

The only thing that saves us is that there are too many of us, and there's just too much going on for them to ever figure out. Unless, of course, it's too late.

Anyway, the old zoot suiter tore himself away from leering at El Muertonto, and introduced us:

"Greetings, Amigos and amiguets, cowboys and cowgirls, tonight, we here at Galaxia Tejana are proud to present, some very talented young people . . ." He winked at El Muertonto. ". . . who have been really attracting a lot attention on the webs, and in various seedy dives, and vacant lots around town, so we've decided to give them their big break here at Galaxia Tejana, so let's make some noise for them . . . Paco and Los Freetails!"

They made a glorious noise. Alcohol and other chemicals were having their effect.

We made some back at them. They responded. Good. I gave the nod and Los Freetails cranked it up — including Tongoléléita delivering a killer high note that qualified as a sonic weapon in some of the more civilized parts of the planet. We drowned them out. They quivered in spastic ecstasy.

As Mr. Zoot Suit said, "Once they have that decibel-driven orgasm, you could play like squashed armadillos, and they'll love it."

I was determined that we not play like squashed armadillos. I saw this as our big break and was determined to send shock waves all over Earth and leaking out into the developed Solar System.

"Hola, Galaxia Tejana!"

The crowd roared.

"I'm Paco, and these are Los Freetails."

More roar.

"You've probably heard some of what we've got buzzing around the webs."

Laughter. Cheers.

"Like this little diddy that's been getting some criticism from certain gente in high places."

A wave of approval. They knew what was coming.

"It's damnear close to being a hit. It's all about how aesthetics isn't about giving in to your anal-retention and obsessive-compulsive disorders. It's isn't about control. It's just the opposite. It's not about perfection. Or purity. Control, perfection, purity . . . that shit's for losers. We call it Texanization Without Representation!"

They went, what they used to call in the old days, apeshit as we laid down the beat. El Muertonto and Búmbúmi got to work. Tongoléléita wiggled up to the edge of the stage, nearly knocking me over as she shook her implants. Individuals in the primo seats reached up and got zapped by the security system.

She bumped, grinded, giggled and worked the crowd into a state of premature esctasy. At the right moment, she threw a wink at me, and we harmonized:

"Texanization!"

The verbal explosion blotted us out.

Texanization was the big word back then. Ever since the secession. Some folks loved it, some folks hated it.

She then took it away with:

> "Since when are rules and
> regulations Texas style?
> Who says your cowboy hat
> is more Tejano than mine?
> Billy-Bob Paolozzi
> why don't you just
> go and die?"

With that the audience explodes with a mass ejaculation of approval that drowned out our amps.

Then they were blasted off any sensory range.

Several flash-bangs went off.

We were all blinded with ringing ears.

I closed my eyes, positioned my guitar so it could be used as an instrument of self-defense. I'd been through this before. I knew the drill.

The chaos I felt thrashing around me hit me a few times. Soft impacts, arms, legs, Tongoléléita's implants. No boots, cubs, or gun butts.

Yet.

As my distorted eyesight and hearing crept back, I could hear:

"EVERYONE STAY WHERE YOU ARE! DO NOT MOVE, OR YOU'RE GONNA GET A TASTE OF A QUASI-LETHAL ENFORCEMENT DEVICE! YOU ARE NOW IN THE CUSTODY OF THE BUREAU OF TEXANIZATION!"

Speak of the devil.

"THIS PERFORMANCE HAS BEEN STOPPED BECAUSE THE SONG INSULTED THE HONORABLE BILLY-BOB PAOLOZZI, CEO OF THE FREE, INCORPORATED NATION OF TEXAS UNLIMITED!"

And flowing out of the club's dark corners they came, shadowy hulking figures with cowboy hats, gas masks, and body armor that bristled with weaponry, lighting equipment, and combat electronics.

I was tempted to start playing *Ghost Riders in the Sky*, but the flash, zap, and thud of someone being tased stopped me.

Like giant, intelligent termites, they sorted through the crowd, checking IDs: "Hey! Looks like we got us an illegal here!" **Flash! Zap! Thud!**

They zeroed in on us. Targeting lasers seemed to pin us in place.

Tongoléléita stood there, her arms crossed, causing her breast implants to stick out in that way never found in nature. You could almost see steam coming out of her ears. Her eyes darted around — they couldn't decide who she was the most mad at for ruining her big night. But she did keep shooting lethal looks my way.

El Muertonto smirked with his usual "fucked again" look.

Búmbúmi shook and sweated with her mouth wide open. Her drug cocktail de noche was sending her over the jagged edge instead of inspiring her.

Soon we were zip-cuffed and packed into urban aerial assault & transport, being flown off to an undisclosed location.

After being bashed around in low-light, airless environments a while they left me in a dark room to wait for my interrogators.

I knew they had arrived when the lights and air-conditioning came on.

As my eyes painfully adjusted, I couldn't believe them. Maybe I had caught a contact high from Búmbúmi when she hugged me before the show. This had to be some kind of hallucination.

I was expecting to face a team of enforcement industry-types ready to play good-cop/bad-cop, but instead, hovering like a supernatural apparition, was CEO Billy-Bob Paolozzi himself.

This was the early days of autonomous hologram corporate icons. It was a primitive, flickering thing created in Billy-Bob's image. Since Billy-Bob was pretty damn predictable, it was essentially like being interrogated by Billy-Bob himself.

"Great," I said, "I'm hallucinating. I'm never kissing Búmbúmi again."

"No, boy. This is for real. And don't look at me like that. You could end up a hologram someday, too, y'know. You're in the custody of the Bureau of Texanization!"

"So to what do I owe the honor of your holographic presence, Mr. Paolozzi?"

"That's pronounced Pow-Oh-Law-Ze Texas style — I ain't no Eye-talian. I ain't no Americano. I'm a Texan! Hell, I'm *the* Texan!"

"Sorry, I used to go out with this Europhilic arty gal."

"Bet she's been shipped back to Europe by now." Billy-Bob grinned big. "We all gotta be Texan, you know! It's the law, dag nab it!"

"Speaking of which, just what are we all doing here?"

Pause. Static. "What wrong with you, boy? Don't you know what's been going on in the great nation of Texas Unlimited for the last few years? Ain't you hear about the Great Succession? You spend the whole revolution doped up on drugs and that bad music of yours?"

"Some people like it."

"Do I detect some sarcasm in your mode of expression, boy?"

"I don't know. I always talk like this."

"We're beginning to think that you ain't the kind of citizen we need here in Texas."

"I'm Texas born and bred, amigo."

They liked occasional Spanish words, but you had to pronounce them Gringñol style with a Texas twang.

"Born in El Paso. Mother Texas-born Mex. Father Texas born Jewish."

"What?" Billy-Bob lit up. "You got Jewish blood in you?"

"You some kind of racist?"

"Don't you try to pull that Americano political-correct mumbo jumbo on me, boy! We're still working the bugs out of a lotta things. It isn't enough for Texas to be corporate and install me as the constitutional CEO — I think we need an official religion to go along with Texan as our official language . . . but at least for now, the great nation of Texas Unlimited does not believe in racism. To be Texan is more about attitude than blood or skin color."

"You saying I'm not Texan enough for you?"

"Too bad we can't come up with a genome to define Texan purity. I wish we could create some kind of nanohudu stuff like what they're using on Mars, y'know, instead of making people into purple Martians, we could make 'em all into proper Texans, with all the right attitudes — if you know what I mean!"

"What, I'm not rebellious enough for you?"

"Rebelliousness is part of the e1s1s000000ential Texan identity, but it's more than that. There has to be a balance. You have to have loyalty to the Texan way of life. Besides, we're the ones who decide who's Texan and who's not."

"What, you mean things like my being born here don't count?"

Billy-Bob grinned. His teeth were unnaturally white, and symmetrical. "No, boy, Texas Unlimited ain't gonna recommit that fatal error that them there United States of Americans did. Letting anybody sneak across the border to drop anchor babies all over the place. Being born here is no longer enough."

"Since when?"

"It's a recent development. Folks have been yakking up over it all over the planet. Haven't you been keeping up with the news?"

"Well, I have been busy lately, with my career talking off . . ."

"Oh, you have been a busy buzzer. With that song popping up on some of the sleazier net sites I've ever seen. My sainted mama would turn over in her grave if she ever dreamed such things would come to be. Like this song Texanization Without Representation — downright shameful."

"Why? There's no sex, drugs, or glorified violence in it."

"You don't need to get dirty to be a menace to the society that we're heroically struggling to perfect here! This slop-bucket of sonic trash just oozes with disrespect, disloyalty, and subversion!"

"What ever happened to freedom of expression?"

"You can't go around expressing anything that twisted excuse for a brain in your pointy little head can come up with! We have to work to achieve a balance. In New Mexico, and Arizona the Indians and Hispanos have taken over. California looks like part of Asia or Africa. We can't let that happen in Texas. We can't let things get skewed too far to the dark side — like they used to say in those old-time rocket-ship movies. Everyone needs to undergo the Texanization process, after all, this is Texas, and if you don't like it you can run for the border."

"So, you're going to Texanize me?"

He flashed those big fake teeth again, and yukked like a happy idiot.

"No, Paco, my boy, I'm afraid that we've determined that you're a hopeless case. Just trying to log your information into our database confuses our algorithms! All our social pathology specialists say your influence will ruin our plans for a pure Texan society."

"And I thought I was just being me." I blushed a little.

"You're in a heap of trouble, boy. I've got a very creative legal staff that can come up with all kinds of ways to get you put away for the rest of your natural life — hell, they could even find a way to justify the death penalty. They've done it for me before. So, what you may be thinking about is just getting your half-breed ass out of Texas. Go to the U.S., Mexico, or some other God-forsaken place that will take you. If I were you, I'd get off the planet — I hear some of these corporations need folks to do menial labor for their developments on Mars. Y'know, I heard that some nerds somewhere are working on a gadget that could turn the entire planet into liquid assets. We should kidnap them, and force them to work for us . . ."

"I need to think about it."

"Think about it? You should have done that before you started all this! And you better do it fast!"

"I need to talk to my mom about it."

Another static-y pause. The mother reference must have triggered some algorithmic distress.

Eventually, some officers came and got me. I was tracker-chipped and released into my mother's custody.

"Mijo, I don't know what's going on in this world! Why should you have to go to Mars, just because of songs that kids like?"

"Ask Billy-Bob."

"He's a meshugana pendjo!"

She'd cry, hug and kiss me, and feel the lump where the chip was.

Then she collapsed and had to be taken to the hospital.

I didn't hear from El Muertonto or Búmbúmi again.

I tend to imagine him killing himself. His entire life was one long excuse to give himself to his beloved Santa Muerte.

I imagine her running off to some cyberpsychedelic commune.

I hope they found some degree of happiness.

Tongoléléita, was another story. Suddenly, she was all over every screen you saw. It wasn't quite the fame she wanted, but the world — or at least Texas — was paying attention to her for a while.

Seems Billy-Bob went crazy for her state-of-the-art body. Soon he was parading around with her as First Fiancé.

She was constantly being interviewed, giving tearful confessions about how I had manipulated her in singing subversive songs and having illicit sex: "I'm just a poor, innocent girl, all I ever wanted was to become mondoultramegasuperstar! I didn't know what those strange, big words they used meant. I didn't know that those sex acts were unnatural!'

Soon people were calling to have me hung on live pay-per-view broadcast.

"The way I see it, if enough legitimate citizens of Texas decide that someone deserves killing, the state should provide that service."

Death Penalty Live was the most popular show in Texas, and Tongoléléita was leading the campaign to put me in front of their celebrity firing squads.

That was about the time my mom went into a coma. It wasn't long after that that she died.

I blame Billy-Bob. And Tongoléléita. And Texas.

For a while I considered doing a maddog assassination on his ass, but I kept thinking about what Mom would think, kept hearing her saying:

"Mijo, don't be a yutz."

This was when people were checking themselves into the Texanization Reprogramming Camps for reeducation:

"It's a crazy, mixed-up world, amigos, and you can never be sure if you've picked up some unhealthy, unTexan influences. They can hang around for years, festering away in your brain, until one day — KA-POW! — you find yourself committing a shameful act that will get you a guest shot on Death Penalty Live. So I recommend you do what I did, go through a Full Volunteer Reprogramming Course at your local camp. They use proven reeducation techniques that some fuzzy-headed types used to call brainwashing — but what's wrong with a clean brain? Especially one that's one hundred percent Texan!"

Then I was seeing bugs everywhere. Big ugly ones that looked weaponized.

Life was horrible, and I was never one for suicide — besides, it would have made Billy-Bob and Tongoléléita happy, so I signed up to go to Mars instead.

It was just in the nick of time, too. I didn't like the look of the bugs that were following me around, and the votes of Texans who wanted me dead kept coming in.

It was a relief to get rid of the tracker chip, and get out of Texas, and off Earth.

Billy-Bob just loved to shoot his mouth off. Kept saying things that pissed people off not just in what was left of the United States of America and Mexico, but the rest of the world. As he like to put it, "I've got nukes, if you don't like what I say you can kiss my ass."

I was approaching Mars' gravity well when Austin went up in mushroom cloud, taking Billy-Bob, Tongoléléita, and a lot of other poor bastards along for the radioactive ride. They were never sure who did it. The list of suspects went on forever.

Some of them were even Texans.

Of course, with the fallout and all, Texas, and all of Greater Norteamerica got weirder than ever. New improved Texas! Wild, weird, and radioactive! Yee-haw, pendejos!

I was sure glad, Mom didn't live to see all that shit.

No matter how crazy it gets on Mars — it'll always be a lot saner than Texas!

MONSTRO

Junot Díaz

Yunior, the distinctive narrator in *The Brief Wondrous Life of Oscar Wao* (2007), comments on his protagonist Oscar: "You really want to know what being an X-Man feels like? Just be a smart bookish boy of color in a contemporary U.S. ghetto. Mamma mia! Like having bat wings or a pair of tentacles growing out of your chest." Díaz not only uses the language of science fiction and fantasy, he is also a piercing theorizer of the genres he loves, making clear that the colonialism endured by the Caribbean is deeply intertwined with science fiction and fantasy. He says in interview: "... if it wasn't for race, X-Men doesn't make sense. If it wasn't for the history of breeding human beings in the New World through chattel slavery, Dune doesn't make sense. If it wasn't for the history of colonialism and imperialism, Star Wars doesn't make sense." Born in Santo Domingo, Dominican Republic, Díaz has a BA from Rutgers University and a MFA from Cornell University. His collection of short stories *Drown* (1996) took the country by storm and he received the Pulitzer Prize for Fiction for his novel *The Brief Wondrous Life of Oscar Wao* in 2008. He is currently a professor of writing at MIT.

At first, Negroes thought it *funny*. A disease that could make a Haitian blacker? It was the joke of the year. Everybody in our sector accusing everybody else of having it. You couldn't display a blemish or catch some sun on the street without the jokes starting. Someone would point to a spot on your arm and say, Diablo, haitiano, que te pasó?

La Negrura they called it.

The Darkness.

These days everybody wants to know what you were doing when the world came to an end. Fools make up all sorts of vainglorious self-serving plep — but me, I tell the truth.

I was chasing a girl.

I was one of the idiots who didn't heed any of the initial reports, who got caught way out there. What can I tell you? My head just wasn't into any mysterious disease — not with my mom sick and all. Not with Mysty.

Motherfuckers used to say culo would be the end of us. Well, for me it really was.

In the beginning the doctor types couldn't wrap their brains around it, either.

The infection showed up on a small boy in the relocation camps outside Port-au-Prince, in the hottest March in recorded history. The index case was only four years old, and by the time his uncle brought him in his arm looked like an enormous black pustule, so huge it had turned the boy into an appendage of the arm. In the glypts he looked terrified.

Within a month, a couple of thousand more infections were reported. Didn't rip through the pobla like the dengues or the poxes. More of a slow leprous spread. A black mold-fungus-blast that came on like a splotch and then gradually started taking you over, tunnelling right through you — though as it turned out it wasn't a mold-fungus-blast at all. It was something else.

Something new.

Everybody blamed the heat. Blamed the Calientazo. Shit, a hundred straight days over 105 degrees F. in our region alone, the planet cooking like a chimi and down to its last five trees — something berserk was bound to happen. All sorts of bizarre outbreaks already in play: diseases no one had names for, zoonotics by the pound. This one didn't cause too much panic because it seemed to hit only the sickest of the sick, viktims who had nine kinds of ill already in them. You literally had to be falling to pieces for it to grab you.

It almost always started epidermically and then worked its way up and in. Most of the infected were immobile within a few months, the worst comatose by six. Strangest thing, though: once infected, few viktims died outright; they just seemed to linger on and on. Coral reefs might have been adios on the ocean floor, but they were alive and well on the arms and backs and heads of the infected. Black rotting rugose masses fruiting out of bodies. The medicos formed a ninety-nation consortium, flooded one another with papers and hypotheses, ran every test they could afford, but not even the military enhancers could crack it.

In the early months, there was a big make do, because it was so strange and because no one could identify the route of transmission — that got the bigheads more worked up than the disease itself. There seemed to be no logic to it — spouses in constant contact didn't catch the Negrura, but some unconnected fool on the other side of the camp did. A huge rah-rah, but when the experts determined that it wasn't communicable in the standard ways, and that normal immune systems appeared to be at no kind of risk, the renminbi and the attention and the savvy went elsewhere. And since it was just poor Haitian types getting fucked up — no real margin in that. Once the initial bulla died down, only a couple of underfunded teams stayed on. As for the infected, all the medicos could do was try to keep them nourished and hydrated—and, more important, prevent them from growing together.

That was a serious issue. The blast seemed to have a boner for fusion, respected no kind of boundaries. I remember the first time I saw it on the Whorl. Alex was, like, Mira esta vaina. Almost delighted. A shaky glypt of a pair of naked trembling Haitian brothers sharing a single stained cot, knotted together by horrible mold, their heads slurred into one. About the nastiest thing you ever saw. Mysty saw it and looked away and eventually I did, too.

My tíos were, like, Someone needs to drop a bomb on those people, and even though I was one of the pro-Haitian domos, at the time I was thinking it might have been a mercy.

I was actually on the Island when it happened. Front-row fucking seat. How lucky was that?

They call those of us who made it through "time witnesses." I can think of a couple of better terms.

I'd come down to the D.R. because my mother had got super sick. The year before, she'd been bitten by a rupture virus that tore through half her organs before the doctors got savvy to it. No chance she was going to be taken care of back North. Not with what the cheapest nurses charged. So she rented out the Brooklyn house to a bunch of Mexos, took that loot, and came home.

Better that way. Say what you want, but family on the Island was still more reliable for heavy shit, like, say, dying, than family in the North. Medicine was cheaper, too, with the flying territory in Haina, its Chinese factories pumping out pharma like it was romo, growing organ sheets by the mile, and, for somebody as sick as my mother, with only rental income to live off, being there was what made sense.

I was supposed to be helping out, but really I didn't do na for her. My tía Livia had it all under control and if you want the truth I didn't feel comfortable hanging around the house with Mom all sick. The vieja could barely get up to piss, looked like a stick version of herself. Hard to see that. If I stayed an hour with her it was a lot.

What an asshole, right? What a shallow motherfucker.

But I was nineteen—and what is nineteen, if not for shallow? In any case my mother didn't want me around, either. It made her sad to see me so uncomfortable. And what could I do for her besides wring my hands? She had Livia, she had her nurse, she had the muchacha who cooked and cleaned. I was only in the way.

Maybe I'm just saying this to cover my failings as a son.

Maybe I'm saying this because of what happened.

Maybe.

Go, have fun with your friends, she said behind her breathing mask.

Didn't have to tell me twice.

Fact is, I wouldn't have come to the Island that summer if I'd been able to nab a job or an internship, but the droughts that year and the General Economic Collapse meant that nobody was nabbing shit. Even the Sovereign kids were ending up home with their parents. So with the house being rented out from under me and nowhere else to go, not even a girlfriend to mooch off, I figured, Fuck it: might as well spend the hots on the Island. Take in some of that ole-time climate change. Get to know the patria again.

For six, seven months it was just a horrible Haitian disease — who fucking cared, right? A couple of hundred new infections each month in the camps and around Port-au-Prince, pocket change, really, nowhere near what KRIMEA was doing to the Russian hinterlands. For a while it was nothing, nothing at all . . . and then some real eerie plep started happening.

Doctors began reporting a curious change in the behavior of infected patients: they wanted to be together, in close proximity, all the time. They no longer tolerated being separated from other infected, started coming together in the main quarantine zone, just outside Champ de Mars, the largest of the relocation camps. All the viktims seemed to succumb to this ingathering compulsion. Some went because they claimed they felt "safer" in the quarantine zone; others just picked up and left without a word to anyone, trekked half-way across the country as though following a homing beacon. Once viktims got it in their heads to go, no dissuading them. Left family, friends, children behind. Walked out on wedding days, on swell business. Once they were in the zone, nothing could get them to leave. When authorities tried to distribute the infected viktims across a number of centers, they either wouldn't go or made their way quickly back to the main zone.

One doctor from Martinique, his curiosity piqued, isolated an elderly viktim from the other infected and took her to a holding bay some distance outside the main quarantine zone. Within twenty-four hours, this frail septuagenarian had torn off her heavy restraints, broken through a mesh security window, and crawled halfway back to the quarantine zone before she was recovered.

Same doctor performed a second experiment: helicoptered two infected men to a hospital ship offshore. As soon as they were removed from the quarantine zone they went *batshit*, trying everything they could to break free, to return. No sedative or entreaty proved effective, and after four days of battering themselves relentlessly against the doors of their holding cells the men loosed a last high-pitched shriek and died *within minutes of each other*.

Stranger shit was in the offing: eight months into the epidemic, all infected viktims, even the healthiest, abruptly stopped communicating. Just went silent. Nothing abnormal in their bloodwork or in their scans. They just stopped talking — friends, family, doctors, it didn't matter. No stimuli of any form could get them to speak. Watched everything and everyone, clearly understood commands and information—but refused to say anything.

Anything *human*, that is.

Shortly after the Silence, the phenomenon that became known as the Chorus began. The entire infected population simultaneously let out a bizarre shriek — two, three times a day. Starting together, ending together.

Talk about unnerving. Even patients who'd had their faces chewed off by the blast joined in — the vibrations rising out of the excrescence itself. Even the patients who were comatose. Never lasted more than twenty, thirty seconds — eerie siren shit. No uninfected could stand to hear it, but uninfected kids seemed to be the most unsettled. After a week of that wailing, the majority of kids had fled the areas around the quarantine zone, moved to other camps. That should have alerted someone, but who paid attention to camp kids?

Brain scans performed during the outbursts actually detected minute fluctuations in the infected patients' biomagnetic signals, but unfortunately for just about everybody on the planet these anomalies were not pursued. There seemed to be more immediate problems. There were widespread rumors that the infected were devils, even reports of relatives attempting to set their infected family members on fire.

In my sector, my mom and my tía were about the only people paying attention to any of it; everybody else was obsessing over what was happening with KRIMEA. Mom and Tía Livia felt bad for our poor west-coast neighbors. They were churchy like that. When I came back from my outings I'd say, fooling, How are los explotao? And my mother would say, It's not funny, hijo. She's right, Aunt Livia said. That could be us next and then you won't be joking.

So what was I doing, if not helping my mom or watching the apocalypse creep in? Like I told you: I was chasing a girl. And I was running around the Island with this hijo de mami y papi I knew from Brown. Living prince because of him, basically.

Classy, right? My mater stuck in Darkness, with the mosquitoes fifty to a finger and the heat like the inside of a tailpipe, and there I was privando en rico inside the Dome, where the bafflers held the scorch to a breezy 82 degrees F. and one mosquito a night was considered an invasion.

I hadn't actually planned on rolling with Alex that summer — it wasn't like we were close friends or anything. We ran in totally different circles back at Brown, him prince, me prole, but we were both from the same little Island that no one else in the world cared about, and that counted for something, even in those days. On top of that we were both art types, which in our world of hyper-capitalism was like having a serious mental disorder. He was already making dough on his photography and I was attracting no one to my writing. But he had always told me, Hit me up the next time you come down. So before I flew in I glypted him, figuring he wasn't going to respond, and he glypted right back.

What's going on, charlatan, cuando vamos a janguiar? And that's basically all we did until the End: janguiar.

I knew nobody in the D.R. outside of my crazy cousins, and they didn't like to do anything but watch the fights, play dominos, and fuck. Which is fine for maybe a week — but for three months?

No, hombre. I wasn't *that* Island. For Alex did me a solid by putting me on. More than a solid: saved my ass full. Dude scooped me up from the airport in his father's burner, looking so fit it made me want to drop and do twenty on the spot. Welcome to the country of las maravillas, he said with a snort, waving his hand at all the thousands of non-treaty motos on the road, the banners for the next election punching you in the face everywhere. Took me over to the rooftop apartment his dad had given him in the rebuilt Zona Colonial. The joint was a meta-glass palace that overlooked the Drowned Sectors, full of his photographs and all the bric-a-brac he had collected for props, with an outdoor deck as large as an aircraft carrier.

You live here? I said, and he shrugged lazily: Until Papi decides to sell the building.

One of those moments when you realize exactly how rich some of the kids you go to school with are. Without even thinking about it, he glypted me a six-month V.I.P. pass for the Dome, which cost about a year's tuition. Just in case, he said. He'd been on-Island since before the semester ended. A month here and I'm already aplatanao, he complained. I think I'm losing the ability to read.

We drank some more spike, and some of his too-cool-for-school Dome friends came over, slim, tall, and wealthy, every one doing double takes when they saw the size of me and heard my Dark accent, but Alex introduced me as his Brown classmate. A genius, he said, and that made it a little better. What do you do? they asked and I told them I was trying to be a journalist. Which for that set was like saying I wanted to molest animals. I quickly became part of the furniture, one of Alex's least interesting fotos. Don't you love my friends, Alex said. Son tan amable.

That first night I kinda had been hoping for a go-club or something bananas like that, but it was a talk-and-spike and let's-look-at-Alex's-latest-fotos-type party. What redeemed everything for me was that around midnight one last girl came up the corkscrew staircase. Alex said loudly, Look who's finally here. And the girl shouted, I was at church, coño, which got everybody laughing. Because of the weak light I didn't get a good look at first. Just the hair, and the vampire-stake heels. Then she finally made it over and I saw the cut on her and the immensity of those eyes and I was, like, fuck me.

That girl. With one fucking glance she upended my everything.

So you're the friend? I'm Mysty. Her crafted eyes giving me the once-over. And you're in this country *voluntarily*?

A ridiculously beautiful mina wafting up a metal corkscrew staircase in high heels and offering up her perfect cheek as the light from the Dome was dying out across the city — that I could have withstood. But then she spent the rest of the night ribbing me because I was so Americanized, because my Spanish sucked, because I didn't know any of the Island things they were talking about — and that was it for me. I was lost.

Everybody at school knew Alex. Shit, I think everybody in Providence knew him. Negro was star like that. This flash priv kid who looked more like an Uruguayan fútbal player than a plátano, with short curly Praetorian hair and machine-made cheekbones and about the greenest eyes you ever saw. Six feet eight and super full of himself. Threw the sickest parties, always stepping out with the most rompin girls, drove an Eastwood for fuck's sake. But what I realized on the Island was that Alex was more than just a rico, turned out he was a fucking V—, son of the wealthiest, most priv'ed-up family on the Island. His abuelo like the ninety-ninth-richest man in the Americas, while his abuela had more than nine thousand properties. At Brown, Negro had actually been playing it modest — for good reason, too. Turned out that when homeboy was in middle school he was kidnapped for eight long months, barely got out alive. Never talked about it, not even cryptically, but dude never left the house in D.R. unless he was packing fuego. Always offered me a cannon, too, like it was a piece of fruit or something. Said, Just, you know, in case something happens.

V— or not, I had respect for Alex, because he worked hard as a fuck, not one of those upper- class vividors who sat around and blew lakhs. Was doing philosophy at Brown and business at M.I.T., smashed like a 4.0, and still had time to do his photography thing.

And unlike a lot of our lakhsters in the States he really loved his Santo Domingo. Never pretended he was Spanish or Italian or gringo. Always claimed dominicano and that ain't nothing, not the way plátanos can be.

For all his pluses Alex could also be extra dickish. Always had to be the center of attention. I couldn't say anything slightly smart without him wanting to argue with me. And when you got him on a point he huffed: Well, I don't know about that. Treated Dominican workers in restaurants and clubs and bars like they were lower than shit. Never left any kind of tip. You have to yell at these people or they'll just walk all over you was his whole thing. Yeah, right, Alex, I told him. And he grimaced: You're just a Naxalite. And you're a come solo, I said, which he hated.

Pretty much on his own. No siblings, and his family was about as checked out as you could get. Had a dad who spent so much time abroad that Alex would have been lucky to pick him out in a lineup — and a mom who'd had more plastic surgery than all of Caracas combined, who flew out to Miami every week just to shop and fuck this Senegalese lawyer that everybody except the dad seemed to know about. Alex had a girlfriend from his social set he'd been dating since they were twelve, Valentina, had cheated on her at least two thousand times, with girls and boys, but because of his lakhs she wasn't going anywhere. Dude told me all about it, too, as soon as he introduced me to her. What do you think of that? he asked me with a serious cheese on his face.

Sounds pretty shitty, I said.

Oh, come on, he said, putting an avuncular arm around me. It ain't that bad.

Alex's big dream? (Of course we all knew it, because he wouldn't shut up about all the plep he was going to do.) He wanted to be either the Dominican Sebastião Salgado or the Dominican João Silva (minus the double amputation, natch). But he also wanted to write novels, make films, drop an album, be the star of a channel on the Whorl — dude wanted to do everything. As long as it was arty and it made him a Name he was into it.

He was also the one who wanted to go to Haiti, to take pictures of all the infected people. Mysty was, like, You can go catch a plague all by your fool self, but he waved her off and recited his motto (which was also on his cards): To represent, to surprise, to cause, to provoke.

To die, she added.

He shrugged, smiled his hundred-crore smile. A photographer has to be willing to risk it all. A photograph can change todo.

You had to hand it to him; he had confidence. And recklessness. I remember this time a farmer in Baní uncovered an unexploded bomb from the civil war in his field — Alex raced us all out there and wanted to take a photo of Mysty sitting on the device in a cheerleading outfit. She was, like, Are you *insane*? So he sat down on it himself while we crouched behind the burner and he snapped his own picture, grinning like a loon, first with a Leica, then with a Polaroid. Got on the front page of *Listin* with that antic. Parents flying in from their respective cities to have a chat with him.

He really did think he could change todo. Me, I didn't want to change nada; I didn't want to be famous. I just wanted to write one book that was worth a damn and I would have happily called it a day.

Mi hermano, that's pathetic to an extreme, Alex said. You have to dream a lot bigger than that.

Well, I certainly dreamed big with Mysty.

In those days she was my Wonder Woman, my Queen of Jaragua, but the truth is I don't remember her as well as I used to. Don't have any pictures of her — they were all lost in the Fall when the memory stacks blew, when la Capital was scoured. One thing a Negro wasn't going to forget, though, one thing that you didn't need fotos for, was how beautiful she was. Tall and copper-colored, with a Stradivarius curve to her back. An ex-volleyball player, studying international law at UNIBE, with a cascade of black hair you could have woven thirty days of nights from. Some modelling when she was thirteen, fourteen, definitely on the receiving end of some skin-crafting and bone-crafting, maybe breasts, definitely ass, and who knows what else — but would rather have died than cop to it.

You better believe I'm pura lemba, she always said and even I had to roll my eyes at that. Don't roll your eyes at me. I *am*.

Spent five years in Quebec before her mother finally dumped her asshole Canadian stepfather and dragged her back screaming to la Capital. Something she still held against the vieja, against the whole D.R. Spoke impeccable French and used it every chance she got, always made a show of reading thick-ass French novels like "La Cousine Bette," and that was what she wanted once her studies were over: to move to Paris, work for the U.N., read French books in a café.

Men love me in Paris, she announced, like this might be a revelation.

Men love you here, Alex said.

Shook her head. It's not the same.

Of course it's not the same, I said. Men shower in Santo Domingo. And dance, too. You ever see franceses dance? It's like watching an epileptics convention.

Mysty spat an ice cube at me. French men are the *best*.

Yes, she liked me well enough. Could even say we were friends. I had my charming in those days, I had a mouth on me like all the swords of the Montagues and Capulets combined, like someone had overdosed me with truth serum. You're Alex's only friend who doesn't take his crap, she once confided. You don't even take my crap.

Yes, she liked me but didn't *like* me, entiendes. But God did I love her. Not that I had any idea how to start with a girl like her. The only "us" time we ever had was when Alex sent her to pick me up and she'd show up either at my house in Villa Con or at the gym. My crazy cousins got so excited. They weren't used to seeing a fresa like her. She knew what she was doing. She'd leave her driver out front and come into the gym to fetch me. Put on a real show. I always knew she'd arrived because the whole gravity of the gym would shift to the entrance and I'd look over from my workout and there she'd be.

Never had any kind of game with her. Best I could do on our rides to where Alex was waiting was ask her about her day and she always said the same thing: Terrible.

They had a mighty strange relationship, Alex and Mysty did. She seemed pissed off at him at least eighty per cent of the time, but she was also always with him; and it seemed to me that Alex spent more time with Mysty than he did with Valentina. Mysty helped him with all his little projects, and yet she never seemed happy about it, always acted like it was this massive imposition. Jesus, Alex, she said, will you just make it already. Acted like everything he did bored her. That, I've come to realize, was her protective screen. To always appear bored.

Even when she wasn't bored Mysty wasn't easy; jeva had a temper, always blowing up on Alex because he said something or was late or because she didn't like the way he laughed at her. Blew up on me if I ever sided with him. Called him a mama huevo at least once a day, which in the old D.R. was a pretty serious thing to throw at a guy. Alex didn't care, played it for a goof. You talk so sweet, ma chère. You should say it in French. Which of course she always did.

I asked Alex at least five times that summer if he and Mysty were a thing. He denied it full. Never laid a hand on her, she's like my sister, my girlfriend would kill me, etc.

Never fucked her? That seemed highly unfuckinglikely. Something had happened between them — sex, sure, but something else — though what that was isn't obvious even now that I'm older and dique wiser. Girls like Mysty, of her class, were always orbiting around croremongers like Alex, hoping that they would bite. Not that in the D.R. they ever did but still. Once when I was going on about her, wondering why the fuck he hadn't jumped her, he looked around and then pulled me close and said, You know the thing with her, right? Her dad used to fuck her until she was twelve. Can you believe that?

Her dad? I said.

He nodded solemnly. Her dad. Did I believe it? The incest? In the D.R. incest was like the other national pastime. I guess I believed it as much as I believed Alex's whole she's-my-sister coro, which is to say, maybe I did and maybe I didn't, but in the end I also didn't care. It made me feel terrible for her, sure, but it didn't make me want her any less. As for her and Alex, I never saw them touch, never saw anything that you could call calor pass between them; she seemed genuinely uninterested in him romantically and that's why I figured I had a chance.

I don't want a boyfriend, she kept saying. I want a *visa*.

Dear dear Mysty. Beautiful and bitchy and couldn't wait to be away from the D.R. A girl who didn't let anyone push her around, who once grabbed a euro-chick by the hair because the bitch tried to cut her in line. Wasn't really a deep person. I don't think I ever heard her voice an opinion about art or politics or say anything remotely philosophical. I don't think she had any female friends — shit, I don't think she had any friends, just a lot of people she said hi to in the clubs. Chick was as much a loner as I was. She never bought anything for anyone, didn't do community work, and when she saw children she always stayed far away. Ánimales, she called them — and you could tell she wasn't joking.

No, she wasn't anything close to humane, but at nineteen who needed humane? She was buenmosa and impossible and when she laughed it was like this little wilderness. I would watch her dance with Alex, with other guys — never with me, I wasn't good enough — and my heart would break, and that was all that mattered.

Around our third week of hanging out, when the riots were beginning in the camps and the Haitians in the D.R. were getting deported over a freckle, I started talking about maybe staying for a few months extra. Taking a semester off Brown to keep my mom company, maybe volunteering in Haiti. Crazy talk, sure, but I knew for certain that I wasn't going to land Mysty by sending her glypts from a thousand miles away. To bag a girl like that you have to make a serious move, and staying in the D.R. was for me a serious move indeed.

I think I might stick around, I announced when we were all driving back from what was left of Las Terrenas. No baffler on the burner and the heat was literally pulling our skin off.

Why would you do that? Mysty demanded. It's *awful* here.

It's not awful here, Alex corrected mildly. This is the most beautiful country in the world. But I don't think you'd last long. You're way gringo.

And you're what, Enriquillo?

I know *I'm* gringo, Alex said, but you're *way* gringo. You'd be running to the airport in a month.

Even my mother was against it. Actually sat up in her medicine tent. You're going to drop school — for what? Esa chica plastica? Don't be ridiculous, hijo. There's plenty of culo falso back home.

That July a man named Henri Casimir was brought in to a field clinic attached to Champ de Mars. A former manager in the utility company, now reduced to carting sewage for the camp administration. Brought in by his wife, Rosa, who was worried about his behavior. Last couple of months dude had been roaming about the camp at odd hours, repeating himself ad nauseam, never sleeping. The wife was convinced that her husband was not her husband.

In the hospital that day: one Noni DeGraff, a Haitian epidemiologist and one of the few researchers who had been working on the disease since its first appearance; brilliant and pretty much fearless, she was called the Jet Engine by her colleagues, because of her headstrong ferocity. Intrigued by Casimir's case, she sat in on the examination. Casimir, apart from a low body temperature, seemed healthy. Bloodwork clean. No sign of virals or of the dreaded infection. When questioned, the patient spoke excitedly about a san he was claiming the following week. Distressed, Rosa informed the doctors that said san he was going on about had disbanded two months earlier. He had put his fifty renminbi faithfully into the pot every month, but just before his turn came around they found out the whole thing was a setup. He never saw a penny, Rosa said.

When Dr. DeGraff asked the wife what she thought might be bothering her husband, Rosa said simply, Someone has witched him.

Something about the wife's upset and Casimir's demeanor got Dr. DeGraff's antennas twitching. She asked Rosa for permission to observe Casimir on one of his rambles. Wife Rosa agreed. As per her complaint, Casimir spent almost his entire day tramping about the camp with no apparent aim or destination. Twice Dr. DeGraff approached him, and twice Casimir talked about the heat and about the san he was soon to receive. He seemed distracted, disoriented, even, but not mad.

The next week, Dr. DeGraff tailed Casimir again. This time the good doctor discerned a pattern. No matter how many twists he took, invariably Casimir wound his way back to the vicinity of the quarantine zone at the very moment that the infected let out their infernal chorus. As the outburst rang out, Casimir paused and then, without any change in expression, ambled away.

DeGraff decided to perform an experiment. She placed Casimir in her car and drove him away from the quarantine zone. At first, Casimir appeared "normal," talking again about his san, wiping his glasses compulsively, etc. Then, at half a mile from the zone, he began to show increasing signs of distress, twitching and twisting in his seat. His language became garbled. At the mile mark Casimir exploded. Snapped the seat belt holding him in and in his scramble from the car struck DeGraff with unbelievable force, fracturing two ribs. Bounding out before the doctor could manage to bring the car under control, Casimir disappeared into the sprawl of Champ de Mars. The next day, when Dr. DeGraff asked the wife to bring Casimir in, he appeared to have no recollection of the incident. He was still talking about his san.

After she had her ribs taped up, DeGraff put out a message to all medical personnel in the Haitian mission, inquiring about patients expressing similar symptoms. She assumed she would receive four, five responses. She received *two hundred and fourteen*. She asked for work-ups. She got them. Sat down with her partner in crime, a Haitian-American physician by the name of Anton Léger, and started plowing through the material. Nearly all the sufferers had, like Casimir, shown signs of low body temperature. And so they performed temperature tests on Casimir. Sometimes he was normal. Sometimes he was below, but never for long. A technician on the staff, hearing about the case, suggested that they requisition a thermal imager sensitive enough to detect minute temperature fluctuations. An imager was secured and then turned on Casimir. Bingo. Casimir's body temperature was indeed fluctuating, little tiny blue spikes every couple of seconds. Normal folks like DeGraff and Léger — they tested themselves, naturally — scanned red, but patients with the Casimir complaint appeared onscreen a deep, flickering blue. On a lark, DeGraff and Léger aimed the scanner toward the street outside the clinic.

They almost shat themselves. Like for reals. Nearly one out of every eight pedestrians was flickering blue.

DeGraff remembers the cold dread that swept over her, remembers telling Léger, We need to go to the infected hospital. We need to go there now.

At the hospital, they trained their camera on the guarded entrance. Copies of those scans somehow made it to the Outside. Still chilling to watch. Every single person, doctor, assistant, aid worker, janitor who walked in and out of that hospital radiated blue.

We did what all kids with a lot of priv do in the D.R.: we kicked it. And since none of us had parents to hold us back we kicked it super hard. Smoked ganja by the heap and tore up the Zona Colonial and when we got bored we left the Dome for long looping drives from one end of the Island to the other. The countryside half-abandoned because of the Long Drought but still beautiful even in its decline.

Alex had all these projects. Fotos of all the prostitutes in the Feria. Fotos of every chimi truck in the Malecón. Fotos of the tributos on the Conde. He also got obsessed with photographing all the beaches of the D.R. before they disappeared. These beaches are what used to bring the world to us! he exclaimed. They were the one resource we had! I suspected it was just an excuse to put Mysty in a bathing suit and photograph her for three hours straight. Not that I was complaining. My role was to hand him cameras and afterward to write a caption for each of the selected shots he put on the Whorl.

And I did: just a little entry. The whole thing was called "Notes from the Last Shore." Nice, right? I came up with that. Anyway, Mysty spent the whole time on those shoots bitching: about her bathing suits, about the scorch, about the mosquitoes that the bafflers were letting in, and endlessly warning Alex not to focus on her pipa. She was convinced that she had a huge one, which neither Alex nor I ever saw but we didn't argue. I got you, chérie, was what he said. I got you.

After each setup I always told her: Tú eres guapísima. And she never said anything, just wrinkled her nose at me. Once, right before the Fall, I must have said it with enough conviction, because she looked me in the eyes for a long while. I still remember what *that* felt like.

Now it gets sketchy as hell. A lockdown was initiated and a team of W.H.O. docs attempted to enter the infected hospital in the quarantine zone. Nine went in but nobody came out. Minutes later, the infected let out one of their shrieks, but this one lasted twenty-eight minutes. And that more or less was when shit went Rwanda.

In the D.R. we heard about the riot. Saw horrific videos of people getting chased down and butchered. Two camera crews died, and that got Alex completely pumped up.

We have to go, he cried. I'm missing it!

You're not going anywhere, Mysty said.

But are you guys seeing this? Alex asked. Are you *seeing* this?

That shit was no riot. Even we could tell that. All the relocation camps near the quarantine zone were consumed in what can only be described as a straight massacre. An outbreak of homicidal violence, according to the initial reports. People who had never lifted a finger in anger their whole lives — children, viejos, aid workers, mothers of nine — grabbed knives, machetes, sticks, pots, pans, pipes, hammers and started attacking their neighbors, their friends, their pastors, their children, their husbands, their infirm relatives, complete strangers. Berserk murderous blood rage. No pleading with the killers or backing them down; they just kept coming and coming, even when you pointed a gauss gun at them, stopped only when they were killed.

Let me tell you: in those days I really didn't know nothing. For real. I didn't know shit about women, that's for sure. Didn't know shit about the world — obviously. Certainly didn't know *jack* about the Island.

I actually thought me and Mysty could end up together. Nice, right? The truth is I had more of a chance of busting a golden egg out my ass than I did of bagging a girl like Mysty. She was from a familia de nombre, wasn't going to have anything to do with a nadie like me, un morenito from Villa Con whose mother had made it big selling hair-straightening products to the africanos. Wasn't going to happen. Not unless I turned myself white or got a major-league contract or hit the fucking lottery. Not unless I turned into an Alex.

And yet you know what? I still had hope. Had hope that despite the world I had a chance with Mysty. Ridiculous hope, sure, but what do you expect?

Nearly two hundred thousand Haitians fled the violence, leaving the Possessed, as they became known, fully in control of the twenty-two camps in the vicinity of the quarantine zone.

Misreading the situation, the head of the U.N. Peacekeeping Mission waited a full two days for tensions to "cool down" before attempting to reëstablish control. Finally, two convoys entered the blood zone, got as far as Champ de Mars before they were set upon by wave after wave of the Possessed and torn to pieces.

Let me not forget this — this is the best part. Three days before it happened, my mother flew to New Hialeah with my aunt for a specialty treatment. Just for a few days, she explained. And the really best part? *I could have gone with her!* She invited me, said, Plenty of culo plastico in Florida. Can you imagine it? I could have ducked the entire fucking thing.

I could have been safe.

No one knows how it happened or who was responsible, but it took two weeks, two fucking weeks, for the enormity of the situation to dawn on the Great Powers. In the meantime, the infected, as refugees reported, sang on and on and on.

On the fifteenth day of the crisis, advanced elements of the U.S. Rapid Expeditionary Force landed at Port-au-Prince. Drone surveillance proved difficult, as some previously unrecorded form of interference was disrupting the airspace around the camps.

Nevertheless a battle force was ordered into the infected areas. This force, too, was set upon by the Possessed, and would surely have been destroyed to the man if helicopters hadn't been sent in. The Possessed were so relentless that they clung to the runners, actually had to be shot off. The only upside? The glypts the battle force beamed out *finally* got High Command to pull their head out of their ass. The entire country of Haiti was placed under quarantine. All flights in and out cancelled. The border with the D.R. sealed.

An emergency meeting of the Joint Chiefs of Staff was convened, the Commander-in-Chief pulled off his vacation. And within hours a bomber wing scrambled out of Southern Command in Puerto Rico.

Leaked documents show that the bombers were loaded with enough liquid asskick to keep all of Port-au-Prince burning red-hot for a week. The bombers were last spotted against the full moon as they crossed the northern coast of the D.R. Survivors fleeing the area heard their approach — and Dr. DeGraff, who had managed to survive the massacres and had joined the exodus moving east, chanced one final glance at her birth city just as the ordnance was sailing down.

Because she was a God-fearing woman and because she had no idea what kind of bomb they were dropping, Dr. DeGraff took the precaution of keeping one eye shut, just, you know, in case things got Sodom and Gomorrah. Which promptly they did. The Detonation Event — no one knows what else to call it — turned the entire world white. Three full seconds. Triggered a quake that was felt all across the Island and also burned out the optic nerve on Dr. DeGraff's right eye.

But not before she saw It.

Not before she saw Them.

Even though I knew I shouldn't, one night I went ahead anyway. We were out dancing in la Zona and Alex disappeared after a pair of German chicks. A Nazi cada año no te hace daño, he said. We were all out of our minds and Mysty started dancing with me and you know how girls are when they can dance and they know it. She just put it on me and that was it. I started making out with her right there.

I have to tell you, at that moment I was so fucking happy, so incredibly happy, and then the world put its foot right in my ass. Mysty stopped suddenly, said, Do you know what? I don't think this is cool.

Are you serious?

Yeah, she said. We should stop. She stepped back from the longest darkest song ever and started looking around. Maybe we should get out of here. It's late.

I said, I guess I forgot to bring my lakhs with me.

I almost said, I forgot to bring your dad with me.

Hijo de la gran puta, Mysty said, shoving me.

And that was when the lights went out.

Monitoring stations in the U.S. and Mexico detected a massive detonation in the Port-au-Prince area in the range of 8.3. Tremors were felt as far away as Havana, San Juan, and Key West.

The detonation produced a second, more extraordinary effect: an electromagnetic pulse that deaded all electronics within a six-hundred-square-mile radius.

Every circuit of every kind shot to shit. In military circles the pulse was called the Reaper. You cannot imagine the damage it caused. The bomber wing that had attacked the quarantine zone — dead, forced to ditch into the Caribbean Sea, no crew recovered. Thirty-two commercial flights packed to summer peak capacity plummeted straight out of the sky. Four crashed in urban areas. One pinwheeled into its receiving airport. Hundreds of privately owned seacraft lost. Servers down and power stations kaputted. Hospitals plunged into chaos. Even fatline communicators thought to be impervious to any kind of terrestrial disruption began fritzing. The three satellites parked in geosynch orbit over that stretch of the Caribbean went ass up, too. Tens of thousands died as a direct result of the power failure. Fires broke out. Seawalls began to fail. Domes started heating up.

But it wasn't just a simple, one-time pulse. Vehicles attempting to approach within six hundred miles of the detonation's epicenter failed. Communicators towed over the line could neither receive nor transmit. Batteries gave off nothing.

This is what *really* flipped every motherfucker in the know inside out and back again. The Reaper hadn't just swung and run; it had swung and *stayed*. A dead zone had opened over a six- hundred-mile chunk of the Caribbean.

Midnight.

No one knowing what the fuck was going on in the darkness. No one but us.

Initially, no one believed the hysterical evacuees. Forty-foot-tall cannibal motherfuckers running loose on the Island? Negro, please.

Until a set of soon-to-be-iconic Polaroids made it out on one clipper showing what later came to be called a Class 2 in the process of putting a slender broken girl in its mouth.

Beneath the photo someone had scrawled: Numbers 11:18. *Who shall give us flesh to eat?*

We came together at Alex's apartment first thing. All of us wearing the same clothes from the night before. Watched the fires spreading across the sectors. Heard the craziness on the street. And with the bafflers down felt for the first time on that roof the incredible heat rolling in from the dying seas. Mysty pretending nothing had happened between us. Me pretending the same.

Your mom O.K.? I asked her and she shrugged. She's up in the Cibao visiting family. The power's supposedly out there, too, Alex said. Mysty shivered and so did I.

Nothing was working except for old diesel burners and the archaic motos with no points or capacitors. People were trying out different explanations. An earthquake. A nuke. A Carrington event. The Coming of the Lord. Reports arriving over the failing fatlines claimed that Port-au-Prince had been destroyed, that Haiti had been destroyed, that thirteen million screaming Haitian refugees were threatening the borders, that Dominican military units had been authorized to meet the *invaders* — the term the gov was now using — with ultimate force.

And so of course what does Alex decide to do? Like an idiot he decides to commandeer one of his father's vintage burners and take a ride out to the border.

Just in case, you know, Alex said, packing up his Polaroid, something happens.

And what do we do, like even bigger idiots? Go with him.

Room for Rent

Richie Narvaez

Richie Narvaez was born and raised in Williamsburg, Brooklyn. He has a master's degree from the State University of New York at Stony Brook and attended the Humber School for Writers. Narvaez has primarily published short stories in mystery venues and his story, "In the Kitchen with Johnny Albino," appeared in *Hit List: The Best of Latino Mystery*. However, a number of the stories contained in his first short story collection *Roachkiller and Other Stories* (2012) are science fiction, and the protagonists in these stories often inhabit the same sort of noir worlds as his mystery fiction. *Roachkiller and Other Stories* received the 2013 Spinetingler Award for Best Anthology/Short Story Collection and the 2013 International Latino Book Award for Best eBook/ Fiction. In "Room for Rent," Hala, a space alien of the Pava species seeks out shelter in a new part of town for the impending birth of her children.

Hala stood in the black rain outside the landlord's door. Cold, sooty water soaked her tunic, but he did not invite her in. Although cramped and filthy, the room behind the landlord radiated warmth and the smell of food.

"I would like to see the room you advertised, if that is possible," Hala said. "Can you show it to me, please?"

"It's on third floor. Do I look like I'm making it up there today?"

Indeed, it didn't.

"Then may I have the key to go see it myself?"

"I don't hand over keys without three months' rent and three months' security, paid up front."

"But I need to see if it is appropriate — a good room."

"It's a room with a door, a floor, and walls, okay? I don't have time to bargain with every Pava that comes by. You want the room or not?"

"Yes, we need it."

The landlord extended a moist gray-green flipper. Hala dropped all the money she had in the world into it.

"Oh, yeah," the landlord said, "and you gotta evict the current tenant."

"But I understood the room was vacant."

"What's vacant anymore? But don't worry, it's just vermin."

"Is it sentient vermin? An animal?"

"What's not sentient anymore?"

Hala and her mate Zangano had been living at the terminal since their arrival. It was filthy, overcrowded. She would be giving birth soon, and she wanted a clean home for all the children. This was the cheapest unit she had found. And now she knew why.

"May I see how infested it is first?"

"Go right ahead. But I got your money in my hand, and it's going to stay there."

The landlord was Cangri, invertebrate, covered in slime. A large dirty crack ran down his shell. He ran a shabby building in the poorest part of the territory. But he was still Cangri. It was not her place to argue with him.

"Hey, you could always eat the vermin," the landlord said. "I know you people eat anything, even each other." He laughed to himself, his enormous moist belly jiggling.

"That is a lie!" she said, blurting it out.

The landlord gave her a long look. "Careful now," he said finally. "You don't want me to call the law." He threw the key at her. "Third floor, in the back." One of his eye stems turned to show the direction. "Enjoy your new home."

She could still hear his laughter after he closed the door.

The narrow stairs creaked under her great weight. She was heavy, with the children inside her. Her belly glowed hot when they were hungry, and they were hungry now.

The hallway was filled with a vile smell — almost worse than at the terminal. She clumsily held the key and, as soon as she opened the door, she heard them. The vermin. They scurried into corners behind boxes and what seemed to be furniture and bedding. They sounded large.

The apartment itself had a low ceiling, a small area that radiated heat, and a tiny cold room with a circle of water in a container. The windows were dark with dirt, which was perfect. It would a good place. Just then, one of the vermin crawled out from behind a box. It stood. As she had feared, it was a human.

It had a frail body, about a third of her height, and stood on just two thin appendages. It had long hair on what must have been its face. It screeched at her.

Hala clicked back but clearly it did not understand.

She opened the door and used her pincers to indicate that she wanted it to leave.

The human shook its head.

Then others came out. There were about a dozen of them, different sizes, different colors. Clearly, an infestation.

She pointed again at the open door.

The human who seemed to their leader hopped up and down with its lower appendages and then crossed its upper appendages across its torso. She understood that.

This was not going to be easy.

Zangano would tell her to hire an exterminator, but they had no money for that. She needed a translator.

Through the rain, Hala rushed to her job at the atmosphere factory. She knew that her boss, a Pava named Gargaho, had a translation device.

"Please tell me you're dying," Gargaho yelled when she saw her, "so I can hire someone who will show up to work on time." Gargaho had been badly mistreated by the Cangri — she was missing both antennules and wore three eye patches.

"I had to find a room," said Hala, dripping wet. "I told you."

"And that took you all morning?"

Hala bowed her head. "I need a translator. I know you have an old one, and I was hoping to borrow it."

"What do you need a translator for?"

Hala kept her head low. "I have vermin. Humans."

Gargaho sat down abruptly and crossed a broken pincer over her mouth. The stumps of her missing antennules fluttered. "Oh, that is truly awful. I had them in my first room. It took them forever to die off. I had to help them a little." She opened his desk and gave Hala the translator. "Good luck, Hala," she said. "With the birth, as well."

"I will return this," Hala said, looking up.

"Keep it. I have a better one."

Hala saluted her boss and traveled quickly back to the room, barely aware of the cold, sooty rain.

When she entered the room, the vermin came out again, scurrying from their corners. Hala spoke, trying the language that was set as the former dominant language of the planet: "가셔야 합니다."

The human leader shook its head.

She tried several more — <"Nyt jätät,"> <"پ کو علاقے سے چلے جانا کاہیے."> ... — before she found one that the vermin responded to.

<"You must leave,"> the translator said for her.

The human threw its appendages in the air. <"Finally!"> it said. <"No. We're not leaving. This is our home. We've been here for years, long before you people, and the slugs.">

<"The slugs?">

<"The other aliens. The ones with the eyes that go like this.">

The human approximated the eye stems of the Cangri, and Hala found that she was amused.

<"Those are the Cangri. I am not one of ... it does not matter. You must find new shelter.">

<"That slimy slug from downstairs sent you.">

<"I have paid for this room.">

<"That's not the way it works. We were here first.">

<"You can no longer stay here.">

<"Where will we go? There is nowhere to go. There is nowhere on the planet good for us anymore. You think we have a spaceship stashed around here? Where, under the radiator? Do you see one? Because I do not.">

<"But you must go.">

<"Yeah. And what about the children?">

Children? She had not recognized the smaller ones as immature vermin before. Of course. Their limbs were smoother and their eyes were still full of light. Children.

Hala waited for Zangano outside of his job at the soil processing plant. She watched the other workers leave at the end of the shift but did not see him.

Suddenly, she felt a pincer tap her shoulder. He was behind her.

"You frightened me," Hala said.

"I did! Here, I got you a bag of miyeok."

"Zangano," she said, grabbing the bag. "We have no money —."

"I stole it from a cart!"

She was too hungry to scold him. She sucked in the fluorescent green leaves that smelled of the sea and let her stomach chew the food. Zangano was half her size and looked up at her as she ate.

"Not long ago," she said, swaying, "these were dancing in the sea. Then there was a storm, a frightening storm."

"Do you love it?"

"It is delicious."

"It is more delicious because it is free."

"Zangano! Did you leave work early to get this?"

"Yes. So what?"

"Zangano, you cannot risk losing another job."

"You do not have to worry. Mr. Moco likes me. Tell me you love the miyeok again."

"I do, yes. It is the only good thing about this planet."

Then Zangano asked her if they were going back to the terminal, and Hala told him about the room and then about the vermin.

"Why not just throw them out?" he said.

"There are too many of them. I did not want to get into a struggle in my condition. Besides, they have children. They are a family."

"That does not mean we have to live with them."

"You should be happy they have agreed to remain in the small room behind the door."

"I will smell them. They will stink."

"You will get used to it."

"When the time comes, they must leave."

"When the time comes," Hala said, "they will have left."

At the apartment, Zangano screeched at the vermin to make them scatter. Hala made him stop.

"To be reduced to this," he said, "when we once had a home with green all around us."

"You must learn to understand our role in the universe. There will always be the ones who feed on the weak. But in time the weak will become powerful. And then become weak again. The cycle continues forever."

"I hate it when you get religious. I don't want to stay weak in my lifetime."

"Then join the rebels, Zangano. Although then it will not be likely that you will see your children grow."

He turned sullen and curled into a ball by the window, cuffing any human that came near him.

Zangano stayed out of the room as much as he could, and he would return late at night, surly and silent. So Hala was often left alone with the vermin. The adult ones avoided her, but the immature ones would often gather around her. So much so that she began to differentiate them, and to name them. She realized how sickly the children looked, even for humans.

She began to regurgitate the worm mash she ate at midday. She let it pool on the floor, and then she gestured to the humans to consume it. At first, they ran away, but soon they understood, and they ate, and they came to expect the food.

<"I'm so hungry!"> said the one she called Blin Blin, as it scooped the food into its face.

<"Hi! Hi! Hi! Hi!"> said the tallest one. Hala called it "Mimil."

<"Can I hold the translator for you?"> asked the small one, "Confley," as it did every day.

<"No. That is very kind of you. But no.">

<"What do you eat where you come from?"> asked Chot.

<"We heard the Pava eat each other,"> said Yerba.

<"That is a lie! It is a cruel lie the Cangri always say about Pava. But it is a story used to frighten Cangri children, the baby slugs.">

The children laughed when she used their word.

<"It is an excuse,"> she said, <"used by Cangri to subjugate an entire civilization. It is untrue, could never be true. The Pava are empathic, inside. When we ingest another life form, even a dead one, we feel its consciousness, its feelings, its heart. If we ate animal flesh, we would feel it screaming in pain, desperate to continue life. But plants are wiser, are different. Plants understand their place in the universe. They surrender willingly, sometimes with joy.">

<"Wowwww,"> said Mimil.

<"What is subjugate?"> asked Confley.

Eventually, the adult humans also began to eat her food. But none of them conversed with her. Except for Fo, their leader.

<"I need to talk to you,"> Fo said. <"I am not happy with this situation.">

<"The children seem to be happy.">

<"That's because they're stupid.">

<"Very well. Tell me what is upsetting you.">

<"Where do I start? First we have to all squeeze together in the damned closet,"> it said. <"And then you defecate in the corner. It's disgusting.">

<"I am building a nest for my children. I will give birth soon.">

Fo would stomp its appendages and sulk in a corner or stomp into the closet. But then it would come back out and want to talk about the Cangri.

<"It's them, you know,"> it said. <"They're the problem. I never liked them. Everyone else was excited. *Ooh aliens have landed! Aliens have landed! Hurray! Aliens!* But I knew they were trouble. They came in three little ships and said they just wanted a place to live. Hah! Soon a few more ships arrived, and then dozens, and then hundreds. We saw what was happening and tried to fight back. But we had nothing, no defense. They just moved in and took over.">

The story was much like that of her own people's. Except that while the humans had proved too frail to exploit, Pava had been forced to become laborers.

<"We are a noble, peaceful species,"> said Fo, waving its arms about in a way that always amused Hala. <"We lived in peace with each other. We were peace loving and intelligent and creative and inventive. We made no war. And we were willing to share our planet. But those slugs—those slugs wanted it all.">

She tried to make Fo understand about the universe, about its place in it. But it only seemed to want to sulk and to complain.

Hala stood in a circle with the human children, all of them facing inward. She held the translator but saw little use in it as the human child Confley kept saying the same word as he moved behind them: <"Button.">

The purpose of the game was to determine who held this "button," in this case, a short, sharp stick one of them had made.

Before the game could end, there was a knock on the door. Hala told the humans to hide.

<"But why? Why? Why?"> asked Mimil.

<"Do not ask. Go into your room.">

Hala opened the door, and there stood a tired-looking Pava holding a light pad and wearing a vest usually worn by Cangri clerks.

"Good day. I am here from the Pava Registry and Social Welfare Agency," he said, reading from the pad. "The government sends us out to make sure that all Pava are receiving good care and shelter. Are you receiving good care and shelter?"

"Yes, yes, I am," Hala said.

"Have you missed any work days in the past month?"

"No," she said.

"Have you had any contact with the rebellion or any nonconformist factions?"

"No, not at all."

The clerk was about to leave when he finally looked at Hala. He said, "I see that you will have children soon. This is excellent. So few Pava are being born these days."

"They say it is because we are so far from home that —"

At that moment Mimil and Broki tumbled from the closet and began to wrestle on the floor. The clerk's limp antennules flew up.

"Are those humans?"

"There are just a few," Hala said. "They are no bother."

The other humans emerged and gathered around Hala, since it was near feeding time.

"It's disgusting," the clerk said. "This place is infested. I can't allow you to have children in such squalor. This is no place to raise a family."

"If you . . . if you like, we can call an exterminator?"

"There will be no need. We've been investigating this area and found many groups of vermin like this. But I've never seen so many in one place. Tomorrow, we will come to collect them all. And you will be fined for their removal."

"But we can't afford ... Wait, will they be relocated, placed in a zoo?"

"A zoo? Oh no, my, no," he said. "The Cangri have finally found a better use for them: They make excellent fertilizer."

"I told you," Zangano said when he heard about the clerk that night. "Now we will have to find a new place. And how will we find one in time? I will not go back to the terminal."

"We will hide them."

Zangano rubbed his antennules with his pincers, as if he had not heard her correctly. "Hide them? The vermin? You want to protect the vermin when the children are so close?"

"But they are living beings. We cannot allow them be killed. The universe —"

"Hala, please, no more about the universe. I will kill them myself if you will not, and then discard the remains. If we are very lucky when the clerk returns and finds them gone, we may not have to pay the fine."

"No, Zangano, there must be a kinder solution."

"Hala, really, I have had enough of your —."

That was when Fo attacked. The human appeared behind Zangano with the lid from the room with the circle of water. It began striking Hala's mate with the heavy lid.

"Please! Stop!" she said. She looked around for the translator and saw that Confley had it and was struggling to hold it above his head to show to her.

<"We heard everything,"> Fo said. <"We know what's happening. You want to kill us. You're just like the slugs.">

Fo again hit at Zangano, continuing even after it had cracked her mate's carapace. The other humans moved in, even the children. One of them — Mimil? — held the sharp stick from the game.

What choice did Hala have? She had to save her mate. She moved quickly.

With her left pincer she speared the human Fo through its torso. It flailed and screeched and to quiet it, she put its head in her mouth and twisted.

In an instant, its feelings flooded her mind.

Fear. Anger. So much anger. Loneliness. And then, it had lied: The humans had not been peaceful after all. Soon after the slugs — the Cangri — arrived, the humans had had tried to destroy them, using weapons that had harmed their own lands, killed their own kind. And seeing farther back, Hala realized that this species had always made war. They had always been selfish and cruel and complaining. And they had been powerful. But the Cangri had been more powerful.

It was all part of the cycle, and Fo had never been able to see that.

She flung its corpse off her pincer and left it on the floor. The other humans scurried into the closet. Only Confley stood for a moment, looking at her, then it dove in after the others.

Hala excreted a paste to cover Zangano's wounds. His colorless blood turned blue as it seeped from his body. This filthy, worthless planet. This unholy world. She hated it, she hated it. She rocked her mate gently, and she hated.

Then, at this, the worst time, heat began to grow like fire in her belly. It was too early, she thought. But children must be born.

They began arriving, dozens of them. They hobbled around, finding their balance, examining their new home. She wanted to show Zangano, but he was dead.

Hala clicked maternally at her children, reassuring them. Limbs smooth and eyes full of light. But still she felt anger, that human anger. It was irresistible. It was delicious.

Her children would be hungry. They needed to eat. They circled around Fo's body and then she knew what she must do.

There would be screams. But it would be for the best. The humans will be remembered, their feelings and memories carried by her babies. Her children will never forget these children, these humans, the species who did not, could not understand its place in the universe. And her children will learn from those memories and they will understand.

She broke the knob on the closet door and pulled it open. Following her gaze, her children climbed in.

ARTIFICIAL

Edmundo Paz Soldán

Edmundo Paz Soldán has a B.A. in Political Science from the University of Alabama-Huntsville, and a M.A. and PhD. in Hispanic Languages and Literatures from UC-Berkeley. He is currently a professor of Spanish with a focus on Latin American Literature at Cornell University. Along with Alberto Fuguet he was the editor of an anthology of U.S. Latino fiction: *Se habla español. Voces latines en USA* (2000). Paz Soldán is a prolific writer and two of his many novels have been translated into English: *The Matter of Desire* (2004) and *Turing's Delirium* (2006). Paz Soldán lives in the U.S. but publishes in Latin America and so his work has been strongly identified with the McOndo literary movement which sought to move Latin American literature towards engaging technology. The short story "Artificial" is set in the same world as his science fiction novel, *Iris* (2014). When the narrator's father is critically wounded in battle and is reconstituted by technological means, his human identity is put in question.

It rained all morning the day they declared Dad artificial and Randal and I stared at each other, not knowing what to do. It had caught us by surprise after weeks of filling out forms in the Department of Reclassification, which had been especially hard because we were on our own; Mom, the coward, had left home after the first operation, when the doctors informed her that his injuries were serious enough that he was probably going to become an artificial. We'd tried everything: we woke up at dawn and stood in long lines to get into over-packed, under-ventilated buildings with windows so high and so small it was like being in a war zone. Mornings and afternoons that got us nowhere, because the system was down or was being updated and we would be asked to return the next day. In the faces of the others, we'd see dramas about to unfold or that already had: the hope or the pain—or the hope and the pain — when a sibling or spouse was declared artificial, or not. It was an endless melodrama that wore us out, but we couldn't escape it, even if we had wanted to.

At our last stop — an office where a lean, long-faced woman scribbled away without even glancing at us, surrounded by pictures of wild birds sketched with such hyperrealist precision that I thought they were holograms — Randal and I meekly, dutifully presented the documents that showed how good and dedicated Dad had been with the race, a real model human, always in a good mood, always ready with a word of encouragement. He wasn't a typical soldier, one of those sullen types all about physical strength: he'd organized a neighborhood reading group, played socc12 with the kids in Blind Square. A war hero, to boot. The time they sent him to the Malhado observation post and he saved his whole platoon, seven grateful soldiers: he'd figured out that the men of Orlewen were preparing an ambush, and instead of telling the others, he went in and fought on his own. That should count for something. It was bad luck, what had happened a month later: on his way back to the city, he'd tried to help an old lady lying in the street in front of the market, the apparent victim of a heart attack. He wasn't the only one. Four soldiers died, and he ended up in such bad shape that his children now had to fight to save him from becoming an artificial.

That morning, the woman in the Department of Reclassification who conveyed the final ruling to us said that we'd done the whole thing by the book, and that Dad's documents had been read and discussed by the committee. She said they were surprised that he would have been given patrol duty, at his age. I told her that he'd been put on desk duty once, but he had requested a transfer because he missed getting out there and pounding the pavement, risking his life to protect ours.

One of those intense types, she said with disdain. I don't know why you're so upset, he's going to love being artificial.

We insisted that we could provide witnesses to go before the committee to convince them not to do it. The woman looked at us, tired and ready to move on. She didn't understand why we were fighting so hard to be able to call Dad a human. Being artificial could and should be considered an upgrade. They had lots of advantages over humans: they were more efficient and were given better jobs. The hormone injections they got every so often kept them in excellent physical condition, and their memory, oh, their memory, was purged of traumas that could negatively affect their development. We weren't seeing what was right in front of us. All you had to do was to turn on the news to see who was really in charge.

Artificials born as artificials are one thing, my brother said, humans reclassified as artificials are another. And anyway, it isn't about better or worse: it's about being what you've always been.

Artificials have their humanity, too, she said, why stigmatize them?

They're another category, I said, why be one of them if Dad is fine being one of us?

If there were a war between humans and artificials, Randal said, Dad would be on their side, and he wouldn't be able to stand that.

The woman laughed, showing us her deformed arm. She said that she was 12% artificial and sometimes fantasized about cutting off her other arm, or damaging one of her lungs so they'd have to give her a synthetic one, or maybe even dousing her eyes with acid so her percentage would go up and, who knows, maybe they'd reclassify her. Lots of people had done it, we'd be surprised. Stop exaggerating, she said, there won't be a war between us and them, don't you see that we're working together, that we all want the best for Iris?

And so we left, despondent, and played Rock, Paper, Scissors to see who would tell Dad.

Dad's hospital room wasn't very nice, but it was no one's fault. He'd been convalescing for six months. In the beginning he'd been assigned a big, bright one; later, he'd had to make room for those who had been wounded more recently in battle, which is how he ended up in this dark little corner by the physical therapy wing. When we arrived, the nurses had already gotten his suitcase together and he was ready to go. It was strange to see him, I still wasn't used to it. The doctors had done an incredible job with the reconstruction: the charred face I had seen after the explosion, the chest run through with metal and glass, the missing legs—they had all been replaced remarkably well, and standing before us was a being that looked a lot like Dad, though it wasn't entirely him.

Dad got out of his hospital bed and tried to walk over to us. His steady, energetic gait had been given way to a hesitant one, so we reached him first and gave him a hug. He looked at us, searching for a sign of hope that wasn't there, and his one immobile eye reminded me which side of his body the bomb had ravaged.

He asked about Mom and there were words he couldn't remember; others came out all guttural and we had trouble understanding him, which reminded me of a few things I had read in the report from the Reclassification committee. If there had been no neurological damage, the report had said, the reconstruction would have rendered him 34% artificial according to the algorithms, and Dad would still have been human. But the explosion had also charred parts of his brain, and his long-term memory had been affected, along with his ability to process language and communicate; those adjustments had brought his artificiality up to 48.7%. Dad could just as easily have been human. But in cases like this, right on the line between two fates, the committee had the power to play with the numbers, and after days of deliberation they decided that since his memory would get worse over time it was better to classify him as artificial. We complained, discussed the matter with lawyers, said that we could accept a scientific result but not a final decision in which the personal impressions of the committee added so much arbitrariness to Dad's fate. Another committee might have reached a different conclusion, might have said that he was human and that was it. Only one lawyer gave us hope. There's something there, he said, and added that we should find him when we left the hospital.

He would talk to the media and raise a scandal. Dad could still be human. But when I saw him in the hospital I wasn't so sure, anymore.

As I drove us home through a persistent rainstorm that flooded the streets, Dad asked if we'd heard anything from Mom, and Randal explained that we hadn't. Dad moved his head from side to side, as though he couldn't believe that she could have been heartless enough to leave him, to leave the city while he was still in the operating room. That gesture was a human response, a sign of vulnerability, I said to myself, but what did I know. Maybe it had been programmed; maybe, like they'd said, in his artificial state it was impossible for Dad to be hurt by Mom's desertion. I should be better informed.

All my anger was directed at Mom, who had abandoned us without even leaving a note. I wondered where she was. Fate would catch up with her and make her pay for not rising to the occasion. Dad said that he remembered Trinket, the childhood cat he hunted dragonflies in the garden with, and Panchito, a parrot who could swear in three languages. He remembered his parents, the grandparents I never knew, who were so dedicated to their work he barely even saw them on the weekend. He had grown up with a nanny, Nancy, who would talk about the Devil as though he were someone from the neighborhood. He wasn't one of those who had come to Iris because they'd run out of options; he was drawn to the adventure it promised. Some went to Buddhist monasteries at the foot of the Himalayas, others lived in eco-communities along the Amazon; he and his friends would go to Iris. What an extraordinary time, he said, his voice full of emotion, when adversity made us search out new horizons, leave the familiar behind, reinvent ourselves. When exploring made us what we were.

If you look at it that way, Randal said, wiping the fog from the window beside him with his hand, maybe you could explore your new being that way; that could be good.

It's different, said Dad, very different. Being artificial doesn't make you a new person. You're something else, you're on the other side.

That's not true, Dad, I said, remembering the words of the woman in the Reclassification building, they're on our side, we're fighting together.

I think you meant to say "you're" on our side, said Dad.

You and us, I repeated, but it sounded strange, forced. You'll always be one of us, Dad, I said, no matter what some committee says.

I stopped at a red light and noticed that Dad's eyes had welled up. He wasn't entirely artificial, I thought, at least not yet; he was still shaken by the trauma, though the doctor said that this would change over time. He went back to talking about Panchito and Trinket, he wanted to hold onto the things that had made him human, those things that reminded him best that he was who he was and not what some committee said. As the light turned green, I suddenly got the feeling that something was wrong. Dad had never mentioned Panchito or Trinket before, or any Nancy who'd told him about the Devil when he was a child. Or maybe everything was just as it was supposed to be. Yes, of course. They had rebuilt his memory, too.

The good thing about all this is that only those closest to us will know, I said that night as I brought him dinner in his room, and I tried to believe it because that was what I wanted: no way were my co-workers going to look at me like the daughter of, of who, of what, I didn't know anymore. The room seemed big, now that Mom was gone. He was in bed and tried to eat the soup without help, but he had trouble with it. He was going to need physical therapy every day; it would be a long recovery. That's right, only those closest to us, I said, there's no sign on your forehead that says you're an artificial. I tried to sound optimistic: if the others do find out, though, you'll have better job opportunities. I don't need a sign on my forehead, said Dad, for everyone to know what I know. He repeated the sentence, unsure that either of us had really understood it. His voice was thick, unnatural. It's a matter of intuition, he said. A few officials have fooled me at the Perimeter, sometimes I haven't been sure, but in general I know who is and who's not. I didn't say anything because I knew he was right. Maybe the decades of living side by side with machines had given us a sixth sense, and even when they started to physically resemble us, something always gave them away. Or maybe not and I was being too sensitive, which is what I wanted to believe.

I kept him company in silence, a little uncomfortable at his clumsiness, surprised by how difficult an everyday activity could be, at least, for the moment. The doctor had said that he would be back to normal in a couple of months. A new normal, of course.

I couldn't sleep that night. At three in the morning I turned on the light in my room and the weight of what had happened came crashing down on me. I felt as though my heart had stopped.

I walked up and down the halls, as quietly as I could to avoid waking Randal, and wondered what had become of Mom, who couldn't bring herself to live with a man who wasn't her man anymore, a human who wasn't a human. In trying to understand her, I was able to stop hating her. This was hard on all of us.

I approached the door to Dad's room, which was ajar. One of his eyes was open, but he was fast asleep. I took three steps in, as though I were going to go over and hug him, but I stopped, not sure I was doing the right thing. The sound of crickets filtered through the window. I remembered a trip that Dad, Mom, Randal and I took to the black pine forest just outside town when I was seven. I was certain I hadn't made it up.

I started walking again, toward the side of his bed. He, who used to be such a light sleeper, didn't stir at all. Maybe it was the exhaustion of the past few days, or the painkillers. Or maybe he was just different.

That's what it was.

I couldn't hug him. Not that thing that looked like Dad but wasn't.

Maybe it was time for me to think about leaving, too.

THROUGH THE RIGHT VENTRICLE

Steve Castro

Steve Castro's one-sentence poem "Pillar of Fire," which appears in *Grey Sparrow Journal,* demonstrates the kind of loss and hope for renewal that permeates Castro's work: "The sunbeam that penetrated through the windowpane of their humble shack, seemed to be the only thing holding it up." The prose poem and poem here, "Through the right ventricle," and "Two unique souls" give a similar sense that even in the worst of situations, humanity might just be clever enough to survive. Castro was born in Costa Rica and later moved to southern Indiana. He has a B.S. in Recreation Science and a B.A. in Germanic Studies from Indiana University. He recently completed his MFA in creative writing at American University in Washington, D.C.

I had a choice to become fully robot or die. "A robot has no soul," I said. Complete silence. I knew they could hear me. "Robots do not die, but merely malfunction into oblivion, therefore souls are useless to you bastards!," I screamed, "but me, I refuse to be implanted with any more artificial parts into my being." I was born blind, so as a teenager I was implanted with two cameras that would record everything that I ever saw; those visions were then immediately transmitted into a memory chip that was simultaneously implanted into my brain. I have a photographic memory, I can see perfectly in complete darkness; I can also see through the thickest bank vaults, but I lack the tears to weep. During the brief but deadly twelve day war with Russia over Alaska, I was left paralyzed after my M1 Abrams hit a landmine in Anchorage. Infused with a new metallic spine, I run and swim inconceivably faster than I ever could before my paralysis.

I also lift incomprehensibly much more weight than I ever could previously, but as the door opened and that soulless creature walked into my confinement chamber holding an artificial heart, two artificial lungs and an artificial brain that it threw contemptuously into the stainless steel floor in front of me, I knew what must be done. I opened up my mouth wide, and I fired my artificial boomerang tongue right through that robot's right eye. As my tongue returned to me after exiting through that same robot's left eye, I got up, and with my artificial legs, I ran faster than any cheetah could have ever done through that massive iron door before it was able to close. As I approached the final obstacle to my freedom, I lifted up both of my artificial arms and fired ten lasers out my fingertips that cut the gate to shreds within seconds. As I exited that infernal military compound, I briefly halted as I allowed the fresh morning air to enter my lungs. I then suddenly felt a hollow tip bullet penetrate my heart, but that's expected, 'cause after all, I'm fully human.

TWO UNIQUE SOULS

Steve Castro

So how did you find out that I cannot die?

"I can see forty years into various potential futures,
and the only potential future where I wasn't murdered,
was the potential future when you found out
that I was pregnant with our daughter,
so I focused in on that future alone and followed its path.

I noticed that you lived through situations that no human being
should have been able to survive, so the only possible explanation
was that you couldn't die."

How many will there be?

"Eight, and they'll be here in exactly five hours."

How will they all die?

"You will kill each individual with their very own weapon."

Do we have time to get you pregnant?

As she led me to the master bedroom, she said
"I bought us two first class one way tickets to
Anchorage, Alaska. We leave in eight hours.
We should be there trouble free for nine years,
eight months and three days."

That's good to hear, I thought,
that would shatter my old record,
when I was left undisturbed for
four years and twelve days.

"That would also be a new record for me,"
she told me as she was taking off the belt
that I had previously used to strangle
three would be lovers.

CARIDAD

Alex Hernandez

The first of his extensive Cuban family to be born in the United States, Alex Hernandez writes in a genre of his own making: *Transhuman Mambo* (also the title of his 2013 short story collection). Hernandez's neologism is based on the popular coupling of a science fiction term with a musical form (space opera, cyberpunk) and describes quite accurately his combination of science fiction and Cuban culture. He was deeply influenced as a child by the work of Isaac Asimov, connecting in a personal way to this immigrant whose first language was also not English. While working as an administrator for the Miami Dade College Library, Hernandez has published a number of short stories in science fiction venues, including his story "A Thing with Soft Bonds" which was nominated for a Pushcart Prize and was included in *Near Kin: A Collection of Words and Art Inspired by Octavia Estelle Butler* (2014). "Caridad" is the story of a girl who bears the burden of maintaining, supporting and unifying her large, cybernetically-linked family, possibly at the cost of her own identity.

Tomorrow, Cary Garcia-Martinez will die. She was drawing Ruth in a sexy pose on her bed, when she looked down at the blank outline of a female form reclining suggestively on the white of her notepad and the enormity of the realization hit her. She started to sob, her tears hitting the page loudly, making the blue ink from her copic marker splash and run. Ruth rushed to her side and pulled her close. Now they were both lying in bed, entangled in each other's arms, surrounded by markers and sheets of paper crinkling as they moved.

Cary had known all her life that she would cease to exist on her eighteenth birthday, but the sudden arrival of the date — and the barely-started sketch of a girl — had rattled her with more force than she had expected. She clung to Ruth's plump frame, gripping her like a life preserver, shivering with anger and dread and helplessness.

Ruth kissed her damp cheeks and long, thin nose, whispering some nonsense about "figuring out a way to beat this" as if *this* were simply some lethal disease that could be cured with punishing chemicals and harsh radiation. Her imminent demise wasn't the result of a disease. No, it was something much more caustic — it was duty.

"We won't," Cary simpered and the pathetic, wet sound of her voice made her suddenly ashamed. She tried to get ahold of herself, sucking in deep, ragged breaths. She didn't want to ruin the last few hours she had left wallowing in self-pity.

Ruth took Cary's head in her hands and kissed her on the lips and looked straight into her brown, red-rimmed eyes. "We need to run away. Get as far away from your family as possible."

Something protective stirred within Cary at the negative mention of her family. She sat up, crumpling the loose paper of false starts under her. She hated it when Ruth talked about her family, even if they were trying to erase her from existence. That last thought made the irritation dissipate and a crushing resignation settled within her. "There's no place to run. Surveillance is just too damned tight with networked government employees sifting through and making sense of all the data collected. My family would find me in hours. Besides, where would I go? How would I live? We'd never get any work. No university would take me even if I could afford it without the Garcia-Martinez bank account."

Ruth sat up to face her, the concern in her blue eyes was endearing and infuriating all at once. "You need to talk to them then. Tell them how you feel. Tell them that you don't want this!"

Could it be that simple? Her mother would flip out immediately. She could hear her screaming and yelling already about how selfish Cary was, about how much they'd sacrificed for her, about betraying the family, crushing everyone's hopes and dreams. *What about her hopes and dreams, damn it?* Her father would try to calm her mother down in that soothing voice of his and assure everyone that Cary was just getting cold feet, but in the end he would not entertain the possibility that his daughter, his pride and joy, would not be going through with the procedure. Los abuelos, los primos, las tías and los tíos would push and prod and lecture and encourage Cary until there was a tiny sliver of metal in her cerebral cortex, like a lodged bullet, and she would be gone forever. "They wouldn't understand, or care what I want. Too many people would be screwed over if I backed out now."

"This is crazy, Cary! *You* are being screwed over! Doesn't that count? You can't just go through with this! I can't believe you're actually even considering it?" Ruth's pale face flushed and her cute freckles melted away into red. "This is some hive mind bullshit!"

Cary gently brushed a strand of sandy hair out of her friend's brow then kissed her burning cheeks. "You don't understand, Ruth. You're una Americanita. You're free and independent. You don't even know your family outside of your parents — who don't speak to each other—and one grandmother that lives two states away."

"That's racist!" her friend said without any real offense. *Was it racist? She didn't think so and, in Ruth's case, it was true.*

"My family is massive. All four generations are here, even the branches from Cuba and Venezuela and Spain have come for my birthday party—and to them, independence is pathology, self-reliance is shameful." Too many times she'd heard her mom spit out the word autosuficiente like a curse. "The hive mind is how we've survived brutal Dictatorships and long exiles. We're like fucking bees, but it's a survival strategy that works." *Was she now defending the vile process that would kill her? How fucked up is that, Cary?*

She shook her head violently, but the toxic mix of emotions remained. She was their appointed queen, after all, had been her entire life. They had spoiled her and groomed her since birth for this special responsibility and it had clearly done a number on her psyche. Everyone had pitched in to give her a wonderful childhood, with the certainty that when she turned eighteen and networked her brain to the entire family, she would pay them back tenfold.

Her father had always regaled her with stories of his high school friend, Cody Gonzalez, who became a professional baseball player and bootstrapped his entire family out of poverty. She was their Cody. Only this wasn't baseball. The colloquial term in English was "to become a *familiar*." With a minimally invasive procedure, she would become the Garcia-Martinez family's familiar. Most Latinos though just referred to their familiar as Mi Hija, or Mi Nieta, Mi Sobrina or Mi Prima. You could hear the possessiveness in their voices. She knew that Asian and African families did something similar. The familiar is the member of the family that represented them all, supported them, cared for them, protected them in this cruel, complex world, and bound them together even though politics and economics have scattered them apart. They wore the tacky headbands that constantly transmitted their thoughts to the familiar with pride, the way some people flaunted a brand-name purse or nice shoes or an expensive car. It said to everyone around them, "That's right, bitches, this right here is a direct line to Mi Sobrina, and she's voting in this year's elections for us, or she bought this big house for us with her good job, or she won a Noble Prize in Physics!"

"But you won't survive!" Ruth railed, snapping her out of her reverie. "Not really! You'll become a statistical aggregate of all their thoughts, a human spreadsheet, a puppet shuffling around like Megan Choi at school when she's on her meds! You won't be Cary anymore."

"I know!" Cary pushed Ruth away roughly. She loved this girl. They had everything in common; they gushed over the same books, obsessed over the same games, binged on the same Korean anime, liked the same music and movies, crushed on the same boys and girls, and recently started fooling around in bed. Cary wasn't sure what that meant yet, if anything, but it made her sad that she would never get to find out. "I've always known! The problem is I never thought I'd like myself so much in the end." *My God, this was the end.*

"Promise me you'll talk to your parents. They can't force you to put that thing in your head. That's illegal. You have to be a consenting adult, right? So don't consent."

"It won't make a difference."

"But there will at least be a chance! If you don't try, for sure you're a goner. If you talk to them — cry, throw a tantrum — they might feel guilty and back off."

Throw a tantrum? Cary had never thrown a tantrum in her entire life. Her family had always given her what she wanted and instead of making her a vapid, materialistic monster of a teenager, it actually had the opposite effect. She had become desensitized to *stuff*, it just wasn't important to her. And what she did value, she was about to lose. "I'll talk to them. I promise."

"I'll be there at your party, no matter what."

"Can we stop talking about this? Just come here and snuggle with me because I'm scared shitless and you're only freaking me out more." She pulled Ruth back down to the bed.

"Is that all, just snuggle?"

"Yeah, it's all I can manage right now."

The house buzzed with activity. Her grandmothers, mother and about twelve aunts swarmed in and out of the kitchen, wiping and polishing everything until it shone like stainless steel. The men in her family were outside: mowing the lawn, hosing down the screened-in porch, and waging war on the aggressive bougainvillea, with its lipstick-colored flowers and perilous thorns, that had the audacity to grow a little too high or too far. And they set up la caja china, both coffin and barbeque, for the pork. Kids of all ages ran around screaming like maniacs. Their constant chatter, in three different Spanish accents as well as various degrees of English, rose above the four TV screens blaring the news or novelas throughout the house.

Ruth had left late last night and Cary was now paying for it, but the din mingling with the astringent, artificial lemon scent jolted her more fully wake. She wondered if this is what it would be like, their voices always chittering in her head like invisible insects on a balmy night. Would her own Miami accent, with its imperfections and superimposed English grammar, be reduced to something flat and boring and precise like the news anchors on TV?

An aunt, Tía Mari, grabbed her as she shambled down the hall and squeezed her tight. "Happy birthday! I'm so proud of you!"

Cary nodded and struggled lose. Everyone exploded with glee as she stepped into the family room, embracing her, congratulating her, praising her, wearing her down with words the way they rubbed at the grime on the furniture.

She went into the kitchen, picked out un pastelito de guayaba from the white box someone had gotten at the bakery early in the morning and dropped on the table. The harsh glare from the window hurt her eyes so she focused on her mom's butt moving rhythmically back and forth. It was the only part of her sticking out of the oven. Cary opened her mouth to say something, announce that she wasn't going to go through with the procedure, but with everyone around she felt outnumbered so she shoved the pastelito in her mouth and watched the bustle instead. And she chewed, working the gummy guava jelly out of her teeth, building up courage.

"Where's Papi?" she mumbled when she could speak again.

"He went with Yovany to buy headbands for everyone," her mom's butt said, then the rest of the woman crawled backwards and reared its head. For an instant, it struck Cary how much she looked like her mother: milk chocolate skin, bouncy, curly hair, only Cary had her father's prominent nose and almond-shaped eyes. "¡Que robo! Those things have gotten so expensive. You'd think that as the technology gets better, the prices would get cheaper." She talked about the things as if they were nothing — phones or personal fabricators — not the devices that would turn her daughter into an automaton.

"I'm scared," Cary whispered, when the last of her aunts scurried out of the kitchen hauling a large bottle of Clorox. Her mom didn't acknowledge her statement, instead she wiped her brow, sighed heavily, and dived back into the oven. "I don't know if I want this?" Cary continued, a little louder over the vigorous scrapping. The words coagulated in her throat like thick guava. "I don't want to lose myself."

Her mother, no longer able to ignore the topic emerged once more and — still on her knees — glared at Cary. "Aye, don't be so dramatic! You'll still be yourself, you'll just be all of us too."

She wasn't sure if that was entirely true. Cary had read articles that questioned whether the familiar added to the dataset of experience or if they were just a hollowed-out receiver. "I don't know if I want that."

"What do you want, then?" her mother asked in a low hiss, as if she had already dismissed any answer to that question as utter foolishness. It was like the vague sex talk they'd had a few years back that had inexplicably blown up into a week-long fight.

"That's the point," Cary shrugged, trying to stay calm. "I haven't figured myself out yet, and after today I never will."

Her mother sucked through her teeth. Beads of sweat vibrated on her face with mounting anger. "Eso es la Americanita putting ideas in your head again!"

"No, these are my ideas!" The irony that it was, in fact, her entire family that were quite literally going to shove their ideas into her head escaped her mother entirely, of course. She always blamed Ruth. "I've been thinking about this for a while, reading up on what it means to be a familiar."

Her mother threw her soapy sponge into a bucket, splashing dirty water on the already clean floor. "Mira, I don't have time for this right now so let's break this down, okay? What is it that you think you want to do with your life? Draw? Become an artist? A designer?" She nodded as if those were perfectly sensible options. "What school do you think you'll be able to afford? And if you get loans, like your little American friends, you'll be an indentured servant for the rest of your life. Also, there are no jobs out there! Don't you watch the news? Ivan has a Civil Engineering degree from Venezuela, Yanexy was a Doctor in Cuba, Hector was in computers. They can't get work! Y tu prima, Karen, did exactly what you're considering right now, she took out an insane loan to get her law degree y que esta haciendo ahora? Putiando!"

Her mother always threw her cousin, Karen, in her face whenever they argued, but in her fury she failed to mention that some people were getting by. Xiomara was running a daycare out of her house, same as Lizet's unlicensed hair salon, and Marcos was doing well with his insurance fraud.

"Why would anyone hire fifty different people, when they can hire one who's smarter and who's got more experience than fifty people? You know very well como están las cosas ahora! And to make matters worse, there are no manufacturing or retail jobs anymore. The fabricators took care of that!"

Cary bottled up. She dropped the rest of her pastelito into the white cardboard box and laced her fingers. Her mother had always been the pragmatic one. She could cut down any squishy dream with a quick swipe of hard reason. Soon that particular skill would be hers; she would have all of their accumulated capabilities, she would be an engineer and a doctor and an under-the-table childcare provider, a beautician, a programmer, a lawyer and a kinda-sorta prostitute. All of their likes and dislikes would be buzzing in her head like worker bees, their opinions and beliefs.... And when confronted with any decision, big or small, her augmented brain would instantly average out all of the possible reactions and solutions streaming in from her family and come out with the statistical mean, which, according to the experts, would almost always be the correct response.

Her mom looked at her for a long time. She knew she had won the argument, but she didn't radiate the usual smugness or sadness she did when defeating her stubborn daughter. She just looked very very busy, which scared Cary more. Things were barreling forward to their inevitable conclusion, and in a few hours the sterile citrusy smell would be replaced by the rich aroma of roasted pork, boiling black beans and yucca, the sizzle of fried plantains and the rest of her family—both blood relatives and married-in—would be drawn to her house like insects following pheromone trails.

"Please don't bother your father with this," her mother warned. "Y cuidadito con formando un show in front of the family when he comes to take you to the clinic."

She felt like a child bride on the day of an arranged marriage and she needed to run.

Cary had no plan. She frantically threw some clothes and all her money into a backpack, gathered all of the portfolios she'd naively been working on since the ninth grade and crammed them in. She picked up her phone, hesitated for a second, then turned it off, and tossed it in her closet under a pile of dirty laundry. She wanted to message Ruth, tell her she was coming, but any electronic communication would be easily tracked by assiduous government familiars whose members numbered in the thousands.

Her heart pounded in her chest as she thought of an exit plan. She was surrounded by family, her best bet would be to make her way to her great grandmother's room, because it had its own side door so Mimi could come and go as she pleased. She would run through the neighbor's yard to the corner of the block and start walking to Ruth's house, careful to avoid any family member, including her father, who would be on his way home from the store. *Good plan!*

She peered out into the hall, backpack over her shoulder. When it was all clear, she dashed into her great grandmother's room and quietly closed the door behind her.

Suddenly, the blood in her veins froze when she saw the old lady perched in her recliner like a fat pigeon on a wire, the blue glow from the wraparound TV screen gave her an avian iridescence.

"Mimi?" she said softly. It's what she'd always called the current matriarch of the family, even her own kids called her Mimi instead of Mami or Mamá. Mimi didn't respond. She was fast asleep, snoring softly. Cary took a deep breath to settle her nerves, but also to take in some of her great grandmother's particular fragrance. She always smelled of honey and violets and fried food and Cary would miss her profoundly, probably most of all.

She tiptoed like a cartoon to the door that led outside, but her eye caught a gleam on her great grandmother's nightstand. It was her little shrine to La Caridad del Cobre. The saint's brown, porcelain face surrounded by the resplendent gold of her dress and mantel stood out like a sunspot. An impressive halo arched over her head and shoulders with a blazing corona. A solitary squat, white candle flickered inadequately before her. *Caridad.* Cary had been named after this little doll, and Mimi had named her.

Now that her mind was racing with a pronounced sense of doom, the name became pregnant with meaning. *Caridad?* Yes, she was the embodiment of charity for these people, the living, breathing, cybernetically-wired patron saint of the Garcia-Martinez family! Even her nickname became a nasty portent! Was she expected to carry her entire family forever? Intercede for them? The thought made her want to smash the altar to pieces.

"¿Te vas?"

Cary wheeled around at her great grandmother's hoarse voice. She was panting with built-up rage, her shoulders flexing, but she steadied her voice. "No, Mimi, I'm just going to drop off some things at Ruth's house."

The old lady was eighty-seven, but still sharp; the look on her heavily lined face said, *Do you think yo soy una come mierda or something?* But instead she reached out her arms and said, "Dame un beso y un abraso, cariño. Felicidades."

Cary cautiously set her pack by the door and leaned in to give her Mimi one last hug and kiss. Proximity allowed that powerful, maternal scent to invade her nostrils and grip her chest. Without warning, Cary dissolved into a puddle of tears on Mimi's large bosom. Her great grandmother was not a slight woman; she was sturdy and big-boned with a helmet of chemically-treated, burgundy hair that deflected other people's opinions — being stubborn was a family trait — and Cary clung to her like a frightened chick under her protective wings.

"You're scared?" Mimi asked in English. She had never fully trusted the alien language, but she had started making an effort with her great grandchildren, especially in times of distress.

"Yes!"

"It is very scary." She patted the back of her head, massaging her neck. "Responsibility. Sacrifice."

"I don't want to sacrifice myself! I don't know who I am yet, who I want to become. I feel like I have so much potential ..."

"You will find a way to be yourself, it will be hard — very hard — but you are strong like me. Tenemos el mismo carácter, tu y yo. All those people out there," she said, jutting toward the rest of the house with her chin. "They are small. You will devour them, you will see."

Mimi didn't really understand. It wasn't a matter of character. It was all transcranial magnetic stimulation and neural signal decoding. It was intricate aggregating software running in place of soul and metal and plastic embedded in flesh.

Mimi cooed and rubbed Cary's back in pacifying circular motions. "I left the girl I was at fifteen in Cuba. I had un noviesito, you know — his name was Fernandito — he was skinny and ugly, with big teeth, but I loved him and would write very passionate poems for him. I wanted to be a poet. I think I loved writing more than I loved Fernandito." She clucked to herself. "But then I came here and I started to work in a factory sewing socks. I married your great grand-father, had six kids, made sure everyone ate, worked and studied, but at night I would steal an hour or two and write that ugly, skinny boy some love poems."

"I won't have an hour or two. We have family on three different continents across whole hemispheres, from Spain to California. There will be no time for me, there will be no *me*." Cary shivered.

Mimi gave her a reproachful frown, as if she had bared her soul — In English, no less! — and this idiot girl had understood nothing. "Aye, niña, no exageres! We don't have family en la China!"

Cary smiled despite herself. And it was true. There were still time zones free of the cloying Garcia-Martinez horde. *Could there possibly be a time when all of her family in the world were asleep and not actively transmitting? She would have to do the math.*

Mimi stroked her shoulder gently. "If you want to go, go. I won't say anything. It is your life and your decision. You make it."

"But the family ..."

"I will handle them," she said sternly, and Cary believed her.

In a surge of excitement, Cary kissed her great grandmother and scrambled to her feet, slinging her pack over her shoulder in one swift move. She felt lighter than ever. She felt free. She took a step toward the door, but turned, without thinking, and asked, "What will they do about a familiar?" She regretted the question the instant it left her lips.

Mimi waved that away as if it were no longer the girl's concern. "No sé. They will probably pressure your prima Victoria to do it."

Vicky? The girl was only thirteen, blithe and unsuspecting. She was also kind of an airhead and would probably evaporate under the intense heat of the family's collective brainwaves. *Could she condemn a younger cousin to oblivion, just to save herself?* She might never know the woman she would become, but Cary knew instantly that she wasn't that kind of person now. She made the decision to drop her pack. "I won't go."

Mimi nodded sagaciously, satisfied in the certainty that she had chosen the right name for her great granddaughter eighteen years ago. "Listen to me, I don't understand all the technology of esta cosa." She swirled her arthritic finger around her head to simulate the headband. "But I know that as of today tu mandas aquí! You can make the rules. Find a way to save at least a little bit of yourself. Dale, yo te apoyo."

She was right. As the familiar she made all the decisions for the family. She could set the terms. So what did she value? What did she want? She needed to think fast.

Cary's father cried the entire way to the clinic. He apologized once while they were stopped at a red light, but when it turned green he continued driving, as if he were just taking her to an out-of-state college instead of her execution, and as far as he was concerned, that's exactly what he was doing — getting his daughter to college, no matter what!

Her mom was dead silent in the back seat, wringing her hands the way she did while waiting up late for Cary to get home. *Only this time she wouldn't be coming home*, Cary thought bitterly. The drive felt eternal and torturous, but it gave her plenty of time to think.

An inkling of an idea had started to bloom as they pulled in to their destination. The clinic was nicer than Cary had expected. It looked more like a spa than a place where they performed minor brain surgery. The familiar business was booming, apparently. They admitted her quickly, and her parents hovered as a nurse with a bald head and huge biceps gently helped her onto a gurney and administered the anesthesia. "You have a few minutes before this kicks in," he said. "The doctor will be here shortly."

"You need to buy more headbands," Cary said, the second the IV was in place. She knew this was the time her parents would be the most vulnerable. When the doctor arrived, they would be kicked out of the room. These were their last few minutes with their only daughter.

"What? Why?" her father asked, startled.

"I want to add more of the family to the network, more kids."

The doctor walked in, but waited patiently by the door.

"Those things are too expensive and we already had to buy fifty four of them, there's at least that many kids in the family."

"You don't have to get them for the really little ones, just like ten-years-old and up. I'm serious about this."

"Why?" her mother finally spoke up. To her credit, she did look like she was trying to understand, for once.

"Everyone in the network would be an adult. I'm thinking including some of the kids would balance me out — I'm half kid myself—besides, I've been researching this and the more diverse the group is, in age and education and gender, the more accurate the system is. Is that true?" she asked the doctor, and her parents looked back at the vacant-faced woman in confusion and supplication.

"That's right," the doctor, a plain, middle-aged Indian woman, said and smiled beatifically. Of course, she was a familiar, Cary realized. It was the only way she'd get a job like this. She was probably maintaining people in India or Trinidad or both. The doctor was Cary's future and she got the odd desire to sketch her.

"If you don't promise, I won't consent." Cary said casually, there was no need to put any heat into her words, the doctor's presence made her statement threat enough.

"Coño, Cary." Her father looked pained. He ran a hand roughly through his thinning hair, unable to think clearly. This wasn't the emotional good bye he had readied himself for. *Well, too bad.*

"Okay," her mother sighed suddenly. "We can probably buy twenty more, and that's it." She turned to Cary's father. "Tell Yovany to go back and get twenty more headbands. We'll pay him back."

Her dad eyed the doctor, but gave a jerky nod.

"Okay," Cary said, deflating. The drowsiness had begun to take over. "I love you."

The procedure was over in no time at all. When she was out cold, Dr. Rao drilled a tiny hole in through the top of her skull, like the opening of an anthill, and injected the miniature device. Once in place, the implant sprouted artificial dendrites, branching outward like a micro family tree. They tangled with her neurons, touching different parts of her brain. It laced itself thoroughly and then the doctor sealed the hole with synthetic bone paste.

When Cary awoke, she was only a bit queasy, and that was probably due more to the anesthesia and her nerves than the actual procedure. With the infinite imperturbability of a bodhisattva, Dr. Rao reported that everything had gone smoothly and that Cary could go home.

Outside, the sky crackled an electric blue and the pitiful breeze smelled of rain and asphalt. Cary's stomach churned. There must have been a torrential downpour while she was inside, but now everything was bright and soaked and hot. The bulky nurse winked at her as he wheeled her to the car and whispered, "Easier than getting a boob job, no?"

Cary half-nodded, still in a daze. She would know soon enough, though, as her cousin, Karen, had gotten one a year ago.

The party was bigger and more elaborate than her quinces, and much like that particular ordeal, she arrived after it had already started. Everyone clapped and cheered as her parents helped her into the house like an invalid and sat her in a makeshift throne at the center of the room. Beer and salsa music flowed freely around her. She thought it rude, that some of the guests were already wearing their transcranial headbands like party hats, is if they couldn't wait to snuff her out.

Ruth showed up right when they were going to start singing happy birthday and cut the cake. She looked scared, like an unsuspecting European stumbling into the middle of a Mayan ritual sacrifice. Seeing her, made the sorrow and nausea well up all over again; Cary clenched her teeth and waved her over.

"You did it?" she asked, tentatively.

"Yeah. I almost ran away with you, though."

"Why didn't you?"

Cary shrugged, "I couldn't."

"That's fucked up."

Too late for all that now, Cary thought. "I'm glad you're here. I wanted to ask you a favor."

"Anything." Ruth kneeled before her and clasped her clammy hands, as if she were going to propose marriage in front of all her family on her birthday.

Cary inhaled and exhaled to steady herself; she had a much less romantic proposal in mind. "I want you to join the family network."

"What?" Ruth let go of her hands and backed away. Cary wasn't prepared for the clear hint of revulsion twisting her friend's face.

"Hear me out. Please! I can help you, support you, give you a chance in this world and you can leave the network whenever you like. You can come to school with me. No loans!"

"I don't care about that stuff!"

"I know, but I'm trying to shore myself up here." Cary wanted to cry, but the tears would no longer come. She wondered if she had been brain-damaged somehow. "I've added a lot of the kids, trying to average in some of their raw potential, but you ... You know me so well ... I don't know if any of me will survive when we synch these things up, but if you're a part of it, some of me will — a lot of me will, I think. I just need you there for a little while until I can figure things out."

"That's not going to work, Cary. Look around at all these people. I'll just be a rounding error to the sum total." Ruth was crying now, crying for both of them. They were a bubble of grief at the center of a raging, celebratory hurricane.

"It's all I've got."

Someone was banging on a beer bottle with a fork and making a speech, thanking Cary for her selflessness and bravery. In her periphery, people were putting on their headbands, powering them up, and synching them. Cary's mouth went dry, her fingers cold, reaching desperately for Ruth.

Her great grandmother, Mimi, leaned in and dropped a headband into Ruth's lap. "Coge, niña, no pienses mas." Then she came around, kissed Cary on the crown of her head, right where the implant had gone in and puttered away.

Ruth shook her head in disgust. She took Cary's hands, kissing them. "I love you," she said almost angrily and managed, with trembling fingers, to slip the thing on.

When the end came, it wasn't as an abrupt, violent supernova of information, like Cary feared. It was more like a slow and incremental sunrise. With each person to enter the network, the world grew brighter and the transient being that had been allowed to exist for only a brief moment in time, receded and faded like a shadow, until only the sun remained.

The vast, widely-distributed intelligence that emerged—Caridad Garcia-Martinez — began to see her sprawling family, not as a collection of individuals, but as luminous rays emanating from her core. This realization dazzled her. *She* was, in fact, the sun. She watched/felt the lancing rays vector out, strengthening her, aggrandizing her with each person that came online.

When the brilliance of this novel reality subsided fractionally, she understood something that wasn't in any of the research the little shadow had read. The flow of information moved both ways — Of course it did! — she could reach out with electromagnetic fingers and nudge her component parts in subtle, but significant ways. They were one, after all. All the waste and inefficiencies and poor decisions of their messy lives suddenly burned away like clouds and she could work at correcting the wayward trajectories of her many beams of light.

Caridad was running calculations to do just that, when something else drew her near-omniscient attention: a blemish had appeared amidst all the glory, like an ugly, little sunspot, a freckle. This triggered an association cascade that rippled through at least three different minds in the link. Her vision, through seventy six pairs of eyeballs, focused on the conundrum — Ruth Ann Tremper — it was the only part of her that didn't shine.

Another association cascade, this one much more turbulent, like a roiling solar storm. Then, understanding: this particular ray was creating a feedback loop, like a great arch of plasma swerving and crashing back into the sun, penetrating deep into its fiery heart. *Interesting.*

"Are you in there?" Ruth's whisper carried as much mass as a photon.

Caridad Garcia-Martinez smiled magnanimously from the center of herself and Ruth smiled back, her expression fraught, tears still streaming down her face.

The algorithm churned, curiosity flared, and Caridad peered through Ruth's eyes to better understand the question. She saw a serene, young girl smiling contently at her. More memories tallied from all across her being produced an output: *Cary.* This was the core that had fused all of these tiny, zipping, separate bits into a substantial, cohesive whole.

After a while, Ruth buried her face in her hands, blocking the view of the girl. "If you're in there give me a sign," she demanded into her palms. From all around the room, Caridad watched Ruth flicker with fury and desperation, prostrated before the radiant brown-faced girl.

Using the processing power of seventy six interconnected brains to search for the appropriate response, Caridad began to trace the query in lines of light and code pulled from each of her components parts — some of them knew Cary very well and others barely at all — but the girl started to take shape.

"Stop smiling like an idiot and tell me that you're in there!" Ruth wiped her tears with her sleeve and grabbed her core, shaking it, interrupting the detailed rendering. "I need to know!"

Caridad recalculated, holding the incomplete image of Cary across many minds, like lines on paper. She would continue this work at another time — the project seemed important somehow — but a new, more immediate response emerged.

Slowly, she raised her core's hand and brushed Ruth's bangs out of her blue eyes. They crackled with anticipation. The move felt strange and familiar to Caridad. She watched herself watching herself and, when she was sure that her answer was the correct one, she pulled Ruth in with almost gravitational force and kissed her in the mouth.

DIFFICULT AT PARTIES

Carmen Maria Machado

K. Tempest Bradford writes: "Carmen Maria Machado's stories build and build until they surround and ensnare, and at the end you're always glad to be all tangled up." Machado is a fiction writer, critic, and essayist whose work has appeared in *The New Yorker, Granta, The Paris Review*, and elsewhere. She is a graduate of the Iowa Writers' Workshop and the Clarion Science Fiction & Fantasy Writers' Workshop, and the author of the forthcoming collection *Her Body and Other Parties.* As to why she writes speculative fiction, she writes: "From my earliest years, the currency of my Cuban grandfather's communication with me was storytelling. Every tale about his life - from his poverty growing up in Santa Clara to his immigration and McCarthy-era deportation and return, his military service, and his life in DC with his wife and children - was told through a lens of humor and hyperbole." In "Difficult at Parties" a woman discovers that, in the aftermath of a sexual assault, she has taken on some strange new powers.

Afterward, there is no kind of quiet like the one that is in my head.

Paul brings me home from the hospital in his ancient Volvo. The heater is busted and it's January, so there's a fleece blanket wedged at the foot of the passenger seat. My body radiates pain, is dense with it. He buckles my seatbelt, and his hands are shaking. He lifts the blanket and sets it down on my legs. He's done this before, tucking it around my thighs while I make jokes about being a kid getting ready for bed. Now he is cautious, fearful.

Stop, I say, and do it myself.

It is a Tuesday. I think it is a Tuesday. Condensation on the inside of the car has frozen into ice. The snow that I can see is dirty, a dark yellow line carved into a space near the curb. The wind rattles the broken door handle. Across the way, a teenage girl shouts to her friend three unintelligible syllables. Tuesday is speaking to me, in Tuesday's voice. Open up, it says. Open up.

Paul reaches for the ignition. Around the hole there are long scratches in the plastic where, in his rush to get me, the key had missed its destination over and over again.

The engine struggles a little, like it doesn't want to wake up.

The first night back in my house, he stands in the doorway of the bedroom with his wide shoulders hunched inward and asks me where I want him to sleep.

With me, I say, as if it's a ridiculous question. It is a ridiculous question. Lock the door, I tell him, and get into bed.

The door is locked.

Lock it again.

He leaves, and I can hear the stifled jerks of a doorknob being tested. He comes back into the bedroom, flips back the covers, buries himself next to me.

I dream of Tuesday. I dream of it from start-to-finish.

When the thin light of morning stretches across the bed, Paul is sleeping in the recliner in the corner of the room. What are you doing? I ask, pushing the quilt off my body. Why are you there?

He tilts his head up. Around his eye, a smoky-dark bruise is forming.

You were screaming, he says. You were screaming, and I tried to hold you, and you elbowed me in the face.

This is the first time I actually cry.

I am ready, I tell my black-and-blue reflection. Friday.

I draw a bath. The water gushes too-hot from the spotted faucet. I peel my pajamas away from my body and they fall like sloughed skin to the tiled floor. A halo of flesh gathers around my ankles; I half-expect to look down and see the cage of my ribs, the wet balloons of my lungs.

Steam rises from the bath. Somewhere in this room I am remembering a small version of myself, sitting in a hotel hot tub and holding my arms rigid against my torso, rolling around the churning water. I'm a carrot! I'm a carrot! I shriek at a woman, who might be my mother. I'm a carrot! Add some salt! Add some peas! And from her lounge chair she reaches toward me with her hand contorted as if around a handle, the very caricature of a chef with a slotted spoon.

I add a fat dollop of bubble bath.

I slip my foot into the water. There is a second of brilliant heat that slides straight through me, like steel wire through a block of wet clay. I gasp but do not pause. A second foot, less pain. Hands on the sides, I lower myself down. The water hurts, and it is good. The chemicals in the bubble bath burn, and they are better.

I run my toes along the faucet, whispering things to myself in a low voice, lifting up my breasts with both hands to see how high they can sit; I catch my reflection in the sweaty curve of the stainless steel, tilt my head. On the far side of the tub, I can see the tiny slivers of red polish that have receded from the edges of my toenails, crescent moons ebbing into nothing. I feel buoyant, weightless. The water goes too high and begins to threaten the lip of the tub. I turn the faucet off. In the absence of the roar of rushing water, the bathroom echoes unpleasantly.

I hear the front door open. I tense, until I hear the rattle of keys on the hallway table. Paul comes into the bathroom.

Hey, he says.

Hey, I say. You had a meeting.

What?

You had a meeting. You're wearing a dress shirt.

He looks down at himself. Yes, he says, slowly, as if the choice of his shirt has not occurred to him before this moment. Actually, he says, I went and looked at some houses on the other side of town.

I don't want to move, I tell him.

You should find another place. He says this with force, as if he has spent his entire day building up to this sentence.

I shouldn't do anything, I say, I don't want to move.

I think it's a bad idea to stay. I can help you find a new apartment.

I wind a hand into my hair and pull it away from my skull in a wet sheet. A bad idea for who?

We stare at each other. My other arm is crossed over my chest; I release it.

Unplug the tub for me? I ask.

He kneels in the cold puddle on the tile next to the tub. He unbuttons the sleeve at his wrist and begins to roll it up in a neat, tight coil. He reaches past my legs, into the water still thick with bubbles, down to the bottom. Suds catch on the roll of fabric around his upper arm. I can feel the syncopated drumming of his fingers as he fumbles for the beaded chain, weaves it around them, pulls.

There is a low *pop*. A lazy bubble of air breaks the water's surface. He withdraws, and his hand brushes my skin for a moment. I jump, and then he jumps.

My face is level with his shins when he stands; there are wet circles on the knees of his dress pants.

You're spending a lot of time away from your place, I say. I don't want you to feel like you have to spend every night here.

He frowns. It doesn't bother me, he says. I want to help. He vanishes into the hallway.

I sit there until all of the water drains, until the last milky swirl disappears down the silver mouth and I feel a strange shiver that starts deep within me, worryingly. A spine should not be so afraid. The receding bubbles leave strange, white striations on my skin, like the tide-scarred sand at the beach's edge. I feel heavy.

✦

Weeks pass. The officer who'd taken my statement in the hospital calls to say they might have me come in to identify someone. Her voice is generous, too loud. Later, she leaves a clipped message on the answering machine, telling me it's not necessary. The wrong person, not the right one.

Maybe he left the state, Paul says.

I stay away from myself. Paul stays away, too. I don't know who is more afraid, me or him.

We should try something, I say one morning. About this. I gesture to the space in front of me.

He looks up from an egg. Yes, he says.

We lay out suggestions on a hot pink post-it note that is too small for many solutions.

I place an order for a DVD from a company that advertises adult films for loving couples. It arrives in a plain brown box, neatly placed on the corner of the cement stoop in front of my apartment. When I pick it up, the box is lighter than I expect. I tuck it under my arm and grope the doorknob for a minute. The new deadbolt sticks.

I put the box on the kitchen table. Paul calls. I'm coming over soon, he says. His voice always sounds immediate, present, even when he's speaking over the phone. Did you get the —

Yeah, I say. It's here.

It will take him at least fifteen minutes to get to this side of town. I go to the box, which is sitting quietly where I've left it. I pull a perforated tab marked *pull*, and the cardboard opens like a book. I remove the plastic case: shiny, wrapped in cellophane. I tear open the corner of the wrapping with my teeth, wincing at its high squeak.

The number of limbs tangled on the front cover doesn't appear to match the number of faces. I count, twice, and confirm that there is one extra elbow and one extra leg. I open the case. The disc smells brand new and doesn't snap easily from its plastic knob. The shiny side gleams like an oil slick, and reflects my face strangely, as if someone has reached out and smeared it. I set it down in the DVD player's open tray.

There's no menu; the movie plays automatically. I kneel down on the carpet in front of the television, lean my chin into my hand, and watch. The camera is steady. The woman on the video looks a little like me — the same mouth, anyway. She is talking shyly to a man on her left, a built man who has probably not always been so — he seems to be straining out of his shirt, which is too small for his new muscles. They are having a conversation — a conversation about — I cannot make out any of the individual pieces of the conversation. He touches her leg. She takes the tab of her zipper and slides it down. There is nothing underneath.

Past the obligatory blowjobs, past the mouth-that-looks-like-mine straining, past perfunctory cunnilingus, they are talking again.

the last time, I told him, I told, fuck, they can see my —
I can't hold this down, I can't hold this down, I can't —

I sit up. Their mouths are not moving. Well, their mouths are moving, but the words dropping from those mouths are expected. Baby. Fuck. Yeah. God. Underneath, something else is moving. A stream running beneath the ice. A voiceover. Or, I guess, a voiceunder.

if he tells me again, if he says to me that it's not okay, I should just —
two more years, maybe, only two, maybe just one if I keep going —

The voices — no, not voices, the sounds, soft and muted and rising and falling in volume — blend together; weave around each other, disparate syllables ringing out. I don't know where the voices are coming from — a commentary track? Without taking my eyes off the screen, I reach for the remote control and press the pause button.

They freeze. She is staring at him. He is looking somewhere out of the frame. Her hand is pressed down on her abdomen, hard. The swelling knoll of her stomach is vanishing beneath her palm.

I un-pause it.

okay, so I had a baby, this isn't the first time that's —
and if it's only a year, then maybe I can follow —

I pause it again. The woman is now frozen on her back. Her partner stands between her legs, casually, like he's about to ask her a question, his cock curved to the left against his abdomen. Her hand is still pushed into her stomach.

I stare at the screen for a long time.

When Paul knocks, I jump.

I let him in and hug him. He is panting and his shirt is damp with sweat. I can taste the salt in my mouth as I press my face against his chest. He kisses me, and I can sense his eyes flickering the screen. You okay? I ask.

I was running, he says. I had to park a few blocks away. How are you? How was class?

I didn't go. I don't feel well, I say, turning off the television.

He looks concerned.

I feel sick, I tell him.

He asks me if I am soup-sick or sprite-sick. I tell him soup-sick. He goes into the kitchen and I lie down on the couch. In the sharply focused dark I can hear the *thunk* of the cupboard door striking the cabinet next to it, the dry sliding of cans being sorted through, the sloshing of liquid, the tap of a pot on a burner, the metallic clink of him using the wrong spoon to stir. When he brings it out to me, chicken broth hovering precariously at the top of the bowl, napkin resting beneath it, I thank him. He warns me that it's hot. I sip it too quickly, and bite down on the spoon in shock. Vibrations resonate through my skull, and I burn my mouth.

His friends invite us to a housewarming party for their new home out in the country. I don't want to go, I tell him, the pale blue light from the television making shadows on my face as three men intertwine with each other, each mouth full.

I'm worried that you're spending too much time in the house, he says. It'll be mostly women.

What?

At the party. It'll be mostly women. All people that I know. Good people.

I wear my turquoise dress with black stockings underneath and take a small aloe plant as a gift. In my car, we speed out of the dim lights of our small town and onto a country road. Paul uses one hand to steer, and rests the other on my leg. The moon is full and illuminates the miles of glittering snow that stretch in every direction, the sloped barn roofs and narrow silos with icicles as thick as my arm hanging from their outcroppings, the herd of rectangular and unmoving cows huddled near the entrance to a hayloft. We drive in straight lines, and turn at right angles. I hold the plant protectively against my body, and when the car makes a sudden left some of the sandy soil spills out onto my dress. I pinch it from the fabric and drop it back into the pot, brushing a few crumbs of dirt off the thick, fleshy leaves. When I look up again, I see that we are moving toward a large, illuminated building.

So this is a new house? I ask, my head pressed against the passenger window.

Yeah, he said. They just bought it, oh I don't know, about a month ago. I haven't been there yet, but I hear it's really nice.

We pull next to a row of parked cars, in front of a renovated, turn-of-the-century farmhouse that glows with the lights inside.

It looks so homey, says Paul, stepping out and rubbing his gloveless hands together.

The windows are draped with gauzy curtains, and a creamy honey color throbs from within. The house looks like it is on fire.

The hosts open the door; they are beautiful and have gleaming teeth. I have seen this before. I have not seen them before.

Jane, says the dark-haired one. Jill, says the red-headed one. And that's not a joke! They laugh. Paul laughs. It's so nice to meet you,

Jane says to me. I hold the small aloe plant toward her. She smiles again, so deeply that her dimples look carved into her face, and takes it. Paul looks pleased, and then leans over and scratches the ears of a large white cat with a smooshed face that is rubbing against his legs.

We've made a coatroom out of the bedroom, Jill says. Paul reaches for my coat. I slip it off and hand it to him, and he vanishes up the stairs.

A man in the hallway with buzzed hair and pale skin is holding an ancient camcorder on his shoulder. It is gigantic and the color of tar. He swings it toward me, an eye.

Tell me your name, he says.

I try to pull away, out of its view, but I cannot shrink tightly enough against the wall.

Why is that here? I ask, trying to keep panic out of my voice.

Your name, he repeats, tipping the camera towards me.

Oh Jesus, Gabe, leave her alone, says Jill, pushing him away. She takes my arm and pulls me along. Sorry about that. There's always some retro-loving jackass at parties. And he's ours.

Jane comes up on the other side of me and laughs down a scale. Paul, she says, where'd you go?

He reappears. Onward, he says, sounding giddy.

They ask us if we want the tour. We wander from the living room to a wide-open kitchen, shiny with brass and steel. They tap each shiny appliance in turn: dishwasher. Refrigerator. Gas stove. Separate oven. *Second* oven. There is a door toward the back with an ornate, bronze-colored knob. I reach for it, but Jane grabs my shoulder. Stop, she says, careful.

That room is being renovated, says Jill. There's no floor. You could go in there, but you'd go straight down to the cellar. She clasps the knob with her manicured hand, and turns it. The door opens, and yes, the no-floor yawns at me.

That would be terrible, says Jane.

The camera follows me around. I stand near Paul for a while, awkwardly smoothing my dress. He seems anxious, so I move, a satellite released from orbit. Away from him, I feel strange, purposeless.

I do not know these people, and they do not know me. I stand near the hors d'oeuvres table, and eat one shrimp — meaty, swimming in cocktail sauce — tucking the stiff tail into my palm. Another one, then a third, the tails filling up my hand. I swallow a glass of red wine without tasting it. I refill, and drain another. I swirl a cracker in something dark green. I look up. In the corner of the room, the single eye of the camera is fixed on me. I turn toward the table.

The cat saunters over and paws playfully at a hunk of pita bread in my hands. When I pull it away, she swipes at me and takes a chunk out of my finger. I swear and suck at the wound. In my mouth, I can taste hummus and copper. I'm so sorry, says Jill, who swans up as if she has been waiting offstage for the cue of my blood. He does that to strangers sometimes, he really needs anxiety medication or something. Bad pussycat! Jane touches Jill's arm lightly and asks her to come and help clean up a spill, and they both vanish.

Friendly people I have never met ask me about my job, about my life. They reach across me for wine glasses, touch my arm. Each time, I move away, not directly back but a half-step to the right, and they match my movements, and in this way we move in a small circle as we speak.

The last book I read, I repeat slowly, was —

But I can't remember. I remember the satiny cover beneath the pads of my fingertips, but not the title, or the author, or any of the words inside. I think I am talking funny, with my burned mouth, my numb tongue fat and useless inside my mouth. I want to say, don't bother asking me anything. I want to say, there is nothing underneath.

And what do you do?

The questions come at me like doors thrown open. I begin to explain, but as soon as the words leave my mouth I find myself searching for Paul. He is in the far corner of the room, talking to a woman with short hair and a strand of pearls that wraps around her neck like the coils of a noose. She touches his arm familiarly; he bats her away with his hand. His muscles look taut enough to snap. I look back at the woman who asked me what I did. She is curvy and taller than most and has the brightest shade of red lipstick on that I have ever seen. Her eyes flicker over to Paul. She takes another long swig of her martini, the olives rolling around in the glass like eyes. How are things with the two of you? She asks. A pimento iris lolls in my direction. The woman with the pearls touches Paul's arm again. He shakes his head, almost imperceptibly. Who is she? Why is she —

I excuse myself and walk into the dim hallway. I press my palm into the iron sphere at the base of the railing, and swing myself up onto the staircase.

The coat room, I think. The coat room. The bedroom full of coats. The repurposed —

The stairs move away from me, and I rush to catch them. I search for the door, a darker patch among darkness. The coat room is cool. I press my hand on the wooden panel. The coats will not question me.

In the shadows, two figures are struggling on the bed. My heart surges with fear, a fish with a steel hook through the ridge of its lip. As my eyes adjust to the darkness, I realize that it's just the hosts, writhing on the heaps of shiny down jackets. The dark-haired one — Jane? Or is it Jill? — is on her back, her dress gathered around her hips, and her wife is over her, grinding her knee between her legs. Jane — maybe Jill — is biting her own wrist to keep from crying out. The coats rustle, slide. Jane kisses Jill or Jill kisses Jane and then one leans down and rolls down the top of the other's stockings, a rolled line of underwear, her face disappearing into her.

A pleasurable twinge curls inside of me. Jill or Jane writhes, pulls up fistfuls of down coat with her hands, makes a soft noise, a single syllable stretched in two directions. A long red scarf slides to the floor.

I don't wonder if they can see me. I could stand here for a thousand years and between coats and syllables and mouths they would never see me.

I close the door.

I get drunk. I have four flutes of champagne and a strong gin and tonic. I even suck the gin out of the lime wedge, the citrus stinging the scratch on my finger. Gabe finally puts the camera down on a chair in deference to its extraordinary weight. It sits there, quietly, but it holds me inside, somewhere, for precious seconds that I cannot take back. A face that I have yet to really look at, resting deep in the coils of its mechanical innards.

I walk past the camera and take it, my fingers tightening around the handle. I am sure that when I lift it from its perch the handle will give way. It will crash to the floor, tremendously, and the heads will all turn. But it comes up easily. I control it now. As I begin to walk nonchalantly toward the front door, taking care to point the lens away from my body, I see the white cat with the smooshed face, watching me from the landing. His pink comma tongue slides out and makes a leisurely trip over his upper lip, and his blue eyes narrow accusingly. I stumble. I do not bother to get my coat before I walk through the front door.

Outside, my boots crunch loudly through the glittering ice and mean snow. Near the end of the path that leads to the driveway, someone has emptied a half-full coffee cup, and dark brown is splattered grotesquely across the white lawn. Narrow tracks in the snow suggest a deer has seen this sight, too. My skin is stippled with goosebumps. I realize I don't have the keys, but I reach for the trunk handle anyway.

It's unlocked. The trunk opens to me, and I thump the camera down into its shadows.

I go back inside and have a glass of wine. Then a shot of something green. The world begins to slide.

Instead of passing out like a dignified person, I stagger out to the car again, sit in the cold passenger seat, recline it, and stare out the sunroof at a sky crowded with delicate points of light.

Paul gets into the driver's seat.

Are you all right? He asks.

I nod, and then throw open the door and vomit cocktail shrimp and spinach dip onto the gravel driveway. Pink chunks and long dark strands like hair settle among the stones and snow; the puddle gleams and reflects the moon.

We drive. I recline and watch the sky.

Did you have fun? he asks.

I giggle, laugh. No, I guffaw. I snort. Fuck no. Fuck —

I feel something cold on my face and I pick it off. Spinach. I roll down the window. Icy air hits my face. I throw it out of the car.

If that were a cigarette, I say, it would spark. It should be a cigarette. I could use one of those.

The cold stings.

Can you roll the window up? Paul asks loudly over the rushing wind. I roll it back up and lean my heavy head against the glass.

I thought it would be good for us to get out the house, he says. Jane and Jill really like you.

Like me for what? I pull my head away, and there is a circle of grease obscuring the sky. I see a black stain flash briefly under the headlights, then a huddled mass on the side of the road — a deer, blasted apart by the tires of an SUV.

I can almost hear the line between Paul's eyebrows deepening. What do you mean, like you for what? What does that even mean?

I don't know.

They just like you, that's all.

I laugh again, and reach for the window crank. Who is that woman with that pearl necklace? I ask in the sudden silence.

No one, he says, in a voice that doesn't fool either of us.

At my house, he carries me to bed. When he lies down next to me, I reach over and touch his stomach. He doesn't ask me what I am doing.

You're drunk, he says. You don't want this.

How do you know what I want? I ask. I inch closer. He takes my hand and lifts it away. He holds it aloft for a minute, not wanting to drop it, not wanting to put it back. He settles for resting it on my own stomach, and then rolls away from me.

I reach for myself. I don't even recognize my own topography.

Most mornings, Paul asks me what I dreamt about.

I don't remember, I say. Why?

You moved around. A lot. He says this carefully, with restraint that betrays itself.

I want to see. I set up the camera to record my sleep, tucked on the highest shelf of the bookcase next to my bed. The DVD from the other day is obviously broken, so I put it in the garbage can, shoving it deep in the bag past potato peelings curling like question marks. Then, I order another DVD. It shows up on my cement stoop.

This one is in many parts, smaller parts, like film shorts. The first one is called *Fucking My Wife*. I start it. A man is holding the camera — I can't see his face. The woman is blonde and older than the last woman and she has meticulously applied mascara.

How do I say, how do I say, how do I say —

I cannot hear him. I look at the video case again. *Fucking My Wife*. I don't understand the title. I can't hear him. All I can hear is her voice, tinged with desperation.

How do I say, how do I say, how do I —

I don't want to hear her anymore. I hit mute.

How do I say, how do I say, how do I —

I turn off the DVD player. The television blinks to the news network. A blonde woman is staring gravely at her audience. Over her left shoulder, like an advising devil, there is a square graphic of a bomb, blasting apart the pixels that make it. I unmute the sound.

—a bombing in Turkey, she is saying. Viewers should be advised that the following images are —

I turn off the TV. I yank the plug out by the cord.

Paul comes over. How are you feeling? he asks.

A little better, I say. Tired. I lean into him. He smells like detergent. I lean into him and I want him. He is solid. He reminds me of a tree — roots that run deep.

The DVD player is broken, I say, heading off the question before it can be asked.

Do you want me to look at it? he asks.

Yes, I say. I plug in the TV again. As the DVD begins to play, and the bodies begin to unfold, I can hear it again. That voice, that sad, desperate sound, the questions repeated over and over again like a mantra, even as she smiles. Even as she moans and her mind flits between her question and the pattern of the carpet. Paul watches with a determined courtesy, absently stroking my hand as it plays. Nothing on his face indicates that he can hear what I hear. As the scene draws to a close, he looks over at me and asks me what's broken about it.

Can't you hear it? I feel the nails of my free hand digging into my jeans.

He cocks his head to the side and listens again. He shakes his head regretfully.

I turn the TV off. I stand in front of him, my hands dangling heavily at my sides. He stands up and puts his arms around me; rests his chin in my hair. We rock back and forth slowly, dancing to the sound of the heating vent struggling to keep us warm.

I think I found you an apartment, he says into my hair. It's on the third floor of a building on the other side of the river.

I don't want to leave, I say into his chest.

His muscles tense, and he pulls me away from his body by the length of his impossible arms.

You can't keep doing this, he says, his voice loud, upset, pitched into the ceiling. You have to find a new place.

Please don't yell, I say. Please just listen.

It's like you're not even in there. He grabs the sides of his arms. You're responding to all of the wrong things.

Please stop, I say. He reaches for me, but I knock his hand away. I need you to be simple and good, I say without looking into his face. Can't you just be simple and good?

He looks straight through me, as if I already know the answer.

Each morning, I slide the monstrous cassette out of the camera, rewind it, and watch it in the VCR. I fast forward through the stillness, though there is not much of it. Camera-me flails. She grabs for the air as if she is trying to pull party streamers down from the ceiling. She knocks her limbs against the wall, the oak headboard, the nightstand, and does not recoil in pain but goes back to them, over and over. The slender lamp crashes to the floor. Paul gets up, tries to help, holds her arms, holds my arms, trying to pin them to her sides, then looks guilty and releases them. She comes down. She struggles against the blankets. She slides down onto the floor, rolling half-under the edge of the bed, partially hidden by the pulled sheets. Paul tries to get her back up onto the bed and she takes a wild swing at his head, and I can hear her steady no, no, no, no, no, no, no even as he tugs her back up onto the mattress, getting close enough to talk into her ear, something too low for the camera to catch, and then getting her down, down onto the mattress, down into his arms in a grip that looks both threatening and comforting. This lasts for a moment before she — before I — am up again, and Paul pulls me into him, even as I hit his chest, even as I slide again to the floor. A whole night of this.

When I am done, I rewind it to the beginning and replace it in the camera.

I stop ordering DVDs by mail. I begin free trials at four different websites. There are no voice tricks in internet porn, no weird commentary tracks.

I can still hear them. A man with slender wrists wonders endlessly about someone named Sam. Two women are surprised about each other's bodies, the infinite softness. *No one said, no one said,* a tanned woman thinks in a whisper. It echoes around her mind, around mine. I lean in so close to the screen that I cannot even see the picture anymore. Just blotches of color, moving. Beiges, browns, the black of the tanned woman's hair, a shock of red of which, when I pull back, I can't see the origins.

A woman mentally corrects a man who keeps referring to her *pussy. Cunt,* she thinks, and the word is dense and sits in the air like a wedge of underripe fruit. I love your pussy, he says. *Cunt*, she repeats, over and over again, a meditation.

Some are silent. Some have no words, just colors.

A woman with a black harness around her fleshy hips prays as she fucks a thin man who idolizes her. Each thrust punctuates. At the end, she kisses his back. Benediction.

A man with two women on his cock wants to be home.

Do they know what they are thinking, I wonder, clicking through videos, letting them load like a slingshot being pulled back. Do they hear it? Do they know? Did I know?

I cannot remember.

At two in the morning, I am watching a man deliver a pizza. A woman with breasts that float wrongly against gravity opens the door. Not the right house, of course. I think that I have watched this before, maybe. He sets the empty cardboard box on the table. She takes off her shirt. I listen.

Her mind is all darkness. It is full, afraid. Fear rushes through it, white hot and terrified. Fear weighs on her chest, crushing her. She is thinking about a door opening. She is thinking about a stranger coming in. I am thinking about a door opening. I can hear him clutching the doorknob. I cannot hear him clutching the doorknob, but I can hear it turning. I cannot hear it turning, but I hear the footfalls. I cannot hear the footfalls, I cannot hear them. There is only a shadow. There is only darkness blotting out light.

He, the delivery man, the no-delivery man, thinks about her breasts. He worries about his body. He wants to please her, really.

She smiles. There is a smear of lipstick on her teeth. She likes him. Below this, there is a screaming, rushing tunnel. No radio signal. It fills my head, it presses into the bone of my skull. Pounding, pushing it apart. I am an infant, my head is not solid, these tectonic plates, they cannot be expected to hold.

I grab my laptop and hurl it across the room at the wall. I expect it to shatter, but it doesn't — it strikes the drywall and hits the ground with a terrific crash.

I scream. I scream so loudly the note splits in two.

Paul comes running out of the basement. He cannot get close to me.

Don't touch me, I howl. Don't touch me, don't touch me.

He stays near the door. I slump down onto the floor. My tears run hot and then cool on my face. Please go back downstairs, I say. I cannot see Paul, but I hear him open the basement door. I flinch. I do not get up until my heart slows.

When I finally stand and walk over to the wall, I tip the computer right side up. There is a massive crack down the center of the screen, a ruptured fault line.

In the bedroom, Paul sits across from me, his fingers tapping idly on the denim of his pants.

Do you remember, he says, what it was like before?

I look down at my legs, then up at the blank wall, then back to him. I do not even struggle to speak; the spark of words dies so deep in my chest there is not even space to mount them on an exhale.

You wanted, he says. You wanted and wanted. You were like this endless thing. A well that never emptied.

I wish I could say that I remember, but I do not remember. I can imagine pumping limbs and mouths on mouths but I cannot remember them. I cannot remember ever being thirsty.

I sleep, long and hot, the windows open despite the winter. Paul sleeps against the wall and does not stir.

The voices aren't happening, not now, but I still perceive them. They drift over my head like milkweed. I am Samuel, I think. That's it. I'm Samuel. God called to him in the night. They call to me. Samuel answered, Yes, Lord? I have no way of answering my voices. I have no way of telling them that I can hear.

I hear the door open and then close but I don't turn my head. I am staring at the screen. An orgy, now. The fifth. Dozens of voices, too many to count, overlapping, tangling, making the air tight, crowding it. They worry, they lust, they laugh. Sweat glitters. Badly placed tungsten lights cast shadows, slicing up a few bodies for a few moments into slick skin and canyons of darkness. Whole again. Pieces.

He sits down next to me, his weight sinking the cushion so far that I fall into him. I do not take my eyes off the screen.

Hey, he says. You okay?

Yes. I curl my fingers tightly against one another, my knuckles locking in a line. This is the church. This is the steeple.

He sits back and watches. He looks at me. He settles his fingers lightly on my shoulder blade, catching the strap of my bra and running his finger on the curve of my skin beneath the elastic. Gently, over and over.

A woman at the center of a male orbit reaches up, up over her head, so far up. She is thinking about one of them in particular, the one filling her, making her whole. She thinks about the lighting for a bit, then her thoughts drift back to him. Her leg is falling asleep.

Paul talks very close to my skin. What are you doing? He asks.

Watching, I say.

What?

Watching. Isn't this what I should be doing? Watching this?

The way he is still, I can tell that he is thinking. Then he reaches and puts his hand over mine—covering the church.

Hey, he says. Hey, hey.

One of the men is sick. He thinks he is going to die. He wants to die.

Bodies linking, unlinking, muscles twitching, hands.

Through the woman's mind, a ribbon of light tightens and slack-
ens and tightens again. She laughs. She is actually coming. The first
time we kissed, Paul and I, on my bed, in the dark, he was almost
frantic, humming with energy, a screen door banging in the wind.
Later he told me that it had just been so long, *so long*, that he felt like
he was coming out of his skin. *Skin.* I can still hear them thinking,
echoing around my head, slipping into the crevices of my memory. I
cannot keep them away. This dam will not hold.

I do not realize that I am crying until he stands and brings me
with him, pulling me from the couch. On the screen, Pearly arcs of
come crisscross the laughing woman's torso. I lift easily. He holds me
and touches my face and his fingers are wet for the effort.

Shhh, he says. Shhh. I'm so sorry, he says. We don't have to watch
it, we don't have to.

He weaves his fingers through my hair and supports the small
of my back. Shhh, he says. I don't want any of them. I only want you.

I stiffen.

Only you, he says again. He holds me tightly. A good man. He
repeats, Only you.

You don't want to be here, I say.

The floor rumbles; a large truck darkens the front window. He
doesn't respond.

He sits there quietly, radiating guilt. The house is dark. I kiss him
on the mouth.

I'm sorry, he says. I'm so—

Now it is my time to *shhhh*. He stammers to silence. I kiss him,
harder. I take his hand from my side and rest it on my thigh. He is
hurting, and I want it to stop. I kiss him again. I trace two fingers
along his erection.

Let's go, I say.

I always wake before him. Paul sleeps on his stomach. I sit up and stretch. I trace the rips in the comforter. Sunlight streams through my curtains. I can hardly sleep through such daylight. I get up. He does not stir.

I cross the room and pull the camera from its spot. I carry it into the living room. I rewind the tape, and it whines as it whirs back over itself.

I insert the cassette into the VHS player. I run my finger down the buttons on the machine like a pianist choosing her first key. As I press it down, the screen goes snowy, and then black. Then, the static diorama of my room. The wrinkled sheets with the spray of blue-china pattern, unmade. I fast-forward. I fast forward, spinning through minutes of nothing, unsurprised by how easy it is for them to slip away.

Two people stumble in, my finger lifts, the rush-to-now slows. Two strangers fumble with each other's clothes, each other's bodies. His body, slender and tall and pale, leans; his pants hit the floor with a *thunk*, the pockets full of keys and change. Her body — my body — mine, is still striped with the yellowish stains of fading bruises. It is a body overflowing out of itself; it unwinds from too many layers. The shirt looks bulky in my hand, and I release it onto the floor. It sinks like a shot bird. We are pressing into the side of the mattress.

I look down at my hands. They are dry and not shaking. I look back up at the screen, and I begin to listen.

DEATH OF A BUSINESSMAN

Giannina Braschi

In the R.E.M. song "Electrolite" Michael Stipe croons: "20th century go to sleep. Really deep. We won't blink." Giannina Braschi's challenging novel *United States of Banana* (2011) is also a dirge to the 20th Century, to all its injustices and worn out dilemmas. "Death of A Businessman" is the opening section of the first part of the novel, a collection of essays and stories centered on the 9/11 terrorist attacks and the economic life of the U.S. "Burial of the Sardine" opens the second part, in which the fictional Giannina and the literary figures of Hamlet and Zarathustra go on a quest to free Segismundo from the dungeon of the Statue of Liberty. What is at stake in the novel is the independence of Puerto Rico. Braschi extrapolates from the colonial status of Puerto Rico into the future, showing what would happen if the U.S. were to sell Puerto Rico to China. Born in San Juan and based in New York, Braschi holds a PhD in the Spanish Golden Age from SUNY Stony Brook. Her major works include the poetry collection *Empire of Dreams* (1988) and the ground-breaking Spanglish novel *Yo-Yo Boing!* (1998).

It's the end of the world. I was excited by the whole situation. Well, if everybody is going to die, die hard, shit, but what do I know. Is this an atomic bomb — the end of the world — the end of the millennium? No more fear of being fired — for typos or tardiness — digressions or recessions — and what a way of being fired — bursting into flames — without two weeks notice — and without six months of unemployment — and without sick leave, vacation, or comp time — without a word of what was to come — on a glorious morning — when nature ran indifferent to the course of man — there came a point when that sunny sky turned into a hellhole of a night — with papers, computers, windows, bricks, bodies falling, and people running and screaming.

I saw a torso falling — no legs — no head — just a torso. I am redundant because I can't believe what I saw. I saw a torso falling — no legs — no head — just a torso — tumbling in the air — dressed in a bright white shirt — the shirt of the businessman — tucked in — neatly — under the belt — snuggly fastened — holding up his pants that had no legs. He had hit a steel girder — and he was dead — dead for a ducat, dead — on the floor of Krispy Kreme — with powdered donuts for a head — fresh out of the oven — crispy and round — hot and tasty — and this businessman on the ground was clutching a briefcase in his hand — and on his finger, the wedding band. I suppose he thought his briefcase was his life — or his wife — or that both were one because the briefcase was as tight in hand as the wedding band.

I saw the wife of the businessman enter the shop of Stanley, the cobbler, with a pink ticket in hand. The wife had come to claim the shoes of the businessman. After all, they had found the feet, and she wanted to bury the feet with the shoes. There, I was talking to Stanley, the cobbler, because I too had left my shoes, a pair of pink boots, in Stanley's cobbler shop. He told me — you won't believe what I saw. I saw Charlie, the owner of Saint Charlie's Bar 'n Grill, watching the burial of the 20th century. Charlie goes out to hang the sign, closed for business, he looks up, and jet fuel burns and melts him down. And do you know how, how the torso hit the ground, how it landed. What I saw hitting the ground was a little bubble of blood, a splash that hardly felt itself, soundless, and dissolving into the cement, and melting without a sound.

I saw a passenger hanging on the edge of a bridge — with his feet in the air — his legs kicking — and both hands holding onto a steel girder hanging loose from the bridge — about to collapse — with the passenger — kicking his legs — as if he could peddle his way to the other side — where there is sand — sand and water — deep water — as if he could swim to shore and survive. The sand and the era of the camel are back. The era of the difficult. Now you have to climb sand dunes of brick and mortar. The streets are not flat, but full of barricades, tunnels and caves, and you have to walk through the maze, and sometimes you'll get lost inside, finding no end — and no exit — and you'll fall into despair — but you'll see a dim beacon of light — appearing and disappearing — and when it fades away — your hope will fade — and you'll be amazed — because your pace will change. I used to be Dandy Rabbit and now I am Tortuga China — not that I have lost my way — only my pace — because of the dead body I carry on my back — on the hump of the camel — in the desert storm — with no oasis in sight — but the smiling light of the promised land.

I saw the hand of man holding the hand of woman. They were running to escape the inferno — and just when the man thought he had saved the woman — a chunk of ceiling fell — and what he had in his hand — was just her hand — dismembered from her body. Now we no longer have the Renaissance concept of the Creation of Man — those two hands reaching out to each other on the Sistine Chapel — the hand of God and the hand of man — their fingers almost touching — in unity of body and soul. What we have here is a war — the war of matter and spirit. In the classical era, spirit was in harmony with matter. Matter used to condense spirit. What was unseen — the ghost of Hamlet's father — was seen — in the conscience of the king. The spirit was trapped in the matter of theater. The theater made the unseen, seen. In the Romantic era, spirit overwhelms matter. The glass of champagne can't contain the bubbles. But never in the history of humanity has spirit been at war with matter. And that is what we have today. The war of banks and religion. It's what I wrote in *Prayers of the Dawn*, that in New York City, banks tower over cathedrals. Banks are the temples of America. This is a holy war. Our economy is our religion. When I came back to midtown a week after the attack — I mourned — but not in a personal way — it was a cosmic mourning — something that I could not specify because I didn't know any of the dead. I felt grief without knowing its origin. Maybe it was the grief of being an immigrant and of not having roots. Not being able to participate in the whole affair as a family member but as a foreigner, as a stranger — estranged in myself and confused — I saw the windows of Bergdorf and Saks — what a theater of the unexpected — my mother would have cried — there were only black curtains, black drapes — showing the mourning of the stores — no mannequins, just veils — black veils. When the mannequins appeared again weeks later — none of them had blond hair. I don't know if it was because of the mourning rituals or whether the mannequins were afraid to be blond — targets of terrorists. Even they didn't want to look American. They were out of fashion after the Twin Towers fell. To the point, that even though I had just dyed my hair blond because I was writing Hamlet and Hamlet is blond, I went back to my coiffeur immediately and told him — dye my hair black. It was a matter of life and death, why look like an American. When naturally I look like an Arab and walk like an Egyptian.

I had four characters in my head: Hamlet, Giannina, Zarathustra, and Segismundo. Hamlet will give me the poetry. Giannina will give me the epic — I will write my own story. Zarathustra will give me the philosophy. And Segismundo will give me the plot. The truth is that the plot came first.

I was thinking: Should the statue come down. After all, a statue is just a statue. But inside a man is buried alive. We should destroy the statue to save the man. The man is more important than the symbol. But I was also thinking: he should not be able to break out. Let's keep him inside to prove that liberty exists. A statue is just a statue. But to have a man inside that statue — claiming he wants to become free — and never becoming free. We should charge to see him, but never free him. If he can't liberate himself — neither the crowd nor the police nor the firemen nor the army should liberate him. He has to do it himself. And if he grows old pushing the columns — and has no energy left to push, push, and push — and the media's attention deficit disorder turns the spotlight on someone else and the crowds forget all about him — too bad for him. There are enough problems in this city to worry about one man. And if he dies and the smell of his rotten body invades the city and brings diseases and plagues — will that be reason enough to split open the mausoleum of liberty? If an oracle says that unless we split open the statue — the body will continue plaguing the city — and there will be no peace — nobody will be able to sleep in peace.

It's not that we can't rescue him. We could if we wanted to, but we would lose a fortune. Segismundo thinks he depends on me, but the truth be said — I have more need of him than he of me. The more he rattles his shackles and chains, the more tickets he sells. The military is afraid that some terrorist group will plot to rescue him. The people want to liberate him. Especially his own people — immigrants and prisoners from around the world. So, in order to prevent the coming insurrection, we create a voting system to give the people the impression that Segismundo's destiny is in their hands. They are given three options:

Wishy

Wishy-Washy

Washy

If they vote for Wishy — Segismundo will be liberated from the dungeon. If they vote for Wishy-Washy, the status quo will prevail. If they vote for Washy, he will be sentenced to death, and nobody will have the honor of hearing his songs rise from the gutters of the dungeon of liberty. Every four years the citizens of Liberty Island vote for Wishy-Washy. They can choose between mashed potato, French fries, or baked potato. But any way you serve it, it's all the same potato.

I was living on 50th Street in midtown — and moved downtown — two blocks south of the World Trade Center — six months before the attack — so that I could study up close, from the shore of Battery Park, the Statue of Liberty. I took ferries to the statue and bought books about the sculptor, Frederic Auguste Bartholdi, who on a trip in 1871 to Liberty Island, at that time called, Bedloe's Island, saw a stone fortress in the shape of an 11 pointed star — and realized — here on this 11 pointed star will be my statue. When I saw a cartoon of Bartholdi, in a children's book, drawing sketches for his sculpture, I was thinking that same fortress over which Bartholdi erected the Statue of Liberty will be the fortress where Segismundo will be imprisoned.

I read in the *Post* on August 11, 2001 about an attack by a suicide bomber on Jaffa Street, in Jerusalem, at Sbarro Pizzeria — and I was impressed by the mention of a little girl, 3 years old, who stood up among the rolling heads like Lazarus back from the dead, back to tell them all — *wake up* — and she saw her mother — sleeping beauty on the floor — and called her:

> — *Mommy, wake up.*

The mother was dead. At this point a little piece of my glazed donut fell on the little girl's face and another crumb fell on her mother's legs. I picked up the pieces of my donut and ate them — the way I pass beggars in the streets — the worse they appear and the more they beg the more I ignore them, avoiding eye contact with the poor and thirsty — and as I turned the page — I saw the torso of a businessman whose testicles were blown off. He was screaming to a policeman who was passing by:

> — *Please, help me! I don't want to die!*

When the policeman saw the man, he vomited on the stumps of the man's legs — and I felt the horror — but I ate my donut anyway, thinking:

> — *I'm glad I'm not there. I'm here dunking my donut while others are blown to bits and pieces. Good luck. Keep hope alive.*

One month later I would be eating a glazed donut of the same kind when the first airplane hit the World Trade Center.

> — *Tess! Tess! Where are you? Let's go!*
> — *I have to get my camera. And my pink ticket.*
> — *For what?*
> — *To pick up my shoes.*
> — *Where?*
> — *At Stanley's cobbler shop.*
> — *Are you crazy! Let's run!*
> — *No* — Tess said — *I have to contemplate life from the highest point of view. That's what Emerson said it is to pray.*

So we went to the penthouse terrace — and from there we saw the second plane hit the second tower.

> — *They're going to fall!* — I screamed.
> — *If they fall, they will fall on themselves* — Tess said.

Bull's eye. What a prophet. I had told Tess when I was apartment hunting earlier that year:

> — *My only concern is the proximity of the towers. They will crush my building. If the Arabs came once to take them down — they will come back to finish the job. I know them. They were in Spain for eight centuries. They have a different way of measuring time. They are turtles. We are rabbits.*
> — *But they were designed by the Japanese* — Tess said. *If they fall, hari-kari, they will fall on themselves.*
> — *I don't want them to fall* — I said.
> — *They won't fall* — Tess said — *but if they fall, they will fall on themselves.*

So I signed the lease, on February 5, 2001, my birthday.

It is amazing, you know, when I was a kid we used to say, my friends and I:

> — *How old will we be when the new millennium comes?*
> — *I will be 45, an old lady* — I used to say — *and by then I'll be dead.*

But look at me now, running for my life, and wanting to go on forever and ever. I tell you, when my friends heard about the collapse — some of them smiled and wished me dead so they could relate more closely to the tragedy. I hate telling my story to these splinters who don't understand — and they don't care to understand — all they want is the scoop — and they're happy with the splinter and the splint. It's like misery loves company. Join the club of splinters and split your hair with a bobby pin. One of them said:

> — *Finally, the empire is falling. This is the begin-ning of the upset. What a defeat.*
> — *Not because they fall, will you rise. Why are you gloating?*
> — *Because the fall will make other towers rise.*
> — *Okay, okay. But the towers that will rise will not be the ones that laughed when our towers fell. It's not the laughter that rises. What rises is the curtain.*

A cop stumbled into the lobby, bent over, and started hacking up on the floor, while the walkie-talkie in his back pocket blared:

> — *Evacuate Battery Park! The gas lines are going to blow!*

That is when Tess grabbed my hand and said:

— *Now.*

I had tried to convince Tess to leave before but she insisted on going up to the penthouse. And when we came down to the lobby — I realized I had no shoes on. So, we went back to my apartment, got my shoes and my manuscripts, and came down again. To the lobby. By then the building was rumbling — smoke everywhere — dogs running — doormen crying — mothers with baby strollers. My neighbor gave me her dog. And the handyman broke open the first-aid cabinet and gave out masks. Outside it was snowing debris. We couldn't see where we were going. We ran toward the strobe lights of a patrol car — and knocked on the window:

> — *How do we get to the other side?*
> — *On a prayer.*
> — *Which way do we go?*
> — *Choose your own destiny.*

We headed south toward Clinton Castle, past the Chapel of Elizabeth Seton, the home of the first American saint and the birthplace of one of my masters whose bust is in the wall with the inscription:

> — *Here was born Herman Melville, the author of*
> *Moby Dick.*

On the shores of Battery Park I saw a boat, and the captain was Charon sailing us through the waterways of Acheron — Tess was Virgil — and these were the waters that would lead us through hell. The captain announced the destination:

> — *Liberty Island!*

At that moment, I held my neighbor's dog tight to my soul, reminding me of my own long lost Scotty Dulcinea — and looking back at the black clouds of Manhattan — the smell of Dulci's hair, greasy and soothing — I breathed deeply. At my side, I saw Hamlet and Zarathustra — with dead bodies on their backs — and I saw the burial of the 20th century — with all the memories that have flashed through my mind — like black clouds on movie screens.

— How is it that the clouds still hang on you?

I don't know how is it, but I can tell you they are always pregnant — with milk in their breasts — and they are leaking — those breasts — giving milk to the world — and I suck those milky breasts — that is where my inspiration comes from — from those white breasts — two breasts leaking — two towers falling — and the clouds keep hanging on — hanging on — and I feel the pressure of the hanging, that can hang me from a rope — tie me in knots — drive me into a toil — it is the hanging of expectation — of not knowing when or how — because we know not how it will fall, with fire, with choler, with water, or with death.

We arrived at the Statue of Liberty — only to hear Segismundo blaming us for a crime we never committed:

> *Ay mísero de mí, Ay infelice*
> *Ya que me tratais así*
> *Que delito cometí*
> *Contra vosotros naciendo*
> *Aunque si nací ya entiendo*
> *Que delito he cometido*
> *Pues el delito mayor del hombre*
> *Es haber nacido*

— Start the bucket brigade! There's a man alive! He's caught beneath the rubble!

— Keep hope alive! Keep digging. Maybe you'll find Segismundo in an air pocket where a bird laid an egg.

— We have to destroy the statue to save the man. The man is more important than the symbol.

— Don't you think we had enough? What more are we going to lose? Our liberty? As far as I know, it could be Osama Bin Laden himself like a horse of Troy with a ploy to destroy another national landmark.

— When those two towers fell — I felt a dentist had pulled out my two front teeth. I could not laugh anymore. And I have the smile of a smiling damned villain. But I also felt the hole in my mouth became a garage, and entering that garage were terrorists in trucks full of explosives and French diplomats — to fuck us more with other nations — to run over our dead bodies.

— Bury the one — bury the other — bury the twins — Muslim and American — Arab and Jew. Don't be unilateral. See the other's point of view. You are the whipper, cowboy. You whip and whip and whip — and attack, attack, and attack. Don't you know how to cover your ass? The attacker is never prepared to cover his ass. And to be fucked up the ass. But you will be fucked up the ass because you have fucked up other nations too many times. Nobody knows you better than the one that you abuse. And I can talk. I know you well.

— You thought legs are not important — but now that liberty has no legs — it can't walk. And you thought legs mean labor — and you can find cheap labor in Mexico and in China. So you broke Lady Liberty's legs off — looking for cheap labor — and you found terrorists with explosives.

You went for cheap — forgetting that cheapness is cutting liberty off at the knees. Now we cannot walk. What do you want us to do? Find cheap legs in other countries that will walk for us? We always thought: if you want to walk — it's because you're poor. We go by cars and jets. But we forgot that fuel is a luxury and that it would end. Oil is coming to an end — and now we have no legs to walk.

— I thought the brain could rule over the legs. And I thought the brain was white and the legs were yellow or brown. And I thought I could rule with my brain — and even if I cut my legs off — I would find cheap legs in other parts of the world. But now I am a mutilated body. I lost my legs in Korea. I lost my arms in Vietnam. I lost my head in Kuwait. I lost my torso in the World Trade Center.

BURIAL OF THE SARDINE

Giannina Braschi

There at the Fulton Market — where three roads intersect — was the point where Hamlet, Giannina, and Zarathustra first met. The three had been walking the streets like mad — without stopping to rest — until they came to the South Street Seaport — where flies were harrowing around the halo of the fish market that smelled like the rot of Chinatown. They recognized one another and walked towards each other with dead bodies on their backs.

Giannina: I'm burying the sardine — the dead body I carry on my back.

Zarathustra: A little fish — in a little coffin. And for this — for this little stinky thing — we came from so far?

Giannina: Look, it's moving. It's still alive.

Zarathustra: Pica y muerde de fea y de salada que esta.

Giannina: It worked its whole life in the sludge of oil and vinegar. I'll sprinkle incense, myrrh, and a pound of gold to be buried with it under the sand.

Hamlet: Hurry up. The ferry will leave without us.

Giannina: You have no idea how much I've suffered under the influence of this rigorous but retarded sardine. Not a warrior, but a soldier. Making me vow to its regiment of passive-aggressive work. No traveling was allowed.

No smoking allowed. No pets allowed. No one could get near me because the sardine would stink — and its stink would bite. Sometimes it would fly around the rim but it would always dive back into the can of sardines — looking for its paycheck. Every two weeks — it brought me a salary — the stinky sardine — and I brought home all I could buy with that salary — confinement, imprisonment. Depending on a salary made me salivate — but it blew my mind to dust — the dust that blows around and makes you cough — but you hardly can see it because it's made of dust. But I'm not made of dust — I'm made of flesh — and making love to the little sardine drove me crazy. It was such a little fish it barely filled my mouth. I could hardly eat it. I grew hungry — hungry for a big fish. God help me — no more fish! Please no clams, no oysters! Please — nothing shelled or scaled! Nothing salted — nothing finned or fanged! Because it had fangs — the sardine had fangs — and it bit me like a rabid squirrel. It must have known I wanted to bury it. Its fangs were long — and its screams were shrill — and it held grudges — and it had bones to pick. It blamed me for keeping it down — but all I wanted was its liberation from the can. I wanted it to breathe clean air — and to sing. Your mouth is already open — now take a deep breath, little fishy, and sing — sing a song of love. You know my cords are made of vibrant colors. You know I too come from the sea — but I don't come with grudges in my fangs. I come with wings to fly from your stink. I hate sardines.

Zarathustra: Then why do you eat them?

Giannina: Because I detest their helplessness. I wouldn't eat a lion. It would eat me first. I eat what is weaker than me. I like lamb. I watch a grazing lamb, and my mouth waters. I could eat it alive. But not sardines. They're already dead. They never lived. They're dead even when they're alive. Always with their mouths open. Begging for water. And I don't mind beggars. But sardines are not beggars — they're squirmers. They beg for water — but what they really want is to eat you alive — with their deadliness — which is a plague — a virus — bacteria — something contagious that kills you without killing you. They open their mouths to beg for water — but do nothing but gulp the draught and wait for water — with their mouths open — as if snoring which is worse than imploring — they're beggarly beggars that don't even beg — they're too dead to beg — and they're deadly contagious. It's their deadliness that lingers over me everyday of my life — the dead inertia of the sardine that obeys and begs for water, gallons of water, and does what it's asked to do in spite of no water and denies itself so much — that it doesn't realize it doesn't have a being anymore — and it lets itself be canned — always with its open mouth saying:

> — *Drop dead but give me drops of water.*
> *I don't want to be buried alive. I want to*
> *survive. I'm a salaried sardine. Give me*
> *more money.*

That's why they're so salty and ugly, they itch and bite. Because they're salivating for salty salaries—salty salaried sardines.

Zarathustra: It is not a sardine. It is a big fish.

Giannina: The coffin is small, but the stench is immense.

Zarathustra, would you allow my little pet to be buried in the same hole of the hollow tree where you left the tightrope walker?

Hamlet: And may I please leave the putrefied carrion in the same hollow tree?

Giannina: We are burying sameness — the aesthetic principle of sameness — the three together — at the same time — holding hands — burying bodies in the same hollow tree — and running free from freedom. Free.

Hamlet: More myrrh, more gold, more incense — to purify the air. And there is no blood spill.

Giannina: Not this time. This is the burial — the enclosure of the deed. This dust will purify the air. Hang in there while I finish the rites.

Zarathustra: I have been hibernating.

Giannina: I have been stagnating.

Hamlet: I have been trying to figure out what I should do with Polonius' body. I might as well do what you did, Zarathustra, leave the body in the hole of a tree — but before I leave it in the hole of a tree — find a hermit to give me two pieces of bread so I can give a piece of bread to the dead.

Zarathustra: I already left the corpse in the hole of a tree. Now I need to find the overman — somebody who rescues me from the principle of equality:

— All men are created equal.

Maybe that is why they are men because they have equal eyes, ears, and noses — and they have voices that howl to the infinite. But I am looking for inequalities. My thirst is unequal. Satiety is not satiated. And it's not water I need, but networkers.

Giannina: So, after all, you are a networker. You work the Internet.

Hamlet: I am a fishmonger at the market smelling everything that is putrefied. I smell the stench of death — and I have not gotten to my goal.

Zarathustra: I am still walking the tightrope — trying to get to the other side.

Hamlet: Do you realize we are posthumous? We are talking after.

Giannina: Speak for yourself. I'm not. Not yet.

Zarathustra: But you don't count — with your broken English —
you
             cut the line — you're not invited — little fox. You think you are a visionary just for saying: I am going to bury the 20th century. In 1998 you said it — and here we are in 2006 — and you are still trying to bury the body.

Hamlet: All these bodies are pestering the annals of literature. We have too many unresolved issues.

Giannina: When I said I will bury the 20th century — everybody — not just me — went looking for a dead body. When Princess Di and Dodi died — people thought

— oh, this is the funeral we've been waiting for! And when John-John Kennedy died, Americans appropriated the death of Lady Di — and said — this is our American dead prince. But they were inconsequential deaths — deaths that were not the beginnings of a war — nor the end of a century — but accidental incidentals — and their bodies were buried.

Hamlet: Wait a minute, the death of Polonius was an accidental death, so was the death of the tightrope walker. And Antigona's brothers were casualties of war.

Giannina: I am not here to analyze literary texts. You did what you did. I do what I do. What we have in common is our brotherly love — we bury bodies — and we never give birth — although I am in labor most of my life. In labor like Zarathustra. Not like you, Hamlet. You're a suicide bomber — and a camel with too many grudges. You should have been what you are — a poet — but instead the hunchback took center stage — because you were possessed by your father's ghost which was the absence of present life in you. You did not live. You remembered. That's why you didn't have an objective correlative. What you had were regrets that you didn't become the poet that you should have been. You should have given up the crown — and followed the path of Yorick — the path of music and love. Your feelings were overwhelming — and they overwhelmed you. Why didn't you write them down?

Hamlet: Words, words, words.

Giannina: What were you reading? That is the question. Instead of writing, loving, living — in the experience that is — not in the regrettable state of what was. I don't want to fall into the pit of Ground Zero again. Why are we here? Let's state the facts of our last supper.

Zarathustra: We are gathered here to break bread with our dead bodies.

Giannina: I found my dead body in a manhole — two blocks south of the World Trade Center where I was living when the Twin Towers collapsed. Even now, they are finding bones in manholes — and as long as there are bones — I still have lines to write. I like dead bodies and leftovers. I can see clearer when nobody is looking. When everybody goes to sleep — very late at night — I see what I saw when I lived at Ground Zero. I walk like a hunchback with a knapsack on my back.

Zarathustra: Clear our purposes. Revise our expectations. Set our goals a deadline. Revisit our analysis — explore new consequences — stabilize our instability — take a piss — before we embark on our journey to hear the speeches of Segismundo, the overman.

Giannina: Not an overman. A prisoner of war, a slave of liberty.

Zarathustra: The slave is liberty, trapped in the Statue with Segismundo.

Giannina: Talk to her. Ask for advice.

Zarathustra: She won't listen to us. She hates us. She is a feminist.

Giannina: She will listen to me. She is French.

Statue of Liberty: What do you want from me?

All Three Together: Orient us. Are we are on the right track?

Statue: I am a trophy. They played a game — a tennis match
               — between the French and Americans at the tourna-
               ment of liberty — and I became the prize. Do you
               believe in liberty?

Zarathustra: As much as I believe in God, in Santa Claus. God is
               the enemy of philosophy. If God exists, why should I
               exist? If I exist it is to question the possibility of God.
               God is always trying to put a stopgap in my brain.

Hamlet: Ghost is the absence of work.

Zarathustra: Madness is the absence of work.

Hamlet: What is madness but the ghost of my father. I didn't
               do what I should have been — a poet. The absence of
               work is madness.

Giannina: Entertain me a little more while I finish my supper.
               What have you been doing after death?

Zarathustra: Sleeping on laurels. Listening to the voice of critics. I
               can't stand what they say about me. I could never
               stand myself. That is why I had to disappear après my
               time. I could have waited longer. But I lost patience.
               And faith. No, faith I never had. But patience I lost.
               Being alone is not easy. Always alone — without even
               a platonic dialogue. Despotricando — and preaching

— always having to say something wiser than what another just said — using his argument to upset my own — to displace my argument — to take it out of context. And once my argument was taken out of context, I would always find a parking lot in that empty space where I would park my car. And give my speech — from the highest point of view. Even though blind — I could see the bridge over the cliff — and the abyss between the bridge and the cliff — and my eyes would shine more astounded than ever — looking over the ridge — at the abyss — and the cliff. Poets don't mean what they say. They take no responsibility — no accountability — they have light feet — they run like rabbits after carrots — intuitions — and leave the tortoise behind — with jetlag — and myopia and eyeglasses — studying studiously the flight of the rabbit.

Giannina: I have a lucky rabbit's foot and tortoise shell glasses.

Hamlet: I have crab legs. If like a crab I could walk backwards — and resurrect the body of my ghost — and as a crab — walk backwards — behind the tortoise crawling behind the rabbit eating carrots.

Giannina: What are carrots but flashlights of intuitions?

Hamlet: And what are flashlights but the spotlights of ghosts.

Giannina: I prefer track lights. They put me on track.

Statue of Liberty: I have inspired empires. I have destroyed empires.

Giannina: How did you become a mummy? Weren't you supposed to be a good wind that makes everything feel good? Your torch — wow — it's the spotlight over my head.

Statue: Let me tell you a story. I was once told that my genie would be liberated when the three come together. That moment has arrived. You are the three together — you, Zarathustra, Giannina and Hamlet. Let me tell you my secrets. Oh, my prophetic soul! I am the spirit of Joan of Arc. I liberated France from Anglo-Saxon freedom in the Middle Ages — and was burned at the stake. I came back to lead the French Revolution — and was sent to the guillotine. I reincarnated into the spirit of Napoleon. The French sent me to America as their horse of Troy. Under American surveillance, I've been the unhappiest woman on the planet. They turned me into the mausoleum of liberty. They say: Freedom! Freedom! But freedom means Anglo-Saxon Protestant rule oppressing the Latin, African, Asian, Arab, and Jew. When immigrants come looking for freedom, I suck their juice — under the surveillance of dread of labor without labor — of jobs without lightness of feet and creativity. I kill music. I kill love. Banks are banking my juice into credits and debts. But something is changing. I was Sleeping Beauty for too long. But life is not a dream. I have been waiting for a Prince of the Gutters to rise and seal my lips with a kiss that will awaken the winds of Joan of Arc, the French Revolution, and the spirit of Napoleon Bonaparte. With one kiss on the lips — I will come alive again. The moment has arrived. I am already feeling the signs. My cheeks are blushing. My knees are shaking. I feel vulnerable again. This Prince of the Gutters will make love to me. I will make love to him. We will become one and bring an era of peace and prosperity. Throughout the Americas, from the tippy top of the Yukon to the tippy toes of la Tierra del Fuego. Let me tell you another secret. Anglo-Saxon dominance is doomed. It wants to be the head of the elephant, but it's the tail of a mouse. The worst is ruling our shores.

Zarathustra: Pity the country that is ruled by the worst. And I don't pity anyone — not even the country ruled by the worst.

Statue: You don't know, Zarathustra, how many repressed emotions I've had to bury in my chest. I was almost diagnosed with breast cancer a few years ago. But I did something illegal — and if the authorities knew about it — they would have hammered me down to pennies — searching for the terrorist who sucked the milk from my tits. Since then I have not been the same — I cry, I weep. I am not supposed to feel — I am a mummy. My job is to gag and bind the prisoners of war — and the illegal aliens — and whip them into submission. But I feel for Segismundo. I nursed him. He might steal my crown one day. Unless, unless I realize I am not a dominatrix but a genie with human feelings that can love and be loved — even by one called terrorist. Segismundo is not a terrorist, I assure you. He is a liberator.

Zarathustra: He is the overman.

Giannina: He is a poet.

Hamlet: He is a conqueror. I see him rising up from the dungeon. He will make Puerto Rico a state. Then he will become the president of the U.S. and in the spirit of Napoleon go south and conquer all Latin America.

Giannina:	Again! The same mentality of domination! Can't we come up with a better system where the ones on top aren't whipping the ones on the bottom into hard labor, bankrupting creativity. Give me your social security number.
Statue:	My social security number is 009-11-2001 — the day the towers fell, I began to shrink.
Giannina:	Is that your expiration date? I still see you standing there.
Statue:	The day Segismundo takes the crown.
Giannina:	As a product you have an expiration date. But you're not a bottle of champagne or perfume — you have the stench of sweat — you have blood on your hands — you are a revolutionary — you are change — you mean business. You weren't meant to be a product — to be sold on free markets. You don't believe in free markets or free trade agreements or freedom fighters. Marketers have misrepresented you. You've become a symbol of the establishment but you were meant to abolish slavery — overthrow the status quo — blow winds — inspire change. Instead they bottled your essence so they could sell you. That's why you have an expiration date. Products are meant to expire. But once your genie is out of the bottle — you will become a creative process again. Your genie wants to be liberated. Who among us doesn't want liberation? We are on a quest for something higher than material dispossession.
Statue:	Can I sing again as the fat lady you've all been waiting for?

Zarathustra: Why do you think I became a hermit? I entered the stage of the world — and my exit was fast. I gave my speeches. I said what I had to say. I gave what I had to give and when I had no more to say — silence sealed my lips.

Hamlet: The rest is silence.

Giannina: I used to hear the voice of the people in taxi drivers — but now their voices are hooked up to cell phones, iPods, or BlackBerries. If you talk to them — they disconnect only for a second — and return to their gadgets. Human beings can't bear very much reality. They need a prop in their hands. It used to be the cigarette. Everybody was smoking in the streets. And now they use electronics to formalize the fact that they're busy with the dread of daily living that produces nothing creative but the monotony that they call pragmatism. They're busy producing dust, frenemies, intrigue. They're fire-breathing dragons foaming at the office of their mouths. What would happen if we snipped the wires of their busyness. Progress would happen — as it did to us on September 11. Inspiration made an installation that day.

Zarathustra: That whirling of the Muslim world — that earthquake. We were walking with our dead bodies on our backs.

Giannina: I thought — more delays — I'll never get to the statue. But the delay turned out to be progress. I had to move from Ground Zero back to midtown again. I lost track of the Statue of Liberty and of Segismundo. Even they lost touch with themselves. Segismundo, who was milking the breast of Lady Liberty, retreated into the dungeon — receding into seclusion and silence. I said:

Enough! Let's start our voyage again. We were set to take a ferry to Liberty Island when the Twin Towers melted down. I thought: Am I melting? Where is my creative energy? Where is my progress? Where is Zarathustra? In what part of the city is Hamlet? If like a crab I could walk backwards. Backwards I walked — and like a crab I found Hamlet crawling into a manhole where he thought he would find Ophelia's funeral procession — instead he found the bones of the businessman.

Hamlet: Alexander died, Alexander was buried.

Giannina: It's not over until it's over. Do you think I came to this country to shrug and say: Well, every empire has to expire.

Hamlet: Our empire is over.

Giannina: It might be over for you. But for me it has not even started. I'm starving. You ate all the food. And left me leftovers. I'm hungry. I'm an illegal alien. My strength is not satiated like yours. You might be disintegrating into body parts. But not me, honey. I am not over. It's over for you, but for me it's only just beginning.

Entanglements

Carlos Hernandez

Born in Aurora, Illinois, Carlos Hernandez has a Ph.D. in English from Binghamton University and now serves as Associate Professor of English at the City University of New York. He is a game designer currently working as the lead writer on the Lewis and Clark CRPG Meriwether, now in beta. In his story "Entanglements," Jesús, who had not known that Karen was married when they had an affair, finds out in just about the hardest way imaginable: when her husband, Chase, returns from his deployment in Iraq after having lost his legs to an IED. In a fit of guilt and unresolved emotion, Jesús vows to help Chase using the experimental technology at his Basic Energy Sciences (BES) lab.

I didn't know Karen was married until her husband Chase was wounded in action and was coming home. An IED took both his legs at the knee. She couldn't leave him, not now. She had to break it off with me.

I should have been angry, but all I felt was a vacuous shock. I had no idea how I should react. So I tried to imagine what a decent person would say in this situation and parroted that. "What do you need?"

She didn't answer for a while. Her kitchen smelled like a Pennsylvania July. The mason jars lining the high shelf broke the morning sunlight into rainbows. Through the window I watched the corn swaying like the crowd at a revival. I leaned against her counter sipping orange juice; she sat at the table double-clutching her mug and letting her tears fall where they may.

"Chase can't have children anymore," she finally told her coffee. "I will never be a mother."

I thought terrible things. Among the least savage was, *We were planning a family together. You and me. Remember?* But out loud I said, "Right now you need to focus on Chase."

She looked at me, her smile full of self-loathing. "Do you hate me, Jesús?"

"No," I said automatically. "You're human. You made a mistake."

She laughed through her nose; no sound, just bitter air. "I don't get you. I don't get you one bit."

I swirled my juice. "You want me to yell and scream?"

"I want you to feel something! Jesus Jesús. Do you know what Chase would do to me if he found out I'd been cheating on him all this time?" She was about to sip more coffee, but she stopped suddenly and yelled, "Aren't Spanish guys supposed to be passionate?"

I stopped leaning, stood straight. I dumped out the rest of my juice in the sink, washed the glass, dried it with the rag, set it oh so carefully in the rack.

"What are you doing?" Karen asked.

I stepped away to admire my work, made a box of my fingers like a cinematographer framing a shot. That glass was perfectly clean. Still looking at it, I said, "Spanish guys come from Spain. I'm Puerto Rican." And without another word I left.

As I drove to the lab where I work — I'm a physicist with the BES—my thoughts turned to Chase. I felt for him the kind of barrenness only fields of burgeoning corn can inspire.

His service to his country had left him mutilated. He'd suffer for the rest of his life, physically. But worse, there was the secret pain of his wife's betrayal waiting to reveal itself to him. Maybe someday when he was feeling stronger, maybe when he was starting to feel like he'd gotten a bit of his life back, Karen would unburden herself and tell him about us. Or maybe one day when she just felt like hurting him.

I had to pull over for a minute to collect myself.

Like everywhere in Pennsylvania this time of year, a cornfield abutted the road. I got out of the car and walked up to the six-foot-high wall of stalks. Took deep breaths.

These fields always remind me of my research. If there are Many Worlds, that means that there are many versions of me out there: an infinite number, maybe. Uniqueness is our most pervasive illusion. I'm just one of many cornstalks in the field.

I pushed a stalk gently, set it swaying. Flexible, but solid. Vibrantly alive. Indistinguishable, yes, from the thousands of others in this field: until you get up close. Then it becomes uniquely itself. For now. A farmer would soon mow it down, it and all its buddies. This whole field of slightly different stalks would be razed to the dirt. Where was the lesson in that?

There was none; it was just a field of corn. But even if the universe has no use for right and wrong, humans do. My affair with Karen had left me feeling very, very wrong. I needed to make amends.

So, with the stalks of corn as witnesses, I said aloud, "I'm going to help you, Chase."

I met Chase in person for the first time three months after he'd come home. I invited him and Karen—she pushed his wheelchair—to the BES superportation lab late on a Tuesday afternoon, when I was sure I could be alone with them. After I met them at the door and we introduced ourselves, they followed me to our experiment chamber. Karen rolled Chase carefully behind me; she was terrified of crashing into some multi-million dollar piece of government equipment.

The first time I heard Chase speak, he said to Karen, "Why the fuck are you going so slow?"

"There's no rush," she replied.

"Fuck you there's no rush. The game starts at 7:30."

Karen stopped moving; though I was studiously pretending not to hear any of this, I paused too. "You said you'd hear him out."

Chase craned to glare at her.

When he turned back to me, he was smiling: but like a hyena sizing me up. I sized him up right back. His hair was bristly and straw-colored, like he'd picked up a handful of hay and stuck it on his head. Harley Davidson muscle shirt, cargo shorts, nothing to cover the puckered, scarred ends of his legs. The tan he must've developed overseas had largely faded and his skin was returning to its default papier-mâché color, though freckle-specked. His solid build was starting to slacken and fatten; he was starting to melt into his wheelchair.

And he had good hyena-teeth. He was smiling when he said, "Before we go any farther, Doc, why don't you explain to me what I'm doing here? See, that way, once Karen hears how full of shit you are, we can go home and I don't have to miss the opening pitch."

I put my hands in my pockets and paced toward him. "You're not talking about the All-Star Game, are you? You actually watch that?"

He said nothing. He was shocked that a scientist could know anything about baseball.

"Look, Chase," I said, "I get it. You think this is just a waste of time. You think I'm some clueless egghead, or worse, some fraud who's out to rip you off. You're only here because of Karen. She's the only person in the world right now who could've gotten you here on a Sunday."

He folded his arms. "So?"

I closed the distance between us and took a knee in front of him. "You're here because you love her. Because you want to make her happy, even when you know she's wrong. Because now she makes your life possible. What would you do without her, Chase? If she got sick of your foul mouth and your bad attitude and the burden of caring for you, and left you?"

I glanced up at Karen. She was stone-faced. It had taken me this many months to convince her I wasn't plotting some kind of secret revenge on her, like some morning talk-show revelation/confrontation/conflagration. She kept telling me she still loved me, that she only wanted the best for me, and why would I ruin the wonderful memories we had shared together by destroying her life, or Chase's, who, I should remember, was a war-hero and deserved better?

Only after weeks of repeating that I only wanted to help Chase did she finally halfway believe me. Now, though, her strained face told me she thought I was indeed about to betray her. She was stoically preparing herself for the ugliest moment of her life.

Chase, meanwhile, reacted just like I thought he would. A guy like him is a tea-kettle; his shame at being disabled always boiled just under his skin, looking for any weak point through which it could escape, whistling. He bowed his head and, with a voice thick with self-pity, said, "Karen is the one good thing I have left in my life. I would do anything for her."

I smiled and nodded. Karen tilted her head. Then she squeezed Chase's shoulders and, looking at me with a face somewhere between relief and wariness, said, "I'd do anything for you too, baby."

I stood up. "What you're feeling right now, Chase—that's what I need you to hold onto. And Karen, you too: hold onto every bit of love and loyalty you feel for Chase. Love is entangled across universes. We're going to use the love you feel to find good matches for you."

"The fuck you talking about?" said Chase, staring at me, hard. I'd exposed his vulnerability, and now he needed to assert himself. He was used to making people look away whenever he wanted these days. A legless man glares at you, you avert your eyes; that's the rule.

I didn't look away. I even smiled a little. One hyena to another.

"I'm part of a team that's researching a process called superportation. That over there," I said, pointing to the 320 sq. ft. gray-concrete cube in the center of the room, "is the heart of what we call our Classical Information Aggregator. ClassAgg for short. It's where we conduct our experiments."

Chase, like any good Pennsylvania farmer, scowled at all that mumbo-jumbo. But to my face he said, "Well, don't stop now, Egghead. Tell me how it works."

"I'd have to lecture you for a year on current entanglement theory to even scratch the surface," I said. I opened the door to the ClassAgg and flourished like a New York City doorman. "Why don't I show you instead?"

I love watching the faces of people when they first get a look inside the ClassAgg. It looked like a homey efficiency apartment, featuring a 12-point stag-head presiding over the faux fireplace and framed, embroidered psalms hanging on the walls. The quilt on the full-sized bed was a gorgeous example of the local art. On the gingham futon sat an oversized Raggedy Ann. Coffee and whoopie pies—Karen loved whoopie pies—waited for us on the Amish kitchen table.

"This room is so darling!" said Karen. I'd showed it to her several times back when we were lovers, but she had to sound surprised for Chase. "I want to move in!" she flourished.

Chase didn't seem able to see through her lies. Glad I wasn't the only one. "This is science?" he asked, not without humor. "How is this science?"

"Let's eat and talk," I said.

So we dipped our fingers in cream filling and spooned sugar in our coffee while I did my best to explain uncertainty and entanglement in layman's terms.

"The room's a little goofy by design," I said. "To a lot of locals, it looks like Grandma and Grandpa's house, and if not, it's still campy and funny. Either way works for us. For our experiments, we need people to be as relaxed as they can be."

"That sounds like something a shrink would say," said Chase, suddenly suspicious. "Is this all a trick? Are you a fucking shrink? I ain't going to no shrink!"

Karen pinched his arm. He turned to her and dared her with a "What?"

I just kept talking. "We're not trying to help you get in touch with your inner child here. For superportation to work, we need to get you in touch with the other Chases out there, ones that are similar enough to you so that we can copy information from them."

Chase stopped mid-chew. "What do you mean, 'the other Chases?'"

"Like that one," I said, gesturing with my chin.

I'd gotten lucky; the timing was perfect. I had started the ClassAgg before I entered the chamber, and now, as if on-cue, Chase and Karen looked across the table and saw a silvery, liquidity form sitting across from them. It looked exactly like Chase. It was speaking to someone we couldn't see. A second later it started laughing like a silent movie. It was standing on two perfectly healthy legs.

"That's me?" said Chase. Then: "That's not me. That's some trick. Is this a movie set? Is this reality T.V.?"

"Science is full of tricks," I said. "This trick allows us to translate information of Chases from other universes and bring it here, into the ClassAgg. We call it superportation."

Some Chases joined the army but were never deployed. Some Chases were, but were never hit by the IED. Some were hit by the IED but made a full recovery. Some died in action. Some Chases never joined the army at all; they became poets and classical violinists and waiters and civil engineers and started businesses that failed and businesses that succeeded and were arrested for tax-evasion and became congressmen. Some Chases died when they were kids; some became the richest men in the world. Some married Karen, but most didn't: they died virgins, or married other women, or were gay and moved to states to marry men or stayed here and lived with men out of wedlock, or lived in universes where Pennsylvania allowed gay marriage.

But the most important thing I explained to Chase is that, out in the cosmos there were innumerable, luckier Chases who had perfectly functioning lower halves. I could sneak him into the ClassAgg a couple of Sundays a month and—using his love for Karen and Karen's love for him—find other Chases. Then I could superport information from those other universes onto his own body.

The upshot was, through an enormous expenditure of energy, and only while he remained in the ClassAgg, for a couple of hours every month I could give him mercurial legs. For as long as it lasted, Chase would be whole again.

If you want to know what happiness is, give someone his legs back. Even if it's temporary or incomplete. Even if it helps heal the marriage you wished every second of every day would fail, because you want Karen for yourself, even after everything that's happened. Tell the love you feel for her to go fuck itself. Bring happiness back to a body the world has ravaged, and some of it will vicariously trickle down to you. You will rediscover what agency feels like. Agency, you will suddenly remember, feels good.

If, on the other hand, you want to feel like a lovelorn teenager, drive into a cornfield and lie on the hood of your car next to someone who: 1. has already betrayed you once, but; 2. you want more than anyone else in the world, yet; 3. is utterly forbidden to you, and thus; 4. is even sexier because of it. Just lean back on the windshield with your hands pillowing your head and listen to the rustling stalks and look up at the stars. Try to be honorable. Try to be a good friend.

"Thanks for dessert," I said to Karen. She and Chase were constantly finding ways to thank me for sneaking him into the ClassAgg for the past four months. That night's thank-you had taken the form of a homemade four-berry pie. It sat on the back seat now, untouched, tepid.

"It was the only excuse I could think of to see you tonight," said Karen, her eyes locked on the moon. "I have to tell you something."

"You couldn't text me?"

"No."

"Okay. What?"

She swallowed. "Chase wants a baby."

I thought this through for several seconds before I responded. Then: "He figures there are some universes where you are pregnant right now. He thinks I can superport that information to our universe, the same way I've been superporting legs."

She laughed joylessly. "Our very own immaculate conception."

I waited a few seconds to make sure what I said next I could say completely without affect. I said, "Is that what you want?"

"First I want to know if you can do it."

The last thing I wanted to do in any universe, ever, was to help Chase and Karen have a baby together. Because that would be it. Karen would be gone forever.

Only thing is, the scientist in me wouldn't stand for it. I'd betrayed my professional ethics more than enough for the sake of my stupid, stupid heart. Being good at my job was one thing over which I still had control. So I thought through the idea dispassionately, scientifically. And I can honestly say the best answer I could give was, "No. It's impossible. It'd be just like Chase's legs: the information vanishes as soon as you turn off the ClassAgg's power."

There was relief in her voice. "That's what I thought."

"There are other options." This was me still being professional and self-sabotaging. "I could show you what your child or children look like in other universes. I could superport them a while into the ClassAgg. Maybe Chase would like to see them. Maybe you would, too."

She shook her head. Her voice was raw and tender when she said, "It'd be like seeing ghosts. That would break poor Chase's heart."

At least she sounded raw and tender. I realized then I had no longer had any idea how to interpret her words. She had become a cypher to me, a placeholder zero of herself. Her words were dialogue from an audition-script: a good actor could play them a million different ways.

Yet I still wanted her. What the fuck was wrong with me?

I was awoken from my reverie by a touch. Karen's hand had cautiously crawled over to mine, like a crab seeking a mate. I lay very still. She interlaced her fingers with mine. Neither of us said anything for a time.

Eventually, her eyes jumping from star to star, she said, "Chase is coming back to himself. Those months when he first came home, there was nothing left of the man I'd fallen in love with. He was pure rage."

"He'd lost both his legs."

"Yeah. Who wouldn't be angry?" She squeezed my hand a little tighter. "And I thought, 'Karen, you slutty bitch, this is exactly what you deserve. You deserve a hateful husband who will treat you like shit for the rest of your life.'"

"No one deserves that."

She looked at me for a second. Then she turned back to the sky and, rueful, said, "You should think that. You have every right to think I deserve every bad thing that could happen to me. What I did do you, Jesús—unforgivable.

"Yet here we are. Not only did you forgive me, but you've given Chase his hope back. He's feels like he's living a miracle, thanks to you. You know what he says? He says, 'I feel like every Chase in the universe is coming together to help me get through this.'"

It was the longest we'd held hands since Chase had returned. "That's a nice thought," I said.

"He's not nearly as angry anymore. He can envision a future. He wants kids now."

"I can't give him kids."

"But you made it possible for him to dream about the future again. You gave him his vision back. It's the greatest gift anyone can give."

"Glad to help."

She laughed. "'Glad to help.' Really, that's it? That's all you want to say?"

"What else should I say?"

She shook her head and smiled. "Always so practical. So understated. You know why I fell for you, Jesús?"

"Yep. Because I'm 'Spanish.'"

She squeezed my hand, hard, as punishment; I giggled evilly. "Never going to let me live that down, are you?"

"It was pretty racist, m'dear."

"I know. I mean, now I know. I didn't realize I was being racist. I'm sorry."

"It's okay. If I'm being really honest," I said, letting go of her hand so I could roll on my side to face her, "I'm not really all that Puerto Rican. Really, I'm white."

Now that cracked her up. "Jesús, honey, have you looked in a mirror? You are not white."

"I know I look brown. But I've forgotten all my Spanish. I have a Ph.D. in Physics from an American university. I have money, a white ex-wife, a white ex-lover, and a split-level I bought 17 years ago. I don't live the life of someone who has to struggle against racism every day. It's not fair for me to call myself Latino."

I looked up. The moon pulled a curtain of clouds around itself like a magician, and the field grew a little darker. "Can I be really honest, too?" Karen asked.

"Sure."

"I did fall for you because you're Spanish. Latino. Whatever. I mean, your name sounds super-Latino—Jesús Camacho!—and you have brown skin and kinky hair. But you're right. I mean, you speak perfect English. Better than me."

"Better than 'I.'"

Her laugh ascended to the stars. "See? So yeah, fine, you're white. But off-white. I was lonely without Chase, and you were different enough to be exciting. But not too different. Just enough."

Maybe some people in my shoes would've been offended by Karen's words. I wasn't. Because—again, being totally honest—I thought of myself in exactly the same way: Latino enough to be interesting, but white enough to fit in. Before Karen, I had no idea how much racism I'd internalized.

"You know why I fell for you, Karen?" I asked her.

"Seriously, no idea. I'm an administrative assistant with a high school diploma who eats too many whoopie pies and goes to church mostly for the gossip. You could do a lot better."

"I fell for you because you're so honest. Even when it makes you look bad. Everyone else keeps their evil parts hidden. Not you. You share everything you're thinking: good, bad, ugly, whatever. It's so refreshing."

Her face became mannequin hard. She told the moon, "You mean, except for the part where I was lying to you about my husband, and lying to my husband about you."

What could I say? "Yeah. Except for that."

I thought I had ruined the moment, but I saw her squint a little; she was thinking, and the thought seemed to amuse her. "You know what I want, Jesús? I want to know how the other Karens did it."

"Did what?"

She rolled over and got make-out close to my face. "How they managed not to fuck up our relationship. In some universes right now, there are Karens and Jesúses who are perfectly happy together, even after Chase came back. Every possibility can happen, right? Somehow, some brilliant Karens out there figured out a way to keep seeing you."

As gently as I could I said, "That sounds impossible."

"With all the gagillions of universes out there, you're telling me there isn't a single Karen in the entire cosmos who figured out how she could keep you and Chase?"

"I don't know. Maybe. But we still only get to live in this universe. And in the here and now, I don't see how to make that happen."

"But we have a ClassAgg! Don't you see? That thing is a fucking crystal ball! We can search for those universes. Find out how they made it work." She took my hands. "Jesús, there's a way! A way we can be together again!"

She was almost crying she was so happy. She wanted so much to be right. And she was, kind of. But when physicists use the word "information," they mean mass, particles, position in space and time. They don't mean philosophy and morality. It's true that we could spy on all the Karens and Chases and Jesúses living their lives across realities, but we couldn't talk to them or ask them how we should fix our broken lives. The ClassAgg only let us spy on others. It had no opinion about what anything meant.

It was Chase who called me. "Jesús, it's time, man, it's time! Her water broke!"

"I'm on my way. What do you need?"

"Nothing man, just get your ass to the hospital! Wahoo!"

I wasn't family, so they wouldn't let me in the delivery room, even though Karen and Chase told everyone in the hospital I was more than family. But rules are rules, so Chase came out regularly to update me, and every time he reported, he thanked me for the miracle I'd given Karen and him. He called me his angel. Twice he summoned me into a hug, and each time I locked his wheels so I wouldn't lose my balance, then stooped over and embraced him until he had finished crying.

At 4:40AM, Karen and Chase became the proud parents of a healthy 8lb. 11oz. boy with ten fingers and ten toes and his whole life ahead of him.

It was hours more before they would let me in to see the baby and the proud parents. When I did finally enter the room, Chase was cradling the sleeping newborn in his lap, while Karen lay on the bed with her eyes closed, looking like a vampire's most recent meal, black-eyed and enervated.

I whispered from the door, "Hey, happy parents!"

Chase gestured me over; I tiptoed so as not to wake the newborn. "He's just the most beautiful thing I've ever seen," Chase whispered. Only surface tension held the tears against his eyes; they would fall the next time he blinked. "It's like he's made of 'perfect information,' right Jesús? Like you gathered all the best ideas from every universe and put it into our child. That's what you did. There in the ClassAgg, you made all this possible. It's a miracle. You gave Karen and me a child of our own."

"Yeah," said Karen, "a child of our own." I looked at her and found she was staring at me. Through her exhausted rictus I could see that same infuriating look of hers. Once again she was waiting for me to betray her.

I knelt next to Chase's wheelchair and brought my face close to the child's. The sleeping baby took easy, sonorous breaths. "My God," I said, and I meant it. It was hard to imagine the universe had any problems at all when it had babies in it breathing so peacefully.

But the truth is, babies are born into a whole universe of problems. My son's skin was as brown as mine.

THE DRAIN

Alejandra Sanchez

Alejandra Sanchez has a BA in English from California State University, Los Angeles and a MFA in Creative Writing from Antioch University, Los Angeles. Her work has been featured in the independent film, *I Stare At You and Dream*, KPFK's *Pacifica* Radio, Radio Sombra's *Red Feminist* Radio, *Mujeres De Maiz*, *La Bloga*, *UCLA Young Writers Anthology*, *Hinchas de Poesia*, *Duende Literary Journal*, and PBS Newshour's *Where Poetry Lives*. In "The Drain" Anahita who normally relies on a morning shower for personal healing, finds that a strange substance has invaded her sacred space.

Anahita entered her bathtub and stepped in something like a pool of curdled buttermilk that slid between her finely manicured toes and crept up her ankles.

Eew! What the hell is that?

She jumped out and wiped her feet with a towel that hung from a hook on her bathroom door. Entering her bedroom, Anahita fished around her closet for a hanger. Straightening the hook, she went back to the bathroom and stuck it in the drain. The water struggled to go down but stuck, emitting a gargling sound and spurts of phlegmatic bubbles.

Anahita needed a plumber. But had no idea where to find one at 6:00 AM, when what she desperately required was her morning shower. Today was huge for her. It was the deadline for a crucial grant proposal at the non-profit where she worked as Resource Development Manager. What would Teresa, the Community Health Coordinator say to her four-year old on his birthday if mommy suddenly lost her job and had no money? Or poor Steven, who had cried to her in the breakroom when his wife was diagnosed with ovarian cancer and medical bills were sky high?

Everybody was counting on Anahita.

Who could she call to fix the drain?

He had always taken care of those things. And Anahita did not want to call him. Not after the last time.

Anahita, I'm so sorry baby. Please. Please forgive me. I will never do that to you, ever again. I promise.
I love you
Ana.

She had tried to leave. They were standing at the bar and Vincent squeezed her wrist so hard she couldn't feel her fingers. He poured her glass of cabernet onto her white dress, staring at her with a crazed look in his eyes. His pupils were so dilated, melted into his irises—like pools of black obsidian. *I told you I don't like you to drink Anahita*, he said in a hoarse whisper. It almost looked like he was smiling, with those frantic, liquid eyes that really scared her. As if trying to contain something behind them that seeped through and scared the shit out of him.

She ran outside. He followed her to the parking lot. She thought he was running after her, with apologies. Anahita put her hand on the car door handle. It was cold, hard, lifeless. She heard his footsteps behind her. Anahita turned around as his hand rose, and saw with her eyes, but didn't really see.

His hand loomed huge, as if bulging out from some other body — not Vince's — and hurled towards her. The parking lot whirled like a carnival twister, though somehow felt slow motion. All the blood drained from her head and sunk to the pit of her stomach.

A sting burned a hole through one side of her cheek. Her head throbbed. Anahita's face felt misshapen, lopsided, as if her face was a mask that had been attached — now ripped off, hanging from her cheekbone.

Her vision blurred. The parking lot, with all its shiny metal cars, looked slanted.

He stared at her.

She saw him. He looked like a completely different person to her. Not Vince, not her lover. Through eyes almost swollen shut, she saw. He was a mass of unlighted shadow, no eyes, no face. She got into her car and locked the door.

She did not know him. He was a stranger.

Anahita's shower was the one place where she escaped all the oppressive forces in her life that dammed her: her boss, coworkers, family, friends, and her hard exterior, which, she knew, was really fake. She had to fit in and fit herself in to all these other worlds that were not her own.

How she envied the water. Anahita wished she could flow freely outside of her bathroom, outside her skin even.

She sweated in the shower, cried in the shower, bled in the shower. The water cascaded all over her glistening brown body, releasing, cleansing, and healing her. Anahita emerged from the baptismal steam — reborn. Profanely accessible, yet immaculately sacred, inside the temple of her shower she was water. The steam of her authentic self rose all around her, opening her pores, her body becoming a pulsing, singular breath, inhaling every molecule of hydration and clarity.

Anahita wanted to cry, sweat, and make love all the time. But she had to hold it in. Her desires had a way of slipping through, though. In bashful little doses, but still. Always these slips were immediately sanctioned. Sneezes were sanitized by *excuse-me's* and dismissed by *God bless you's*. Pure sweat was contaminated by icky-sweet, perfumey anti-perspirants. Tears were censored by tissue, quarantined to poking corners. *No, NOT in public Anahita. Ana, don't make a scene!* Or, *Oh my God, are you crying?*

How she resented those nagging voices! Especially the voice inside of her that took the shape of the others, echoing them.

Sometimes Anahita stared at herself in the mirror and saw a complete stranger glaring back at her.

Every morning she dressed for work, pinching her voluptuous curves into too tight slacks that weren't much for breathing, and applied *Ivory Beige* face powder to her chocolate skin. She straightened her hair with an iron that sizzled and spat while it tamed her unruly curls. Anahita's grandfather, true to the Latin American colonial legacy of caste based on skin color, always told her: *Ay mija eres muy quemada. Cover yourself when you go out in the sun or you'll get negra.* He stretched out the word *negra*, like saying it produced a bad taste his mouth really wanted to spit out. He blamed Anahita's cocoa skin and kinky hair on her love of going to the beach, saying the salt in the air and water gave her hair its dense curls. Anahita was the only one in her family who was dark skinned. Most of her tias and tios were European looking, proudly flaunting milky skin and straight hair. Anahita was like a silent reminder of some dark sin, some taboo that no one liked to talk about unless to negate what she truly was, blaming her darkness on the harsh, unforgiving forces of nature: the saline air and water, the blistering sun.

Every 6:00 AM Anahita offered her beautiful bronze body: its undulating peaks and curves, resilient arms, giving hands, high breasts, dipping navel valleys, small triangle of pubic hair, ample, round bottom, abundant thighs, and strong legs to the water. As she stood under her personal waterfall, naked and elemental, all of her cells breathed as if for the first time. Her abundant lips, rising broad nose, and crown of spiral ringlets — all reminding of the universal laws of physics — became vibrant with life. Anahita's hour of beauty in her shower was only a drop of sacrament to appease the daylong massacre of her senses.

Anahita made her decision.

She stared at the muck in her shower, took a deep breath, holding it tight in her chest, and went in.

She winced when her feet sloshed through the scum that looked like a swamp of sour milk turned ecru. She turned the circular metal knob slowly, unsure of herself. It shined brightly in the light of her bathroom, revealing Anahita's reflection in its silvery gaze. She looked distorted: elongated at her head, neck, and face and morphed and globular at her ass, tummy and thighs. Anahita squeezed her eyes shut, raising her chin to the clear water. The showerhead squirted out unevenly, in bursts of hot and cold. It spat at her, then slobbered like a messy kisser. The muck at her feet rose, filling the tub. Warm and slimy, it curled around her calves, clinging to her skin. Anahita felt a strong pulling sensation grip her legs.

She started to panic, unable to catch her breath. She tried to jerk her feet away but couldn't budge. The thick sludge was like quicksand, clamping onto her knees. Each time she tried to move the scum slithered higher up her thighs.

Anahita suddenly knew, *she was stuck.*

She gripped the shower curtain, screaming. Then realized, *who would hear her?*

She was totally alone.

The clear water at the top of the tub overflowed, spilling onto the floor. It had escaped the scum that now stuck to her skin. She tried to wipe the scum away but it solidified, plastering to her skin as she scrubbed and scratched to get it off. In desperation she bent down, feeling for the drain.

The water near the drain was hot on her fingertips. She felt a whirling force that instantly froze her. Ripples of fear numbed Anahita's hand, weighing her down deeper in the bath. The fluid spun furiously, building momentum.

Anahita felt the liquid grip her arm. It pulled her and she slipped, losing her balance, forcing her head to plunge into the vortex of hot water. She squeezed her eyes shut, thrashing her hands wildly, flinging chunks of hardened mush to dislodge the muck and clear the drain.

As her cheek hit the bottom of the tub, she felt heat emanating from the tiny cave of the drain. It burned the tips of her fingers and eyelids as she blinked hard and struggled to the surface for air, spitting out pieces of grit that lodged between her lips.

Suddenly, there was a flash of light.

All the untainted water in the tub rushed down the drain, as if sucked in one incredible gush by an invisible, cyclonic vacuum.

With the force of the drain eddying like a maelstrom, the water tripped her over, sending her whole body crashing against the tub.

She landed with a hard thud. The last sound Anahita heard before her head hit the porcelain, slipping into unconsciousness, was her own voice cursing her shower — her sanctuary.

She awoke to the sound of a muffled voice yelling, "This is Caesar, where the hell are you?! Anahita?" It was her boss. It sounded so far away.

Then Vincent's voice. "Baby girl? Everyone's looking for you. I spoke to your boss, he says you haven't been to work in three days. Where are you, mija? Ana? Are you there? Ana? ... who are you with? What the fuck are you doing? Answer me! I'm coming over."

Vincent's voice sent chills piercing down Anahita's spine, leaving a tattoo of cold sweat in its wake.

She tried to move.

Nothing.

Anahita was covered head to toe in something like a body cast. She couldn't even move her head to see what it was. Each second the clay-like material covering her body tightened, hardened, choking her insides. Pain impaled her whenever she tried to move. Her thoughts hazed and jumbled together, nailed to the far sides of her brain. Somewhere her mind was there. Anahita searched desperately, but her reason was like a stack of neglected mail sealed in a corner of a very dark, windowless room. Her thoughts were unreadable, unreachable, eclipsed by drilling pain.

Anahita closed her eyes and gave up understanding what she was doing there — naked in her bath covered in a substance quickly hardening to cement — or why.

She slipped in and out of sleep and consciousness. Dream and reality whirled together. *Yes ... wait, no ... swirled. Yes ... swirled together like water — water — yes. Like water going, going ... down. Down the drain. The drain? The drain! Oh, NOOOO!* Anahita tried to scream. No sound came. It felt as though an unseen hand held her fast, suffocating her. She couldn't fight; she could not see her enemy.

Someone was knocking on her bathroom door. Or was it the front door? Someone was calling her name.

Vincent.

Anahita felt the old fear rise in her throat, throttling her. She did not want it to be him. He was not her knight in shining armor—as if there were such a thing. She tried to yell, *Leave me alone!* but had no voice.

Again she tried to move. Nothing. Now Vincent's voice was pleading. The side of his mouth and cheek sounded pushed against the door. She heard him thrust his body against the wood. He was banging hard on the door with his shoulder, kicking it with his feet. The barricade didn't give, not even a crack. His pounding was loud, making Anahita's head feel like jagged glass hammered into it. With each of Vincent's thrusts her head clamored. She threw up and felt warm vomit dribble down her chin.

"Ana, hold on baby girl. I'm coming back. With a locksmith." She heard heavy footsteps rush down the stairs.

Shivers of fear trembled in her gut, burning her skin. She felt needles of perspiration all over her.

Then they came.

Not Vincent. Not a locksmith.

Anahita could feel them running all over her like millions of tiny ants. They were in her hair, crawling up her nose, in her ears and eyes. They crawled between her legs. They squirmed, spontaneously multiplying, swarming like maggots. Depositing themselves into her pores, they burst open, exploding. Connecting to one another, they created a fault line of burning that throbbed beneath her skin. Filled with puss they sucked from her vital fluids, they grew. Reemerging as huge boils, they cracked her skin, bursting the cast that covered her.

Anahita realized with crystal clarity: the cast was the substance that had invaded her shower and contaminated her bathwater.

Anahita gasped and panted but her lungs did not fill with air. Unable to breathe through her nose or mouth, Anahita wheezed in heaves as her whole body struggled to respire through the sores on her skin. Her chest surged; her legs quaked.

Anahita saw her belly swell, becoming a humongous balloon of brown flesh. Pain tore at her in places she'd never known existed. Her womb dilated; her insides pulled apart. She saw clumps of her bright red blood unfurl into the clear water.

One by one, the abscesses on Anahita's body burst — and life emerged.

"We have reversed the process!" the voices declared in high-pitched, singing unison. They shone brilliantly. Tiny orbs of white, blue, and pink light swirled before her.

Anahita thought they were the visions she'd had as a small child. But no, she thought, that could not be. The daydreams she'd had in her mother's garden of shimmering, diaphanous creatures as tiny as ants and voluminous as nematodes that spoke to her in other languages, telling her stories of ancient times, calling her by another name were not real. *No, of course not.*

They were glaring at her. One screamed, "REVOLUTION!!" Her skin prickled and itched as they retched all over her. She felt stinging pinches everywhere, as the holes on her body from where the abscesses had burst seemed to suck in the vomit.

"More! More!" they screamed.

"Yes! We must rid ourselves of this sickness!"

"Yes! Back to the Source!"

The Source? Sickness? What are these things? What the hell is happening to me?

The beings glistened before Anahita's eyes and swayed on her body in a unified hum, reverberating a singularity that could only come from one corpus, yet they were millions. They seemed endless.

She heard a loud, piercing drip wrench at her insides, clamoring in her ears. It seemed as if she were … melting. *Melting? Yes that was it!* Her bodily fluid was being drained with a vicious suction. She felt weaker and weaker with each *dripdrip dripdrip dripdrip* down the drain. She realized with a horrifying lucidity — and tried with the entire logical, safe reasoning she could muster to fight it — that she was going down the drain!

Dripdrip. Dripdrip. Dripdrip.

With each *dripdrip dripdrip* all her safehouse doors — the doors to her repression, the doors to her fear, the doors to her obsessive control were unhinged wildly with the force of an island typhoon. All the rusty nails that held those doors in place were ripped from her body, exposing gaping holes, releasing all her pain and fluids in gushing torrents.

Anahita's doors could not hold the obesity of one single idea that bulged behind them: *She was going down the drain!*

Melting, melting, melting. Dissolving like a plastic doll in a blazing pyre.

NO! NO! NO! This is not possible! 'You lost it baby girl. I always knew that would happen. You are fucking crazy!' What? Nooo!! This is MY voice! Not yours, Vincent! Get the fuck out of my head, you ASSHOLE!! YOU are the one who is crazy!!!

No, she told herself. No. The last real thing that happened was Vincent trying to get in the door. She was sure of it.

Yes. He was trying to get in the minute just a door ago. Wait — what? Oh no! This is happening! This is real! Wait. Wait! Wait! Hold on to Vincent. Hold on to him! Any minute he'll be back. Any minute … Oh! Why didn't I just give him my keys?

She had never given Vincent her key. No matter how he assumed and asserted her space as his own. No matter how many of his grey suits were hanging in her closet, or how he slept stretching himself across her bed, as if by some wizardry shrinking her bed and blankets to fit only him. No, she had never given him the key. Not to the front door nor to her bathroom, which had a keyed lock also. She'd made sure of it. The bathroom was hers only. And she had never regretted her decision. Until now.

She tried to will herself to lose consciousness.

But she could not shut herself down any longer. Anahita's ignorance refused to bounce her safely in place like an inflatable, plastic punching doll. That doll had already melted down the drain.

She pinched her eyes closed. Then, without her brain willing her eye muscle to open, she saw. A thick, mucousy film slid down her eyeball, past her cheek, dribbling down the sides of her face. She tried to blink and with that came immense, stabbing pain that seemed to shoot through her head and out of her, bouncing into the light all around. She felt as though a piece of her consciousness had been excavated out of her brain.

Anahita did not experience the lapse of vision or flash of light to dark that accompanies blinking. There was no abrupt phosphine, no rustling of eyelash to skin. Anahita realized with certain horror that she had not opened her eyes at all.

Her eyelids had melted away!

Anahita awoke in a vast darkness. Tiny spheres of light shimmered and trembled like a million pearls, moving in a thrum of glowing whites, blues, soft pinks, and yellows set against an immense void. The lights appeared to move together, in and out of each other seamlessly — like an ocean of radiance, glimmering in a womb of blackness.

She did not feel her body. She did not remember her body.

She did not remember the glossy, tight curls of her childhood when boys tugged at her hair, marveling at how it bounced back. *Boing-boing curls,* they called them.

She did not remember the swoon of moist warmth between her smooth, pubescent thighs at twelve, when she slow danced with a boy for the first time.

She did not remember the implosion of electricity rise from her belly into her throat when he pressed against her and she felt his hot, pink tongue flicker at hers.

She did not remember the blossom of friendship as a young woman, talking with her girlfriends, sipping hot coffee swirled with cinnamon and cream, or chilled champagne splashed with orange juice. She did not remember the bursts of their shared laughter. She did not hear the clink of crystal glasses, toasting a birthday, a graduation, a job offer, a proposal.

She did not remember the brine of tears choked in her mouth, the salted swallow of betrayal, or the vinegared knot of loss that had lain lead-weighted in her stomach for so many years.

All of that was gone now.

She did not remember her image in her full-length mirror; how she squeezed and pinched her body, frowning when it didn't fit into some elusive, unnamed — already reserved — space of beauty. Even when so many poured praise onto her she couldn't figure out why — why couldn't she accept the compliments? Why couldn't she breathe under the weight of them? Why wasn't she satisfied with herself? Why was she never enough? Always too dark, too curvy, too smart even? Of course, she knew why intellectually — she had gone to college, developed an analysis, read bell hooks, *This Bridge Called My Back*, knew very well the self-hate women of color have mastered.

Although Anahita longed for self-love, she could not change the emotion that became a jagged stone in the pit of her womb.

She did not see herself frowning at herself, while her own reflection stared back at her, some stranger in her mirror, asking: *Why? Why do you hate me so?* She did not see herself dismissing in a red-cheeked flutter the compliments of: *You are beautiful,* that no matter how many times she heard, she could not find a home for.

All of that was gone now.

She did not remember the blood caked on her cracked lips after she opened the car door and let Vincent in. She did not judge herself, asking like so many other times, *why the hell had she done that?* She did not blame or punish herself for what happened later, which was so much worse than the parking lot.

She did not even remember the cold porcelain tub against her skin. Or the immense pain that wracked her body just moments before.

She did not remember any of it.

Unafraid for the first time in all of her existence, Anahita let go.

No longer perpetually clenching, no longer holding back — she felt liquid. Anahita was finally herself. Unconditionally, unapologetically, perfectly, imperfectly *herself.*

She moved with the seamlessness of water and the quickness of light. No longer hiding, *She was hers.* And she was completely free.

She heard chanting.

Iba se Yeye! Iba se Yeye! Iba se Yeye! Iba se Yeye! Iba se Yeye!

Somehow she knew the language, although it seemed ancient. But still, she knew it — *she remembered it.*

Voices thrummed out of the blackness, warbling over and over, *Iba se Yeye! Iba se Yeye! Iba se Yeye!* creating a vibration that welled inside of her, rising, entering her essence, filling her with infinite prisms of joy. She began to weep in ecstasy.

Suddenly, the cacophony of voices stopped and a single voice spoke to her from the darkness:

Iba se, Yeye. All praises to you, Mother.
Welcome home, Yeye. You are our story that lives in our cells,
existing forever. You are a part of us and we of You. We will love
You, care for You, praise You, and offer to You, always.
You are our Goddess, You are our Mother!! You are Osun!!!

The voice stopped and one by one all of the circles of light disappeared. Slowly, with each extinguished illumination all the remaining story strands from Anahita's human life left her. She became filled with the expansive realization that she had become what she'd always been. Spirit, Goddess, eternal, free, beginning, spinning, whirling, now, then, always.

When Vincent returned with the locksmith the door was wide open, as if someone had left. The bathtub was smeared with blood. In it were remnants of Anahita's DNA: bits of teeth, hair, and tissue.

Although the blood on Vincent's hands had long been washed away, traces of his abuse were found and he was questioned and detained on suspicion of Anahita's disappearance and possible murder.

Hours later, Vincent was found in the holding cell, dead. It appeared as though he had been forcefully drowned in the toilet.

When the guards found him his face had been eaten away, as if dissolved. The toilet was filled with a unknown, clay-like substance that filled the drain, clogging it.

All that was left of Vincent's face was covered in the substance. It looked as if it had molded his visage into a mask where a man's face once was.

She whispered to the fire, delicately dropping the mask into the flames. She placed her left palm over her womb and stretched her right arm out to Her people. In unison they waved long fans of peacock plumes, making the conflagration blaze. The iridescent feather eyes gleamed: royal blue, emerald, and turquoise spirited in the incandescent light. The mask that was Vincent's face crackled and dissolved, sputtering in the blue and orange flames.

She exhaled.

She bowed Her head at the pyre for a long time.

When the fire breathed its final breath and the last of the smoke cleared, she lifted Her eyes, threw up Her arms, and began to dance.

Slowly, Her people arose, singing:

Omi O!!
Iya mi, ile oro
T'alade mo'ro gbogbo Orisa!

Oore Yeye Osun!!
Ora Yeye O!!!!!
Sacred Water!!
Mother mine, house of our lifeways
Sovereign Woman who guards the lifeways of all the gods!
All hail the benevolent Mother, Osun!!
Ora Yeye O!

RED FEATHER AND BONE

Daniel José Older

In the world created by Daniel José Older, a giant ghost bureau-
cracy, the New York Council of the Dead, rules over the spirit
world of New York. As Carlos Delacruz, a "soulcatcher" agent who
works for the council, declares "death isn't the great equalizer it's
made out to be." Carlos, a hybrid, half dead and half alive, adeptly
weaves through the living and the dead, rich and poor, and the
cultural mix of New York. Born in Cambridge, MA, Older earned
a BA from Hampshire College and a MFA in creative writing
from Antioch University Los Angeles. In the story included here,
"Red Feather & Bone," which appears in his debut ghost noir collection, *Salsa Nocturna,* Carlos is at the top of his game, fighting
the system and working for the cause of justice, even when he has
been assigned a bird watching case.

There it is: A flash of crimson against the gray, gray sky. I jot
down some notes and squint back into my eyepiece. Its ragged siren
song reaches toward me through the cold skyscrapers. The cawing
replaces my irritation with sorrow — a gentle, blues that reminds me
that I'm every bit as singular and lonesome as that bright red flicker
of feather and bone.

I'm not used to this bird watching shit. I'm the guy the New York
Council of the Dead brings in for the really nasty jobs. The headless
bastards trying to make it back to tell their ex-wives some bullshit,
the homicidal midget house ghost — all these wayward souls with
grudges that won't stay where they belong — that's my turf. Unlike
the rest of the NYCOD, though, I'm only half dead. Yes, my skin is

more gray than brown — a weird neither-here-nor-there hue, just like me, and I'm eerily cold to the touch. But I've perfected the forced easy grin of the living, the authoritative cop snarl, the just-walking-by shrug. In short, I pass. It allows me access to places that fully dead COD agents could never get their translucent asses into, so the ghouls upstairs dispatch me only on those good juicy messes.

At least, that's how it was right up until three weeks and four days ago, when my partner Riley Washington disobeyed orders and did away with the child-killing ghost of a long dead plantation master. Riley went rogue and the Council went batshit — sent the full raging force of their soulcatchers on him. Everyone's been out there looking, except for me. They knew I'da sooner hugged the dude than taken him out, so I'm stuck staring at the Manhattan skyline, watching this stupid long-necked bird trouble the skeevy business men with its beautiful, pathetic song. Below me, the tall shadows of the elite COD soulcatchers roam back and forth, looking for my friend.

To top it all off, it's the middle of day — that horrible, bright lull when there're no shadows and no mercy. I put down the binoculars and walk back to the rooftop shed. A small, translucent child is waiting for me inside. He's about five or six, sipping absentmindedly from my two-day old coffee and staring much too closely at the scribbled over maps and bird drawings plastered across my walls.

"What you doing there, youngin?"

"Minding mine," the child says.

"Actually, you're minding mine. Why don't you go help some dead geriatric cross the street?"

The boy gives me such a haunted, intense stare that I'm not sure what to do with myself. He looks familiar — one of these lost soul child phantoms that haunt the outer boroughs running odd errands for folks like me in exchange for toys and candy. This one, as I recall, is only interested in rusted-out car parts and electrical wiring.

"You want a light bulb?" I try. He scoffs and hovers his little body to another corner. His bulgy eyes scan the floor plans to a building my bird was sighted in.

"What do you want?"

"You think the ghost bird came from the burial ground?"

"Seems likely," I say. The thing started its midday cooing in a high-rise beside the weird shaped, corporate rock that comemorates some forgotten African slaves. "I don't know where else it would come from down here. The thing is old, from what I can tell, and not any species I can find in the bird nerd books. All the buildings it shows up in are within a five block radius of the site. It's starting to add up." The boy grunts thoughtfully and floats over to an old map I found of the financial district in 1863.

"Where'd you get this map?"

"Ganked it from the research room at the historical society. But this is a nonsense assignment, kid. What you care?"

He hovers for another minute and then turns, looks up at me and says: "Just curious. Thank you for the nice visit." He moves out the door and then pokes his little head back in. "Oh, and I have a message for you. Almost forgot."

It can't be from the Council — when they want to get in touch they just blare another staticky transmission directly into my head with that creepy dead people telepathy they got. My slow, slow heart quickens by a fraction. Could it be—

"It's from Riley?"

"Gimme a battery charger."

"I don't have one, man, just tell me who it's from."

"Give to get, get to give. You got a blender?"

I briefly consider going for my blade. It's that kind of day. "You want my extension cord?"

He considers for a few seconds. "Yes, it's from Riley."

I unplug the cord from the wall and my lamp and start wrapping it around itself. "I'm really not in the mood to bargain any more — what's your name, shorty?"

"Damian."

"Damian, I'm done playing." I toss him the cord. "What's the message?"

He sizes me up carefully. "Where ass meets Anderson at eight." A pause. "Bring that map along." And he's gone.

In the Chambers Street train station, commuters are cluttering around a street musician. The music is wack, but the crowd is huge, which means it's either a midget in a costume or a hot chick. Turns out to be neither. When I shoulder my way deep enough in to get a good look, I find a half visible, shiny fellow doing an old fashioned jig to some scratchy canned music. He's tall and frail, dressed in baggy, rotting trousers and seems to have some kind of circus makeup on. Folks are just gaping at him obtusely and he's yukking it up.

If there's one thing the NYCOD is really, really uptight about, it's dead folks appearing to the living. Course, the high-up afterlifers do it whenever they see fit, work their way deftly through and around whatever bureaucratic loopholes they can find, but those of us on the streets know there's no leeway when it comes to human interactions. So I'm not surprised when a burly, translucent team of patrol ghouls comes swooshing down through the turnstiles towards the giddy dancer. The crowd feels the chill circulate and begins to disperse. The performer chuckles, grabs his radio and shoots off like a rocket into one of the train tunnels. The patrol team disappears into the darkness after him, cursing and snarling as they go. I shake my head and get on a Brooklyn-bound train. Something is definitely fucked up in ghost world.

When Riley and I first started working together — back when I was still coming to terms with having died in some horrific, unknown way that wiped out all my memory and then been partially resurrected — we used to have a constant caller named Anderson. He was a suicide — I think he'd been a banker or something in life — and he was crazy about Puerto Rican ass. He couldn't even really do anything with it, being a ghost and all, but for some damn reason the dude wouldn't stop showing up at this one spot in Bushwick and harassing the girls. It was dumb shit — tying two ponytails together or giving invisible wedgies — but it was noticeable enough to show up on the

COD's disturbing-the-living radar and land me and Riley out there again and again.

Now it's a quarter to eight, a dim September night and Bushwick is alive with bustling, laughing, gossiping Puerto Ricans, Dominicans and Ecuadorians. They mingle in and out of the cuchifritos spots and fruit stands, sending ruckus spanglish prayers and flirtations up into the rumbling train tracks above. I'm quiet and a stranger hue than the rest of them, but still, I am home. I never get the stares here that I do downtown. The occasional brand new whitey wanders past, sometimes in cautious bands of two or three.

I'm not surprised to see my old friend Riley sitting in the little triangular park just off Broadway where Anderson used to pester women. I am, however, a little disturbed to see his ghostly ass sitting directly across the chessboard from an overweight and very much alive fellow in a bulging guayabera. They're both laughing, probably each thinking he's got the other one's king three moves from checkmate. I reconcile competing urges to hug and slap Riley by pulling up a folding chair and lighting my smoke like it's no big deal.

"Whaddup," Riley says without looking up from the game.

"It is what it is."

He gestures towards the fatso sitting across the table. "Gordo, Carlos, Carlos, Gordo." Gordo extends a hand to me. I don't usually touch the living. I'm corpse cold and can find out way more information than I'd ever need to know about someone from a casual tap. But this man's face regards me with such genuine kindness I'm caught off guard. I shake his hand and he doesn't flinch when he feels my chilly skin. He looks me dead in the eye, smiles, and then helps himself to one of my cigars.

"I'm done with the invisible bullshit," Riley replies to my unasked question.

"So I see."

"It's not like they don't know we here. Especially chubby old Cubanos like this motherfucker."

Gordo chuckles. "It's true!"

"And COD coming for me anyway. What I got to lose?"

I just shake my head. He has a point. "You wanted to talk 'bout something?"

"Yeah, what you have on the bird situation?"

"It's BS. They just throwing grunt work at me. Why's everybody so interested in it?"

"What you got?" Riley's still staring at the game but I can tell his mind is elsewhere.

"What I told the Damian kid. He didn't let you know 'bout his spy mission?"

Gordo's lost in thought. I can see the strategic little lines twirling around his head and by his self-satisfied grin I'm guessing it's paying off on the chessboard.

"Alright, I'll level with you." Riley finally looks at me. "I didn't want to get you too deep in this, for your own sake, but we need your help."

"Check," Gordo says.

"Fuck." Riley lurches a pawn one square further into a suicidal last-ditch get the queen back mission.

"Mate."

"Fuck-fuck. Alright, we have to go anyway. C'mon, Gordo, let's show Carlos what we building."

"The kid's been working on this thing for a while actually," Riley says as he sends a metal gate clamoring loudly out of our way. "I guess Gordo here started helping him out a few months back, just putting pieces together that the little guy couldn't manage with his little ghost hands." He makes pathetic flapping motions with his arms.

"I can hear you, dickface," a voice says from the darkness inside. We're somewhere along the ambiguous line between Williamsburg and Bushwick, down a deserted backstreet. The empty warehouses will soon be swank million dollar lofts, but for now they're just canvas for young graffiti writers.

Gordo leads us into a vast, open room that was probably once full of either endlessly-sewing Chinese ladies or churning machinery. Tiki torches throw flickering illumination onto a pile of junk sitting in the back of a rusty old pickup truck. Damian is floating circles around it, appraising each piece and occasionally tinkering with a little silver tool.

"You guys are opening a mobile second hand store?" I say. "That's exciting."

Riley and Damian look miffed, but Gordo lets out a grandfatherly belly laugh. "No, no, Papi. It's a machine!"

"What's it do?" I think I see my extension cord in there, along with a few car parts I'd traded to Damian the last time I needed a message run.

"It opens things," Riley says, looking at me as if I should know what the hell he's talking about. I make go-on-with-it hand motions at him. "It makes new doors. To things."

"No." The meaning is slowly trickling down to me now. "Doors to...places?" I say. Riley nods. "Places where dead people live?" I need to sit down. "You're building an entrada-making machine?"

An entrada is an entrance to the Underworld. There's only about a dozen in the City; they're all old as shit and very well hidden. I've never met anyone that can remember when or how they came about — had always just figured it was a natural phenomenon actually. "Are you sure?" I say, cocking an eyebrow.

Damian floats over to me. "Allow me to explain the situation, Carlos, because Riley would prefer being cryptic and Gordo's just gonna sit there and chuckle."

"It's true," Gordo confirms. He eases his wide ass into an easy-chair and lights up a Malagueña.

"About three weeks ago, the ghost bird starts showing up downtown."

"Right."

"NYCOD puts their best man on it. He is perhaps of questionable allegiance when it comes to certain recent defections, but when it comes to getting the job done, second to none."

"Now, that I'm gone, of course," Riley puts in.

"Go on."

The boy's more animated than I've ever seen him. He floats in little figure-eights around his junky invention as he speaks. "Strange, right? Such a star agent on something as trivial as an irritating bird?"

"That's what I'm saying."

"And all those patrols downtown..."

"Right!"

"Well, you and I both got wise to the bird having something to do with that Burial Ground Memorial, as we spoke about earlier. Turns out the thing ain't supposed to be around at all. It's like the one that got away, three hundred years later."

"Eh?"

"Let's drive and chat," Riley says. "We don't have much time."

The Williamsburg Bridge is backed up with party kids trying to make it on time but still be fashionably late. The city sparkles on either side of us, those emptied-out skyscrapers looming like old gods in the autumn night. We're squashed four across the front seat of Gordo's old pickup, the two ghosts sandwiched in between the one and a half living bodies. Damian partially unrolls a yellowed piece of parchment and hands it to me.

"What's this?"

"The missing piece, I believe." It's a chart of some kind. Little squares with writing scribbled over them sprawl across the page in a crooked hectagon shape. "The placement map for the African Burial Ground." I squint at one of the boxes. LITTLE THADDEUS, B. 1730 - D.1746, ORIG: DAHOMEY is written in tiny, elegant script. The one below it says: MISS LUCY TRINIDAD, B. ? - D. 1750 APPROX 82 YEARS OF AGE. HEALER. ORIG: KONGO.

I look at Damian.

He nods. "Everyone."

I unroll further. The little boxes go on and on. "There's thousands of them!" Damian nods again. "Where did this come from? Who made it?" Damian puts his tiny finger to the bottom left corner of the map. CYRUS LANGLEY, it says in the same delicate handwriting. MADE WITH LOVE & LIGHT THAT THE CHILDREN OF OUR CHILDREN'S CHILDREN MAY KNOW FROM WHENCE THEY COME & UPLIFT THEIR SPIRITS & OUR OWN.

"Who's Cyrus?" I ask, but Damian's already directing my attention to a box near the center of the map. CYRUS LANGELY, B. 1725 - D.1755. CONJURER IN THE OLD TRADITION. ORIGIN: UNK. EDUCATED IN THE MAGICAL ARTS OF BOTH WHITE FOLKS & THE NEGRO. BORN SLAVE DIED FREE & FREE WILL 1 DAY AGAIN BE.

Gordo leans on his horn, breaking my reverie.

"Get the fuck out of the way you scrawny hipsters!" Riley screams out the window. "Tell 'em, Gordo, I don't think they heard me."

"¡Comiendo mierda y gastando zapatos!" Gordo yells.

Riley eyes him suspiciously. "Did you say what I said?"

"Basically," Gordo chuckles. The mini-coop in front of us jolts into motion and catches up with traffic further down the bridge.

I could drown myself in this map. The names and histories seem to go on endlessly. "It's bigger than I realized."

"Bigger than anyone realized," Damian says. The line of cars is picking up pace again.

"So the monument itself..."

"Just the tip of the iceberg," Riley says.

"And this Cyrus fellow?"

"Made the map after he was dead and buried down there obviously," Damian says. "They discovered it with the first few bodies that came up at the construction site, tracked down some surviving descendants of Langley and returned it to them. This is what I think happened: When the last African was interred at the burial ground and the property started looking juicy for real estate, the NYCOD from way-back-when did their little lockdown spell maneuver, entrapping the dead within. Far as anyone in the afterlife is concerned, the place never happened."

"Which is basically what they did up here too," I said. "Best I can gather."

"Right, but then some pesky bones turned up in the nineties and they had to make amends."

"So they picked a choice few," Riley says, "you know, fill the color quota, and let the rest rot. The Council of the Dead basically did the same thing. The burial site is still sealed shut, no souls get out, no souls get in. Without interaction, without change, movement, they'll all go into a coma-like state and eventually waste away."

Some folks die and never show up in the afterlife. They just float out into nothingness. The ones that do make it through as ghosts could turn up any damn place, and usually get confined within the district limits of whatever city or county they end up in. But to have your soul locked perpetually in your own subterranean grave? I shudder just thinking about it. Thousands of imprisoned spirits, cramped into a tiny space after a lifetime of slavery — they must've gone insane with rage.

Gordo's smoking again. "It's a very sad estory," he says.

"But?"

"But," Damian says quietly. "They didn't count on Cyrus the Conjurer."

"That's Cyrus The Mothafucking Conquerer, crackers!" Riley yells out the window. The car full of hoochies next to us exchange concerned glances. "I think they heard me that time."

"It must've killed him not knowing where he was from," I say. "Seeing as how he put down an origin for most of the others buried down there."

"We think he's gotten out," Damian says.

"Gotten out?" I stammer. "The only way he could get out is..." Oh, the pieces. Turn them. Rearrange them. Fit them together. "...by making an entrada."

"With whatever combination of traditions he ended up mastering," says Damian. "But still — it must be tiny. Even with all that magic."

"Too tiny for a human spirit to fit through?"

"Exactly."

"Hence, my brightly-colored little friend," I say.

"Indeed," mutters Damian. His spooky little eyes are elsewhere though. "He must've been down there for years, watching all his contemporaries waste away, gathering strength, preparing. Drawing from their wisdom."

The river below is as inky black as the sky around us. Little flickering reflections of the city dance and disappear in the current. "Council must be pissed." I say, smiling.

"They throwing everything they got at him," Damian says. "That's why we have to move fast. I believe they're quite close to catching their prey."

Of course! All those swarming patrols weren't looking for Riley — they were on the same assignment I was. "That's why we're driving downtown with that machine?" I say. "We're going to finish the job Cyrus started and break open a new entrada to release thousands of entrapped souls of the first African New Yorkers?"

"Exactly," Riley and Damian both say. Gordo just laughs.

It's still the wrong century for two brown men to be driving a pickup truck with mysteriously tarped cargo towards lower Manhattan. Angry, suspicious eyes whirl around to glare at us as soon as we cross the bridge. Gordo cuts a hard left on Allen and barrels towards Canal. I'm relieved no one can hear the obscenities Riley's yelling out the window at them.

"You got the map I told you to bring?" Damian asks as we jolt to a halt outside one of the federal buildings. I retrieve the photocopied, taped-together sheets from my pocket and unfold them across the dashboard. Gordo switches on the inside light. "No one knew how large the gravesite really was," our tiny companion explains. "At least they never demarcated its true borders on any of the white people cartographies."

He places Cyrus's ancient, yellowed chart on top of my crisp printer paper. "The entrada should be over Langley's grave. We have to line these two up. Look for landmarks."

A silence falls over the cramped front seat as four pairs of eyes scan the two pictures. Riley's transparent finger traces a diagonal line marking the edge of the African Burial Ground on the conjurer's map. "This looks like it moves along the coast here, the South Street Seaport."

"Yes," I say. "That would make the memorial site about here." I stretch my hand from the border of the map halfway across towards the middle."

"And Cyrus's grave..." Riley tiptoes his fingers along five paces, checking back and forth between the two documents as he goes. "... here."

Damian looks past Riley at Gordo, who's fallen into a pleasant nap. "Ernesto," he says.

"Eh?"

"You brought the map I asked you for?"

"Glove compartment."

I pop it open and find an MTA train map. We spread it across the other two and dart our eyes back and forth.

"Chambers Street train station!" Riley and I yell.

Gordo's eyes pop open. He cranks the gear shift into drive and speeds off down Broadway. We all throw our hands to the ceiling as the truck two-wheel tips, screeching around a corner to Chambers. We blow through a light and pull up beside the subway entrance on Church, heaving collective sighs of relief.

We hop out of the truck and that's when it hits me. "Of course!" I yell, slapping a palm to my gray forehead. "Could Cyrus return to his man form once he was out?"

Little Damian considers for a moment. "I imagine so," he says. "But his powers would be diminished. Probably he couldn't leave the immediate area."

"I believe I saw our man earlier today." Everyone spins around to stare at me. "He was dancing to bad 80's music for change on the A train platform."

"Damn," Riley says, "times really are tough."

"He's reaching out any way he can," Damian says. "The birdsong. The train dance. He's trying to let us know he's ready."

Gordo lumbers over to us from the driver's side. "How we going to get this damn thing down there?"

It takes me, Riley and Damian hauling it step by step down the stairs and through the handicap entrance while Gordo runs interference on the station agent, pretending not to speak English, but we eventually make it with the entrada-maker intact. We stand at the edge of the platform, gazing into the utter blackness of the tracks.

"I'll cover the entrance with Gordo here," Riley says. "Carlos, you and the youngin head in. Something comes that we can't handle, I'll give a shout."

"What if a train comes?" I say.

"Ju kidding?" Gordo laughs. "It's after midnight. We have plenty of time."

We all nod gravely at each other and I hoist up the machine and follow the kid down some metal stairs into the tunnel. It's completely dark except for his little glowing form ahead of me. He's got both maps stretched out and he's muttering quietly to himself. We round a bend and my eyes start to adjust. It's all drip-drops and scurry-scurries in the shadows around us, plus the distant rumbling of late night trains.

"How'd you get this map away from the family anyway?" I ask Damian.

"I didn't," he says simply and quietly. "It's an heirloom." I'm left to ponder the significance. Connect-the-dot constellations form around my head. I stagger along behind my little floating glow-in-the-dark guide. *That the children of our children's children may know from whence they came and uplift their spirits and our own.* Langley hadn't been kidding. Maybe it's because it wasn't so long ago that I stumbled upon a long lost ancestor of my own, but the realization that Damian is in it for his bloodline strikes a chord deep inside me.

"How this mechanical doohicky gonna do anything in the spirit world?" I ask.

"A little sorcery will help."

"Another heirloom, I presume."

Damian doesn't answer. A few minutes later, he stops and hovers perfectly still, scanning the dark walls. "Should be...right about...here!"

I place the machine carefully on the damp ground and step back. Damian is on it instantly, fuddling around, muttering to himself, pouring little vials of liquid into some plastic piping. Soon, a mechanical churning grinds out, accompanied by a low, angelic hum. A dim glow emanates from the wall in front of us.

"It's working," I whisper. Damian just creases his little brow with determination.

I'm trying to fathom how many years this moment has been in the making when Riley's voice comes echoing down the tunnel.

"Company!" he hollers.

"What kind?" I yell back. My hand wraps around the blade handle that's stored securely in my walking stick.

"Soulcatchers. I got this." He does, too. Riley's been waiting for an opportunity to get into it with some COD loyals ever since he went on the run. The clanging and groaning sounds of spirit warfare drift out from around the corner. "Yeah, what?" Riley's yelling. "What? Thought so."

The light is burning bright from the tunnel wall, now. Damian's still fiddling with levers and liquids, looking up occasionally to see how the work is progressing.

"More company!" Riley yells. There's an uncomfortable pause. "Lots more!" Reinforcements. Those dickheads always roll deep. If they see me it's a wrap. I had just begun having visions of all the good work I could do from the inside, especially being linked up on the DL with Riley's band of rogue ghosts. So much to consider and so little time. "I'm coming towards you, man, there's too many of 'em." Another pause. "And they got cops with 'em too!"

That's bad. "Real cops?"

"No rent-a-cops. Of course real cops. Transit, I'd say. Two of 'em."

"Ew. What's Gordo doing?"

"Pretending to be homeless and mumbling to himself."

"Works. Come to us, we're better off closer together." I look over to Damian. "How we looking?"

"Close. But not there." It's downright bright in here now. The light's throwing giant shadow versions of me against the far wall. When Riley comes flashing around the corner I throw myself into one of those sarcophagus-shaped inlets and wait. He pants up and we both draw our blades.

"How's it look?"

"Looks bad," he says. I resist the cheesy 'just-like-old-times' remark that I know we're both thinking. "A lot of 'em out there. Probably got tipped off when Homeboy the Magnificent decided to put on the A train minstrel show."

"Almost...there," Damian reports. I peek around the corner and see the anxious flickering of flashlights. Boots are echoing towards us, along with the ominous swoosh of many, many angry spirits.

"What's going on down there?" an authoritative and terrified voice demands. "Come out and let us see your hands!" The two cops burst around the corner, guns drawn, faces contorted into tense frowns. They immediately throw their arms in front of their faces to block the sharp glare of the brand new entrada.

"Done!" Damian yells. The glow becomes unbearably bright for a moment and it sounds like two tectonic plates are getting it on somewhere beneath us. The light dims slightly and I see the skinny dancing ghost from earlier burst out of the wall and hover directly in front of the stunned policemen. Further behind them, a crowd of fuming soulcatchers hovers in wait.

"What the fuck is that?" one of the cops yells.

"I'm the magic negro from all your worst nightmares," Cyrus laughs. "Now scatter!" He swirls his arms like he's gonna shoot a fire-ball at them and they take off, tearing through the ranks of NYCOD agents and disappearing around the corner.

"I like this dude," Riley whispers.

Cyrus directs his attention at the angry ghost mob that's glaring him down. "You want some too, fools? I got some for you, don't worry." The mob advances towards us and I flatten myself deeper against the wall. Cyrus floats away from the glowing entrada entrance, there's a swooshing sound like an invisible rocket just blew past and then a flood of old African souls comes surging forth. They pour out into the tunnel, thousands and thousands of them, and barrel through the COD goons without stopping. They're wearing head scarves and rag-gedy clothes, carved jewelry and beaded necklaces; a few even have chain links around their arms and legs. I feel the wind of hundreds of years of pent up rage and frustration release across my face. Riley's screaming as loud as he can beside me and we're both laughing hys-terically and crying at the same time.

Everything is bright light and holy terror and then the souls scatter through the tracks and out into the fresh New York night. When the air finally clears, a peaceful silence descends on us. Riley and I let go of each other's hands and smile awkwardly. In front of the entrada, Damian has his arms wrapped around Cyrus. His little body is heaving with occasional sobs. Cyrus just smiles that big grin of his and pats the boy on the back. "Hush boy," he says. "It's all over now. We're free."

"¡Coño, mi gente! The fuck happened?" It's Gordo, stumbling blindly towards us around the corner.

"Go help him," I tell Riley.

Damian has collected himself by the time Gordo and Riley get to where we stand near the entrada. The entryway is just a swimmy black void now that the souls have all escaped. Cyrus looks the four of us over carefully. He's replaced his rags with an elegant zoot suit. A bright red feather sticks out of his crisp Stetson hat. Tightly wound braids stretch around the back of his head. "You've done well," he says. "Each of you played your part." He died young, but Cyrus's deeply-lined face beams like a proud old grandfather. "A very capable team."

"What're you gonna do now?" Riley asks.

"Oh, there's so much mischief to make; this is only the begin-ning." Cyrus looks like he can't control the grin breaking across his face. "I believe I'll stick around in this city for a little while. I think I could be a very unpleasant presence for certain deserving individuals and institutions."

Riley beams at him. "I was hoping you'd say that."

"Besides," Cyrus says, "this isn't the only entrada I been working on." We all perk up and gape at the ancient conjurer. "There's one go straight into the New York Harbor. Been slipping through as a little guppie fish, pestering the cruise boats and them. It's a whole other kinda gravesite out there, boys. You can only imagine."

We make our way slowly towards the platform. Each of us is in our own little daze, dreaming up futures pregnant with Cyrus's swashbuckling adventures and the roles we each could play. For the first time, I can imagine using this ridiculous both/neither status for something I believe in. The idea gives me an unfamiliar feeling, like a hundred baby birds are jumping up and down in my stomach — giddiness, you could call it. "There's much to be done, lads," Cyrus is saying, his voice fluttering with laughter in the dark tunnel around us. As we walk together towards the station lights, the old spirit starts humming — it's a gentle, melancholy blues, a ragged siren song that reminds me again and again that I'm every bit as free as that bright red flicker of feather and bone.

A SCIENCE FICTION

Carl Marcum

Carl Marcum was born in Nogales, Arizona and his BA and MFA were awarded by the University of Arizona. Marcum is the author of *Cue Lazarus*, a vibrant collection of poetry released by the *Camino del Sol Series* at the University of Arizona. He was a Wallace Stegner Fellow in Poetry at Stanford University and a recipient of a creative writing fellowship from The National Endowment for the Arts. He taught for several years in the Creative Writing Program at DePaul University in Chicago, and now lives in Pittsburgh. In Marcum's poetry, red vinyl backsets and whiskey bottles are invoked at the border where "Barbed wire fence runs down the axis of a heart." "SciFi-Ku" is an imaginative series of haiku poems focused on nature at the interstellar level. In "A Science Fiction," the narrator falls into a black hole and his experience is expressed linguistically through shifting tenses which for him are a single moment.

When the sun rose it was smaller
than in my dream. I had been asleep
for what felt a long time, and woke
confused and claustrophobic.
The texture of sky still magnetized me,
a desert bright day. But the light is streaked
like too much everything pulled to the edges
of a window in storm. What little of me exists
as aperture. I wanted so little for my birthday,
a moment's peace on a hill. And where
did that get me? Into the stars themselves?

To hitch myself to a salvage run,
thirteen years round trip? A distress signal,
a freighter the company had written off
the summer I learned to kiss a girl until she
shook with desire, when the engines
fired no one thought to think,
could even know this uncharted
singularity. At night on Earth I am all of Orion,
at night on Earth I fell tangential into a puddle
of cold rain and rippled the muddied reflection of light
—blurred the confusion of New Chicago
into circuit and solder. This is what I can expect:
gravity, density, volume dissipating. I am
all at once. I studied all night for an exam
I wouldn't pass, slept through a snowfall
that piled itself upon itself. Death isn't the door
you would expect—isn't a carriage kindly
stopping. I celebrated my birthday on a
science rig surveying a binary system.
The galley scrounged up a cake and candle;
I wished myself into consciousness. Proximity
alarms should be blaring, but sound is stretched
to color, color stitched to light, light solidifying
to absence, absent of sequence.

SCIFI-KU

Carl Marcum

Eve of chilled stars stuns
the night dark blue. Gravity
holds my place, twirling.

> The rings of Saturn
> shimmer, it is said, like white
> sand and shells, the shore.

Venus, Jupiter
dance like forlorn lovers,
each bright birl, pining.

> Asteroids are hurt-
> ling in their field. Unlucky
> leftovers, poor rocks.

Telescopic eyes
and such enormity. So
little light squeaks through!

> Robots venture where
> we can't. Do servos whir where
> there is no sound?

Earthrise: now we see
how we are seen—enviable,
blue world. So small.

          When stars explode they
          color clouds that look like crabs
          —even if they don't.

Starship Enterprise,
its continuing mission
so boldly going.

          Beam me up, Scotty.
          Damn it, Jim! I'm a doctor!
          Live long and prosper.

Some neutron stars pulse
accurately as atom-
ic clocks—a heartbeat.

          Gauzy ribbon, our
          own galaxy, spilled milk sky
          —we are but an arm.

We should be a space-
faring people, if only
to leave and come back.

TRADITIONS

Marcos S. Gonsalez

Marcos Gonsalez has a BA in English from Pace University and is currently enrolled as a PhD student at the CUNY Graduate Center. He has just completed the manuscript of his first novel about a hustler MexiRican on the streets of 90's New York. His story included in *Latino Rising* is his first literary publication. "Traditions" is set in a futuristic New York City where the Mexican population that once came from far away has now been long settled. Their children and grandchildren, U.S citizens born and raised, deliberate and question what connections they still have to Mexico, to being Mexican, and to traditions. The story concludes the anthology, expressing the hope that traditions will continue to adapt to the technologies of our collective, our speculative, futures.

"Como asi," Josie coos, her arthritic hands guiding Máquina's, whipping the ingredients gently in the bowl. "Suave, mija, don't overdo it. In baking a cake or brewing a remedio, remember that the secret to success is texture. If the texture ain't right, te jodiste! No one wants mashed mierda."

Máquina giggles in a tinny voice as her heavy hand whips the flour, and the moment Josie turns her back to check the temperature in the oven, she manages to turn the kitchen into the American Dust Bowl. Not that Josie or Máquina would know this historical connection that Mictan makes, since the history from that period is a forbidden subject of inquiry. Mictan, Josie's granddaughter, who is standing at the edge of the kitchen watching Máquina's baking buffoonery through holospectacles, only knows because she once created a sim-game set in 1930's America. The research she did was extensive and exhausting. It's hard to find holobooks on the net about anything before the year 2050. Yet, for Mictan, cyberpunkista that she is, forgotten or restricted history is not a problem when all it takes is a simple hack into the Archival Database (A.D.) and history is hers for the taking.

Josie sighs at Máquina's cooking skills, fanning the smoky and dusty kitchen with her laced apron. She doesn't mind La Máquina's failures. At least La Máquina, she tells herself, shows interest in the traditions, unlike Mictan, who leans against the door frame of the kitchen, smirking at Josie and Máquina. Her nutmeg skin glistens from her grandmother's homemade crema. A cream, which, according to Josie, is the exact rejuvenation recipe her grandmother has passed down to her — with some minor technological updates — Mictan says all kittenish. She puts it on every day, religiously and dutifully, one of the few suggestions from her grandmother that she follows. Otherwise, hard-headed Mictan, dedicated to doing things her way, like a true XicanaYork, dismisses her grandmother's archaic life advice. Mictan thinks it's cool her grandmother is a devout curandera, even appreciating how she employs some innovative biotechnologies, she just wishes her grandmother would upgrade completely to the techno-curanderismo so popular with the other healers. Update to the modern age, she complains, and Josie, in her typical fashion, simply shoos Mictanita with an "andale" and withered hands.

Mictan has just gotten in from a night out in Jackson Heights with the Razarobos, the underground techie group. The group is pro-automaton, pro-cybernetics, pro-information-accessibility. All of them young radical Latinos who come together to express their non-aesthetics against the mainstream and their refusal to be swept up by the propagandist initiatives calling for the natural, the organic, the pre-mechanical. All the older Latinos, like Josie, feel that the Razarobos are stirring up more trouble than is needed. We need respectability, the elders all reason. The techies, who invest in illegal information exchange and recovery, most of them history connoisseurs like Mictan, don't believe in respectability politics. Save that for the distant future, they cry out in cyberspace chatrooms.

"You two always in this kitchen concocting some helluva new way to make a mess. What's it today?" Mictan asks over the tumult of hovercraft sirens blaring into the apartment.

"A lemon and strawberry cake that gives super strength!" Máquina squeaks, in her automaton voice calibrated to be in a chirpy buzzing register. She cracks an egg into the bowl, egg shells slipping into the batter. Josie rushes her ancient body over and delicately extracts the little shells from their creation. Mocking, Mictan makes an O with her mouth. On cue, the pulsing from the subterranean hovertram, sprinting to its next destination and swollen with travelers eager to get off the congested metal boxes, disperses through the kitchen making Josie's knick-knacks tremble. La Máquina's body chitters, the electric pulse surging through her and producing magnetic friction. Mictan's holospectacles buzz.

"Is that how you come into this pinche house Mictan? No beso for your grandmother? You never know when the last kiss will be."

"Abuelita, you been alive over 150 years. Look at you. You still running your curandera business and you still strutting down 116th in your nightgown like it's your damn runway. Just because you got a back hunch the size of Mrs. Lopez's obese gato don't mean nothing. You ain't going nowhere, vieja."

"Oh thank you, mija," Josie purrs, flattered, beads of sweat dropping into the quicksand of her forehead wrinkles, as she primps a few rogue pelitos from her face. "Let's be real, though. I ain't gunna be here forever. Who's gunna carry on my legacy of being the best curandera in New York City—correction, in all of North America? The art of la curandera is dying and you insist upon not taking it up, Mictan, pero"— winking at La Máquina, prideful—"I have La Máquina here who wants to learn the traditions."

Mictan grows noticeably agitated. Another one of her grandmother's jabs. Twenty-four years on this Earth and her grandmother still preaches the same porqueria: Mictan why do you want to be a simulation developer? Are you sure you don't want to be a curandera? Mictan, blazing bitterness, stares through her holospectacles at her plump grandmother and the flacita Máquina. She loves her grand-mother and would do anything for her. However, she cannot be a curandera. The future of the Mexican people, as Josie moans every other night during the trio's favorite telenovela *no soy de aquí, ni soy de allá*, depends on the youth. Mictan snaps back that the world would have to settle for a robojunkie as their representative for Mexican culture. The conversation usually ends there, La Máquina quickly changing the subject to the pobre automaton maid, or the cyborg migrant worker too unfashionably hybrid to be a lead character on the holochannels.

Having enough of her grandmother's badgering, Mictan grum-bles down the hall to her room. Josie, humming the ancient tune of her childhood, *Amor Prohibido,* doesn't notice Mictan's pouty exit. La Máquina notices though. After all, Mictan is the reason La Máquina even exists—an intimate connection that binds them forever.

La Máquina drives her spindly legs to Mictan's room, each step pattering against the tile. She knocks on the door. No response. The only sound comes from upstairs where Chevy Lopez sings Dominican merenguerobo in her wolfish voice to her live-in automaton aid Florita. Chevy doesn't really want Florita in the house but the family, tired of taking care of the vieja and tired of paying for an expensive human aid, sent an automaton to care for the energetic old woman.

No being, living or mechanical, deserves such sonic abuse, Josie always jokes.

Máquina doesn't bother with a response and walks in. She knows Mictan sometimes likes it when you try hard to win her affection. Just as she expects: Mictan has her holospectacles on and is immersed in some virtual world she has most likely created.

"Is everything ok? Máquina asks, her voice box speaking a but-tery lilt, adjusting itself to be more soothing rather than its typical chirpy register. As she closes the door, the hinges squeak terribly. Despite La Máquina's own bodily composition, she hates the sound of metal scraping against hard surfaces. It irritates her audio receivers, sending them into screeching dissonance. Even though wood has long ago become a nearly extinct resource, she prefers it, sleek and smooth, rich in olfactory sensations. For all her talk, Máquina has never even seen a tree, and as she so often laments, the majority of the tree species in the world can only be encountered in simulation games.

"It's all good, Máquina, all good." Mictan says brusquely, keeping her eyes in the spectacles.

Máquina lingers in the room, thumbing her fingers through one of Mictan's holobooks on ancient British culture of the 1800's, pondering why the people during the period had such odd names: John, Arnold, Stuart, Thomas, Elizabeth. Máquina can barely say them, least of all pronounce them correctly. Mictan guzzles up as much history as she can, using the forgotten stories and mythologies as inspiration for her virtual games. If history isn't being taught in schools anymore, Mictan reasons, she would bring it to the masses through virtual realities. La Máquina finds her fervor for knowledge inspiring.

"As you know, your grandmother worries about the future of the Mexicans here in New York City." La Máquina blurts, her voice box screeching from some reason, veering away from its usual buttery or chirpy calibration. She hammers against the side of her neck, remedying the jarring noise. She in dire need of a voice tune-up. "You know how history works better than anyone. Cultures get permanently lost in the A.D., with only a small percentage having any access. Your grandmother sees that the preservation of her culture—our culture— is in passing down the traditions."

"Well, it's not like I'm not interested, Máquina. I am, it's just I don't want to live my life the way she wants me to live my life. I've learned so much already with her but, damn, I can't be her. She has to come to terms with the fact that traditions do die."

La Máquina nods her head in approval, her joints creaking. She deliberates what to say next.

"She doesn't want you to be her. She just wants you to—"

"I know, I know. It's just frustrating cause my grandmother always be doing stuff with you. Ever since I created you, you been her prize possession."

La Máquina pauses, a grim expression materializing over her coppery face.

"You know I never wanted to replace you, Mictan. And it's not like I have."

"I know. It's just you're her perfect Mexican girl. And that leaves me asking: what am I? The perfect failure? How could I create a machine that could be more Mexican than me? I created you to be my companion, Máquina, not hers. Y, mira, you're interested in the cooking, in being a curandera, in learning her ways. And I'm over here like some traidora to la raza."

Mictan bites her lip. Tears well up in the corner of her almond eyes. Schematics of code run across the glass of the holospectacles, glistening like prisms from the wet drops trickling behind them. She knows that what she is saying, regardless of its honesty, hurts La Máquina. Máquina's eyes flicker, a valve siphons air, and her mouth sputters out her version of a sigh. She feels something. In many ways, Máquina is human.

Machines, a long time ago, programmed with an abundance of protocols equipped for any engagement with human kind, were supplied with advanced affective sensors and modules that allowed for their own emotions to blossom. Unexpectedly, emotions started emerging that even humans could not decode or figure out how they came to be. Some were amalgamations of disparate feelings, synthesizing, coming together in odd harmony, and completely perplexing their creators.

Máquina embodies all of these strange arrangements of emotions, and at times is sullenly jovial, irritated silly, or tenderly agitated. The affective combinations are endless and strange. Mictan always finds it astounding how her home-made automaton, constructed from the scraps and junk around her grandmother's neighborhood, could evolve so much. No wonder why one of the most popular programs of study at Susan Calvin University, where Mictan picks up classes every now and then, is now The Department of Emotional Consolidation. Automatons are unpredictable creatures, and no programming, no amount of modeling, engineering, can predict who they can become.

La Máquina, after ten years of being with the two women, plays the simultaneous role of daughter, granddaughter, sister, mother, friend, and companion. Mictan and Josie love her; La Máquina loves them back even more. They are their own oddball family unit. Even though most Latino households have gotten over their machine-phobia and are employing automaton units for babysitting, tutoring, handiwork, and other functions of everyday life, there is still a stigma for having one living in the family full time. The distrust of technology runs deep, understandably. The machinations of war and espionage, like specters, haunt the diaspora: patrias invaded, pueblos burned, barrios demolished, and campos gentrified. The metal apparatuses of squabbling governments are brutal in their methods, relentless in enterprise, and undeterred by morality, no matter what poor soul is being annihilated by their precision weaponry. Service automatons can be just as dangerous as war machines if the programming falters or if they are even a tiny bit modified. Neither human nor machine can be fully trusted.

Yet, regardless, Mictan and Josie want La Máquina around, love her as if she were flesh, como familia. Mictan smears the tears away, face pouting, becoming stern and composed.

"I'm the death of the Mexican culture. And she sees you as its future." Mictan says sullenly.

La Máquina doesn't move. Her facial expressions shift. She is about to speak, but her mouth joints creak, remaining locked in the slight frown her face set itself in. A smile appears on Mictan's face.

"You need a tune-up, chica."

La Máquina smacks her two pieces of dull, silvery lips together, attempting to exercise the kink out of them. Her frown spreads into a weak crescent moon smile, and then her coppery lips open, screeching. Outside, the ever-present low hum of voices and feet moving, marching, pounding the streets in protest, in unison, drift into the room. Siren lights spin in all directions lighting up the sky, a visual show of action. Mictan and La Máquina peer out the window, briefly, interests peaked. Mictan thinks she probably knows someone out there, resisting, screaming. Máquina stares eagerly, wondering if there are any automatons present. Secretly, the two itch to be out there, together, one with the mass, reaching out, pollinating change into the polluted atmosphere. They return to their conversation.

"Mi Mictanita, óyeme. Your grandmother loves you. You need to understand that there *is* no death of the Mexican culture. Just adaptation. Cultures change, mix, overlap, even mutate depending on context. I know the A.D. has nearly erased history, but remember the Great Global Migration," she said matter-of-factly. "During PostAmericanismo, when Mexicans, Guatemalans, Hondurans, and other Central Americans fed up with the injustices of el norte, migrated to all corners of the globe and there was a new age exodus to the Promised Land. Those events proved to your grandmother that nothing stays the same. Not to mention being here in the United States for over a century! It's a lesson she had already learned, but being as hard-headed as you—" La Máquina knocks on her durasteel noggin for added emphasis—"she chooses to ignore it. Let her be stubborn. You have to be whatever kind of Mexican you want to be and pass down whatever it is you want, Mictan. She was you, 'a long time ago in a galaxy far, far away,'" La Máquina quipped. "And look at me? Am I what anyone would consider Mexican?"

La Máquina starts to pound and point to the pieces of her body. The upper body a remnant of a hovercar muffler with "Made in Thailand" inked on the top right corner where a heart would be if she were flesh. Her head, some kind of recycled, shimmery brass, is smoothed over into a perfectly circular dome. The other parts of her body are metals of all different shades, rust levels, and textures. Mictan finds La Máquina's body, an assemblage of leftover parts and unwanted pieces, an artistic masterpiece.

"Nothing tells you I am Mexican, but I still am. Being Mexican means many things. Many of which we can't see." La Máquina says confidently, knocking her metallic hands near the writing on her chest. "If anything, I am Thai."

Mictan laughs, taking off her holospectacles, looking at Máquina lovingly. La Máquina forces her jammed facial joints into a smile. The sirens outside wane, float away. The lights penetrating the sky disappear. The majestic darkness of New York City, a glowing haze, blankets the tired skyscrapers, returning the groggy motion of night to El Barrio.

"Mictan darling," Josie yodels from the kitchen. "Come show us your new game! I've always been interested in Japan, especially this Sei Shōnagon you're including in this one."

Mictan smiles at La Máquina. Josie's sundried brown face materializes at the door, like a patchwork quilt, intersecting lines crossing and moving, each furrow a story, all of them trenches of memory that Josie can recount vividly.

"Sabes algo, muchachas? Over a hundred years ago a flock of Mexicans moved to Japan and started a little village in the mountains. You know how the story goes. Well, let's hope you didn't forget that we even had some cousins who were in that group. None of them knew where their Japanese started, and where their Mexican ended. And when they moved to Egypt, olvidate! Make a game on that identity crisis! Now come and let's finish this cake."

ACKNOWLEDGMENTS

This anthology certainly would not have happened without the work of the many people who are recovering and supporting multi-ethnic science fiction and fantasy. The results of past anthologies such as *So Long Been Dreaming* and *Dark Matter* in particular have been enormously positive in opening up the possibilities for writers of color and to these I am indebted. This book was originally supported by a wonderfully generous grant from the Speculative Literature Foundation. In turn, that grant allowed us to organize a successful Kickstarter campaign. I can only bow in gratitude to the 321 people who believed in the vision and took the risk to make this anthology happen. Special thanks in particular to Alexis Madrigal, Sabrina Vourvoulias, and the Otaño-Gracia family for stepping up to support the campaign in a big way. Finally, I am deeply grateful to the authors who were enormously patient throughout the process.

PERMISSIONS, PUBLICATION HISTORIES & TRANSLATION CREDITS

In order of appearance.

Frontispiece illustration, "El Muerto: Los Cosmos Azteca," by Javier Hernandez is previously unpublished.

"Foreword" by Matthew David Goodwin is previously unpublished.

"Introduction: Confessions from a Latin@ Sojourner in SciFilandia" by Frederick Luis Aldama is previously unpublished.

"The Road to Nyer" by Kathleen Alcalá is previously unpublished.

"Code 51" by Pablo Brescia first appeared in Spanish as "Código 51" in *Gente ordinaria* (Mexico: Librosampleados , 2014), 31-41, and in Sdl #*revista de horror*, 1.1, (2014): 12-14. It was translated by the author with contributions by Matthew David Goodwin. Brescia expresses his heartfelt thanks to the editors for allowing him to translate this story.

"Uninformed" by Pedro Zagitt was originally published as "Desinformada."

"Circular Photography" by Pedro Zagitt was originally published as

"Fotografía Circular." Both stories wer translated by Nahir Otaño-Gracia. Both stories first appeared in *Historias de Las Historias*, ed. Alberto Chimal (México: Solar, 2011).

"Sin Embargo" by Sabrina Vourvoulias is previously unpublished.

"Accursed Lineage" by Daína Chaviano was originally published as "Estirpe Maldita." It was translated by Matthew David Goodwin.

"Coconauts in Space" by ADÁL was first presented in 2004 at the Taller Puertorriqueño in Philadelphia, Pennsylvania. Previously unpublished.

"Cowboy Medium" by Ana Castillo is previously unpublished.

"Flying Under the Texas Radar with Paco and Los Freetails" by Ernest Hogan is previously unpublished.

"Monstro" by Junot Díaz first appeared in *The New Yorker*, June 4, 2012.

"Room for Rent" by Richie Narvaez is previously unpublished.

"Artificial" by Edmundo Paz Soldán was translated by Heather Cleary. It is previously unpublished.

"Through the right ventricle " and "Two unique souls" by Steve Castro are previously unpublished.

"Caridad" by Alex Hernandez is previously unpublished.

"Difficult at Parties" by Carmen Maria Machado was first published in *Unstuck: 2*, ed. Matt Williamson (Austin: Unstuck Books, 2012).

"Death of the Businessman" and "Burial of the Sardine" are excerpts from *United States of Banana* (AmazonCrossing, 2011) by Giannina Braschi, reprinted under a license arrangement originating with Amazon Publishing, www.apub.com.

"Entanglements" by Carlos Hernandez first appeared in *The Assimilated Cuban's Guide to Quantum Santeria* (Rosarium, 2016).

"The Drain" by Alejandra Sanchez is previously unpublished.

"Red Feather & Bone," first appeared in appeared in *Salsa Nocturna* (Crossed Genres Publications, 2012) by Daniel José Older. By permission of the author.

"A Science Fiction" and "SciFi-Ku" by Carl Marcum are previously unpublished.

"Traditions" by Marcos S. Gonsalez is previously unpublished.

ABOUT THE EDITOR

Matthew David Goodwin is an Assistant Professor in English at the University of Puerto Rico in Cayey. His work is centered on the topic of migration in Latino/a literature. In particular, he looks at the ways that science fiction, fantasy, and digital culture have been used to express the experience of migration. He completed his PhD in Comparative Literature at the University of Massachusetts–Amherst in 2013. He has published a number of essays on Latino/a speculative fiction for journals such as *MELUS* and for a number of essay collections including *Black and Brown Planets, Alien Imaginations,* and *Putting the Pop in Latino Culture.* He has co-authored an article for Oxford Bibliographies on "Latino/a Science Fiction" with Ilan Stavans. Goodwin has travelled and worked throughout Latin America and the Caribbean, and has long been involved in the Latino/a community. From 1997 to 2006 he worked in the Latino/a community of Northwest Arkansas, serving as the director of two non-profit organizations, one focused on legal aid for immigrants and the other focused on worker rights. He now lives in Cayey, Puerto Rico where he teaches courses on Latino/a literature, science fiction, and digital literature.

AUTHOR OF INTRODUCTION

Frederick Luis Aldama is University Distinguished Scholar as well as Arts & Humanities Distinguished Professor of English, Spanish and Portuguese, at Ohio State University where he is also founder and director of the White House Bright Spot Awarded LASER (Latino & Latin American Space for Enrichment & Research) that creates a pipeline for Latinos from 9th grade through graduate and professional school education. He specializes in Latino and Latin American literature, comic books, and film—and pop culture generally. He is the author, co-author, and editor of over twenty-four books, including recently *The Cinema of Robert Rodriguez* and *Latino Literature in the Classroom*. He is the editor of two book series, *Latino Pop Culture* (Palgrave) and *Latino and Latin American Profiles* (University of Pittsburgh Press), and co-editor of three other series: *Global Latino/a Americas* (University of Nebraska Press), *Cognitive Approaches to Literature and Culture* (University of Nebraska Press), and *World Comics and Graphic Nonfiction* (University of Texas Press). He is a member of the standing board for the Oxford Bibliographies in Latino Studies.

WINGS PRESS

Colophon

This first edition of *Latino Rising: An Anthology of Latino Science Fiction and Fantasy*, edited by Matthew David Goodwin, has been printed on 60 pound Anthem Plus Matte paper containing a percentage of recycled fiber. Titles have been set in Aquiline Two, Bickham Script and Adobe Caslon type; the text in Adobe Caslon type. All Wings Press books are designed and produced by Bryce Milligan.

On-line catalogue and ordering:
www.wingspress.com

Wings Press titles are distributed
to the trade by the
Independent Publishers Group
www.ipgbook.com
and in Europe by
www.gazellebookservices.co.uk

Also available as an ebook.

Books By

Drew and David VanDyke

SUPERNATURAL SIBLINGS SERIES

MoonRise - Book One

MoonFall - Book Two

BloodMoon - Book Three

Visit our website at:
www.davidvandykeauthor.com

MOONRISE
Copyright © 2013 by Drew VanDyke and David VanDyke
All Rights Reserved.
Printed in the United States of America.

Published by Reaper Press

ISBN-13: 978-1-62626-185-3

ISBN-10: 1-62626-185-7

MOONRISE

Supernatural Siblings
Book One

Drew VanDyke

and

David VanDyke

Drew's Acknowledgements

For Leslie Suzanne:
You always were and always will be
My better half
Love, Andrew

Thanks to Dave for believing we could do this and for making it happen

Thanks to Caitie Daphtary for being my (IDTBR) "identical twin beta reader."

Thanks to Dad and my hometown of Turlock, California for giving us such fertile ground to grow our stories, and thanks to my mom, Joan Elaine, whose presence continually haunts me, for better or for worse.

David's Acknowledgements

Thanks to Nick Stephenson, Ryan King and Bella Roccaforte, great authors all, for the feedback provided that made this a better book. Thanks to my lovely and talented wife Beth, my first, last and best beta reader, for all her hard work and support.

Cover by Molly Phipps

-Prologue-

Dear Diary:

Life is really a pain in the butt right now.

Now, before you start going off on me, let me tell you that this pain is not metaphorical. It's not merely because I've been relegated to staying with my identical twin sister back in our hometown of Knightsbridge, California, for the first time in years, or having to figure out how I feel about my old boyfriend Will.

No, this pain is due to some overenthusiastic animal control officer with a dart gun, plus poor adherence to Steam Room Sterilization and Sanitization Techniques by an unnamed resort and spa somewhere near the border of Idaho and Washington State.

So, armed with a secret I can't tell my other half and a chunk taken out of my derriere that hurts like a son of a bitch, I'm playing invalid to my own twin version of holiday misery.

Let's just hope we make it to Christmas alive.

–1–

"Ashlee Scott! Get that ruler away from your rear end!" My usually sweetness-and-light twin sister Amber grabbed it out of my hand before I could take care of the itch I'd been dealing with all day.

"Amber, you give me back that ruler or so help me…"

"What? Like you're gonna take me? In your condition?" Amber smiled and turned to her partner Elle, who was planted on the plush and comfy davenport, remote control in hand, trying to catch up on NFL scores. Elle was in her late thirties, which kinda made Amber a trophy chick, I guess. Booby prize, maybe?

"Honey?" My twin flashed Elle that dazzling Scott smile.

"Oh no, you don't," Elle wryly dribbled from the side of her mouth without taking her eyes from the split screen ESPN channel. "I am not falling for that one again."

Amber furrowed her brow, frustrated for the moment.

"Amb, don't frown," I said, mock-sweet. "You'll need to get Botox before you're thirty."

My sister turned to me with a flip of the bob she had going this week and sighed. "And *you* need to keep all sharp objects away from your rear. At least until that butt wound..."

"Bullet wound!" I interrupted.

"Fine. Bullet wound. Only you would manage to get shot in the ass by a hunter's ricochet, hiking around in God-Knows-Where, Idaho."

That was my story, anyway.

My twin tossed her head again and rolled her eyes. "Until that heals..." She turned to JR, her five-year-old son, my nephew, and tickled him.

Seriously, who names their kid after a nighttime soap opera character from the eighties? Okay, it was short for John Robert, but still. At least it wasn't "Junior."

"We're locking up the cutlery until your Aunt Ashlee is all healed up," Amber said. JR giggled as my sister tickled him. Then Elle decided to join in on the fun and took playful swats at him with the rolled-up sports section while he shrieked in fun.

I, on the other hand, seized the moment's distraction to drag myself painfully upstairs to my room – well, the guest bedroom I occupied – while the girls got domestic. Yuck. Sometimes being around the Gordon-Scotts was so sugary I thought I'd develop a whole mouthful of cavities.

I tried to sit on the bed, but having to favor one cheek didn't make things easy, so I rolled over and lay on my stomach. Besides, it still itched like crazy...and then came a knock at the door.

"Hey, Sis." Amber poked her head in. "You know, the sooner you heal up, the sooner you can be back doing what you love to do."

I cocked my head, threw back my own Jennifer Aniston locks, the ones that somehow managed to put Amber's to shame despite sharing a gene set, and said, faux-sweetly, "Don't worry. I'll be out of your hair before you know it."

Amber's eyes narrowed. I knew she'd get the dig. She wasn't happy with her latest stylist and it took time for her hair to grow out. We both used to have the same length tresses, but this year she'd opted for what was supposed to be a hot shoulder-length bob, and it just wasn't quite working the way she wanted it to.

Trying to recover, she turned and tossed over her shoulder, "Yes, well. Remember what I always say." She looked back just as I was pushing the door closed with my foot, which in turn pressed on her retreating bebe-branded ass.

"I know, I know. Guests are like fish and family." I smiled back at her.

We finished in unison, "They both stink after three days."

"Remember what else they say?" I yelled as she retreated down the hall.

"What's that?" my sister yelled back.

"You can pick your nose, but you can't pick your family."

"That makes no freaking sense. Kleenex!"

Sigh. By the time I get out of here, I'll probably be ripe as rotten fruit and smell just as bad. So, tell me, God, what the hell did I do to deserve this?

No answer.

There comes a time in every girl's day when she's just gotta sit down and scratch. Make that in every *bitch's* day, when she's just gotta…even if her ass hurts like a sonofabitch. I'll spare you the details.

See, I'm a werewolf.

Scratch that. No, it's not supposed to be a pun. Never mind. Okay, s*trike that*. I'm technically a lupine. A lycanthrope, some might say.

I had researched the subject after my first change, and gorged myself on as many werewolf tales as I could get my hands on. In my favorite, the goddess Hera was supposed to have made twin girls into wolves to protect a Thracian poet as he wandered the Earth spouting prophecy and oracles to the masses, until they fell prey to the wiles of Romulus and Remus. Something like that anyway. Hey, I'm not a big reader of the classics.

Well, there isn't any Thracian poet in my life, and the only oracle I consult is my daily horoscope when I want an uneasy laugh, and I'm sure not wandering the Earth as much as I'd like to right now. No, the closest thing to any Thracian poet I know is my editor, and he's not too happy

with me lately as my galleys keep coming back redlined
with chunks of text missing.

See, I'm a travel writer. Ashlee Marie Scott by name
and pen. Twenty-nevermind years old, and terminally
single according to my dead mother. Unlike, that is, my
vacuous sister Amber Michelle, who got married young
and had a son before deciding she wanted to bat for the
other team. I might have that out of order, but you get the
idea. They divorced and then she fell in love with a lesbian
chief-of-police-turned-high-powered-city-attorney. Makes
her, well, whatever. In love, I guess. I wouldn't know.
Never really been. Not for sure.

I, on the other hand, specialize in luxury health spas of
the high seas and high mountains, the cities and the
coasts. My latest find had me in a third-world country,
also known as Idaho, with a wicked staph infection and an
HMO surgical team determined to turn a pound of flesh
into an ounce of cure. Thus, as I mentioned before, I am
now grounded, stuck in my hometown of Knightsbridge,
California, staying with my sister, her partner and my five-
year-old nephew in a house that could be photographed at
any time of the night or day for *Good Housekeeping*.

Not my idea of comfortable living: a place for
everything and everything in its place. I'm more the bra-
on-the-doorknob kind of girl, at my loft back in the City.

Did I tell you that I hate my sister even while loving
her? No, really I do. She's perfect. Even my parents think
so. Except for the fact that she's bisexual in a lesbian
phase, but they're slowly coming around to that, too.

Oh, did I tell you I'm also a werewolf? Right. I did. Must be the medication. Snort. Wonder how that one's gonna go over with the in-laws? Oh, right. I don't have any. Never mind. So, let's just say, at certain times of the month, Mother Nature's even more of a bitch with me than with most women.

I'm sure you're wondering about that bullet wound, so I'll tell you a long story short before the short story gets long.

I was doing a piece on Pacific Northwest spas. Hardship, yeah, but the job paid diddly squat so I might as well enjoy the expense account. Besides: cold, *bad*. Heat, *good*, and every now and then I meet a cute guy. I mean, I can rock a bikini with the best of them, and nobody expects me to have perfect makeup in a spa.

But I digress.

For the story I got the full package, comped for the magazine of course. Steak and lobster, Eggs Benedict, and one of everything on the spa menu. It was glorious. I took pictures and my editor got his five thousand words, for which he paid me almost nothing, but that was the deal. Live high on the magazine's dime, cheap on my own.

The resorts all knew who I was, of course, and were happy to oblige. How else would I get the freebies? And I wasn't writing exposés after all. My job was to sell magazines, whether print or online editions, which sold advertisements to paying customers.

Long story short, yeah, yeah.

So I worked my way through lockers, changing rooms and the amenities therein to the pools. I did a full set of lap work to check the workout box for the day and then, ah, the fun started. Sauna, cold dunk, heat lamp, cold dunk, steam bath with herbal infusion, and so on. Wonderful. After that came a mud bath, hot rock massage, lunch at the wine bar, mani-pedi, facial – you get the picture. Most fun a girl can have alone.

I spend a lot of time alone, I guess.

On the afternoon in question, I hurried upstairs to my room and banged out a rough draft, quick and dirty because tonight was MoonFall; that is, a full moon, which for me makes the usual girl's monthlies seem hella tame. Anyway, I packed my day pack – okay, night pack – with the stuff I'd need – change of clothes, wipes, water and food, handheld GPS – what a godsend – and so on.

My usual MO was to hike to a landmark before sunset, like a mountaintop or tip of a lake, load it into the GPS, clip the little unit to a collar and put it on. Then I'd have a nice dinner, a tiny fire if I could, get naked and wait for the change.

After doing it for years, I was pretty lucid in wolf form, but I could easily get distracted, which was where the GPS came in, just in case I changed back somewhere other than the campsite. It would help me sneak in the buff across country to my stash. Either way, I'd clean up and get back to the other twenty-seven days of my life before the next change.

This time, though, someone had shot me with a tranquilizer dart, in the middle of the night no less. Who does that? No idea, never found out, don't want to know. Narcotics don't work well on me in wolf form, by the way, which was why I didn't go down. Nothing less than a bear dose would probably do it. I managed to make it back without trouble.

The next morning I did the steam room, and then the infection showed up. I made up a story about a hunter's ricochet and went to the ER expecting to be sent on my way with antibiotics, but they said it was a drug-resistant strain so *boom*, straight into surgery. From the way it felt afterward, the surgeon used a steak knife and an ice cream scoop to excise the necrotizing tissue. They told me they got it all, and shot me full of the latest thing, gave me pills to take and orders for a regimen of bleach baths for the next three weeks.

I was able to get three more free days at the resort by hinting that the infection was their fault, caught from the steam room bench, but eventually I had to go recuperate where assistance was near. Among my relatives, Amber was my best choice. I really do love her, you know, even if we are like oil and vinegar. We may taste great together but we still don't mix very well.

Want to guess who's the oil, and who's the vinegar?

3

I watched Amber primping in the mirror, envious as sin. She'd bought this darling new turquoise collection from Sephora and was wearing some Jimmy Choos that I would have killed to afford. Sigh.

Don't ever let any of those sparkly werewolf books or movies fool you. Unless our injuries are cured by some kind of magic, we also have to heal over time. Oh, it may happen faster, especially in wolf form, but when it comes to infections, colds and viruses, we're just like the rest of you. And since I was trapped at home nursing an oozing sore, I was stuck with what the girls had on disc in the den or what JR had in his bedroom. Hell, I could always play Singstar, but a girl gets tired of hearing the sound of her own voice. I had my phone, but as I paid for the data myself, I had to go easy on it when I wasn't working and able to expense it.

I couldn't even figure out how to work the streaming TV channels, and the only internet this retro household had was a cheap hotspot from five years ago. I think Elle deliberately made everything complicated so nobody could mess with her sports.

"So, where you going tonight?" I asked as Amber put herself together.

"Oh. Nothing special," she answered. "Elle has this charity function sponsored by the Animal Rights Coalition."

"Animal Rights?" I sneered. "What about people's rights? I mean, some of us treat our dogs better than we treat each other. Don't we Spanky?" I threw that last bit out at the miniature Schnauzer who sat in the doorway staring up at Amber's transformation. I turned back to watch my sister go from beautiful to breathtaking in the Clairol-quality lighting over the mirror. She'd mesmerized me ever since I was child with her ability to use makeup in its most subtle and glamorous ways.

"That's because Spanky's special," Amber singsonged. "Aren't you, Spanky?"

He barked in response and his stubby tail began to wiggle.

Amber sighed and touched up her lips with a darling cinnamon custard. "Don't think you're missing anything. Just a lot of ho-hum and small talk. You'd find it very boring. I know I will."

"Hey, hey, now," Elle said. I watched her look over from where she stood putting on a few last touches of her own in the other mirror. His and hers...I mean, hers and hers mirrors; it was so decadent. "I'm standing right here, you know."

Amber launched another of her dazzling smiles and gave Elle a peck on the cheek as she exited the master bath. I followed, feeling frumpy in my Jaclyn Smith flannel cotton white PJs with the intersecting black, blue, and brown stripes down the side.

"Besides, Jeanetta Macdonald will be there and she can't help but seethe whenever she sees me. Just another perk for looking like you, Ashlee," Amber skewered.

Shane's sister, I thought. Crap. I was hoping she'd get out of this town so I wouldn't have to remember. The truth was, I didn't have to remember, at least not right now, so I flipped a switch in my head and chose to think of other things.

"Anyway, I'm sure you can keep yourself occupied for a couple of hours by yourself. J.R.'s over at his Dad's and Mervin won't be bringing him back till the morning." Amber strode forward out of the bedroom, down the stairs to the landing, and almost fell down the steps.

"Damn it, JR!" She shot into the air as she grabbed for the banister. "Honey!" she yelled. "Did I or did I not tell JR to move his things from off the stairs?"

"You did." Elle's voice came out of the bedroom. When it came to raising JR, Elle was pretty hands-off.

"I thought so." Amber shook the exasperation from her eyes and smiled. "Kids. They may just be the death of me." She bundled up the nylon jacket that JR had left on the floor and tossed it into the laundry room around the corner.

"Elle? You ready?"

"Hold your horses, woman!" Elle snapped from the bedroom. "I'm coming."

I strangled a laugh. "Ah, domestic bliss."

Amber glared and carefully flounced down the hallway.

"Yeah, well, don't you worry, sister." Elle sucker-punched me in the arm as she breezed by. "Your time will come soon and then we'll see who's laughing."

"Not if I have anything to say about it!" I yelled from my position at the top of the staircase, cradling my elbow.

Amber yelled back, "And don't even think about sneaking into my room tonight to try on my clothes. I've booby-trapped the closet."

And with that, the door slammed and my sister and her partner were out for the evening. The dog barked while I tried to do my happy dance. I thought better of it as a twinge of pain reminded me of my wound. So, I just sang.

"I do the hippie-hippie shake...ye-eah...I do the hippie-hippie shake." And I headed off to see what latest additions Amber had made to her wardrobe. Booby trap, hell. I eat booby traps for breakfast.

"I am so depressed," I said three hours later from the Berber-carpeted floor of my sister's humongous walk-in closet. Scratching Spanky behind his ears and calculating the deficiency of my own wardrobe, I realized what having two healthy incomes can do for a woman's choices. Amber and Elle had racks and racks of top-of-the-line name brands, and even JR had designer stuff to work with. "Maybe I should become a lesbian," I said to the uncomprehending Spanky. "Or at least bisexual, and marry a successful lawyer. They seem to get all the attention, and the swag."

The little schnauzer cocked his head at me and bumped his nose up for more pronounced attention. He didn't usually like outsiders, but since we came from the same zygote and he likes my sister, I guess he likes me too. "Huh, Spanky? Should I become a lesbian?" I asked him in my girliest voice, but he only licked my nose and then looked away.

"Ashlee, you would make a terrible lesbian," Amber said as she breezed by me through her walk-through closet into the master bath. I'd heard her come in, of course, but I was too depressed to move. "You like guys too much."

"I do, Spanky," I baby-talked as I rubbed shnozzes with the dog's cute little muffin nose. "I do like guys too much. It's horrible. I know. But I just can't stay away from rock-hard abs and tight butts."

"You are *really* disturbing me," Elle said as she hung up the expensive-looking slick-black-with-pearl-piping power blazer she'd worn that evening and took off the sensible but Amber-influenced brand-name flats she always wore. "Put the dog down and back away slowly."

"I know! I disturb myself." I groaned and rolled onto my back on the floor. "Ow. Ow. OW!"

Amber stuck her head out of the bathroom and looked worried.

"Ash? Are you okay?"

"I'm fine. I'm just so pathetic!" I cried as I cradled my wounded hip.

"Hey Amber. I think I'll let you handle this one." Elle smirked and headed downstairs for a late-night snack. Women of society never eat much at social functions; hence the voracious appetite afterward.

"Ashlee Scott! You are not pathetic!"

"But I am! I am!" I moaned and curled up into a fetal position while Spanky played leapfrog over my aching ass.

"No. You are not. Mother would roll over in her grave if she heard you talking like that. You are a powerful, wonderful girl."

"Amber, shush," I muttered into the dog's fur. I did not want a visit from my dead mother just at the moment.

Oh, didn't I tell you? My mother haunts me. Maybe she haunts other people, but as far as I know, only I can see her. I've spotted some other ghosts from time to time, but I always shy away and act like I don't.

This ability has something to do with the lupine gene, I believe. Amber didn't get it. Only one per zygote. So, I'm the one with the weird menstrual cycle and the need to turn hairy at every full moon. Amber knows nothing, of course, about me or Mom, and I intend to keep it that way.

Sigh.

"What do you know about being pathetic?" I whined, picking up a pair of her Manolo Blahniks and bringing them to my nose to inhale. I was in heaven. They still smelled new.

"Because you and I are two peas from one pod and *I* am NOT pathetic. So, ergo, neither are you."

"Oh, well then. That clears everything up!" I had to laugh. Amber grinned right back at me.

"I love you, you know," I said, and right then I really meant it.

"I know." She did a quick kiss-kiss to the air as she went back into the bathroom to undress. "I am lovable, after all."

I think my sister got all the cute genes in the family. I know I didn't come off half as adorable as she did, even when I was trying, which wasn't often. Where Amber was like Pink Chandon, I was more like any hard drink you had to muddle sugar into to offset the bitters: an acquired taste.

I crawled on my hands and knees back to my bedroom as the dog followed behind me, playfully nipping at my heels. Time to take a pain pill and sleep off the looming depression. Maybe tomorrow would be a better day, I thought. I hoped. I prayed.

I was asleep before my head hit the pillow.

−4−

"Hey Amber!" I called as my sister finally made an appearance at nine in the morning. "I just got the weirdest email!" I continued as she stepped blearily to the door of the den. "Look at this!" I swiveled the screen at her and let her read.

"Who said you could use my laptop?" she said.

I gave her a shit-eating bear grin. "Grrr?"

"Yeah, grrr." She looked and read.

TO WHOM IT MAY CONCERN:

IT HAS COME TO MY ATTENTION THAT YOU MAY NOT BE AWARE BUT THAT YOU HAVE BEEN TARGETED AND I HAVE BEEN COMPELLED TO HELP TERMINATE YOU. I TELL YOU THIS BECAUSE I DO NOT BELIEVE THE ACCUSATIONS THAT MY EMPLOYER HAS LEVELED ABOUT YOU AND FEEL THAT YOU SHOULD KNOW SO AS THIS DOES NOT HAPPEN VERY OFTEN, IN FACT NEVER, AS I AM A PROFESSIONAL, BUT I TRUST YOU AND WANT TO HELP YOU.

SINCERELY,
A FRIEND

The sender's address was nothing but a bunch of characters. It must be some kind of anonymous email server.

"What the fudge?" came the words from my sister's usually righteous mouth.

"That's kinda what I said, but with a *c* and a *k*." I stared at her.

"This can't be serious." Amber looked more like me when she wasn't all dolled up. She the lipstick lesbian and I the tomboy, go figure, but sans makeup, two peas and all that.

"That's what I said. And God, what a hack. JR could write better copy."

"You get a possibly threatening email and you're critiquing the sender's writing skills?"

"I've gotten threatening emails before," I said with an offhandedness I did not feel, "but usually they have something to do with an article I wrote."

We looked at each other with a slight tension in our eyes.

"Hey Elle!" Amber yelled at the top of her lungs. Before we knew it, Elle was at the door with a baseball bat, looking thoroughly disheveled.

"WHAT? What's the matter? What?" Elle brandished the bat like she was trying out for the San Francisco Giants, shook the morning sleep from her eyes and blinked at us uncomprehendingly.

Amber handed Elle some reading glasses, one of the many sets she had lying around the house. "Look at this email." She swung the laptop around some more. "Ashlee just got this and I don't know what to make of it."

Elle read quickly, mouthing the words. When she got to the word "terminate," she looked up at me and her eyes got wide.

"DUCK!" she screamed, and we all did as I heard the sound of breaking glass over my shoulder and caught it on the chin as a baseball sailed into the room.

The sound of quick footsteps padding up the walk and J.R.'s voice were the next things I remember as Amber shook me where I lay.

"Is everyone okay? Why is Aunt Ash on the floor?" JR asked.

"Ashlee! Wake up!" My sister's voice now.

"Am I dead?" I murmured. At least, I thought it was me as I struggled back to consciousness with the dog licking my face.

"Spanky, knock it off." I pushed him away, but he came right back, thinking we were playing some new kind of game.

"Spanky! Go lie down," my sister ordered, and when my sister used that tone, you knew you were in trouble. The dog slunk out the door and collapsed on the tile, laying his head on his forepaws and giving us that "what did I do?" look. "Be careful, JR, there's glass all over."

"Gee, Mom. I'm sorry. I didn't think I could hit the thing that hard. I wasn't even trying." JR apologized profusely from the doorway of the den. My ex-brother-in-law Mervin, and I emphasize the X, as in *crossed out, no thanks, buh-bye*, stood behind my nephew smirking as his face wandered into focus.

"Damn, Mervin. Next time you want to take out the ex, why don't you make sure you're aiming on the right twin sister." Amber sponged me toward consciousness with a cool cloth. "And you can stop that now! I'm up! I'm up!" I growled. Just had to get my knees under me as I rose from the carpet.

"Better put something on that," Mervin joked. "Or you're gonna have rug-burn all over the side of your face."

I snarled, "You oughta know. Doesn't your new girlfriend like to drive?" Let him figure it out. "Amber, can you please get your smarmy sperm donor out of my sight?"

"Mervin. You're not helping," my sister carped as she pushed his sorry ass toward the door. "And you're paying for half the repair."

"Well. Ex-*cuse* me," he called and headed out. "Take it easy, champ. You played a good game today."

"Thanks, Dad!" JR called and waved goodbye. He turned back to me with a cute little pout and said, "I'm really sorry, Aunt Ash."

"I know you are, sport." I gritted my teeth, smiled and waved him off to clean up in his room. Then I turned to my sister.

"I really hate that guy."

"Don't you say that about my son!" she said with a grin.

"I wasn't talking about – never mind." I hobbled back into the chef's grade kitchen.

"You know Mervin has always been a fan of yours," Amber continued. "I have no idea why, but he likes you."

"That's just 'cause I've got all the looks of the woman he married but I don't hate him as much as you do so he thinks he might get some from me sometime. And *I* don't like *him* like I used to, before I wised up. That's bound to make him a little insane."

"Wow. You know, I'd forgotten you liked him back then. Maybe we should have swapped places when I was married instead of getting divorced. Then we would have both got what we wanted. He would have never known the difference."

"Yeah. Right." I laughed ruefully. "Like substituting a sow's ear for a silk purse."

Amber and I used to do a lot of self-swapping in high school, mostly just for grins, but every now and then, when one of us wanted to go out with a guy who asked, but the one he asked didn't, we'd trade without him knowing.

After the first full moon of my sixteenth year, we didn't play that game anymore. Amber still felt guilty it hadn't been her on that fateful date, like it should've been. I was just thankful that if somebody had to die, it wasn't me.

I'm sorry. Maybe being a wolf has made me callous, and Shane was an omega anyway.

Tell you about it later, I promise.

"I'm serious, Ash. I think we need to report this email to the police."

"Elle *is* the police," I said as I grabbed ice cubes from the freezer and stuck them in a plastic bag. A few pieces ended up on the floor. My sister glanced over at me, wondering if I was going to take care of it. I'd get to it, but if it wasn't soon enough, I knew she'd be pissed off. She was already frowning at the floor where the ice was melting.

"Oh, for Pete's sake, Amber! I'll get it!" I said and took a moment to wipe the puddle of water off the floor. Then I stuck the ice-filled bag to my head. Sometimes I hated being a twin.

"And she's right. I am the police." Elle kissed her on the cheek as she went past.

"You used to be the police. But then you took a job with the city," Amber reminded her, all syrupy-like.

"So, maybe I'm out of practice, but I'm still the city attorney. That's gotta count for something." She cocked her head and winked at me. "I've got connections. And a gun."

"Yeah! That's gotta count for something," I echoed and stage-winked right back at her.

Elle was very much a cards-to-the-chest kind of gal, but she could be real amusing when she let her sense of humor show. Amber, on the other hand, had a tendency toward taking things *way* too seriously.

"Still." Amber sniffed at us. She hates any ganging up, unless she does the ganging.

"Still." Elle drew my sister out and did a quick waltz with her around the room.

"Still," she re-echoed, "I think if it happens again, we need to report it."

"I'll report it right now, if that makes you feel better," Elle said. Then she started getting handsy with Amber.

"Um, guys? Can you just…take it somewhere else?" I asked, ever so humbly.

They stopped and looked condescendingly at me.

"What? You homophobic or something?" Elle pulled my sister into a twirl and then dipped her.

"No," I said. Then under my breath as I walked away, "Just envious."

It was true. Total sister-envy, 'cause she had the life. She had the house. She had the child, whom I adored, and the dog that I liked as well. And she had the tall, dark, and handsome S.O., only not so tall and handsome as I imagined, the kind I wished I could come home to each night.

Let's face it, she had it all. And what did I have? A lot of frequent flyer miles, fab trips, upgraded hotel rooms, and free spa treatments.

Okay, maybe I didn't have it so bad.

5

It was day three and I was totally bored. No really! Abso-bloomin-lutely out of my freakin' gourd. And I said so as I perched on one butt cheek on top of the dryer watching my twin fold laundry.

"Move your legs. You're in the way," Amber said.

I scooted over to give her access, wincing.

"You know, when JR tells me he's bored, I usually send him out to play," Amber said, matching pink socks and folding polka-dot underwear.

"Are you crazy? Don't you know? Suburban neighborhoods are incredibly dangerous!" I made a face at her, only semi-mock-horrified.

"Ashlee, this is Knightsbridge, not Oakland. And J.R.'s a smart kid. Besides, he knows not to go far, and we have a Neighborhood Watch program."

"Yeah, after that email, it's the neighbors I'm going to be watching," I ran my hand along the dust-free blinds and peeked out the window of the laundry room, squinting into the morning light. See, I thought: even the dust knows not to mess with Amber.

"Go walk around the neighborhood. Play Auntie Security. The fresh air will do you good." She looked at me, chagrined. "Oh my God! I sounded just like Mom."

"Yes you did."

"DID SOMEONE CALL ME?"

I blanched when I heard my mother's voice coming from the heavens. "Not exactly," I muttered.

"What?" Amber asked, uncertain.

"I think I'll go take that walk." I hopped to the floor, much to my butt cheek's dismay. Then I hobbled downstairs and out the front door.

"Leave the door unlocked. I don't have a key!" I called out behind me, and then wondered if I should have yelled so loud. I mean, Amber and Elle lived in a fairly safe neighborhood, but in places like this, there were always older kids and crimes of opportunity.

"On second thought, I'll take the spare!" I yelled, and grabbed it out of its hidey-hole, sticking it in my shoulder bag.

"Good idea," my sister called back, as I locked the door behind me and turned to greet the day.

Ugh, I thought. It's much too bright out here. What the hell is that hot thing doing up in the sky at nine a.m.?

I grabbed the Donna Karan sunglasses I'd nicked from Amber out of my bag and took a big inhale of the grassy-sweet smell of cow manure. I could still feel the residue of my dead mother's presence and I hurried away, keen to escape from the force of nature that is her spirit. Ghosts naturally retain more power when they are near a symbiotic frequency of shared experiences, an exorcist once told me.

Are you wondering why I was talking to an exorcist? Um...

When people get together, shared desires often manifest visitations from the other side. Put enough people's concentration on one thing and a thought can achieve critical mass; hence the number of Elvis sightings, no doubt.

Amber and Elle lived in a burb-district on the edge of Knightsbridge proper. Directly behind their house, placed at the east end of the development, rose steep hills and a deep cut that led up into Knightsbridge Canyon. To the north and south sides of their subdivision were open acres where the valley began a gentle rolling into a land of almond orchards, horse stables and dairy farms. When we were younger, we actually got milk from one of those dairies, but not anymore. It was cheaper to buy from the grocery store, and safer, so they said.

I liked it better back then. Waah.

With determination in hand and a fresh pack of slim clove cigars – I didn't want Amber to know that I still smoked sometimes, but hey, it was better than tobacco – I headed down the road toward an in-town walking trail. With the pain in my ass, I wasn't ready for any serious hiking.

The path near my sister's home was paved, and it bordered the rows upon rows of similarly styled homes with precisely varied color schemes that housed the upwardly mobile middle class of Knightsbridge's finest. I wondered just how similar and precisely varied the lives of those who lived in them were as I stretched my legs. I stripped off the extra sweater I'd woken up with this morning, leaving myself braless in a tank top and sweats, and I seriously hoped that I didn't run into anyone I knew since I hadn't shaved my pits in a few days.

In contrast to my home in San Francisco where fog was typical, I aimed to soak up the dry San Joaquin sun as I made the rounds. There weren't many people out as it was a bit winter-nippy, but not so bad that you could see your breath, maybe fifty. I continued around the corner away from the house. Before I knew it I'd reached a large park with four baseball diamonds and decided that this was about as good a time as any to light up.

I know nonsmokers look at those of us who have a puff in the morning like we're crazy, but to a smoker the act has the same effect as meditation. Besides, it was nice to not be so distracted by all the other scents that the wolf inside me had access to in its catalog. There's nothing worse than feeling like you're sniffing your way through the neighborhood on two feet. News flash: most smells are disgusting, even the nice ones, if your nose is sensitive enough.

"Ahem." I heard a voice behind me and turned. There, staring at me with the most beautiful blue eyes, was the one guy I was most worried about having to face again: my ex-boyfriend and former star of the Spartans football team, Will Stenfield. Six foot two and stocky, without an ounce of fat on him, he still had the prettiest eyelashes you ever did see. I won't even talk about the abs.

Anyone who doesn't believe God has a sense of humor just ain't paying attention.

"Got another clove, or aren't you willing to share?" he asked as I stared at him, speechless. I realized he was just as breathtaking as I remembered. I'd tried to forget. Hell if I would let him know, though.

"You know, that buzz cut really works for you," I deadpanned, bracing my smoking arm with the other one under the elbow. Hey, he'd caught me off guard and it was the first thing that popped into my head.

"Really? Ya think? 'Cause your sister just calls me cue-ball." He grinned and my knees went weak.

"At least she's consistent. She called you cue-ball when we were growing up too."

"And YOU haven't called at all, Ash. Now, why is that?" Will picked the clove right out of my hands, took a drag, and then handed it back. I stared at the moist filter, thinking of the other places I remembered those lips being. A shudder moved through me for a moment, and then I came back.

"Poor cell plan?" I cracked.

No, the truth is, Will was my first crush and longtime on-again-off-again boyfriend from way back. During an OFF phase, I made the mistake of going out on a pity date with one of my sister's castoffs, Shane Macdonald.

Will and I got to be even more OFF when the guy ended up dead.

Dad sent me away for my junior year to a private boarding school because of the small-town hoopla and what it did to me. Most thought I was shattered over Shane's death the night of our date. Some suspected I was pregnant. Trust me, I was not.

In fact, after the full moon fiasco that set off my first transformation, I was still too messed up to be interested in anyone. When I came back for my senior year, Will and I danced around but never really got back to where we had been. I knew even then that I wouldn't be staying in Knightsbridge, and he was a small-town boy all the way, always intending to take over the family landscaping business. I remembered a lot of tension when I left.

I guess Will got over it, because he was talking to me now.

"I waited, you know." He said it with a serious look on his face. I believed him, but back then I was running away, and Will, well, he was just part of what I'd left behind.

"It was never about you," I told him. It's amazing how much can be said with so few words when you have that connection like Will and I did.

Do?

Maybe.

"I know." He smiled. "Can I at least get a hug? I read all your magazine stories about those fancy places."

Straight to a writer's heart that went, so I obliged. Hell, I did more than oblige. When he opened up his arms, I buried my face in his ratty old sweat-stained lawn-jockey t-shirt, smelling of musk and dead leaves, old wounds and memories.

"So, what are you doing back in town?" Will asked a few moments later as he gently escaped from my clinging embrace and returned to the lawnmower he'd been pushing down the walk.

"Oh, you know. Just slumming." I grinned. Despite it being what, five or six years? I'd come back for the summer after high school and seen him a few times then, but not seriously. Now, it was like no time had passed at all. He was still a redneck and maybe somewhere inside me, I was still a redneck's girl.

California version, of course. We don't drawl. We do drink beer and drive pickup trucks.

I'd heard Will had taken over the family landscaping business when his father semi-retired with a back injury, and more often than not came home smelling of tree sap, grass and loam. It was woodsy, a little nutty and always made my head spin.

"You doing Parks and Recreation now?" I asked as I watched him load the mower into the trailer he had hitched to his Chevy pickup.

"That and everything else under the sun. You know, Ash, if you're not too busy, why don't you slum with me for awhile?" He cocked his head. "Let's go hang out. Talk about old times."

"I don't know," I told him. The pain pill was wearing off and I had no idea how I was going to hobble over to the truck, let alone get up into it. "I kinda had a little surgery."

Will put out his hand, reflexively. "Oh crap. Was it something serious?"

"No. No." I waved the matter aside. "I got shot in the butt up in Idaho. Just hurts to sit down for long periods of time."

"Shot?"

I fed him the same simple half-truth I'd been using with everyone else. "Just a ricochet off a rock. I was hiking, some asshole was hunting and thought my blue North Face looked exactly like a twelve-point buck, I don't know. Whoever it was didn't own up, and I limped back to town, went to a spa the next day and it got infected."

He stared at me like I was a bad little girl, which wasn't all bad.

"I know, I should have gone in to the ER right away and gotten antibiotics, but…"

Will laughed. "Butt." He mock bowed.

"Hey, staying at Amber's is penance enough, and sitting down is a real bitch."

"Then you can stand on the seat with your head out the roof and hold onto the roll bar. Your chariot awaits, my lady." Will held out his hand.

He was so cute, I had to give it a go.

6

"Elle! You are not going to believe this!" Amber stood on the front lawn of the house, cell phone in one hand, talking while she watered the lawn with the other as we drove up. "It looks like Ash and Will are together again." I could hear the sounds of exclamation coming from the other end as Will lifted me down from the tailgate.

"Hi, Will!" Amber called and waved. "I'll talk to you later," she told the phone and hung up on Elle. "Fancy seeing you here."

"Yes, well I found this poor handicapped bag lady wandering the streets smoking a clove and had to stop and lend her a hand," Will said to Amber as he walked me over.

"Don't let him lie to you like that," I said quickly, trying to divert her from the smoking tipoff. "It was me who took pity on the poor schmuck, because he had to stop and ask for directions."

"Now I know you're lying. Men never ask for directions. Besides, he's lived here all his life."

"So sue me."

The diversion did not work. "Ashlee, I thought you'd given up that nasty habit," Amber said, so I whacked Will in the back of the head with the palm of my hand.

"Thanks for spilling the beans, loser." I turned back to my sister. "Will's staying for lunch," I said, hoping to avoid a lecture and almost positive she wouldn't pull rank and nix his invitation.

"Oh no he's not," Amber said.

"Oh no I'm not," Will echoed.

"C'mon. I bet you two haven't talked in a while. It'll be good for all of us," I said. "Besides, I'm cooking."

My sister rolled her eyes. "Now this I've got to see."

"See, I told you I make a mean pot of spaghetti," I teased as I cleared the dishes and set another helping of pasta before the man I realized I wanted to get to know better again.

"Please, Ash. I really couldn't eat another bite," Will said.

"Oh, come on. Just one more wafer-thin mint?"

Will grinned, deliberately stuck his fork into the center of the bowl and started slurping anyway, much to my delight.

"Actually, Ash, that wasn't bad for spaghetti. It was pretty good in fact," Amber added as an aside to her S.O., who had come home for lunch. Benefits of the small town: short commute. "Wasn't it, Elle?"

"It was very good, Ash." Elle played her role as the grownup to the hilt. "If it wasn't for Amber, I'd probably be having another helping myself." Elle laughed as Amber tickled her, pinching the pudge that she never could seem to lose.

"So, why don't we go take that drive?" I suggested to Will, who perked up at the sound and put down his fork. I'd taken another pain pill by now, so I figured I could at least make it through a two-hour reunion tour of the hometown, and besides, I didn't think I could stand the lovey-dovey around here anymore. "Catch up on the dish. Tell me who's divorced who and who's still having babies when they should have stopped years ago. And stuff."

"And stuff," Will echoed solemnly.

"You still have to clean up this mess," Amber tossed over her shoulder.

"I'll handle the dishes." Elle put a hand on Amber's wrist and squeezed. "I think Ash could use the time out of the house for a while."

Amber got it, smiled and then gave me a quick wink. "Fine. Take your time. Keys still in the same place, and don't forget to reset the alarm after you come in."

"Thanks guys!" I gave them a quick hug and limped enthusiastically out the door toward the pickup past Mervin and JR, who were just coming home from soccer practice.

"Hi guys! Bye guys!" I sang.

"Hey, isn't that Will Stenfield?" I heard Mervin ask Amber as he handed her J.R.'s muddy cleats, which she took with two fingers and walked them into the garage.

"I think he dated Denise once," Mervin commented, referring to Amber's replacement and J.R.'s new step-monster, then shrugged and walked away.

"Amber," Elle said in a warning tone as she poked her head into the garage.

Amber turned and put her hands on her hips.

"What?"

"Love you," Elle said.

Hearing that, I was seriously tempted to toss my cookies, but with Will there I was already too far away, reminiscing.

"So, where do you want to go?" Will asked as he revved the engine while I went through his CDs. I pulled out a scratched-up copy of the Cars' first album, one that he'd inherited from his dad. I still remember it playing from the work truck as Stenfield Landscaping groomed the school grounds when I was a kid. We both ended up loving the eighties music of our parents, I guess.

Or maybe it was because Will was frozen in the past and I had no time to figure out "what's a Bieber?"

"Can we go by my old house?" I asked. "I want to see how much it's changed."

"Um. Sure." He hesitated, looking at me funny.

"What?"

"Nothing." Will laughed as he pulled out onto Walnut Avenue and over to the west side of town.

"Tell me."

"Tell you what?"

"Tell me."

"No."

"Weirdo."

"Freak."

"Fine." I folded my arms and faked a sulk.

When Amber and I were growing up, we lived on the good side of the bad side of town, a couple houses down from one of the retired mayors. His raised brick ranch-style sprawled out over a half-acre lot and held lemon trees we used to swipe fruit from during the summer. These weren't the cute little things you get in grocery stores, the ones that look like they were made from plastic lemon molds. These lemons were frickin' monsters, grapefruit-sized. I had no idea why. Anyway, we had this weird thing about sucking the juice from lemons after coating them with salt, kind of like our older brother Adam did with cold sliced potatoes and equally cold slabs of butter.

Had to be there, I guess.

Will drove us down Golden Boulevard, which used to be part of the old highway before they put the by-pass through, and pulled into the parking lot of the Boxcar, an abandoned set of railroad cars that had been turned into a nice restaurant. I had worked there the summer I came home.

For some, Knightsbridge was a college town, for others it was a great place to raise kids, but for single people, it seriously sucked. Just one more reason why I had taken the travel writer's apprenticeship, seldom went back, and didn't look people up.

I know, thin, right? Bad memories, I guess I'll admit to.

"Remember this place?" he asked as we stared at the outside.

"God, yes!" I'd spent that whole summer as the hostess greeter, since I was too young to carry alcohol and too new to serve food and get tips. I did help bus tables. Minimum wage, go me. "I met Palmer Courtland here and he tried to put a hand up my dress. You know, the guy from one of those daytime soaps where no one ever ages? I think he was seventy. Looked forty if he didn't move his face."

"Come on, can you blame him?" Will waggled his eyebrows, mock-lasciviously. Or actually lasciviously. Made me feel all tingly.

"Guess not, but I'm worldly and wise now. Back then...ew." I laughed.

"And what about that Sid guy who used to be the chef?"

"Omigod! That's right. He had such a filthy mouth," I remembered. "If the customers only knew the way he talked about them! They would have just died."

"I think he knew it offended you and if I remember correctly, you told me it got even filthier, that is, until I had a chat with him."

"That was you? I never knew. That was sweet." I lay flat on the bench seat, put my head in his lap and stuck my feet out the window, taking the pressure off my ass. "Remember when we all dressed up in white and played croquet in the park?"

"I wasn't there for that one, but I remember driving by. You looked adorable in white."

He was right. I did. I do. I smiled.

"You're still pretty adorable."

That made me sit up and look at him, searching his face.

Will leaned over and put a peck on my forehead. I lifted my face and he kissed me for real this time. Very softly. My mouth parted involuntarily and his tongue flicked in and touched the tip of my own in an intimate caress.

Was I really doing this?

"Um. Is it hot in here, or is it me?" I asked as I moved away from him, opened the door and climbed out of the cab. Just down the road from the Boxcar was a place called the Nordic Chalet where they still sold winter sports equipment. I marveled how it seemed some things changed and some things never did.

"Come on, let's walk," I said, just to clear my head, and proceeded to stroll down my hometown version of Main Street USA, Will trailing a bit behind.

"I can't believe the Frosty Freeze is still here." I kept up a running commentary as we walked. "And there's the studio where Amber and I took jazz class. Knightsbridge School of Ballet was just around the corner, up there in that window, see?" I pointed and Will sneaked up behind me and wrapped his arms around my waist.

I folded myself into him and looked up into his smiling baby blues. "What are you doing?" I asked, my heart pounding in my ears.

"Reminiscing," he said as he leaned down and kissed me again. Long and slow, and soft, like a lover. My body melted into his. I whimpered as my heart threatened to crack and I knew that I had it bad.

Where the hell did this all come from? Old flames rekindled from banked fires.

"Um, that was nice." I inhaled his scent as I hid my face in the crook of his arm.

"You're welcome." Will laughed and kissed me again on the forehead. Lots of kissing going on here. I liked it.

This was the last thing that I was expecting. But there's something about the people in your hometown, something very familiar, the same familiarity that breeds contempt, but when the right strings are played, it makes you feel like they know you inside and out...even when you know they really don't.

But you can never go home again, though I thought I could right then.

I slipped out of his arms and walked a few steps ahead of him again. "I know what you're doing."

"What am I doing?" he asked, daring me to answer.

"Don't think you can come in here all hella wonderful and worm your way back into my life that easy."

"Hella wonderful?" Laughter from him.

"I got out of this hick town years ago and I'm not going to be dragged back here in the lined bed of a Chevy with intertwined hearts on it," I said, referring to the etching on his back window.

"I never thought you would," he told me, eyes glittering in the sunlight dappled through the maples. I hated it when men did that, with their eyes. Hated it.

Okay, I'm lying.

"Well. Good. So back off, 'cause this girl's not ready to settle." I crossed my arms and looked at him defiantly.

"Since when have you settled for anything, Ash?" he asked and grabbed my elusive hand. "And if I was that kinda guy, I'd be insulted. Come on. I want to show you something."

I let him drag me a few paces, then decided that with his bulk it would be a losing battle anyway and matched his steps. Before we knew it, we were in front of Crave.

Keith and Dawn Snyder had opened Crave Donuts when I was a kid when one of those horrible chain donut shops was the only game in town. Pretty soon the other place closed. How's that for entrepreneurial? They made the best Bavarian crème I have ever tasted in my life, so when he pulled me in the door, I thought I was going to die.

"Hey Ash!" came a voice from behind the counter. "I didn't know you were in town." Jill Snyder, now Jill Blumenthal, came around the corner and gave me a big hug. I was taken aback for a moment. We'd never been that close in high school, but it just goes to show you that people's memories of the past are often more rosy than we expect.

"Yeah. I'm holed up at Amber's for a few weeks recovering from a surgery. Bullet wound on assignment. I see you're still in the doughnut biz."

"Bullet wound?" she said, her mouth a big O.

"Just a ricochet. Nothing serious. Forget I said anything. You look great by the way." And she did. Married life looked really good on her.

Jill's face lit up. "Oh, you're so sweet."

That was the difference between her and a city girl, who would have taken my comment as one-upmanship. She was married to a tall, blonde and dishy silent type I knew from school but not very well, and now they had a few kids. I fought back a pang of annoyance. I was *so* not going to settle, down or otherwise.

You know, God laughs at people's plans, my brother always said, and if you swear you'll never do something, guess what? That's what will happen.

"Hey, Jill." Will gave her a smile. "Can we get some of your custard-filled chocolate bars?"

Jill smiled back and went behind the counter.

"I just made up a fresh batch," she said and I had a sudden déjà vu as I remembered that her mother Dawn used to tell me the same thing. I watched with anticipation as she took the oozingly creamy custard and filled the warm doughy chocolate-covered orgasm before my very eyes.

Will paid her for the donuts and a couple of milks and we sat over at a table by the window. When I bit into it, I thought I was going to die and go to heaven right there. One thing I never had to worry about was getting fat, by the way. Yes, all you girls can envy the hell out of me, but it has something to do with my monthly romp in the woods.

Silver linings? Frankly, I don't think it was a good trade. You try waking up with your face covered in blood. You'll see.

"So, are they as good as you remembered?" Will leaned his forehead into mine across the table in an intimate gesture and I sighed.

"Better," I said, savoring every bite in silence as I watched him demolish his own donut in two seconds flat. I took a napkin and wiped his chin.

Jill was looking at us with interest from behind the counter and I knew that the social media gossip line was going to be hard at work this evening. Local Girl Returns, Reignites Old Passions!

"Let's get out of here," I said under my breath as we downed our milks and headed for the door.

"Bye guys!" Jill called after us. "Don't forget Homecoming's next month! Alumni games are first and then Trojans versus Spartans!" Her voice drifted out. "Everybody would LOVE to see you!"

"Trojans versus Spartans?" I asked. "Since when are Knightsbridge and K-Christian even in the same league?"

"Boy, you have been gone a while, haven't you?" Will teased. "KCHS even has a football team now. It's grown a lot."

"You're kidding," I said as we headed past the Shell station and back to the truck. "Where are they getting the money? We had to buy our own cheerleading outfits when I was in school."

"Yeah, well times change, Ash." He held the door of the truck open for me. "And so do people. The town's not so small, and it got a lot richer with the influx of wealthy conservatives fleeing the Bay Area. K-Christian went from being That Other School to the place the elite all send their kids, at the same time the public schools were cutting their budgets."

"Wow. Weird."

"Yeah, never mind. Back on topic: believe it or not, lots of people remember you with fondness," he said, and I could see he meant it.

I felt bad. I had been a pretty mixed-up kid, and after Mom died and the date-getting-killed thing, which nobody ever talked about – don't worry, I'll tell you about it soon – I had a tendency to see the glass half empty rather than half full. It made me feel small, and I thought that perhaps I needed some new glasses. Half-sized ones, maybe, that would be full, with half the...

Sorry, my metaphor just broke down. Not so good for a writer, but I always swore not to revise my diary, so I'll just keep on telling the tale.

I sighed as he drove me down past the boutique where I'd worked in the basement the summer in middle school, putting price tags on bras before I even had a need for one. He pointed out the old Woolworth's I swiped fingernail polish from and the Safeway turned into a Von's on the corner where we shopped for groceries back in the day. The small-town mansions that fronted the west end of town didn't look so large anymore, and as we turned right onto Broadway and then onto Floral, the street where I grew up, I was floored.

"Wow. This place has really gone to seed," I said. Maybe it was just childhood, but I could have sworn most families in this neighborhood never had more than two cars, and none of them ever on blocks in the middle of the lawn.

Will laughed. "It's not the good side of the bad side of town anymore. All the money went up to the outskirts.

New houses nearer the freeway for all the Bay Area commuters." He looked apologetic.

"You know, I've had dreams of coming back here and buying the old house. Dad sold it when he remarried and we had to move into the house on Devonshire. After that, it wasn't really home-home, you know? Now, I think if I wanted to buy this place, I'd have to move it somewhere else just to feel safe."

We parked outside. It actually didn't look too bad from here. Clearly it was the best-kept house on the block, if the neatly trimmed lawn and new paint job were any indication.

"Let's go in," he said.

I looked at him aghast.

"What?" I shrugged. "Just walk up to the front door, ring the bell and say 'Hey! You know I used to live here. Can I look around your house for a while?'"

"Why not?" He smiled as he got out of the cab. "People are still people. They'll understand."

"No way!" I refused to budge, but I watched as his cocky self walked right up to the painted concrete steps and then he turned to me.

"Are you coming?" He threw his arms wide, like he was in a movie or something. I shook my head, scrunched up my face, then jumped out of the truck. I had to see this.

He rang the bell.

Nothing. I was so relieved.

"See. They're not even home," I said.

"No kidding. Come on, let's sneak a peek inside."

If I really wanted to, I could come back the next full moon in wolf form and check the place out and no one would be any wiser. It would be safer. I wasn't a scaredy-cat when I was in wolf form. In fact, when I was shifted, I wasn't afraid of anything. But now…now I was just petrified.

Will reached out his hand and tried the handle. It turned and he pushed the door open. I was in shock.

"Come on," he said. "Aren't you curious?" He took a step inside the door.

"What? Will. Stop!" I yelped and grabbed his arm, trying to pull him back and away from breaking and entering. Well, entering anyway.

"Hello?" he called as I tried to shush him. "Anyone home?" And then, "Mom?"

Mom? And then it all came crashing into my head and I shoved him.

"You slimy shitbird," I yelled as he turned and I beat on his chest. He grabbed me and pulled me down to the tan-carpeted floor. I was so surprised I didn't even notice my butt pain. "YOU OWN THIS PLACE?"

"I own this place." He grinned and I wanted to wipe that bird-eating kitty grin off his face once and for all. All the feelings that I ever had about this home washed through me and I began to beat on him, slapping him for making me feel stupid and scared, and then I began to cry.

"Well, that wasn't the reaction that I was expecting." Will kissed my forehead, held me and stroked my hair. I heard a sound and turned to see a woman's shoes and stockings out of the corner of my eye.

"Hi Mom," Will said.

I looked up bleary-eyed as his mother bent down to greet me.

"Hello dear. And who have we here?" I buried my face in Will's chest. "Well, Ashlee Scott, as I live and breathe."

"Hi, Mrs. Stenfield," I muttered, as I turned my tear-stained face to her.

Will's mother gently touched my chin. "Now, what's a nice girl like you doing with a rough boy like mine?" she said with a chuckle. "Get up off that floor, young man, and let me greet this girl properly." She stepped back and allowed us to rise.

I smoothed the velvet crush of the fancy sweats I'd borrowed from my sister and ran my hands through my hair, pulling my locks away from my face.

"Come here and give us a hug." She pulled me into her and wrapped her small thin frame around me and I sighed contentedly. Mrs. Stenfield always knew how to make you feel at home. "Why don't you sit down? I'll make us some tea and we can catch up," she said and then disappeared through the dining room and into the kitchen.

"How could you buy this place and not tell me?" I turned on him. "If your mother wasn't here, I'd kick your ass to hell and back."

"Well, then I'm glad she's here. And when was I going to tell you, anyway? You took off so fast after that one summer, and we weren't dating anymore, and the few times you did come back home I hardly saw you, so when was I going to tell you?"

"You could have emailed me. The address is on every article."

"I'm not an email kind of guy."

I knew that. He didn't even have a smart phone, just a beat-up old Nokia that could barely text, and he probably only carried that because his work required it. I always felt Will was born too late, and would have been more comfortable in Mom and Dad's world.

"You could have told Amber. She would have told me."

"I asked her not to," he said. "I wanted to surprise you, if ever..."

"If ever what?"

"Nothing. You know."

Will's mother came back with a serving tray and a tea cozy as I slid into the soft lining of the brown suede sofa. I took the cup she offered, almost overwhelmed with the memories.

"So, what brings you back to town, Ashlee? Last I heard you were doing some articles for Contemporary Cruising."

I forced myself to focus on talking to her rather than reminiscing. "Really? Where'd you hear that?" I avoided the first question. I *so* did not want to talk to her about my bullet wound. Once I started that I'd be sounding like everyone's grandparents talking about their medical conditions. Why is it that the older people get, the more readily they pull out their aches and pains? Probably because there are more of them. I guess I could relate, or at least, my butt could.

"I think you told me, didn't you, Will?" She turned and I looked at him out of the corner of my eye.

"Huh?" He was blushing. "Um, yeah. I guess so."

Mrs. Stenfield turned back to me. "Will has everything you've ever written. Asks Amber to call him when you've got a new article and buys it up before it hits the stand."

"Oh, really?" I looked at him with pursed lips. I wondered what other secrets my dear identical twin had been keeping. I made a mental note to interrogate her when I got home.

"Oh yes," Mrs. Stenfield went on with enthusiasm. "I think my son just might be your biggest fan."

I could not believe it. Will Stenfield? He'd never be comfortable in a five-star hotel and spa. Then again... "Well, then. I guess I'll just have to hit you up when I finally organize my fan club." I laughed.

How natural this all seemed. Smooth. Easy. Not like any of the other conversations I've had with the parents of the guys I've dated. Actually, scratch that. I rarely got around to meeting the parents of the guys I dated, because I normally didn't go longer than three dates with any of them. Sound familiar?

Will settled back and popped the leg rest up from where he sat at the end of the sofa sectional. He looked really comfortable and at home here. In my old home. Who would believe it?

We chatted a bit more, small talk and things.

"You know, you really should go visit Sam and Muriel next door. I bet they'd love seeing you again," Mrs. Stenfield continued. "Darcy's over there a lot, with her husband and the kids. After Oliver died, they needed the grandkids around to fill the place with gladness."

Darcy and Oliver were our neighbor playmates growing up. Ollie died of diabetes complications years before and I didn't get back very often. I sometimes felt guilty about that, but dammit, my life wasn't easy and coming home always intimidated me. I was a moody bitch growing up and still am sometimes, and didn't like being reminded of that fact, which is why I usually avoid things like Homecoming and class reunions.

Forgive yourself, the little voice in my head said. I promised to try.

"Yeah. Maybe I will," I replied to her and myself both.

Will threw the kickstand back on the recliner and pounced out of the chair. "Hey Mom. I'm gonna show Ashlee the rest of the house. Let her see what we've done with the place."

"Of course, dear."

Omigod! Why did he have to be so cute with his mother? And me without mine, since I was eleven. At least corporeally.

But he was, and he pulled me up off the couch and motioned me over. "As you can see, I stripped the paint off the mantel and off all the floor and sideboards, leaving the natural walnut to breathe. This place was made simple, but they used really good techniques in the joins." He rambled on about renovation as I ran my hand over the polished grain. It looked like he'd put a lot of love into the job and I said so.

Will smiled shyly and my heart went pitter-pat. I was such a goner! Inwardly I groaned. What the hell was I doing? This wasn't going to work, me the world traveler and him the small-town guy.

Will showed me how he'd done the same refinishing with the French doors that slid into the wall, and talked about hand-beveling and then showed me the wall with the china cabinet where we used to keep only the best dishes for when guests were over. We usually ate in the kitchen otherwise. The etched panes of crystal seemed to glitter and the light from the chandelier over the dining room table refracted rainbows along the wall as he opened and closed the cupboards, showing me the gleaming burnished solid brass hinges. God, I loved this place, though I really didn't understand as a child how nice it all was.

We hardly ever do.

They'd cleaned up the sun porch that opened off the dining room and added a settee and a breakfast nook and I smiled as I remember how often I'd retreated to this room as a child to read about the Patchwork Girl in Oz, and Nancy Drew and the Hardy Boys. Will then let me out the side door of the house and showed me the well-tended gardens where my father and I had pulled weeds and the now-huge chrysanthemums we'd planted years ago. He walked me around the back and showed me how he'd turned the tomato garden where we used to have mud-fights in the late summer into a small rock garden and how he'd resurfaced the patio and rebuilt the sandstone outdoor barbecue that was still shaded by a couple of plum trees. Sliding open the garage, I caught the whiff of gasoline and the same smell of freshly mown grass that clung to his well-oiled tools occupying the back wall. And he showed me the motorcycle he was building from scratch that looked like he hadn't worked on it for a while, but would get back to, once the landscaping season slowed down in winter.

"Hey! Is that crawlspace still up here?" I asked and climbed up the slatted wall on the left side of the garage to peek my head into a small storage area. On a sleeping bag up there we'd felt each other up for the first time, hiding from the world and discovering clumsy teenage lust.

"Don't go up there!" he said, but I already had.

"Looks like you haven't been up here in a while." I saw it clean and empty. I climbed down, snickering.

"Yeah, well, there's this thing called the internet now," he replied, sheepish.

"What, no girlfriend to take care of your base carnal needs?" I asked with false lightness.

"No, Ash. Not since you."

Wow. I felt honored, and more than a bit pressured. He really had waited. I gave him a peck on the cheek.

"What was that for?"

"Because you're so cute when you turn red." I hugged him again and then stepped away.

"Let me see the rest of the house." I ran toward the garage door, pulled it shut behind me and latched it.

"Don't you dare lock me in here!" he called, but I already had. He pounded on the door and I giggled.

"Ash. It's not funny." He pushed hard against it and I thought the lock was going to snap.

"Okay. Okay. Step back and wait a second." I unlatched it. When I slid the garage door open, I saw anger in his eyes.

"What?" I remarked. Boy, he was actually pissed.

"You of all people should know that that's not cool."

And all of a sudden, it dawned on me how right he was. I'd gotten locked in the garage more than once back when I was a little kid, and the last time I did, it took a couple of hours for someone to find me. It happened to be Will. By that time I was so distraught, I thought the Rapture had occurred and I'd got left behind. I shivered at the memory.

See, there were these movies some friends of ours had been into when I was little, about getting left behind after the Second Coming, and then the Antichrist showed up and everything went to hell, Christopher Walken style. Freaked me out so bad I had nightmares for days and prayed the sinner's prayer every night for the next two years. So, when I got locked in the garage after falling asleep there one day, I was understandably distraught. My brother and Amber had just laughed at me.

"You're right," I said and hugged him. "I should know better." I looked into his eyes and apologized. "Forgive me?"

He nodded. "Of course I forgive you."

People don't apologize enough anymore. Instead, they say something like "I'm sorry," or even worse, "my bad." But forgiveness? Only seemed to happen in certain circles and *I'm sorry* can mean so many different things including *sucks to be you.*

Coming home was hard. It reminded me of all the things I'd done that I was ashamed of. So why was I back here?

Will said, "C'mon. Let's see the rest of the house." He pulled me close and sniffed my hair as we walked toward the back door past the fruitless Mulberry tree that our family had to trim as a ritual every Thanksgiving. I looked up into the newly sprouting branches.

"You know, when I was younger, we had to cut this damn thing back every Turkey-Day. I spent hours here on the ground, waiting for the branches that fell. Amber would drag them over and I would cut them up into manageable pieces that we'd tie with string and when the bundle got large enough, we'd tie it all up and drag it out back to be hauled away on trash day. I always envied my brother Adam, who got to be up in the tree running the chainsaw."

Will laughed. "Well, then. Next Thanksgiving, you can be chainsaw-girl and I'll handle the ground work."

"Aren't you ever afraid you're going to fall?"

"Naw. We strap ourselves in with harnesses nowadays. Too much liability with insurance if we didn't." He opened the swinging door to the back porch where the washer and dryer still sat.

I ran my hands over the cream-colored appliances and experienced a sense of déjà vu all over again.

"I think that's the same washer and dryer your mom used when you guys lived here," Will said.

"How do you know?"

"They came with the house."

I looked closer at them.

"I've replaced a lot of the parts over the years, but they're still the same housings."

"You're so – handy!"

He laughed. "That's me. Jack of all trades, master of none."

"One or two, I bet."

He blushed. I liked that.

Mrs. Stenfield puttered in the kitchen like my mom used to do, rinsing dishes and putting them in the dishwasher as we entered the house. The squared white linoleum floor and the sunny-yellow kitchen were almost like I remembered. Only the trim was different and the countertops had been updated with colored tile and the stove was a new glass-top electric instead of the gas that we'd had years before. Nothing fancy, but I didn't care.

My old house. My old home, now Will's and his mother's. Wow. I remembered his dad and mom had gotten divorced, and that made it seem a little less idyllic, but still, there was this…glow.

A tray with a pitcher of lemonade sat on the sunny kitchen table and Will poured us each a glass.

"Wow. I haven't had real lemonade in forever."

"It's just from frozen, Ash." Will laughed. "Not like your mom used to make off those lemons you and Amber brought home."

"Oh, you remember that?"

"Like it was yesterday."

"I'm glad you like it," Mrs. Stenfield said. "Well, I'll just leave you two alone for a bit. I'm headed downtown to meet Joanne at the White Rabbit. Do you need anything while I'm out?"

"No thanks, Mom." He rose and gave her a quick hug. "I've got everything I need right here."

I thought I was going to die. Alone with Will Stenfield, and with his mother's blessing! In high school, I was always considered the wild one of the "terrible twins" and now I was being left all alone with a man, unchaperoned! What was this world coming to? Of course, objectively I knew we were both in our twenties now, but parents always seem frozen in time, at least in their kids' minds.

"See you later, Ashlee?" Mrs. Stenfield said.

"Um, yeah, sure," I stammered.

"Stay out of the cookie jar, Will." She slapped his hand as he reached for the lid of the Winnie-the-Pooh honeypot on the counter. He cradled his hand in mock injury, but she had looked at me when she said it.

Now I really thought I was going to die. What did she think, I'd jump her baby boy's bones on the sofa while she ate dinner with a friend?

Hm. Not a completely unattractive idea. She breezed out of the house without a word. Will held out the honeypot to me and I grinned.

"No thanks," I said. "I'm watching my figure."

"So am I." His eyes roved me up and down. It felt good, and I loved his laugh.

On impulse I got up and opened the door to the basement and went down. It seemed they'd turned it into some kind of artsy rumpus room.

"Well, this is cozy," I said, as he came up behind me and wrapped his arms around my waist. That was getting to be a habit.

"Yeah it is," Will said, and I elbowed him gently in the gut.

"I was talking about the basement, nerdling." The tiny space contained a La-Z-Boy, a reading lamp, a few shelves of model cars and airplanes and a mysterious work in progress. I walked over to the easel and lifted the tarp from off the canvas that was sitting there.

"Your mom's?" I asked, as I viewed the Italian landscape on it.

"Actually, it's mine," he said, and he blushed.

I turned back to the picture. "It's good. Your perspective is off a bit, here and here. But overall, it has nice composition and your color palette is very Tuscany."

"I didn't ask for a review, but thanks anyway."

Now it was my turn to blush. "Sorry. Force of habit. Travel writer, critic. Goes with the territory." I bit my lip. In my job I was used to being free with my judgments and opinions of the world and sometimes it was hard to turn it off.

"That's okay. I may not always like it, Ash. Like what you have to say. But at least I know where you stand."

"That's rare." I blew a strand of hair out of my eyes. "Most people aren't so appreciative and just think I'm a bitch."

"I'm not most people."

I turned to look at him. Really look at him. He'd grown up since I'd been away and I said so.

"Naw." He stuck his tongue out at me. "I'm still the same old guy. Lucky in life, unlucky in love."

"Well, at least you've got part of the equation." I touched a finger to the painting. It came away tacky, leaving a fingerprint.

"Oh no, Will. I thought it was dry."

He laughed and dragged me over to the sink.

"Don't worry about it." He took a rag, dabbed a little thinner on it and proceeded to wash my finger.

Something inside me stirred and I felt lightheaded again. "Must be the fumes," I whispered. But when he turned me in his arms, my knees wobbled as he pressed his body up against mine.

"I've missed you, Ash." His voice came out low and purr-fect and he leaned his mouth over mine and caught my lips with his own. Warm. Wet. Probing. The tip of his tongue flicked against mine and my breath came out panting. There was a stirring in my belly as I felt him press against my hips.

"Too fast," I said and pushed him away. "Sorry." My head swam and I forced myself up the stairs and out of his reach.

Yeah, I know I wanted him, but thinking about something and then actually doing it are two different things.

Once I was back in the kitchen I relaxed. "You know, when we were kids, we used to have Halloween parties down there. Used blankets to create walkways and strung stringy stuff up for cobwebs, and made things that jumped out to scare each other." I laughed as I ran water into the kitchen sink and splashed my face with it.

Will handed me a towel. "I know. I was one of your victims, remember?" He shut the basement door behind him.

"I remember. We used to blindfold you guys, then make you put your hands into bowls of cold spaghetti and gelatin mixed with fake fur. It was disgusting, but hilarious."

"To you, maybe." He smiled.

"And this was my brother's room," I said as I pushed open the east side door off the kitchen. Apparently Will had turned this into a widescreen TV room. "Adam used to lie on the floor below the turntable with his head between two speakers and blast Coldplay into his ears."

"*You know I love you so, you know I love you so.*" Will sang and strummed an air guitar as we both sounded out the bass line. "Duhdahduhdahduhdah. Duhdahduhdahduhdah. DUN. Dunt DUN. DUn. Dunt DUN!"

We just looked at each other and laughed.

"We are such geeks," I said. "Now, let me see *my* room." I turned and lurched out the other door, through the sun-porch, across the dining room, back into the kitchen and flung open the door off the west wall.

"You mean *my* room now," he said in my ear as he came up behind me.

I don't know why I did it, but all resistance crumbled and I turned and kissed him.

The next thing I knew we were on his bed and groping each other like two kids drowning. Will had his hand up my shirt and I grabbed his jean-clad buttocks as we kissed like starving children. When the phone began to ring, my addled mind suddenly hit clarity and I laughed.

"Aren't you going to get that?" I asked as he nibbled on my ear.

"Ignore it," he mumbled as he nipped my lobe and sent spasms of pleasure through me. His right hand had found the underwire to my bra and his thumb slid over my breast and I gasped.

"You like that?"

"Maybe too much." I was a good girl, after all. Oh, yeah. Aren't we all, in our own minds.

The phone continued to ring, then the machine picked up.

"You still have an answering machine?" I laughed. He kissed me stupid and I shut up.

"You have reached…" The rest of the message fuzzed in my brain as he pulled off my shirt and unsnapped my B-cup, his tongue taking the place of his fingers.

"God, Ashlee. I love you," he whispered into my navel as he slid down my body.

Shock woke me right up out of my lust-filled delirium. "WHAT?" I grabbed his shoulders and pushed back. "What did you say?" My left eyebrow went up and I stared him down like a wombat in a cage, whatever that means.

"Umm…Ashlee, I love you?" He said it as if I hadn't heard it the first time.

"Well, that's just great." I snapped my bra back together and threw my shirt on over my head. "Here we are getting along all fine and dandy and you have to go and drop the L-bomb."

"Ashlee, I've loved you since high school. I've never stopped loving you. I thought you knew that." He looked so forlorn, on his knees, on his bed, in *my* old room.

So, do you really wonder why I'm a mess?

"And how, pray tell, was I supposed to know that?" I asked. "I mean, animalistic teenage lust revisited, I get that! But *love*? Will, you don't even know me anymore."

"I know you."

"Well, maybe I don't."

"You know me."

"I didn't mean – never mind." I growled, "Men are so exasperating!"

"What?"

"You all just think you can cat around until the day you decide it's time to grow up and settle down. Well, I don't want to!"

"I didn't cat around, and I've always wanted to settle down. Ashlee, I'm the same guy."

"Yeah, maybe too damned much the same. Look at it from my perspective. You're a guy who lives with his mom and sleeps in my old room!"

"I thought it would be romantic."

"Argh!" I screamed and I marched out of the house with my buttons all askew.

"Ashlee, where are you going?" he called from the porch as I headed down the dilapidated block into the evening's slanting light.

"Anywhere but here!"

"You know this isn't the best neighborhood to be walking around in," he yelled. "Let me at least take you home."

"I'd rather have a gang-bang with a bunch of Cholos," I yelled back, then looked around as a few faces peered out the windows at me. "Ha ha! Just kidding!" I sing-songed, but I decided that now was as good a time as any to get back to the jogging I'd missed while my ass was healing.

I ran.

I knew it was a mistake, but after the first stabbing pain and the endorphins kicked in I found myself reaching a good steady stride and forgetting about my injury. All I could think about was my breathing and keeping my bag from hitting me right on the wound as I slung it across my back. I cut through a couple of alleys and back onto the Boulevard and then slowed when I hit the tracks and passed into what I felt would be a safer neighborhood.

Night began to fall and soon I found myself walking alone with a designer handbag and a serious ache in my behind, in the dark next to Piccadilly Park. Don't ask me why they called it that. If you ask me, if they wanted a classic London reference they should have called it Hyde Park for its high crime rate.

"Hey! I like your bag," a voice called out behind me.

"Why don't you hand it over," another voice beside me said.

"If you do, maybe we'll let you walk away and keep that pretty face of yours."

My heart skipped a beat and I looked up and around, realizing that in my self-righteous anger, I'd walked right into a herd of biker chicks or something. At least, they had a lot of leather and piercings and ink.

"You know, my twin sister's a lesbian," I said, trying to distract them as I slid away from the phalanx they were creating around me.

"Hey, Arnott. I think she just called you a lesbian," one of the hard-faced girls spoke up.

"No, she didn't. She said your sister is a lesbian," said another.

"I already know that. Although what that has to do with giving me her bag, I got no clue," the more well-spoken leader said. "So, why don't you just hand me that purse and we can all go on our merry way?" The circle began to close.

Oh no, this was not going to happen. I looked at the sky and thought about trying to shift. If the moon was up at all I might be able to induce the change, though most times I no more wanted it than the average girl craved a visit from Aunt Rosie Flow.

"And why don't you take your big old ass…" I began, but didn't get any further, as suddenly the sound of a Chevy V-8 roared up behind me and Will threw open the door, scattering the crowd.

"Get in, Ash," Will yelled and he grabbed for me as I leaped into the truck.

"Ow. Ow. Ow." I yelped as my butt slid across the seat and I could feel skin and stitches tear. "Get me to a hospital."

"I'll do better than that." He said something vulgar. "I'm taking you to my sister." His hands gripped the wheel and he put the pedal to the metal.

Will's big sister Samantha "Sam" Stenfield was a nurse practitioner at Knightsbridge Hospital and worked the swing shift. Used to work graveyard, but when she got the chance she changed to evenings. Too many crazies on nights, she'd said. About ten years older than Will and me, but she looked at least a decade beyond that. I guess that's what the ER will do to you, but she had a good bedside manner and didn't even blink when Will rushed me over.

"Oh, hi, Ashlee. Nice to see you again," she said matter-of-factly. "Strip and let's see what we've got."

"Get him out of here first," I told her.

"Will." She gave him that older-sister-to-younger-brother look and he retreated behind the curtain she'd pulled in front of his face.

I dropped trou and laid face down on the examination bed. I was so humiliated.

"So, you want to tell me what happened?"

"Not really," I said. "Oh, you mean with my bullet wound. I mean, it was a staph infection. Hunting. A ricochet. The bullet wound got infected," I amended.

She scowled. "Doctors these days. Better safe than sorry, they say. So let's just get a surgeon in for a consult, they say. And surgeons love to cut stuff anyway. When you got a hammer, everything looks like a goddamn nail."

I winced and then bit my lip as Will's sister went on her rant. I was so not going to complain. It was my fault anyway I was in this predicament, I figured. I may be from here, but it wasn't my Knightsbridge anymore.

"Well, you may have set yourself back a few days, but I've cleaned the wound and used a little skin seal instead of stitches. What do they got you doin' for wound care?"

"Oh, you know. Bleach baths and fresh dressing."

"Well. Keep it up. Looks like you've got a week or so to go, then you're out of the woods, but I'd continue the bleach baths until the wound is totally closed. Make sure that all the bacteria stays dead."

"Can I come in now?" Will asked.

"No," I warned him.

"Hey Will. Give me your sweatshirt," Sam called, and he handed it to her through the gap. She turned it inside out as it still had a few grass stains.

"Here. Step into this and wrap it around your waist. I'll put your sweat pants in a bag. There's bloodstains on them," she said. "And Will, you take her straight home, you hear? Are you good on pain medication?"

I nodded. "I'm good."

"Cool." She let me get quasi-presentable before she pulled the curtain open and let in her brother.

"Good seeing you again, Ash. Take care of yourself," she said, as if I came in every Friday. Hadn't seen me in years.

Nurses. Can't faze 'em.

I let Will bundle me off to the truck and back to Amber's doorstep. "I'll call you tomorrow. See how you're doing," he promised. Then he drove away.

I kind of hoped he would and I kind of hoped he wouldn't. I sighed as I let myself in the door and slipped upstairs while the rest of the house slept. I was not going to tell this to my sister. No way, no how, I thought as I brushed my teeth and went straight to bed.

7

Will called several times the next day but I didn't answer. I hadn't given him my cell phone number, so he was stuck leaving messages on the landline until my sister got sick of it and cornered me.

"Ashlee. Why haven't you called Will back?"

"I dunno," I mumbled. I so did not want to get into this with my sister.

"You know, you can't run away from all of your problems," she said. "Whatever it is, you're going to have to face it sooner or later. Preferably sooner, 'cause I'm getting sick of making excuses for you."

"I never asked you to make excuses for me." I rounded on her. "So, why don't you mind your own damn business?" Okay, I must be going crazy, because you do not take that tone with Amber.

"As long as you're under my roof, it IS my damn business," she said. "You know, sometimes you are so ungrateful." She was right, but I was mad, and when I had my mad on, my stupid mouth got the best of me.

"Fine. I'm an ungrateful bitch. You hate me. This town hates me and now, probably Will hates me too!" I wailed and I broke down and began to cry.

My sister stared at me like I'd grown another head. I never cried. I was the tomboy. I was the scrapper. I was... I was, I was a big ol' mess.

Amber sat down on the edge of the bed and looked at me with concern. JR and Elle both poked their heads into the room and she waved them away.

"So...do you want to talk about it?"

"Do I look like I want to talk about it?" I sobbed.

Amber patted my foot through the down comforter. She was not making this easy on me.

"I'll tell you about it later," I promised. "Right now, I'd just like to sleep a little."

Amber looked at me with kindness and brushed my hair from off my face. Then, she kissed my forehead like Mom used to do and I about lost it. That is, until she said, "Tomorrow, we'll go get mani-pedis. Just the two of us."

As if that would make it all better. I laughed between sobs as she shut the door.

I was such a schizoid.

"Ashlee Marie Scott!" Mom's voice came out of the woodwork and her disembodied head floated into the room.

Oh, dear mother of God, I thought. Now I'd done it. It wasn't enough to be humiliated and have a nervous breakdown in front of my identical twin, but now Mother had to get involved and I knew that she wasn't going to be put off so easily.

"Stop that sniveling at once," my dead mother said as she halfway materialized into the room.

I say halfway, because the lower half of her body seemed to be having trouble catching up to the rest and was banging its shins against the door. She whistled and her stocking feet finally found their home. "There. That's better. Now what's this all about, young lady?" she intoned and sat down into the bed.

I would have said "on the bed" but it seemed like holding a visual pattern of molecules against the solidity of the real world was a process she hadn't fully mastered.

I opened my mouth, but before I spoke, she plucked the thought from my mind.

"So, Will's in love with you."

I growled, "I really hate it when you do that."

Mom ignored my outburst. "So, why does that bother you?" she asked.

I knew she was referring to Will, but I deliberately called up a brick wall in my head and said, "Because my thoughts should be my own and I'd like to think that there's such a thing as respecting my privacy." If I wouldn't let her read my diary when she was alive, I was sure as hell not going to give her the opportunity to read my mind after she was dead.

"Talk to me, Ashlee," she said. "You know I'm not very good at this."

"Yeah, well that makes two of us."

"So, why does Will loving you bother you so?" she badgered me.

I sighed and threw the covers over my head. "Because I don't even know how I feel! How can he say he still loves me after how many years has it been now?"

"I don't know how to answer that, Ash. Time doesn't work the same for me as it does for you."

"What does that mean?" I asked, suddenly curious. I was always trying to trick Mother into telling me what's on the other side, but she usually saw through my subterfuges.

"Hmm. How can I say it?" Her eyes closed and her head got denser, and the rest of her tea-length gown went diaphanous as if all her energy was centered in her noggin as she thought long and hard about what she could or would say.

"I know." She opened her eyes and the color washed out of her cranium and she got all ghostly again. "See. Time is a continuum, a mental construct created for physical bodies. As I no longer have the same type of physical body that you do and am not bound by time, I see you as a complete entity. You are all ages at once to me. Maybe Will sees you the same way. You're still the girl he fell in love with in high school, and even more so now."

"But people change," I told her.

"Not as much as you would think."

"I'm not sure if that makes me feel bad or good."

"Then don't let it make you feel either," she said. "Feel what *you* decide to feel. Will loves the Ashlee Scott you were and there's something in him, that metaphysical something that is timeless, which loves the Ashlee that you are today."

"But I'm a werewolf, Mother," I let out in exasperation.

"Only temporarily, dear."

"You mean there's a cure?" I said, sitting up so quickly I got a little dizzy from the meds.

"No, I mean, temporarily the rest of your life."

"Oh." What a letdown.

I heard a scratching at the door. Mom turned to look. "That would be Spanky," I said.

"I know that." Mother waved her hand and the door cracked open to let him in. The dog sat at the foot of the bed, looked up at her, and cocked his head.

"He can see you, can't he?" I said, amazed. Even Amber couldn't see our mother.

Mom looked at me before I could get my mental shield up, and we both said what I was thinking. "Must be a dog thing." We laughed as Spanky pawed at the bed. I lifted him up and he curled into my arms and suddenly I got really, really tired.

"Can we talk later?" I asked, and Mother nodded. Spanky and I drifted off to sleep as she floated slowly away.

8

"Damn it! Damn it! Damn it! Damn it! DAMN IT!" I pounded on the keyboard in frustration.

"Hey! Hey! HEY! HEY!" My sister called from the living room as I swore at my outdated computer with the sticking H key. "I hope that's your own laptop you're abusing and not mine this time!"

"Yes, it's mine. And my scumbag of an editor has reassigned my upcoming trip to Cancun. He's giving it to one of his golfing buddies who's been twisting his arm to do the western Caribbean. Listen to this. 'Considering your current physical challenges, we're concerned about your ability to fulfill your obligations at this time.' That shithead word pimp."

"Ashlee. Language," my sister complained as she passed my doorway putting fresh linens into the guest bathroom.

"Is JR home?"

"It doesn't matter if J.R.'s home or not. We don't talk that way in this house," she said, obviously forgetting the F-bombs she had dropped the other night in between Cosmos with

Sheri and Renee. My sister has an inflated sense of propriety until she's had a few and then she can swear like a sailor.

"Sorry. But, if it wasn't for me, he wouldn't even have that assignment. I brought that contact with me and now he's going to try to pull it right out from under my bullet-ridden ass! I don't think so!" I shot off an email to my contact in Cancun. "Let's see him try to fu-, I mean, screw with me," I snarled.

"You're such a lady, Ash," my sister remarked. "And could you please remember to rinse and wipe the tub after you bathe. We have hard water here and it's not easy to get the stains out once they've set in."

"I thought I did," I said, looking up at my perky-nosed sis from where I lay.

She gave me a look that said she didn't believe me.

"Obviously not well enough," I said as she went back down the hall and into her bedroom. "You know, the way you run this house, I'm surprised you don't ask for military corners on all the beds," I muttered.

"I heard that!" Her voice floated back toward me.

"Bite me."

"I heard that, too!"

"Love you."

This time, nothing. Yeah, sure. See? Selective hearing.

I got up and ran myself a bleach bath, then peeled out of my clothes and stared at myself in the mirror. Like my sister I bordered on petite, but I was much more athletic and she hung somewhere around model thin. I'd gotten soft not being able to work out and I was determined that within the next week, I was going to actively pursue some kind of toning regimen.

I turned around and tore off the bandage, wincing as the tape peeled another layer of skin. The wound, which started larger than an everlasting gobstopper, had finally shrunk to the size of a quarter and filled in quite nicely. There was still discoloration and would probably be a slight scar, but surprisingly, it wouldn't be unsightly. Not that anyone that mattered had seen my ass lately.

Which made me think about Will.

I stepped into the bath and settled in, taking the latest Nora Roberts with me. I loved to read in the tub and since baths instead of showers were now a regular part of my routine, it gave me time to catch up.

I had just cracked the spine when Mother materialized in the toilet. Again, I would say "on the toilet," but as usual, her aim just wasn't that good.

"Mother!" I hissed. "What are you doing here?"

"Oh, I just thought I'd check in and see how you're doing." She had that gleam in her eye that told me she was up to something.

There came a scratching and whining at the door and I looked at her, exasperated. "How come he always knows you're here?" I asked.

"Animals are more sensitive to energies and emotion than we give them credit for," she replied. "Or it could be the dog thing again."

Hmph. I laughed. Maybe I should get my own miniature Schnauzer. Use him as an early warning system. *Warning. Dead Mother Approaching.*

"So, Mommy dearest, tell me again how I managed to get lycanthropy and Amber only got allergies?" I settled back for a bath-time story.

"Once upon a time, your great, great, great, great, great, great grandmother Louisa Scott was visiting relatives in Scotland," Mom began.

"Hence, the Scott in our name."

"Am I telling this or you?" She sank deeper into the porcelain bowl.

I bit my tongue and smiled as she continued with her obviously fractured fairy tale. Never tells it the same way twice, no matter how many times it's been. I keep hoping she'll slip and tell me something that sounds true, but hell, how would I know? Nah, I'd know. I'd feel it, right?

That's what I keep hoping.

Mom continued, "The story goes that she was out picking wolfsbane and moonflowers in a fairy circle one starlit night in the Highlands when Titania took umbrage and caused her to fall into a deep sleep. While asleep, Titania enchanted a passing wolf into the circle and turned it into a man, who lay with Louise and on that night she conceived. Upon returning to America, much to her husband's delight, who thought that they couldn't have children, she gave birth to twin girls, the first of many sets down through the generations. One twin is always a lupine, the other, an oracle of some kind: a seer or a prophetess. I don't know what happened this time around to your sister, except for the nightmares and migraines, and the fact that she always seems to win when they go to Vegas, and she has a keen eye for fashion trends...anyway.

You're the one with the more demonstrable powers. Which reminds me of the reason I'm here." She pointed at the ceiling. "Full moon's coming up soon and you're going to have to make a shift."

"I know I have to, but I don't wanna," I whined. "It's such a pain in the ass. Hurts like a son of a bitch. And it's totally disgusting."

"Yes, well. Either you choose the time and the place, or the change will choose it for you. And you know what happened the last time you let that happen."

"I know. I know. I went through a whole herd of sheep before I tired out and changed back. Thank God I didn't hurt anyone. The only good thing about the shift is that I seem to lose most of my body fat when I turn back."

"It's a metabolism thing," my mother said. "And you should be grateful. Some women would kill to have your bone structure." She floated over to caress my face with icy digits.

"So, how many days have I got?" I asked, as if I didn't know. Believe me, I always knew. I sighed and tapped the hot water faucet with my foot to heat up the by-now-lukewarm bath.

"Ten days before the next cycle," my mother said.

"Bummer," I mumbled.

"Oops, gotta run." She apologized and condensed to a small drop of water that plinked into the bowl.

"Aunt Ash?" came J.R.'s voice through the door. "Who are you talking to?"

I cringed. Great. Now even my nephew thinks I'm a freak.

"No one, honey. Just to myself. Do you need something?" I asked sweetly, testing the air.

"No. I was passing by and Spanky was sitting here listening to you talk and I thought it was really weird. I almost thought there was somebody else in there with you. Anyways, I need to brush my teeth and my toothbrush is in there."

"Nope. Nobody but me, myself and I. I'll be out in a sec." I said and stood up, dried off and let the kid have his space, retiring to my room and puttering on my laptop while I thought.

Ten days. Cripes. First the dog, now the kid. And a full moon coming up. I really needed to figure out how I should handle the next change. I supposed I could just do what I used to when I lived in town, which was to leave the basement window unlatched and set so I could enter in whatever form I happened to be at the time.

Only this house had no basement, unlike the one I'd grown up in. You know, the one where Will was now. The one where, if I could just get my head screwed on straight, I could probably stay over and do the same thing. Only, how was I supposed to sneak out of Will's bed without him noticing?

I thought about drugging him. Hey, it was a plan, but there had to be a better way. Maybe I should just go home to my place in the City and take my usual laps around Golden Gate Park.

I was still thinking about this when my email beeped, and I brought it up without even reading the subject line.

Oh, great. Another one.

TO WHOM IT MAY CONCERN:

I AM STILL WARNING YOU ABOUT WHAT MY EMPLOYER WANTS TO DO TO YOU FOR SOME REASON. LIKE I SAID BEFORE I DO NOT BELIEVE YOU ARE WHAT IS SAID ABOUT YOU BUT I HAVE NO CHOICE IN THE MATTER SO JUST BEWARE. THERE IS CERTAINLY A CONSPIRACY SURROUNDING THIS SO TRUST NO ONE NOT EVEN THOSE CLOSEST TO YOU AND DO NOT DO WHAT ANYONE WANTS EVEN IF THEY WANT YOU TO.

SINCERELY,

A FRIEND

I felt like I was back in first-year creative writing class, willing to drive icepicks into my eyeballs rather than suffer through another round of insufferably sophomoric prose. Yeah, I know here in my diary I take liberties with the language but holy freaking Grammar Girl, what are they teaching kids these days in English class?

Then I forced myself to focus on the meaning and ignore the execrable delivery.

It seemed as if he, if it was a he, was trying to give me a friendly warning that someone was trying to force him to do something to me, along with the implication that someone close to me was not to be trusted.

Master of the obvious, right? But I was no detective, and besides, nothing other than these emails themselves had appeared to threaten me since I had returned to

Knightsbridge. Also, there was a kind of lunatic, conspire-acy-nut quality to the messages that made me think the sender wasn't really all there.

So.

I had to figure out whether or not to tell anyone. After a moment's thought, I moved the email to my saved file and decided not to say anything. It would just get everyone spun up again and worried about nothing. I would just have to keep my eyes open and stay away from animal control officers, biker chicks, local hunters or old flames trying to entice me to crawl back into the cozy shell of my former life.

9

Busted. I was busted.

The next morning when I opened the front door, I ran into Will Stenfield camped out on the porch, and he wouldn't leave until I talked to him. I guess I could have slammed the door and not come out, or tried to run out the back, but…he was right, in a John Cusack, *Say Anything* sort of way. I had to deal with him sometime.

"Hi," he said tentatively, waving a sack of sweet-smelling custard-filled chocolate donuts like a peace offering.

"Hi," I replied, not really sure how to feel about anything at this point, but I decided I was not about to pass up a mouthful of Bavarian crème.

"Figured since you weren't returning my calls, I'd need something to get me in the door."

"Well, since you're here, you might as well come all the way in," I told him, motioning from the foyer.

"Where's the rest of the gang?"

"Hell if I know." I went to the fridge. "Milk? Amber only buys the nonfat crap."

"That's okay." He whisked out a couple cartons from the bag he was carrying. "I know how you like whole milk, so I brought some."

"Humph," I said skeptically. "I don't know if that screams stalker or sweet." But inside, I was getting all gooey again, like the donut. I shook it off. "Let's go sit outside on the patio."

Will followed me and Spanky followed him, sniffing.

Amber and Elle had the best backyard. An awning-covered patio with a glass table that seated six comfortably, eight in a pinch, and a black-bottomed swimming pool with an attached hot tub that spilled water over the beveled edge in sheeted columns at just the right height to dip your head under – oh, and at least four chaise lounges for sunning, which I had yet to use. The sound of the water soothed me, and we sat in silence as we ate. The not speaking was kind of nice, until it got awkward.

"So, are we going to talk about it?" Will asked.

"Talk about what?" I replied, dreading the answer. He was going for the RDT, the Relationship Defining Talk, and I had no idea what I was going to tell him.

Sitting there staring at me, all muscly and stuff.

"Fine. Let's talk about it," I finally said.

"I said I loved you."

"I heard you."

"So, how do you feel about me?"

"God, Will. I don't know!" I sat back, exasperated.

"Ouch."

"Give me a minute. I'm not good at this stuff." Now where had I heard that before? "And why is I don't know so bad? It just means I don't know."

"Okay. Pretend you're talking to someone else. Pretend I'm just a sounding board."

"A sounding board. What is a sounding board anyway? Who ever saw one? Is that from when they used to make violins by hand or something?"

"They still make violins by hand, Ash. Pretend I'm an objective third party, who doesn't have anything at stake. What would you say to him? If I were Amber, what would you say to her?"

"Well, first she'd ask me, 'So, Ashlee, how do you feel?'" I said, getting into character. "And I'd say, 'I don't know, Amber. I mean, I like him. I care about him.'"

"But..." Will prompted.

"Butt?" I looked over my shoulder at my ass, drawing a strained laugh from Will. I know, in the middle of an RDT, right? Humor as a defense, that's all. "Not but..." I went on. "*And*...and, and the part of me that knew you back in high school and loved you then, loves you now."

Will moved toward me.

"But I'm not that girl anymore. And you can't try to make me be."

"So, let me get to know the new Ashlee."

"The new Ashlee's a bit more complicated than the old one," I said as I picked Spanky up and cuddled him to my chest while he licked up the crumbs off the tinted table. I think I figured while I held Spanky, Will couldn't hold me.

"Of course. We're both older and wiser. And I like complicated, sometimes."

"Not this kind of complicated you don't."

"How do you know if you don't give me a chance?"

I sighed. "You have a chance."

That brightened him up. "So," he said to me.

"So," I said right back at him.

"So, you've never been what you'd call low maintenance."

"You must be thinking of Amber, 'cause in comparison..."

"I'm not talking about Amber. I'm talking about you. You've got layers, Ash. You've always had them. Only before the..." He stuttered off.

"Before the *incident*."

"Before the *incident*, you were willing to talk to me about them."

"Yeah, well. I've got trust issues."

"We've all got trust issues, Ash," he said. "I keep wondering if it's me you don't trust, or if you just don't trust yourself."

My ego defenses went up. "What are you, my shrink?" I put Spanky down on the ground and got up to pace. *He's getting too close*, a voice in my head started singing. I began walking the edge of the pool, circling it and coming back again.

Will stood and stopped me. "Ashlee. What are you afraid of?" He held my shoulders and bent his knees to look square into my eyes.

Trapped.

"I'd never knowingly do anything to hurt you," he said.

I shrugged him off and collected the trash from the table. "Yes, well, it's the unknowingly hurting that I'm worried about."

"Life is a risk, Ashlee. Nothing ventured, nothing gained."

"No pain, no gain, right, Will?"

"Not the same. Like I said, I won't hurt you Ash. At least not intentionally. I love you."

"I wish I could say the same thing," I muttered, not sure whether I was talking about loving myself or him.

"Ashlee. Stop it." He took the bag of garbage from my hands. "Just tell me, whatever you need to say. I can take it."

My palms began to itch. "God, Will! I'm a bitch. I'm sarcastic, obnoxious, rude and opinionated. I don't look at the bright side and clouds don't have a silver lining. I walk into a room full of people and can't help but wonder what their angles are. That's why I'm a writer. That way I can put everything that I'm thinking into a palatable form, and when I don't get it right, I have an editor who does it for me."

"And…" He put his hands on my shoulders again, and looked me in the eyes.

"You can't love me!" I pushed him away.

"Why not?" Whipping me back around to face him, his voice rose, not caring if the neighbors heard.

"Because, I don't even love myself!" I cried and collapsed into his arms.

"Then that's where we'll start." Will held me and rocked me and let me cry it all out.

10

For the next few days, Will treated me like a queen. I was still pretty wiped, so it was kind of nice being waited on hand and foot, much to Amber's dismay. I found that out when I overheard her talking to our father on the phone one day when she thought I was asleep.

"But Dad," I heard her say. "She needs to get over herself and make a move. *Do* something," she said. "I know we're twins, but where does my responsibility end and hers begin? Well. Yes, she's contributing to the household. She wrote me a check just the other day, but I haven't cashed it...I don't know. It just doesn't feel right. Fine. I'll cash it. But I don't know how much more of this I can take. I mean, Ashlee is one thing, but having Will over here all the time is seriously putting a damper on my own relationship. I mean, I haven't had a guy in the house this much besides JR, since I lived with his father. I know. I don't mean to dump this on you, but can't you take her for awhile? Either that or Elle and I are going to have to go away for the weekend just to get some time to ourselves. And that's not fair, is it?"

I decided that I felt guilty enough as it was without adding eavesdropping to the list of my sins, so I slipped out to the back yard to have a smoke and think. That was where Will found me, lost in thought when he stuck his head over the fence.

"Hey Spongebob."

"Hey Patrick," I popped right back at him, just like we were back in grade school.

"Whatcha thinkin'?"

"Thinkin' about blowin' this popsicle shop."

"Yeah? Where to?"

"Home."

"Home?" he said. "Like Frisco?"

"Yeah," I said. "Home, like San Fran. The City. The Ice Cube by the Bay. The Big Queasy. Don't call it Frisco."

"Come here and help me over." He pushed himself up from the ground on the other side and sort of fell on me as he dangled by his hands.

"You're not as young as you used to be, sport," I said. "Next time you might want to try the gate."

"Hey Ash! Can you tell your boyfriend that we do have gates? Climbing over the fence lowers the property values," my sister called from where she stood in the upstairs window.

"See?" I shot Amber the finger, but thankfully she wasn't looking. "Seriously, Will, I need to get out of Amber's hair," I sighed. "I overheard her talking to Dad today and she actually asked if I could go stay with him and my stepmother."

"Come stay with me," he said.

"Yeah, right," I said. "Your mother would just love that."

"Actually, she would, I think." Will grinned. "Sam works so much and Mom's been feeling deprived. You can be a new daughter figure. And we've got the spare bedroom."

Was I really thinking about doing this? I didn't want to leave, but it sounded like I was becoming a burr under Amber's saddle and I wasn't ready to go back to my lonely loft in the City.

"Say yes, Ash," Will said.

"Say yes, Ash," I heard my sister whisper from where she stood in the bedroom overlooking us on the ground floor.

"Say yes, Ashlee." My mother's voice bubbled up from where she lay at the bottom of the pool.

"Fine. Yes," I said, exasperated. I knew when I was outnumbered. With that, I went upstairs to pack.

"Is there anything I can get for you? Here, let me help you do that," my sister offered, then had my folded laundry tucked into my suitcase and my bag in my hand before you could say Versace. "Now, don't worry about a thing. I'll come visit at least..." She mouthed *four, three* "...no, *twice* a week and you are always welcome for dinner, if you call ahead of time. Bye!" she said as she pushed me out the door and into Will's waiting arms.

We looked at each other and had to shake our heads and laugh. God I loved and sometimes hated my sister. But isn't that the way it always is with family?

11

Will put me in my brother Adam's old room and I had flashbacks of him there – his writing table, his old springy bed that came with the house, his D&D stuff. He'd been such a geek back then, before he buffed up. Now he was all into medieval reenactments, playing knight-errant, wearing real armor and swinging swords. I mean, a grown man, playing King Arthur or something. Real men should take out their aggressions on mature, adult things like football or WWF, right?

If you don't get the irony, try harder.

Will brought my suitcases in and as I began to hang up my clothes in the empty half of the closet, his mother came in to put fresh linens on the bed.

I felt a catch in my throat and choked back a sob.

Mrs. Stenfield looked at me with concern.

"I'm sorry," I said and sat down on the bed with a slight butt-wince. "It's just…" Suddenly the waterworks poured forth. The emotional rollercoaster of what I called PCS, Pre-Change Syndrome, was starting to get me, which really sucked, because it was exactly fourteen days off of my PMS, which meant every damned lunar month I got twice as much insanity as normal women.

And you wonder why I'm a mess?

Will's mother sat on the bed and held me and rocked me as I cried out my sorrow. All of my longing for family. All of my hunger for belonging. All of the heartache from not being able to feel my mother's arms around me came rushing back, here in this place. In my home that wasn't my home anymore, but still felt like it.

"You were very young when your mom died, weren't you?" she said.

How did mothers know just what to say?

"We were eleven," I said, my nose running as I blew long and hard into the tissues she pulled from her pocket. See, I thought. Some women were just born to be mothers. I began to cry even harder. "I forgot how much I missed her," I sobbed, darting glances around the room to see if Mother was going to materialize. I didn't want to seem ungrateful, seeing as how I could still at least talk to her, but I hadn't realized just how much I missed her presence. The softness of her arms around me, the smell of her hair.

Mrs. Stenfield just stroked my hair and held me, waving Will away when he passed by the doorway.

When I came back to myself, I felt awkward and unkempt.

"Why don't I just leave you alone for now?" she said, the unspoken "while you pull yourself together" hanging in the air between us.

I nodded and sniffled as she shut the door behind her and left me alone. I could hear murmuring in the dining room, then the sound of the evening news on television drifting from the living area. With the sounds of normalcy gathered about me, I curled up into a ball on the bed and went to sleep.

I woke up later, in the middle of the night. The clock read 2:23 a.m., and I got the impression I had heard something outside. After looking though the windows and seeing nothing, I went into the kitchen to the back door, carefully turning the deadbolt so it wouldn't make a sound, and left it open. I stood on the screened-in back porch next to the old washer and dryer and stared at the moonlit scene.

Inhaling deeply, I smelled the half-familiar smells of my childhood – wisteria going dormant, wild onions that infested the back lawn, Mexican food from one of the neighbors, damp old rusting steel screens that hadn't yet been replaced with aluminum.

I looked up at *la Luna* hanging there in the sky and felt the tug, the pull, the urge to get naked and change and run free through the backyards like I used to do. I realized I could do the basement window trick, do it tonight, but I had never changed this early. A day before, sure, which hurt like a son-of-a bitch for some reason. Once I'd held it off until the night after, which was painful too, but I'd been aboard a cruise ship that got stranded at sea an extra forty-eight hours and didn't have anywhere to go. Could have locked myself in my cabin but that was its own kind of agony, all that energy bursting from me with nowhere to put it.

If I changed this early, would that mean I was done for this cycle? I really did not know for sure. What if it didn't really count? What if I ended up with some kind of extra bonus change, or what if it threw my cycle off and I have to start changing mid-moon? No, it was safer to just wait a while, do it when it was easiest and I was sure of the results.

Something moved off in the shadows by the fence where the gate to the next-door neighbors used to be. My eyes narrowed and I squinted,focusing on…what? Something small…a striped piece of fur. A cat. Just a cat, doing a bit of nocturnal hunting. I relaxed. See? Nothing to worry about.

I went back inside, locked the door, and settled back to sleep.

12

When I awoke, it was to the sound of a light tapping. Night still reigned and a soft light wove its way through the lace curtains on the windows. Will cracked the bedroom door and stuck his head in.

"Hey, Sleeping Beauty," he said and I rolled onto my back and stretched like a cat. He softly closed the door and knelt down at the edge of the bed and put his arms around me. I curled up against him, my face next to his. His essential maleness assaulted me and I sneezed.

"Ow, ow!" My butt protested the violent explosion.

"Bless you." He laughed.

I groaned, absolutely mortified. "Sorry."

Will chuckled as he grabbed a pillow and wiped his face with it. "What's a few germs among Germans?"

"I'm Scottish."

"I'm English. Who wants to revisit old feuds?"

"You know what I mean."

"Guess I didn't think how being back in this house might affect you," he apologized.

"No. It's not your fault." I paused, thinking. "It's actually really good for me," I said. "I need to face this.

Face my past. Battle my demons." I cleared my throat and inhaled his scent and it stuck in the core of my being.

"Yeah, well. Make sure that you at least leave me something to slay," he teased.

I pulled my head back to get a better look at him, his eyes glittering in the dark. "You know, that's probably one of the sweetest things any man has ever said to me."

He began to make another smart remark when I kissed him. Some men just need to learn to shut up and not ruin the moment. That's why God made women. To kiss them stupid, like I was doing right now.

When we came up for air, he said, "What was that for?"

"Just because," I said and rolled off the bed and onto my feet. "So, what's for breakfast? I'm starving." Nervous breakdowns do that to a girl. They make her incredibly lightheaded and voraciously hungry.

After we ate we decided to go for a drive and watch the sun rise over Knightsbridge. I settled against Will and enjoyed seeing more of the town I grew up in and how it had changed.

"You know, I never get to do this anymore," I told him.

"Yeah, I guess in the city you don't need a car."

"And people don't usually get in a car unless they're going somewhere."

"Guess there aren't many Sunday drivers in Fr-...San Fran." He smiled.

I laughed. "Probably not."

We drove through downtown Knightsbridge again and talked about how we used to cruise Main Street on the weekends. How the city council had threatened to prohibit cruising due to a few small skirmishes that had broken out one summer, until the kids had protested and a band of parents who remembered the glory days of their own youth formed a Main Street watch on weekends to prevent any future violence. What with that and the curfew it for minors at midnight, it appeared to be working.

We drove past our alma mater and I wondered what the kids that went there now were like. High school seemed like just yesterday, and yet, a lifetime ago.

I recalled how when we were younger, we would go swimming in the irrigation canals, even though we weren't supposed to. Later on they ended up fencing them off in the city limits. We talked about simpler times, and a simpler world, and how, even though Knightsbridge had changed a lot, it was still simple.

We held hands. Eventually we parked, and when we kissed, it was without intent. Will was being the perfect gentleman and it felt good to be with him, without the pressure of sex.

Okay, for me anyway. I wasn't thinking about how it might be for him, but like Amber says, sometimes I'm too focused on myself.

I didn't want to think about sex. I don't know how sex is for regular humans, but for a werewolf, it seemed to have extra pitfalls. Speaking of which, I looked out the windows and stared at the waxing moon, and my palms began to itch. MoonFall, the full moon, was in seven days and I'd have to find a way to disappear for the evening, so I could at least make the shift and be back by morning.

Contrary to popular belief werewolves, or lupines, retained most of their capacities for intelligence even in wolf form. When I'd had to go out at night in the City – pretty much anyone from the Bay Area meant San Francisco when they referred to "the City," – I usually hit Golden Gate Park where I could run free and get rid of the excess energy that came after the shift. I wondered where I could do the same around here anymore, what with all the growth. Just out into the hills and the Canyon, I guessed, away from the stupid suburban developments.

Yeah, it would be nice to go back to the Canyon…assuming I could face up to something I'd put off for a long time.

13

We woke the next morning to a call from my sister.

"Ashlee?" Amber's voice came out all echo-ey over the speakerphone. She sounded spooked and Amber was almost never afraid.

"Amber, what is it?" I asked as Will rolled off the bed, fully dressed but plenty rumpled. We'd fallen asleep side by side in the guest room, still in our clothes from the day before.

"Um, we found a coyote's head on the porch this morning."

"Oh my gosh. JR didn't see it, did he?" I asked. How horrible!

"No. Elle put it in a bag before he woke up. But there was a note stuck in its mouth."

"A note?" How strange. "I don't understand."

"The note was addressed to you, Ashlee." Amber's voice took on a tone that could only be disapproval, but for once I couldn't read her intent. "Elle took it all down to the police station. You might want to stop by this morning as they have a few questions to ask you."

"But – what did it say, Amber?"

"I don't know. Elle wouldn't let me read it. She said it's best if I don't worry about it. And then asked me to call. So I did…I'm scared, Ashlee. What is this? This is freaking me out."

"I'll handle it."

"You better."

I resolved to try, though my record with handling things was no better than fifty-fifty most days.

I showed up at the station with Will in tow, asking him to wait outside as Elle met me in the new Chief's office, which used to be hers before she became the city attorney. She handed me a plastic evidence bag with the note inside. It was written with black permanent ink, so even against the dried blood the words were evident.

It said, *I know what you are. I know what you did. Payback's a bitch and so am I.*

My stomach dropped inside me and I sank into a chair. A cup of water was shoved into my hand and I gulped it down. No natural wolves roamed California, but there were plenty of coyotes, the closest thing. This one had been killed as a message to me.

"We pulled your file, Ashlee," Chief Hernandez said in that brittle tone cops use when they are questioning someone they don't suspect, but want to. "You want to tell us what you think this is about?" Like every good cop, bad cop scenario, someone had to start and it looked like the chief was going on the offensive, giving Elle the conciliatory role.

"I – I have no idea," I told him, but I was a horrible liar and I think he knew it.

"Maybe you know something," Elle interjected. "You just think you don't."

"Now listen," Hernandez said. "You got to be straight with us. I've read your file, but I want to hear it from your point of view."

Now, before I write down what happened, let me assure you that what follows is the real story. The Knightsbridge police force got the same account, just without all the furry parts.

−14−

A crisp autumn morning dawned in Knightsbridge. The last of the rising fog was just burning off by the light of the amber sun peeking its way through the clouds and it cast a hazy glow over everything. The leaves had begun to turn and the smells of nature in repose shifted from summer to fall.

Just past my sixteenth birthday, my body had begun to blossom, a bit late by current standards but that's common with exercise junkies. Suppresses puberty or something like that. Or maybe it was the change. Who knows, with this thing?

My metabolism was spiking and I had so much energy to burn that I ended up running just for the meditative aspects of it. I'd finished my early morning climbing run out to the far top of the Canyon – yeah, to the locals it has a capital letter on it, *the* Canyon – and was taking a break before heading back. I'd found a picnic table that had escaped the moisture of the morning dew and I stretched out on its weathered slats, staring up into the dappled canopy of the sunrise through the spreading walnut tree above me. All was peaceful and quiet out here, even if it wasn't in the rest of my world.

I should have known that it was too good to be true.

The sound of a revving engine broke the silence and I sat up quickly, heart beating faster, my pupils dilating as I focused in on the source of the disturbance. Shane Macdonald sat idling his tuned black Camaro, beaming at me from about twenty yards.

Shane was a senior at Knightsbridge Christian High, and was also the new standout on our varsity basketball team, having moved to town during the summer. Starting center on defense and point guard on offense, six foot three with a curly mop of auburn that you just wanted to run your fingers through, a stocky broad frame and shoulders, and big hands to palm the ball. He told me he came from a school down in L.A., where he barely ever got off the bench.

"They were all huge black guys," he'd joked, and I could see he must have been overshadowed and outmatched – not because they were black, but because despite his aspirations, he just wasn't as good as he thought he was. Not in a big city like L.A. Now it looked like he was enjoying his Big Fish in a Small Pond status. Our town was mostly white and brown, and let's face it, Latinos are generally on the shorter side.

"Hey Amber!" he called. "Wanna ride back to town?"

I grinned and grabbed my things. I mean, so he'd got my name wrong. Who was I to look a gift horse in the mouth? And when you're an identical twin, chances are unless people know you really well, they are bound to make that mistake half the time.

"Hey Shane. It's Ashlee, not Amber," I said, leaning down over the open passenger side window and winking at him.

"God!" he laughed. "You guys are really hard to tell apart." Dimples puckered his chiseled Hollywood jaw.

"It's pretty much impossible since you've only been in town what, a couple of months now?" I teased. "Still want to give me a ride? Amber's probably still snoozing, getting her beauty sleep." My sister's idea of the perfect workout was something indoors, with music and a juice bar within reach.

"Sure, no problem." He smiled. "But she ought to know, a little less rest and a little more exercise doesn't seem to be hurting you any."

"Oh, she gets her exercise." I chuckled as I climbed in and belted up. "She just does it through things like cheerleading and being chased by guys like you. I'm the one with the runner's high addiction."

"I'll have to remember that." He glanced over, scrutinizing my face as if trying to memorize the differences between us by analyzing my laugh lines.

"Don't worry. Even most of our teachers can't tell us apart."

"I guess we should be glad that you and Amber aren't in the same classes at school. That would be impossible."

"Yeah, we worked that one out years ago." Different home rooms and class schedules whenever possible. Although in a small town, we still ended up with a lot of the same teachers. We sometimes swapped schedules when we were bored and wanted to liven things up. "Never let 'em see you sweat and always keep 'em guessing," Mom used to say. I bit back a tear and put a smile on my face. I am so not going there today, I told myself.

Instead, I took the time to examine Shane's face as he concentrated on the road. There were quite a few switchbacks coming down the Canyon into the valley and I had to admit, the guy handled the car like a dream.

"So, I guess Amber told you we've got a date tonight."

"Uh-huh." I nodded. "Second date, right?"

"No. Third," he responded.

I winced.

"What?"

"Nothing," I told him. What's a white lie when the truth is a bitch named Amber? Don't get me wrong, I love my sister. But I don't even think she's human sometimes. Like Kim Basinger playing opposite Brad Pitt in Cool World, she rarely spends a day with the rest of us in the third dimension. Speaking of thirds, the third date is when Amber dumps them. She says if a boy's not the one, she knows it by the third date. She said this when we were like twelve and for the last four years my sister has been nothing if not brutally consistent. I don't know how she thinks she'll know he's the one if she's never even met a "one" to compare him to, but she seems to think she's got a handle on it.

"Yeah," he continued. "My big sister thinks I'm crazy. Says I'm playing way out of my league."

She may be right, I thought to myself. "I don't think I know your sister."

"You won't, unless you get caught makin' out on Lover's Leap. She's the new chief ranger up at Knightsbridge Canyon State Park. Ex-Military. You know, the one who usually kicks everyone out just when the fun is starting."

"Oh, right..." I remembered now. "Amber says she looks like she's got a cucumber up her butt and she's trying to scrape off all the pricklies."

Shane broke out in a big belly laugh. "That's so wrong," he guffawed "and so right. That would be Jeanetta. My dad calls her the changeling. You know, like a fairy child, only meaner. Mom says it's a recessive gene from my dad's side of the family. Jeanetta just says that we're all suckers programmed by society to be good little consumers."

"She may be right," I said. I was thinking of my twin and her addiction to whatever brand-name thing was in the latest *Vogue*. "By the way, what are you doing out this way so early in the morning? I thought you lived on the other side of town."

"Can you keep a secret?"

"That depends."

"Depends on what?" he countered. This was getting fun.

"Depends on how good a secret it is."

"Oh, it's good," he assured me.

"So, spill."

"Promise not to tell your sis."

"Promise not to hurt her," I replied, not entirely joking. After all, she was my sister. In fact, sometimes I thought she was almost me. Other times...not so much.

"Naw, this is good. Get this, I drove my trailer up to the ranger station and left it parked on the overlook. For once Jeanetta's ranger status will come in handy, because she said she'd leave the patrol car parked nearby to scare off the townies and catch a ride back home with her creepy boyfriend Sean Gottlieb. She helped me decorate it with Christmas lights, and I had my mom pack us a picnic lunch like they do in the movies. Seafood *ceviche*, oysters, smoked salmon and capers, the works. I even have a bottle of champagne on ice in the cooler."

"Oh my God, that's so romantic," I said. And corny. To his face, I *oohed* and *ahhed*, but as I was listening to him, I was cringing inside. Here he is, going on about oysters on the half shell and I didn't have the heart to tell him that besides being allergic to shellfish, Amber was probably going to dump him anyway, third date and all, and she had yet to go out with anyone, and I mean anyone, on a fourth. Oh, she'd say she loved the date afterward, but more like a good anecdote you told to your girlfriends than even for the sentimental value. It just didn't come with a high enough price tag.

"What type of champagne?" I interrupted his soliloquy. I gotta spare this guy just a bit of heartache, I thought. He is much too nice for my sister. She eats up nice guys and spits them out for breakfast.

"Dom Perignon." I breathed a sigh of relief. At least the alcohol would pass muster, but my sister is truly a brand snob. If you've got caviar, which she won't eat anyway, it better be Beluga. "My parents had a bottle left over from the housewarming. Why?"

"Um, Shane," I began. How the hell was I going to break this to him gently?

"Uh-huh?"

"I'm afraid that Amber's allergic to shellfish." Okay, not so gently. Hey, I don't do gentle.

He slammed on the brakes and I was really glad I'd buckled my seatbelt.

"Are you serious?" He looked over at me and I gave him a sheepish grin. Then he put his head between his hands and I swear I thought the guy was going to begin crying, but he was only pounding his head on the steering wheel.

"Sorry," I said. "But if it's any consolation," I added, "I love seafood."

Shane began to laugh, but it sounded more like a choked scream.

"What the hell am I going to do, Ashlee?" he said. "I am so stupid, stupid, stupid." Shane repeated the word "stupid" and punctuated with the head-banging-on-the-steering-wheel routine. "What kind of idiot doesn't ask if his date likes seafood?" he asked. "I spend all of my money on this one idea and I don't even have a plan B!"

"How much are you out?"

"A hundred bucks!"

"Seriously?" I marveled. "Damn!"

"She's all I think about."

Oh shit. I was really going to have to get Amber to let this one down easy. He seemed really head over hind legs. Infatuated, I think is the word.

"Tell you what…" I made a decision. "Drive by the bank. I've got a Christmas club I can cash out and she will never be the wiser. You can buy something else to make the date special. Maybe a nice filet steak and some fruit."

"Yeah, but what will I do with all the seafood?"

"Eh, I'll take whatever won't keep," I told him. "Yum."

So, when he pulled up to the bank, I hopped out, sauntering by my on-again-off-again beau Will Stenfield, as he was watering the grass in front of the branch. He glanced at me, then at Shane's car, and he almost sprayed a passer-by. It was hilarious. Then I watched him seethe as I sauntered back to Shane's car. Slam and Dunk, Ashlee Scott. Sometimes I really enjoy being a girl. I shoved an envelope of twenties at Shane as I slid into the seat next to him.

"You know Ashlee, I really appreciate this."

"Just remember your promise."

"Promise?" he asked. "What promise?"

Ah, how quickly they forget. I shook my fist at him. "Hurt her, I hurt you. *Capisce?*"

"*Capisce.*" He was kind of adorable when he laughed. Maybe I was gonna have to go out with this one, I thought. Too bad I'm still stuck on Will.

"Hey, you and that Will fella still goin' out?" Shane asked me.

"Not right now. We're kind of in limbo."

"That's too bad." He seemed sincere. "So, who's your plan B?"

"I haven't decided," I said. "Got any ideas?"

"Who, me? No, but if I think of somebody I'll run it by you."

"Yeah, you do that." I smiled.

"Well, here we are."

"Yeah, thanks for the ride."

"Not a problem. Tell your sister I expect to see her ass jogging up the Canyon one of these mornings."

"Yeah, like that'll ever happen," I shot back as I watched him drive away. This guy was much too cute for Amber, I mused as I headed up the walk and went in the front door, only to find my twin sister waiting behind it.

"Shit, you scared me." I held my hand to my heart as it pounded in my chest. "And what is that crap on your face?" I eyed her. She was wearing one of our mother's silky robes, which was always creepy, and like me she had her brunette hair back in a pony tail. It was the gunk on her skin that made her look extra-scary.

"It's an avocado herbalesque masque if you must know. And don't try to distract me. Just what do you think you were doing with Shane Macdonald?"

Crap.

"You're probably going to dump him anyway, Miss Third-Date-Termination Clause. And seriously, Sis, if you don't let him down gently, he might never recover. He's really got it bad, and he's a teddy bear. But what do you care?"

"I don't." She flashed me her most feline grin and flounced back through the entryway into the living room forcing me to follow behind her.

"Amber, it was nothing. I ran out to the Canyon and Shane offered me a ride as I was heading back. No big deal." What was I apologizing for?

My family as a whole can be brutally honest, but when she's got a mad on my sister can be downright vicious. Her voice rose to that superior mothering tone she affected when she really wanted to get my goat. "As you've decided to poach off my leftovers again, let me throw you a bone. I was going to cancel on the guy, but since you two seem so chummy, why don't you be me for the night?"

"You know," I said, "thanks, sis. But I'm really not interested. If I ever go out with Shane Macdonald, I want it to be as myself."

Amber lifted her index finger as if to say 'hold that thought,' then brought the phone that I hadn't noticed in her hand up to her ear. "Shane. Hey." Her morning voice took on a calculatingly manipulative sugary tone. "Hey. It's Amber. I just want to apologize for doing this on such short notice, but you and me, we're just not that compatible. Now I know you're probably disappointed as you were looking forward to our third date, but here's Ashlee. And she just happens to be free." She handed me the phone.

"You are such a bitch," I hissed at her as I held one hand over the speaker.

"Grow up, Ashlee," Amber tossed over her shoulder as she turned and flounced off.

"Why should I bother, since it seems that you are mature enough for the both of us?"

Weak, Ash, weak, but I was never as good at the repartee as she was.

She shrugged and kept walking.

"Hey...Shane." While fuming at my sister, I still felt bad for the guy. "I'm sorry Amber did that to you. But the good news is, I'm not allergic to shellfish."

And with that, it looked like I had a date.

My sister spent the rest of the day in bed with a migraine. Serves her right, I thought, if it's real. Third Date Termination Clause Punishment. And yet, when I looked in on her before running off to volleyball practice, she was tossing and turning with cold sweats and fever. I put our tiff aside and went in to comfort her.

"Don't go, Ash," she said, her eyes unnaturally bright in the room's dimness. I could see her pupils dilated so far her irises seemed almost black, a deep shiny obsidian.

"I wish Mom were here," I told her as I stroked her hair, so like my own. "She was always so much better at this."

Amber grabbed my wrist with surprising strength. "Ashlee, don't go!"

"Oh come on, Amber," I said suspiciously. "You're not going anyway, and the guy bought a hundred bucks of seafood for you. Don't be like that. I'm sorry you got a migraine."

"I'm not being like anything," she said, angry. "I just have a bad feeling about this, that's all."

For some reason this pushed my buttons and pissed me off more than it should have. Amber was always trying to control me and my life, and now she just wasn't going to let me enjoy myself out of some twisted passive-aggressive impulse, I figured.

"Forget it, Amber. I'm going, and that's that." I leaned over and kissed her forehead while prying my wrist out of her grip. "Get some rest."

She closed her eyes and whimpered, rolling over and pulling the blanket over her head.

A part of me was glad she was suffering. I'd sure suffered during the last few years from her bitchiness and rivalry. This was one of the rare times that it looked like I was going to come out on top, to get the guy, to be the winner in one of the innumerable ongoing string of sisterly contests I called life.

I made sure to tell Dad how Amber was doing, and that I was going to go to practice and then out until my curfew at eleven. He nodded absentmindedly and kept grading papers from one of his classes, as he usually did in the evenings. Ever since Mom died, he'd seemed to live in kind of a daze, even after years, like he was stuck in the denial stage of grief or something.

As I went out the front door I made sure to lock it, the glass reflecting me as I did. And though it seemed to be a trick of the light, I thought I saw my sister's face instead of my own.

Sure wish I'd listened to her.

"So, are you horribly disappointed?" I asked Shane as he picked me up from the school gym parking lot after volleyball practice that evening. I'd dressed in jeans and a layering of sports bra, cotton short-sleeved white button-down with epaulets and a sweater over it all. Instead of a pony tail I opted for a French braid so that the one-carat princess cut diamond earrings showed, compliments of a comatose Amber and her jewelry box.

Shane was in the typical uniform of jocks at our school – jeans, white high-tops and a baseball jersey. The car gleamed as if he'd polished it since I saw him last.

"You know, I kinda knew I was hangin' by a thread anyway. All the guys warned me about the Third Date Termination Clause, but I'm actually not disappointed at all." It was the kind of humor that could hide a lot of hurt behind it. "I mean, you are the spitting image of each other."

"Maybe, but we're not interchangeable, you know." I frowned. Guys say the stupidest things and I was really hoping that Shane was more than another dumb jock with threesome fantasies of identical twins running through his head.

"Right. Yeah. No. I mean, I know that." He held the door open for me, smiling. "Your chariot awaits my lady."

"You're such a dork," I told him, and threw my gym bag in the back seat, then settled myself in the already warm car.

It was wasteful, but there is nothing more comforting than driving out into the country on a nippy night with the windows open and the heater blasting. My feet were warm and my face was cool, just like I liked it. I pulled out my cell to check in with Amber. She was my sister. Though I hated her, I loved her.

"Please don't tell me you're texting."

"Amber's sick."

"Aw, tell me you're not texting the evil twin. That would just be adding insult to injury."

Crap. He was right.

"You know what? You're right. Cell phones off," I said, and hit the power button, then made him turn off his.

"Satisfied?"

I smirked.

He laughed and pulled away from the school, my volleyball teammates watching. "So, tell me about yourself."

An open-ended question. *Point in favor, Shane Macdonald.*

"Well, let's see. If we're talking stereotypes, then I'm the tomboy and Amber's the vapid cheerleader."

"And...?"

Score another point for Shane Macdonald. "Well, while I've got my sights set on being Valedictorian, Amber is busy securing the popularity vote for Homecoming Queen."

"Ouch!" He laughed. "Sounds like a little sibling rivalry run amuck. Must be weird having a twin. Well, if it's worth anything, I think maybe I got the better deal." He motioned. "Oh, and your cash is in the glove box, as I didn't need to buy anything after all."

"Thanks!" I pulled on the handle and the envelope flopped out. I took it and slid it in my back pocket. I'd thrown my gym bag in the back seat and I was *so* not carrying around a purse.

He looked at me funny.

"What?" I asked.

"You're not going to count it?" he teased.

"No. Should I?" The verbal sparring was kind of fun. It was the kind I did with my dad and my brother Adam before Mom died of cancer a couple of years ago. The family had seemed to lose its center, flinging us all away from each other. I winced and tried to put it out of my head.

Shane laughed again, bringing me back to the now. He had a nice laugh. Musical, I thought.

"So, what kind of music do you like?" he asked before I could.

"Believe it or not, I'm kind of a country girl," I told him. "Oh, I like most genres, not really into rap or hip-hop unless it's got a melody you can sing to. And though I like alternative rock and contemporary Christian when it's not all 'Jesus is My Boyfriend,' I also like pre-80s classic rock."

"Wow. And here all I wanted to know was what station you wanted to listen to." He hit a few buttons and some crossover country sprang from the speakers.

"Oh." I looked sheepishly at him as he slid his hand into mine. Amber says guys don't like girls who are chatty, but I've got a lot of guy friends, emphasis on the friend instead of the guy, and I was comfortable with them, mostly. Unless things became all, you know.

"Aw, now you're turning red," he needled.

"It's dark, nimnoid. You can't possibly see my cheeks."

But the funny thing was, I could, just fine. See his cheeks, I mean. Over the course of our drive through town and up the Canyon, my vision had taken on an incredibly acute clarity. What had seemed only a pale wash of illumination before had taken on a solidity of the full moon's beams in patterns that I could easily discern. The stars seemed to wink at me, dazzling to my eyes as I gazed out the window and yet when I focused, I could see eerily into the underbrush as it sped by. My senses opened, and I could smell Shane's musky scent overlaid by the acrid tang of evaporating alcohol.

Evaporating alcohol? Huh. Mexican beer is more like it. Corona by the smell, I concluded as I tried to get the cloying taste of it off my soft palate with my tongue. I sneezed, reflexively pulling both our hands toward my face.

"Ew!" He pulled his hand from mine and wiped it off on his jeans. "Bless you!"

"Oh my God! I'm so sorry." Mortified, party of one.

Shane laughed and yanked some tissues from the glove box and handed them to me, taking some handy-wipes for himself. How guys manage to multitask in vehicles when their hormones are cavorting is beyond me. After using the lemon-smelling towelettes, which he told me his mom made him take along, he held out his hand again for me to hold. Good hygiene but not freakishly OCD about it. I chuckled. Gotta give the guy props.

His hand was huge in both of mine and for some reason I became fascinated with it, running my fingers against his palm, exploring every crack and crevice of his skin. His palm was both smooth and rough, a mixture of textures that told a story with every scent and taste that came with my indrawn breath.

"Ashlee, what are you doing?" I realized that we had stopped and I was nuzzling his palm with my face. He stared at me and pulled his hand away.

I wondered what the hell was wrong with me, and pulled an Amber.

"Sorry. I just think hands are fascinating, don't you?" I giggled and exited the car before he could respond. I think hands are fascinating? OMG! Again, what the hell is wrong with me?

"I think you're kind of kinky is what I think." Shane said it as he joined me in leaning against the hood. "It's all right, it's cool. I like it," he continued, as if he was such a worldly senior.

I took a few deep breaths and we watched in silence as the clouds passed patches across the moon. A mouse looked at me from the shadows and my lip curled up in a snarl. Better run, little morsel, I thought as I watched him scamper away.

Shane caught me by my arm and wrenched me to a stop. I was actually moving to follow the mouse. What the – was I insane?

"Hey, Ashlee. Where you going? Camper's over here." He pulled me toward him and it was then that I noticed our now illuminated dining spot. It was enchanting, really. They'd done a good job. Then my stomach began to growl.

"Oh good," I breathed. "I'm starving."

Later I found out that Amber had woken up screaming, my Dad and brother at her bedside holding her down. She was babbling about blood and death and wolves and Ashlee and danger. When she'd calmed down sufficiently she dialed my number, which of course went straight to voicemail.

Sure wish I hadn't turned my phone off.

Shane held the door open for me and I entered the camper. I have to admit, the place was cozy, like a redneck version of a Moroccan restaurant. No chairs, just a couple of matching futons, throw pillows, a fabric-covered makeshift table in the middle and a small refrigerator against the wall. A mass of Christmas lights followed the lines of the flexible A-top and he lit a few candles that let out a waft of evergreen and bayberry. A picnic basket sat on the table waiting and there really was a bottle of Dom Perignon chilling in the cooler on melted ice. A mass of Christmas lights followed the lines of the flexible top and he lit a few candles that let out a waft of evergreen and bayberry.

I promptly blew them out. "You don't use scented candles when you're eating, doofus." I told him. "Messes with the palate." I cringed inwardly as it came out sounding like something Amber would say.

"Duly noted. Now, get comfortable," he told me, handing me a flute. After popping the cork on the champagne, he caught the foam in my glass.

"To Plan B," he joked, and we toasted.

We dug into the smoked salmon with gusto and polished off the champagne with abandon. Maybe I was trying not to feel so guilty about being here with Shane instead of Will because I drank more than the two glasses we were allowed ever since we turned sixteen. Dad was pretty cool that way, but had warned us never to come home drunk unless somebody else drove.

Funny thing is, I was actually enjoying myself. Shane was cute, kinda dorky, very jock-hunky and we were funny together in a city-boy-meets-small-town-girl kind of way. Don't ask me what we talked about, but I seem to remember a similar taste in science fiction versus science fact. The champagne was nice and bubbly, but to be honest, a bit dry for my taste and I kept downing bottles of water like a reverse fire hydrant.

"Damn, Ashlee, you've gone through six of those in the last half hour!" Shane laughed as he threw me another that I caught deftly out of the air.

"I'm sorry! I love seafood, but the salmon is incredibly salty. And it's a bit stuffy in here." I motioned around the cloth-top camper. We sat across from each other, our dwindling gourmet feast between us.

"I can fix that," Shane said as he pulled back the blinds and left the fabric screens in place. I still decided to peel out of my sweater and maneuvered around him to the door.

"I'm gonna get some fresh air. Join me when you're done," I teased as I slipped down the steps and out into the night. I pulled the shirt-tail out of my jeans and unbuttoned my button-down, tying it in a knot at my sternum. I still had my sports bra on so I was perfectly covered, I told my inner critic who sounded just like Mom.

In fact, besides hearing her in my head, I could almost see her ghostly form walking down the trail. I blinked and rubbed my eyes, but she wasn't there, thank God.

The night blazed stunningly clear; the pine trees and eucalyptus opening up into a vast expanse of velvet sky. The breeze felt cool against the patches of my bare skin and my head throbbed with a twinge of a headache. I shut my eyes and took a deep breath, trying to draw in the serenity.

I felt a cold wet trickle of water against the skin of my arm and gasped, then laughed aloud as Shane handed me another bottle of water. I turned to look up at him.

He was so beautiful.

"Are you sure you're okay, 'cause you look a bit flushed."

"I know it's considered cool to be doing it, but I'm really not much of a drinker," I confided.

"Yeah. Unless you count spring water. Wanna walk a bit? Might cool you off. Clear your head."

"Sure," I said, and then immediately strode away, suddenly eager to see if I could find the mouse I noticed earlier.

Shane grabbed his jacket and caught up with me and tried to hold my hand, but the minute we touched, it was like a combustion wave of heat flowed through my body.

"Damn, Ashlee. You're hot!"

I scoffed, "Yeah, I bet you say that to all the girls."

"No, I really mean it, Ashlee. You're burning up, like you got a fever. Are you sure you're all right?"

"I'm fine," I laughed, and I was. In fact, I felt great. Sure, I maybe felt a bit warm and I decided that if I took my shirt off, I was still covered in my royal blue sports bra. I tied my shirt around my waist and kept walking.

Shane jogged up behind me as I finished pulling my hair up and off my neck. It was then that I put on some speed.

"Race you to the promontory!" I shouted, and then took off running flat out.

Now normally I am a distance runner, but at the time I had no idea what it was: the bubbly, the night, a hot handsome guy chasing after me. Before I knew it I'd rounded the bend at the place they called Lover's Leap overlooking the Canyon. Story has it, many people have jumped to their deaths from these rocks over the years, pining for loves they couldn't have.

Only now I was the one out on the tip of the jutting rock past the sign that warned me not to.

"Um, Ashlee, what are you doing?" Shane called from behind the wooden barrier.

"Don't tell me you're afraid of heights," I teased, but when I looked into his eyes, I knew he was. "You are afraid of heights! Oh, that's so...*cute*." Actually I wanted to say "chickenshit," but decided not to spoil things by being the bitch that I sometimes am. I walked back toward him smiling. "Now, catch me!"

I don't know why I was being a show off, but I decided to do a gymnast's dismount off the rock like it was a balance beam. And I gotta hand it to him, he did try to catch me, but it was more like cushioning my fall with his body.

The air rushed out of him as I landed in his arms, taking him to the ground and straddling his solar plexus. He moaned and wheezed, trying to get the oxygen back into his lungs.

When he did, I kissed him.

I didn't plan it. It just happened. I'd meant for tonight to be a simple let-down, a consolation date to offset the wounding of my sister's callous disregard for real people's feelings, but it was turning into a bit more than I expected.

His arms wrapped around me as he gave himself over to the lusts of every teenage boy. Though I normally would have taken it a lot slower and been more hesitant, I wasn't a virgin back then, but almost. I'd only ever been with Will, a couple of times.

I felt like my whole body had turned to heat.

We made out like a couple of bandits, him kissing me and our tongues twining and before I knew it, I was nibbling on his ear, lathering my tongue and teeth upon his earlobe – until I heard a screaming sound, felt a ripping, and smelled the metallic tang of blood in the air.

It was then that I realized that the screams were my own.

Waves of excruciating pain washed through me as my stomach clenched around itself and my body curled up in a fetal position. Shane slid back and away from me and held his head, a look of abject horror on his face as blood poured from where I'd bitten off a chunk of ear.

The pain inside me subsided for a moment. I caught my breath and had the wherewithal to say "9-1-1" through gritted teeth before my body betrayed me again. I would have wondered what was happening if it didn't hurt so bad as I felt my spine snap and my ribs rearrange themselves. I heard in the background a very frightened Shane punching numbers on his phone.

"No. No. No. NO. NO," he cried. "Just hold on, Ashlee, I can't get a signal," I heard him say, and his voice got farther away.

Now, I don't know what it is, but hearing his feet pounding down the trail seemed like the last straw that broke the camel's back and with a primal scream, my body vomited itself into a new configuration. My face broke out into a long muzzle with extremely sharp teeth, a nose for blood, and a hunger for chasing down prey.

I bounded after him on four legs.

On four legs? A miniscule part of me wondered about that, but for the moment, the chase was all I knew.

***

"But, you don't understand, Jeanetta! Shane is in trouble and Ashlee is in danger." Amber banged on the aluminum door of the Macdonald family home, my dad and brother Adam in tow.

"What the hell kind of stunt do you think you're pulling, little missy?" Jeanetta Macdonald pushed Amber back as her boyfriend lurked in the background. She wore what we often call a wife-beater underneath her uniform kaki shirt and she still had her polyester ranger's pants on and her black polished shoes.

Amber wasn't the type to be hysterical, but she sure was doing a bang-up job this evening.

"Just tell me where she is. Tell me where Shane is. I know he was planning something outrageous, but you've got to believe me. Something is wrong! Something bad is going to happen!"

"Oh my God! Listen to yourself!" Jeanetta screeched, her nose reddening with anger. "First you go out with my brother twice, and then you don't even have the courtesy of extending him the Third Date Termination Clause."

"What's the Third Date Termination Clause?" my dad asked.

"I'll explain later," Adam told him.

"And then you pawn your sister off onto him like sloppy seconds and now you want to interrupt his date because you had a bad dream?" Jeanetta ranted. "You are in serious need of professional help."

"Good one, Jen," Sean the loser boyfriend murmured from the background.

"Miss Macdonald," my Dad reasoned. "If you could just tell us where they are…"

"Ranger Macdonald," my brother interjected. "Jeanetta." His voice softened, slipping past her defenses. "I'd really appreciate it if you could help me make sure that Ashlee is safe. I know she can be a pain in the ass, but…she's still my sister."

Adam doesn't assert himself very often, but when he wants to, he can really command attention and response.

Jeanetta looked at him like an aberration, then her brow furrowed as if she seemed confused, which was when she shifted to acquiescence and let out a huge sigh.

My brother has this weird effect on people. It's almost like he can convince you of anything. One Halloween, when we were ten, and he was like, thirteen, as we were dividing up the stash, he convinced me that I loved tootsie rolls. By the time the night was through, he had all the chocolate, and I had…tootsie rolls. It's a great story, but I rarely eat tootsie rolls anymore.

"Fine. They're up at the overlook. But you better just do a drive-by. I was gonna run up there in a couple of hours myself. Make sure the kids aren't trashing the place. So, why don't you just give me a call so I don't have to waste a trip," she called as my family rushed back to the car.

"Crazy townies," Jeanetta muttered as she watched us hurry away and then shut the door.

I felt cool hands on the back of my neck and a whisper of night breezes down my naked skin as I vomited up copious amounts of blood. Bits of flesh surrounded me, and a haze of insects sucked the moisture out of the air as it evaporated from my skin.

My poor dear, I heard. My mother's voice echoed in my head as soft hands petted the pelt of my hair. My throat felt raw from the acid bile, my head in shock, my heart in anguish.

"I think I killed something," I croaked.

I know dear. My mother's arms held me and rocked away my horror till I fell asleep.

My family found me naked and sound asleep in a pool of Shane's blood. And though I know what must have happened, because I've turned every full moon since that time, the sheriff's office, unequipped to deal with the supernatural, named it a tragedy of nature and they even brought back the carcass of a mountain lion to prove it.

Jeanetta Macdonald said she forgave me for "dragging my brother out there." After all, the investigation showed she had allowed Shane to use the camping trailer parked on public land in violation of policy. She tried to claim it was for her own use and that her brother had brought me up there without telling her, but the remains of the feast made it pretty clear what was going on, and with Amber's testimony about what Shane had claimed, Jeanetta was forced to accept at least some responsibility. I heard later she got a bad performance report and was denied a promotion she wanted.

You know what was weird? It seemed like she was more upset over the mountain lion than about her brother.

And now you know what really happened.

15

Chief Hernandez's voice brought me back to the present. "It says here in the file that after Shane Macdonald was killed you got threatening letters like this all of the time."

"Letter, not emails. And not all the time," I protested. "It was every year on the anniversary of his death, and those were direct threats, like, 'You're dead, bitch, for what you did to Shane.' These are more like warnings. And it stopped when I left Knightsbridge for good." Or I thought it had.

"Ashlee, I wish you would have told me, told Amber, told *someone*," Elle said.

"I was in the file. I wasn't hiding anything. Besides, I'd hoped never to have to think about it again."

"Sounds like someone isn't happy you're back," Hernandez said. "Any idea who that might be?"

"Jeanetta Macdonald blamed me for Shane's death, but you guys didn't find anything," I said. By "you guys," I meant the cops in general, of course. Neither Elle nor Hernandez had been with Knightsbridge PD back then.

"What about other friends of Shane's? Some ex-girlfriend or something?" Elle asked. "Or other family?"

"As far as I know Jeanetta and Shane's parents are dead. They have cousins, in Utah or something, but aren't close."

"We're not going to get very far on a cold case like this by questioning the victim," Hernandez broke in, shooting Elle a look. "We need to review all the files and assign an investigator."

Elle glared at Hernandez but the chief spread his hands. "It's a dead coyote and a threatening note. I can't justify some kind of all-out effort unless something happens. Especially not just because it's your family."

Elle relented. "Yeah, I get it. Put someone good on it, though, and start with some decent forensics. I'll back you up at budget time."

Hernandez sighed and nodded. "I'll do what I can."

"Come on, Ash," Elle said. "Let's go home."

"I need to go back by Will's. He can bring me home afterward."

Elle pointed her finger at my nose. "Straight there, straight back, and keep your eyes open, the both of you. If you see anything funny, call me right away."

"Oh come on, Elle. Nothing's going to happen in broad daylight."

"How do you know?" And she was right, I didn't. Except, bad things happened at night. That's what I'd always believed, and ever since that night, I am living proof.

As Elle was licensed to carry concealed weapons, and was clearly on my side, at least for Amber's sake, I wasn't going to argue with her.

On the other hand, Amber wasn't happy, because Elle had invited Will to stay with me, but it eventually saved her from feeling like she had to be hospitable all the time. It probably helped our sisterly relationship in the end, especially since Will turned out to be a better domestic than I was, and kept the house spotless. How humiliating!

Elle ordered spotlights on motion detectors to be installed around the property and my sister seemed to settle into a new rhythm. This was just one of the reasons I imagined my twin loved Elle so much - she was a bastion of safety and security. She radiated alpha during these moments and, knowing my own limits, both of us siblings accepted beta female roles. I think this is where I first began to consider just what it meant to be a pack. Though they weren't lycanthropes, this felt like a home now, as if Amber's attitude had now changed. It seemed I was back inside something, instead of outside, for the first time in years.

Will accepted his beta male role with equanimity, which was funny as there was no alpha male, unless you counted Spanky the Schnauzer, who was about as un-alpha as dogs came. I guess Elle got to play both roles.

Detective Bromley came by and interviewed us all again, and said it would be a couple of weeks before anything came back from the lab. He was a big, florid man who sweated too much and exercised too little, but Elle said he was competent enough. Not much evidence to go on, though, so I didn't get my hopes up. He did say he was interviewing everyone, including my chief suspect, Jeanetta Macdonald, but he wasn't about to disclose any details, not even to Elle apparently.

16

"You know, Will, I think you should take Ashlee out of town," Elle announced at the breakfast table on the morning before the night of the full moon. I'd been wondering how I was going to work that one, and this seemed like a pretty good idea to me, no matter what prompted it.

"Cool!" JR said. "Can I come?"

We all laughed, a bit raggedly I'll admit.

"What?" he asked us, with the most innocent lack of guile on his face.

"Maybe another time, sweetie," my sister said. "I think your Aunt Ash and Uncle Will want to be alone."

"Wait. What?" my nephew said. "When did Will become my uncle?"

"Yes, Amber," Elle teased. "Just when did that happen?"

"Just thinking ahead," she singsonged. "Don't blame me for stating the obvious."

Will grinned and looked at me, but I pouted, not exactly certain why except to reflexively oppose my twin. "The obvious is rushing things, sis. I only just got back into town and you're trying to marry me off to my high school sweetheart?"

"Is that what I am?" Will leaned forward intently.

"And what's wrong with that?" Amber chimed in.

"Maybe you soured me on marriage."

"Ouch," Amber said, and I saw my barb had scored. Perhaps too deep.

"Sorry, low blow," I said. "I know it wasn't your fault."

Her look tried to wither me where I sat. "Been there, done that," she said coldly, and in that moment seemed older than I was, which was actually our usual relationship.

"I love when two beautiful girls fight over me," Will broke in, "but I agree with Elle. We need to get out of this fortress. The investigation's going nowhere and unless whoever is sending the notes makes another move, it won't."

"Yeah, I knew this was too good to be true," I said. Why was I always getting kicked out of places? If I wasn't being asked to leave by boutique hotels that didn't like my reviews or cruises because I had a bad habit of sneaking into the crew's mess in my search for the human part of the story, then I was being passed around from family member to family member like the perpetual problem child. Damn, and just when I thought the crisis had brought us closer.

Then again, I guess I was a handful sometimes. "Fine. I'll take Will back to the city with me."

"Great! I finally get to see how the other half lives," he said. There were hisses and boos all around, except for JR, who laughed uproariously like the kid he was. I doubt he knew what he was laughing at, except his elders' antics.

Elle said, "Actually, I think you and Will should go stay in a hotel. Someone might be watching your place. I'll be guarding Amber and the house back here, and I called in a favor with a bail bondsman I know who has a couple of security guys."

"Why?" I pointed an accusing finger at Elle. "Are you trying to dangle some bait for the, the, what do you call it…"

"Perp. Perpetrator. So what if I am?"

A smile spread across my face. "So what if you are. Anything to get away from here."

"Love you!" Amber said.

"Love you too," I replied, "but I don't see you objecting." In fact, it had been frustrating as all hell, sleeping in the guest room with Will but not, you know, *sleeping* with him. At least, not the full Monty, if you know what I mean and no, I will not give details. You can fill in the blanks. But anyway, fun and frustrating, because I hadn't fully convinced myself getting back with him was the right thing to do and going all the way was just going to make the inevitable breakup that much harder, pardon the pun.

That was our usual pattern, anyway, back in high school. Things would go along good for a while, closer and closer and even, yes, that close, and it was wonderful, but then the explosion would come. My explosion. I knew it was me, always me. Will hardly ever got mad, just irritated, when I would sabotage things when I felt like we were getting too close.

That's what it felt like now, getting too close, so going away would either finish the pattern with fireworks, or maybe we could derail the speeding train and do something different. Maybe if we got away from my family and this pressure and I was on my own home ground, I could get past my fear of flying and think about being with Will the way he wanted to be with me.

Then I thought about what I was, and all the fear came back again. There was just no way I could tell him…if he would even believe me. Until I proved it, that is, perhaps by ripping him to shreds the way I'd done to goofy dorky hunky innocent Shane.

I felt sick.

"Ash," Will jogged my elbow. "I think we lost you."

"Just thinking," I said with a forced smile. I turned to the alpha female. "Okay, boss, what do we do?"

Elle laid down the plan. Will and I were okay with it, and surprisingly, so was Amber. I guess I didn't expect her to be willing to play me in hopes of drawing the threat into the open. Never thought of her as brave, but there are different types of courage.

Will took me to the Claremont Hotel in Oakland, not my apartment after all. The place was a marvel, towering like an ostentatious *grande dame* on the hills overlooking the Oakland-Berkeley line. Like a California version of the hotel Christopher Reeves and Jane Seymour haunted in Somewhere in Time, it nestled among the pines and towering fragrant Eucalyptus trees across the slope. Hard to believe that the old Highway 13 was just over the rise, it gave such an illusion of remoteness.

Since I'd written the hotel a stellar review, the management offered to comp our stay, as I normally couldn't afford a couple hundred a night just for grins. I must admit I did imply that I was going to do a follow-up article, sometime in the future.

I might.

You never know.

Will laughed and said he could handle it. I reminded myself that he had taken over the family business and was actually reasonably well off, if not super-rich. That got me thinking about the fact that none of the local hotties had snapped him up yet, and that I was pretty lucky that he wanted me after all these years.

That led me to wondering about the house he'd bought – my house! Which was so weird, but so romantic. You know, a lot of girls think they would kill for a guy like Will, but like most fantasies, when they actually start happening they aren't quite the same as you think they will be. One girl's romantic beau is another's creepy stalker, and what was I supposed to think about him sleeping in my room – I mean, in my old house – every night? Was that love, or infatuation, or obsession?

We settled in for an afternoon at the pool and a cozy evening on the veranda. Shrouded in secrecy that I claimed was necessary to avoid my legions of rabid fans – ha, ha – the hotel had even let us come and go through the employee entrance.

We stayed up late and got up late the next morning. I dragged Will out to Mill Valley, where I ran him ragged hiking from the shadows of Muir Woods on up and over the Dipsea Trail to the bluff above Stinson Beach and back. MoonFall was coming that evening and I had so much energy, I thought it would just be easier to tucker Will out so I could sneak away and make the change without interference.

We had dinner back on the terrace of the hotel's restaurant. He ate enough for two and me for three. "Damn, girl," he joked, "I'm gonna have to get a side job just to feed you."

"Oh, it's your responsibility to feed me now, is it?" I teased.

"If you want it to be." He took my hand and caressed it, and I let him. "I think Uncle Will sounded pretty good."

"Will…"

"I know, you don't want to talk about it."

"Just not yet, okay? Not until this thing with the threats is resolved, and…"

"And what?"

"Nothing."

"Look," he said, "we can leave Knightsbridge. If it's Jeanetta, she's so attached to the Park and the Canyon she won't follow you, and you'll be gone and once you're out of her field of view she'll stop. She and her animal rights wacko buddies can kiss my ass as we leave them in the dust. I can get a manager for the landscaping business and travel with you, or sell out entirely and start over somewhere far away."

I sighed. "That sounds lovely. Like paradise."

"Then why not?"

I just couldn't tell him. Not yet. Besides, there was Elle's plan, which Will almost seemed like he'd forgotten about. He was such a sweet, live-in-the-now kind of guy, which I guess fit with my personality too, except I tended to be the worry-about-tomorrow kind of girl. You can tell by my bitten fingernails, so different from Amber's long perfect ones.

"It's complicated, Will. Look, I really like you."

"You used to say you love me."

"I...I do love you," I admitted to him. "But that may not mean exactly what you think it does, or it may not be enough, or the timing might just not be right. So can we just leave it at that for a while?"

"That we love each other."

"Pushy bastard, aren't you?" I smiled to soften my words.

"I know what I want, and what I want is you, Ash. Always have."

"You've been waiting around all this time for me? Never went out with anyone else in all these years?"

"Not so many years. I've kept busy."

"You didn't answer me."

Will sighed. "I never asked anyone out. I took Denise Paulos out a couple of times on pity dates, because Carl begged me. We didn't even hold hands. That's all."

"You really did wait for me?" I guess the disbelief came through in my voice, because he showed a touch of anger.

"Yes, I did. You say that as though it was a bad thing." He stood up. "It wasn't. It was a noble thing, a good thing. I wanted to wait, because you're worth waiting for, Ashlee Scott, and I'm really sorry you can't see it. But don't try to diss me for it. I gotta pee," he ended, and stomped off toward the restaurant's facilities.

"Will —" Grrr. I signaled the waiter and ordered a bottle of champagne. That had not gone well. Maybe I could smooth it over. When he came back, face and hands damp from the sink, I had two glasses poured. "A toast," I said.

"To what?" he asked, intrigued.

"To my stupidity."

"Did you order a magnum?" he quipped.

"Watch it, buddy," I winked. "I'm trying to apologize here, okay? Now drink your toast."

"I'd rather drink my champagne." Will raised the glass. "To your stupidity." He drained it.

So did I. "Look…it was really romantic, or noble or whatever for you to have waited for me these past five or six years, but it's a lot of pressure. I've been footloose and fancy-free for all that time and now I come back to my hometown and you want me to just pick back up like nothing has changed."

"Some things have changed, but not others," he said a bit cryptically. "That's life. Okay," he held up a hand, "I'll back off. I've waited this long. I'll wait some more."

I wondered how long he would wait, and for a moment almost gave in to the impulse to polish off the bottle, drag him up to our room and give him the night of his life. Or maybe vice versa, since I hadn't had my ashes hauled in quite some time, and it had never been as good as it was with Will.

That thought stopped me in my musings for a moment. I realized it was true. No sex had ever been as good as with Will, even though it was just early, awkward teenage backseat stuff, mostly. I guess what they say is right: it's not so much about what you do as who you're with, and I had brought Will with me in my mind to a lot of lonely nights on the road.

Then why the hell was I fighting him so hard?

I glanced up at the twilight sky and could feel the moon getting ready to break over the horizon, and that gave me my answer, at least for tonight.

Later I slipped a crushed Ambien into his glass and made sure he drank it all, and then led him up and tucked him in after a hot bath. His snores assured me that I could do what had to be done that night with him none the wiser. Maybe it was just putting things off, but sometimes, that's all I could do.

"Sleep well, Tree Jockey," I whispered and kissed his forehead as I headed out to answer the call of nature and the autumn moon.

17

There's a kind of intoxication in fear. Just a tingle of excitement that leaves a catch in the breath, a chemical reaction that spikes the endorphins and leaves you with the sigh of relief as the tickling jitters pass. The scent of fear that cocks the head of a wolf, sensing prey and the thrill of the chase rushing through the spirit, like a hot flush of blood to the veins. That's what was overtaking me now.

I was ready. It was time, past time. I had to change. I'd put it off too long.

The shift was upon me.

My head snapped back, my back bowed, and my legs collapsed under me as I slid to all fours. A ripple through my belly heaved and I heard my bones crack and felt the slice of pain across every aspect of my synapses. I dry-heaved and the wave of nausea washed the pain through me as my skin slit and slid over my flesh and my muscles took on a meaner and leaner look.

The wolf came over me in waves, like the mirage on a horizon, rippling hair and fur and blood and bone. My feet elongated and it seemed like my fingers splayed from hands to claws and back again. When I thought I couldn't take it anymore, my head snapped out and I screamed as the muzzle slid into place, replacing mangled flesh. I howled and a hundred thousand howls called back. I crouched and shook my pelt, sending blood and gore flying all directions as once again, I was reborn.

I knelt, my forepaws in the grass, then sprang.

On my feet or my paws, whatever word described them best today, I raced along the edge of the patch of forest, past blurring brush and trees. Smells surrounded me, overrode me for a while and humanity deserted me for at least a mile.

I ran.

I ran until I could comprehend what I was once again.

Ashlee Scott. Werewolf. Writer. Sister. Twin. Mate of Will Stenfield, though he didn't know it yet. Nor did my human half, but the bitch part would work on that.

My eyes saw into every shadow. They pierced the depths of the dark with a fluorescence that human vision cannot. I'd forgotten the joy of truly being free. As a wolf, my only responsibility was to my belly, to my heart, to my family.

I thought of my mate asleep back at the hotel room and smelled him on my fur. I licked him from my skin and tasted him upon my lips once again. The musky scent of mown lawns, the rich loam of moist earth, his tangy sweat and salty acrid taste until he showered, all melted into earthy scents of cedar, pine and Vetiver grass.

My man, I marked him and I found myself upon his trail. We'd walked here today, I thought as I bolted out of the trees near the hotel's pool.

Night full of shadows, I slipped beneath the gate to the pool house where I'd left a spare change of clothes earlier that day. As I'd given them a great review, the staff at the Claremont gave me more access to the workings behind the scenes. This served me now as I knew the areas that were often overlooked in the quiet dead of night. I told myself I could just sleep in a corner underneath the benches inside the locker room until the dawn, when Ashlee would take over and the wolf would slip away once again.

My mind seemed so much clearer when I let out the wolf, like cobwebs being swept out of my brain. Everything distilled into its simplest forms. Love. Eat. Sleep. Pray and thank God above that I was what I was.

Right then, I wanted nothing else.

Unfortunately what my mind wanted, what the rational human me said, didn't make the wolf bitch happy at all. She wanted to run and hunt and run some more, to smell and taste and howl and mate under the looming moon. She wanted Will to be there with her. She wanted him to be what she was.

The *she*, the *I*, the *whoever we were* took over and, despite best intentions, ran us out of the pool house, back under the gate, and off into the night of the hills above Berkeley.

Tilden Park and other state and local lands formed a wall against development to the east, and so I ran northeastward along the ridges and hills all the way to San Pablo Reservoir. In that peculiar pellucid state my two minds melded, the animal and the woman, into something more than either.

I knew what I was doing quite clearly. The animal did not control me now, not after threescore or more changes, but neither did I control it. Instead, I was just myself, in a different state of mind.

Have you ever been consumed by desire or other strong emotion – anger, grief, depression? You were still yourself, but changed, different. That's what it was like for me.

In human form the thought of chasing down an animal and sinking my teeth into its warm flesh would have revolted me, but now it seemed like the most reasonable and desirable thing, and I had to have what I desired. If I could not have Will in this form – and oh, wouldn't that be a surprise, a hundred-pound furry wolf bitch leaping into bed with him – then I would hunt, kill, and eat.

I picked up the trail of a yearling buck, full of power and life. He would be small – this part of California was too hunted out of really big racks to ever see the magnificent stags the Pacific Northwest boasted – so I had no fear of being gored. There was a good reason wolves in the wild hunted in packs: not even a great grey male could take down something like a full-grown caribou by himself, much less a beta bitch like me, but this one smelled hardly larger than I was.

He'd meandered here and there, nibbling on shoots and low-hanging branches, dropping scat and leaping small streams. I leaped them too, closing in on the buck until I spotted him in a thicket of Manzanita.

When he spooked, I was after him, and over a short sprint I was faster, with my ranging lope eating up the ground between us. In the night, my senses outmatched his, my strength the greater, my hunger tipping the balance. I sank my teeth into his haunch, and when he shook me off I snapped and hamstrung him. After that, it was a mercy to open his throat and let his life spill out on the ground.

Don't weep for the buck, dear reader. He has his place in the great web of nature. Without him we would have no children of the night, no songs to the moon of wolf and cousin coyote, no grace of puma or, in times long past, no great grizzly or even tribes of Man. And without those ferocious predators, the trees and bushes and all the growing plants would be stripped of their flowers and shoots and bark, and all would soon fall under the predations of the herds of millions of grazing creatures.

Nature is a balance, and for this one night, I was truly part of that.

If you want to weep for something, weep for yourselves, who have never known this kind of life.

Once I had eaten my fill, I left the kill for the others that would come – the bobcat and the vulture and the condor and the other carrion-eaters that must also feed: nature's garbage crew, who would render death into new life in a never-ending cycle.

18

The pool house gave me a place to clean up and change. Despite the joys of the change, I always felt relieved when it had ended. It was so fraught with danger, from trigger-happy hunters to traps, or merely the possibility that my stash would be found and I would have to try to sneak back to the room naked at six in the morning.

Speaking of returning to the room…

"Oh Miss Scott." The concierge waved me over. "You have a package."

My heart thudded against my chest as I stared at the box in his hand. This wasn't in the plan. No one should be sending me anything.

About the size of a compressed oval hatbox, it was shrink-wrapped with my name in black permanent ink on the outside and no return address.

"Um, do you know who left this for me?" I asked as he handed it over. It smelled like flowers and the green scent of grass and cut stems, but that didn't make sense. No one was supposed to know I was here, which meant someone was following us or had bugged us or something, maybe through one of our phones. I was always suspicious of those GPS apps.

"It came in with the flower delivery guy." The concierge tilted his head. "Ooh, maybe it's a gardenia. They sometimes wrap them up on ice like that. Maybe your boyfriend got it for you."

"Maybe," I said, but I wasn't betting on it.

I woke Will up when I got to the room and opened the package. It wasn't a gardenia. It was an animal heart, a canine's to be exact, bigger than a Chihuahua, but just about the size of a cocker spaniel. Before the first change I wouldn't have known that, but now, somehow, I did.

The room phone rang.

"Don't answer that," I said. I was spooked and all I wanted to do was get out of here.

"It's just the wake-up call. I set it for seven, and if I don't answer it'll just keep ringing."

The minute he picked up the hotel landline, my own cell phone went off. I looked at the caller ID. "It's Amber," I said, and answered. But it wasn't Amber, it was Elle, on Amber's line.

"I just wanted to tell you, Ashlee." Elle's voice was muffled, and it sounded hoarse, like there was a catch in it. "Spanky's gone. Got any ideas?"

Elle wasn't usually sentimental, but she was about that dog if anything.

I stared in horror at the heart on ice, dreading the thought that passed through my brain. Nobody could be that sick, could they?

"Umm…" I told her about what I'd just received.

Elle cursed like a sailor, dropping F-bombs left and right. "There goes the plan, having Amber wear a wig and pose as you while we keep her guarded. Somehow the perp figured out where you are."

"Yeah, I got that," I said drily. "What now, Maestro?"

"You're not safe there anymore."

"I'm not safe back at your house."

"Safer than in some hotel."

"Why don't Will and I go to my apartment?"

"There's no one to help protect you there either," Elle argued.

"Come on home, Ashlee," I could hear Amber say in the background. Funny, I think that's the first time I'd heard that in a long time.

Home.

Maybe that was the difference between love and like, between family and friends. Your family might drive you crazy and vice versa, but when the chips are down, they'll be there. It brought a lump to my throat.

"Okay," I husked. "We'll come home." Will nodded solemnly as I clicked off my phone, then I took the battery out. "Yours too," I said, pointing at his old Nokia. "No battery, no tracking."

"Let's search our stuff," he said as he complied. We did, but didn't find anything. Hey, we're not some kind of secret agents, all right? Maybe the police have a scanner or detector gizmo.

I put it out of my mind as we packed, making sure to keep the bloody carton intact for evidence. Come to think of it, I doubted it was Spanky's. I would have known by the smell, wouldn't I?

I hoped.

I prayed.

When we got home, the house seemed like a tomb. Amber stayed seated on the davenport in the family room, a big glass of wine in her hand, and looked at me with accusing eyes red from crying. Elle met us halfway and quivered with energy and anger. My mother floated above them, her ethereal arms outstretched as if she wanted to hold them. They couldn't see her, but it made me feel a bit better to know she was there.

"Where's JR?" I asked as Will dropped our suitcases.

"At his father's," Elle replied. "We thought it best to hold off a few days on telling him. Just in case Spanky comes back."

"He's not coming back." Amber stood up. "Not until Ashlee gets her shit together..." She trailed off as Elle put a hand on her arm. My sister looked at me with wounded resentment and I couldn't blame her.

"I know. I know. I'm sorry."

Amber looked like she wanted to say something nasty and cutting, but held back. You gotta give her credit for that. Like Dad says, we're not responsible for our feelings, just our actions.

Sometimes I can't stand him too, because he's usually right. It's annoying.

Will made himself scarce and went up to my room. We'd dropped off the cooler at the police station on the way into town and had spent a few minutes talking with Knightsbridge's finest.

"This is all my fault, Amb," I apologized again.

"Damn straight it is." Amber sniffed. She looked miserable, and this time that didn't make me the least bit happy.

"Amber," Elle scolded. "We talked about this."

"No," Amber turned on Elle. "You talked, I listened. Well, I'm tired of listening. Somebody's going to have to take matters into her own hands," she said and she headed for the garage.

"Amber, don't do anything foolish." Elle followed her, sounding just like my mother.

I winced, remembering all of those fights we had when we were in high school and I had refused to give my sister the car keys when she had a mad on. She loved to drive recklessly at high speeds when she was pissed off. Hopefully Elle could talk her down.

Alone in the room for the moment — at least, with no corporeal beings — I rounded on my mother, who was looking at me with sorrow in her eyes. "Can't you do anything?"

Mom sighed and looked heavenward as if listening to a voice I couldn't hear. After a moment, she said, "I can tell you this, dear. You are going to have to stop playing the victim and take responsibility for your actions."

"What does that mean?" I railed at her. "I can't just tell everyone I'm a werewolf. How will that solve anything?"

"Blood calls to blood, Ashlee, and you have a blood debt on your hands. Maybe it's time you figured out what the spirits want from you." She said this as she briefly cradled my cheek, and then disappeared.

I sighed and went to the bedroom. Will was sound asleep and snoring, which bugged me. You'd have thought he'd had the best night's sleep last night, going to bed early and all.

Guys.

I pulled my laptop out from under the bed and started scouring the net. By dinnertime, I had some idea of what I had to do. After a glum meal of leftovers, we all went to bed early. I fell asleep immediately; after all, I hadn't had much rest last night.

Will had gone down to the living room and watched television, and I didn't even notice when he crawled back under the covers with me.

–19–

This part I pieced together from talking to Sean after the whole thing was over, and filled in a few details. Okay, I made up a few details, but hell, I *am* a writer.

Sean Gottlieb finished cleaning up after the dog in the pet carrier, cursing the day he ever took up with Jeanetta Macdonald. He stared at the poor little miniature Schnauzer, who looked at him with the saddest eyes. He'd had to kidnap the pet and keep him at his place, as the animal shelter was the first place they would look, or maybe Jeanetta's. Eventually he was supposed to pretend to find the dog, which would give him the opportunity to cozy up to one of the twins.

"I'm sorry, Spanky, but the bitch has got me wrapped around her little finger."

Spanky cocked his head and then settled his muzzle on his front paws to listen.

"Always, Sean do this. Sean do that. Sean take out the garbage. Sean drop your pants and bend over and take it up the ass. Sean, –"

The sound of high heels clicking on the linoleum of his kitchen floor cut him off.

"Sean dear." Jeanetta's sculpted tones matched her sculpted body and Jeff couldn't help but lose his train of thought when she came at him like that. To him, Jeanetta was drop dead gorgeous, and buff as a female bodybuilder. If she wanted to beat the shit out of him, she could, and he knew it.

After her brother had died, she'd turned over a new leaf, went back to school on the Park Service's dime and gotten some kind of environmental degree. She'd eventually become the full-time head of the Animal Rights Coalition as well as keeping her status as part-time ranger at Knightsbridge Canyon State Park. Obviously the salary at the nonprofit suited her better than the pay the government could provide.

If she treated him like a scrub, she definitely made up for it in the bedroom. Today she was dressed in one of her favorite leather and latex outfits, suitable for indoor wear only.

"So, where's the little mongrel?" Jeanetta singsonged in a way that made Spanky cringe. It made Sean think of Cruella de Vil in that dog movie. "Why there you are! I bet your owners are worried sick about you. But don't you worry. You're exactly where you're supposed to be."

With a flick of her single-tail whip, she soon had Sean Gottlieb crawling on all fours behind her. Every time the leather tip hit him, he shuddered with a mixture of pain and pleasure, anticipating what was to come.

It was so bad, but so good anyway.

Spanky hunkered down, put his paws over his eyes, and dreamed about home.

–20–

I woke up the next morning to a silent house and a note from Will:

GONE TO SEE MOM. BACK LATER. STAY SAFE. –WILL. XOXO

I padded down into the living room and got a glass of orange juice from the kitchen when I heard voices coming from the garage. I tiptoed into the laundry room and put my ear to the garage door as my sister began to talk.

"It was him, Elle. It was Sean Gottlieb. He was Jeanetta's boyfriend back in high school and they're still together. I saw it all in my dream. He's been doing the dirty work for Jeanetta, and she's still pissed off because Shane went out with Ashlee that night instead of me, and he got mauled by a mountain lion or whatever it was back when we were in high school."

"What do you want me to do, Amber? Dreams aren't exactly probable cause, not to mention the overtime costs to the city," Elle argued. "I have to have a good reason to request Hernandez put him under surveillance. Something better than my girlfriend had a vision and our dog has been kidnapped."

Holy shit, I thought. Maybe Amber's talents weren't so latent as Mom suggested.

Speaking of Mom – "It's not polite to eavesdrop on your sister, you know," she admonished, sticking her ghostly head up out of the washing machine. I yelped and retreated out to the back yard, Mother following me as I lit up a clove and stared at the sky. Who thought that such a cozy little town could harbor such unknown weirdness? Then again, in all those books and movies, it was always in some little town or remote place, usually in Maine or Idaho or Vermont or somewhere. Amityville Horror. Pet Sematary. The Shining. Misery. Twilight Eyes. Casper the Friendly Ghost. Yeah, that one had scared the hell out of me as a kid.

"She learned that from you and Dad, you know," I snapped at her.

"Learned what?" my mother said as she stepped down onto the twelve-inch sunning slab that cradled one corner of the black-bottomed swimming pool.

"Having your fights out of sight and out of earshot. It's incredibly frustrating, you know. And now Amber's just like you two. No PDA in front of the peasants and no arguing in front of the children. Made the rest of us feel like mental defects, going at it all the time."

"Yes, well your father wanted to show a united front when it came to parenting. And we were much too concerned about what other people thought than what kind of damage we were doing to you kids at the time."

"I think you passed on that little foible to Amber as well. Sometimes I don't think she's even human! Always worried about how it looks on the outside, when who gives a shit about comportment when your family is being threatened. I swear, you wouldn't even think she was gay except she and Elle sleep in the same bedroom." Ouch. Did I really go there? "They're more like…"

"Sisters? Like you two used to be, before you started squabbling all the time? Are you jealous of Elle?"

"No." Maybe. "And when did that happen, Mom? Huh? When did we start squabbling all the time? When you…"

Mom looked sad. "You say that as if I wanted to die and leave you kids alone. If you just thought about it a minute, you'd realize it's just the opposite."

Know what? I did. With all the stress and stuff, maybe this wasn't a good time to have arguments with my dead mother, but then again, when *is* a good time? But I knew what she meant, I think – that she was here now, as best she could be, because she hadn't wanted to leave us.

"I get it, Mom. I'm sorry. Hard to argue with cancer."

"Your father and I did our best, dear," she said sadly. "We were flawed human beings too, just like everyone. Your sister is also doing the best she knows how, Ashlee. Don't judge her until you can walk a mile in her shoes. You can't even fathom the responsibility she feels."

"Responsibility? What responsibility?"

"She has a son now, and she always felt responsible for you, and when I died, she felt responsible for your father and Adam, and now with Spanky gone…"

"Hey, where is Spanky, anyway?" I asked off the cuff, hoping to surprise her into answering.

"I don't know, Ashlee. I'd pass it on if I knew, but even though I'm like this, I can only be in one place at a time. I can't go floating through thousands of houses checking every room." Mom sighed. "You have no idea how much strength it takes to manifest even to you."

I ignored her troubles and said, "Oh, and by the way, when were you going to tell me that Amber's visions were back?" I remembered she'd had a few over the years. They seemed to come in clusters.

"It wasn't my place." My mother gave me that sad smile, the one that said it was only going to get worse before it got better, and then she faded out.

The back door opened right then and my twin came out to join me. The morning was fairly quiet and unseasonably warm. Amber handed me my favorite, a glass of cherry limeade with a sprig of mint on the top, and then crossed her arms and stared into my eyes.

"I need to tell you something," she said, after a few moments' silence.

I kept my mouth shut, and just nodded. When my better judgment was in control, I'd learned that the less I said, the better I did when it came to our relationship. Seems family always takes aim at each other until a common antagonist comes along. Maybe this an opportunity.

"You know those visions I used to have as a kid? Like the night we found you on the slopes of the Canyon near Shane's body?"

"Uh, huh." I sat down on the edge of the pool and wiggled my toes in the cold water, more from an excuse to do something than a desire for relief.

"Well, they never really stopped. In fact, they've been getting clearer and more frequent, lately."

"Uh, huh," I murmured again.

"I think Jeanetta Macdonald wants you dead, Ashlee. Or at least, she wants some kind of revenge. I saw it last night in a dream. Remember her creepy boyfriend, Sean?"

Snort. "You mean her weirdo plaything." I laughed again.

"Yes, well, that. I dreamed that Sean is going to try to kidnap you. I don't know when or how, but it's going to happen and we've got to try to prevent that."

"What did you see?" I asked, an uneasy trepidation creeping over me. Werewolves and shape-shifters, sure, those I could handle. But seers and oracles? I was way out of my depth.

"It was just flashes. But I think you should stay away from the caves up in the Canyon. I think she's going to try to get you up there. And if she does, it's not going to be good."

"We should tell Elle."

Amber shook her head. "She doesn't believe me, not really. I mean, she believes I had the dreams, but she's a cop first and a lawyer second and neither of those professions are big on the visions or clairvoyance or whatever it is."

"So you want to do something behind her back?"

"Not really. Just...without telling her."

"Same thing, Am," I snapped.

"Fine, whatever!" She threw up her hands and started to walk away.

"Amber, Amber...I'm sorry." I got up and put my hands on her arms from behind, turning her around. For a moment it was like looking in a mirror. "I think I'm just so used to saying no when you say yes...I'll try to work on that, okay?"

I could see her eyes tear up for a moment. "Okay." She hugged me for real for the first time in a long time, and I hugged her back, and for a little while I wondered why I was ever mad at her.

"So what are we going to do?" I finally asked as we broke our slightly awkward embrace.

Amber grinned, showing a bit of that cruel streak I knew so well. "I think we need to even the odds."

I wept as my gorgeous tresses hit the floor. No, really. I mean it. You think Bambi cried when his mother died? That was nothing! It had taken me three years to grow my hair out and get the color right. And to add insult to injury, it was my sister who did the cutting. Oh, didn't I tell you? Amber had been a beautician before she got her job with the city manager's office. Unlike other hair stylists, she could never cut her own hair. She could do other people. But whenever she took the scissors to her own hair, it turned out looking like a hack job performed by a weed-eater.

With my hair? I had to admit, she had always been good at it. So, when she got through with my new bob, once again we looked exactly alike.

It was cute. But it wasn't me. I sighed.

"Don't worry Ashlee," Will said. "It's just hair. It will grow back."

"I wish you'd stop acting like it's the end of the world," Amber said. "Better a few strands of hair than getting your head chopped off by a psycho killer."

"Well, gee. When you put it that way."

The key was to make sure that most people, Jeanetta Macdonald and Sean Gottlieb particularly, weren't able to easily tell who was who when it came to Amber and me. We would make sure to never be alone and trade off, swapping cars and outfits and significant others.

I laughed ironically as I looked forward to dolling up in Amber's designer outfits. For once Amber couldn't complain that she was worried I would ruin her clothes. All I had to do was give her some of her own medicine. "Better a few scrapes on the Dior and the Blahniks than getting my head chopped off," I would say.

That was something to look forward to.

–21–

After a couple of weeks of the Amber and Ashlee switcheroo revue, with nothing to show for it but a bunch of pictures of us doing the doublemint twins, no movement on the case and no new threats, we stopped worrying about who was wearing what and where and we just tried to live our lives the best we could.

The hole in the family where Spanky used to be remained constantly in our minds – less in mine and Will's I have to admit, as he wasn't our dog. Amber seemed to take my word for it that the heart hadn't been his, and she hadn't had any bloody visions of his death – or any visions for that matter – so she managed to get by.

Elle was hit the hardest. Cops, or former cops anyway, don't like to be stymied and helpless. They want to do something, solve something, bring the bad guy to justice.

Suffice to say, it was an uneasy two weeks.

My bullet wound was nearly healed, although Will found some sadistic pleasure in tickling the sensitive skin around the area in the few times when we were able to forget about the threat to my life. I snapped at him, he growled good-naturedly at me, and I kept wondering when I would screw things up again.

I thought about going all the way with him, I really did. I know, some of you girls are just screaming at me right now, "Get it done already," but that's an irrevocable step I just didn't want to take right then. Not that my body didn't agree with you. Besides, Mother had warned me that lycanthropy could make hormonal birth control fail, and other methods were too iffy. A girl's gotta think about these things, you know, and I wasn't ready for a baby or a litter of puppies or whatever might come forth.

As long as I held a furry secret, I didn't know how I was going to make it work.

But as I said, we did the best we could, and Will didn't seem like he was going anywhere. What did I do to deserve him? He kept telling me that love wasn't about deserving things. That all of us deserve love, but none of us can earn it, which made no sense to me at the time, but I know it's true now.

My editor had finally called with a new contract for *Spa Review* magazine and a promise never to let the "boys" try to do a guest column again when their patently sexist version of my work was met with extreme disapproval by my female fans. Guys just have no idea what a woman wants in a spa, but us girls know that it's not about how hot the steam bath is or how long the lap pool is. It's about the service and the pampering.

Never send a man to do a woman's job, I smirked internally. Serves them right. And it gave me leverage to take a much-needed vacation until the holidays were over, though I made a mental note to keep some kind of general column in reserve for situations like this. Well, not exactly like this, but you know what I mean — anything unexpected. I tried to draft something but my heart just wasn't in it.

A dark shadow hovered over Knightsbridge and the Canyon that Halloween. We all spent it out at the movies, sick of staying home. Our parents had made this a Scott family tradition, as Mother hadn't approved of all the death and darkness underlying the campy celebrations, and Dad just didn't like all the kids ringing the doorbell. Talk about your total irony, huh? If I can get Mom to stay still for long enough, I think I'll bring that up to her sometime and see what she has to say.

22

At the end of another frustrating day I opened up the newspaper. Yes, Knightsbridge still had one in real print, delivered by real paperboys on real bicycles, in the afternoon. I was taking my life in my hands being the first to see it, because Elle liked to sit down to dinner and be the first, but I figured I could roll it up again and put the rubber band around it with no one the wiser.

I wish I hadn't.

The *Gazette* offered up a one-two punch with an article about Jeanetta McDonald's Animal Rights Commission and their ties to the local animal shelter. Below the byline was a picture of a miniature Schnauzer and although I tried to keep it from my sister, the sixth sense she had didn't let me get that far before she questioned me about what I was hiding behind my back.

Reluctantly, I showed her. "It's not Spanky," I said. "It just looks like him. Will and I already went over to look."

"They're rubbing it in our faces, Ash! What the hell are we going to do?" She looked at me with puffy accusing eyes.

"Something I should have done long ago," I told her, and grabbed the keys to the pickup I'd borrowed. Will hadn't shown up from work yet, so I didn't have to fend him off. I wasn't going to drag him up for a supernatural rendezvous; at least, not yet.

I headed up the Canyon as night fell and a sliver of the new moon showed above. Fortunately I didn't have to worry about being dragged into a change. Lovers' Leap looked just like I left it ten years ago.

Shane Macdonald was still waiting.

"Hello Ash." His ghostly form took solidity as he leaned against the rock, crossing his arms.

"Hey Shane. Been waiting long?" I asked, and then grimaced. What was I thinking? I still wasn't used to this "I see dead people" thing and though I saw ghosts from time to time, I never investigated, never talked to them.

Until now.

Shane laughed sadly. "Seven years too long. Or is it eight? I'm kinda losing track."

"It's been ten. You're my second, you know," I told him.

"Second what?"

"Second real ghost I've talked to. But the other one is Mom, so I guess you're my first non-family haunting."

"How did you know I would be here?" he asked.

"I...I just knew. I've always known you were waiting, not at peace," I said. "If it's any consolation, I'm really sorry I chickened out of coming up here before. Oh, and that I killed you."

"Oh that...no biggie," he said. "So, Ash. Now that you're here, we really need to talk."

"I know why I need to talk to you, Shane. To, pardon the pun, lay some ghosts to rest. Why do you need to talk to me?"

"Same reason, except the ghost is me."

"Same reason?"

"Yeah. You need to forgive yourself, Ashlee."

"I know that!" I pounded the heels of my hands lightly against my head. "In my brain I know that, but in my heart...a hell of a lot easier said than done."

"At least you're facing up to the problem now, instead of running away."

"Yeah. I am, amen't I?"

"Amen't isn't a word, Ash," Shane said with a flash of that smile.

"It is now. I write for a living, so I should know."

"You run away for a living, Ash. You write for a paycheck."

"Yee-ouch. And how do you know all these things? Have you been haunting me?"

Shane smiled. "Now and again. When you do something near enough to here. The farther away, the harder it is to go there."

"That makes sense. Maybe I should become a ghost writer. Interview the spirits."

"Funny. That's what I always liked about you, you know. Your sense of humor. Too bad your sister is losing hers."

I sighed and ran my fingers through my irritatingly short hair. "It's not her fault. Like Mom said, she feels responsible for everything, and she hasn't run. I ran, and now that I've come back, I kinda know what that's like. Feeling responsible, I mean."

"Like for my death. But you weren't responsible. It was your first change. How could you know?" Shane put his ghostly arms around me and I could almost feel them.

"If not me, then who?"

"Nobody, maybe. Sometimes in life shit just happens."

I grunted. "Tell that to your sister."

"I've tried. She won't let it go. Jeanetta hates me, she hates you and she hates herself. In fact, she hates everything around her. I can't even get near her anymore, there's so much black energy coming off her. I don't know what she's gotten herself into but it's not good."

I turned around and Shane's arms blew away into wispy mist before reforming where they were supposed to.

"What about Spanky?" I asked.

"Who?"

"Elle and Amber's dog."

"Oh. I have no idea."

"Dammit!" I rubbed my arms as the wind started to pick up across the plateau. "Can you find out?"

Shaking his head, he said, "Not really."

"Why not?" I snapped, then realized how selfish that sounded. "I mean, I would really appreciate it if you could."

"Because I'm at peace now, Ash. I'm leaving tonight."

"What? You can't be! What about me forgiving myself and all that?"

"You're on your way, Ash, and the other side is calling me. I have to face up to my own ghosts and their judgment now."

My mind whirled, and I wanted to ask him a thousand questions about everything ghosts knew – the afterlife, and souls, and God and stuff like that – but it was too late. Shane had already started to fade. His fingertips brushed my cheek, and this time I did feel them as tears flowed down my face.

"Goodbye, Shane. Forgive me."

"I did. I do," were the last words I heard from him.

Now there's irony for you.

23

"Still no dreams or visions, huh?" I asked Amber the first morning of the Homecoming Week festivities. The Knightsbridge high schools always held theirs later than anyone else, right after Halloween. I'm not sure why. Maybe it was because being in the western foothills of the Sierra extended our autumn weather and people liked to have something between the end of October and Thanksgiving.

"I can't manufacture them, Ashlee. They come when I don't want them, they don't when I do." She changed the subject. "So, I guess you're playing in the game tonight."

I laced up my high-tops, and the smell of leather hit me. I inhaled and relaxed. I was actually looking forward to getting rid of some of my feeling of helplessness, anxiety and aggravation on the basketball court at the alumni games that night.

"Yeah," I replied. "I figured as long as I'm here, it's a good enough reason to slam some backboards."

"Yes, well, don't be alone, and don't take any drinks from strange water bottles."

I looked at her, alarmed. "Will and the team will be with me the whole time. But do I really need to worry about getting roofy'd?"

"Just…be cautious." She pulled me into her arms.

"Yeah, well. You too." I hugged her back then stepped out of Elle's way as she poked me in the side.

"Besides, I'll be there and packing," Elle said.

"Why doesn't that make me feel better?" I teased. But I really did. Feel better, I mean. In a big place like that, surrounded by lots of people.

What could happen?

Shit, I *so* did not think that, did I?

The women's varsity versus alumni game was like a Powder Puff match on steroids. I'd forgotten how good it felt to work as a team and my former classmates seemed to take it all in stride. I still had my jump shot, and my hang time was legendary. But what these girls didn't know was that I had a lupine ace up my sleeve…I could dunk, at least on a regulation high school basket. Like I said, my monthly wolf run seemed to put my body into top physical condition.

Lucky me.

It was late in the fourth quarter when the scent came to my nostrils. I stood at the free throw line after sinking the first of two when I smelled him. Smelled Spanky. At least I thought it was Spanky. But there was a stale aspect to the spoor, as if the vitality of the dog was layered in an olfactory residue of other canines, some of them dead. My lip turned up at the thought of the violation of my pack.

Yeah, somehow, with the scent came the reminder that Spanky was just that. A pack mate.

I nailed the second free throw. As soon after as I could, I ferreted out the location of the Spanky smell.

Sean Gottlieb was wearing the uniform of the Animal Rescue Clinic and stood on the sidelines behind the other basket, holding a covered pet carrier. That was where it came from.

We took up defensive positions around the key and I waited to make my move. Cassandra Jenkins, wiry hotshot and point guard, took a dribble past me when I snatched the ball right out of her hands. Before I could even think, I had loped down the court and, after hitting my layup, I sent my body flying into Sean Gottlieb, knocking the carrier to the floor.

On the ground, I rolled over to look into the crate. Inside I could see a frightened miniature Schnauzer.

It wasn't Spanky.

Sean paled as I looked into his eyes.

"Ashlee, isn't it?" He smirked nervously. "Just couldn't pass up a good game of B-Ball, could you?" It sounded like a line he had memorized.

I snarled and left him standing there. The bastard was taunting me, but his heart wasn't in it, so I knew who had put him up to it.

Amber looked over from the sidelines. She and some of the other alumni cheerleaders had squeezed back into their old outfits and were doing a creditable job of rallying our fans. I shook my head and shrugged.

Time to finish this basketball game, and then we needed to finish the other game that someone was playing. Because I had smelled Spanky on Sean, even though our dog hadn't been in the carrier. His scent had been fresher than the three weeks it had been since he'd gone missing, so the little weasel had to know where he was, had to have been in contact with him at some point.

I hate to gloat, but we toasted those kids. I knew when I was in high school that alumni games were about celebrating the ones who'd gone before. Why not let us bask in being a big shot for one night, even if I'm only reliving the fading dreams of my childhood? Back then I'd thought about going and playing college ball, even maybe working my way to a women's pro league, before the Incident sidetracked me.

I even had a standing offer to assistant coach if I was willing to move back to town. It wouldn't have been hard. I had to admit, it made me feel pretty good to know I wasn't a total pariah as I collected quite a few pats on the back or the ass as I headed back to the locker room. I took a shower with the rest of the team and then hurried back out to the bleachers to watch Amber announcing the year's nominees for Homecoming Court.

Standing there on the sidelines with Will at my back, feeling guilty for feeling so good, I asked myself what kind of person I was and what did I really want? Lonely but glamorous travel all over the world, or coming home to deal with real life and, oh by the way, no more free spa trips and an expense account.

What a quandary.

Then my hackles started to rise.

Jeanetta Macdonald stood behind the platform, next to the stage, and I realized that she was waiting to make an announcement, as she wore that Animal Rescue Clinic uniform and carried a pet crate. If she hadn't come here for something official, she would have been dressed to the nines as she usually was.

I grabbed Will's arm and pointed.

Will turned to where I was looking and said, "Stick close to me," as he pulled me through the crowd.

Elle got there first. "And may I ask what you have there, Ms. Macdonald?" she was saying as we rounded the back of the bandstand where they were waiting.

"Well, since you know the Animal Rights Commission and the Animal Rescue Clinic has long been a supporter of the community, we thought we'd drum up some compassion for the animal shelter by showing one of our adoptees. Hopefully, we can find him a good home."

"Him, eh?"

"Oh, yes. He's just the cutest little thing. A couple of kids turned him in a few weeks ago and even though he was in pretty bad shape, we nursed him back to health and now he's better than before."

"May I?" Elle said. Amber was watching out of the corner of her eye and I shrugged my shoulders. I already knew it wasn't Spanky.

But Amber didn't know that and I could see her disappointment as Elle removed the animal. He looked like Spanky, but up close Amber could see he wasn't.

I looked into Jeanetta's eyes and saw a flash of victory there. Her pulse rate sped up and I gaped at her. She was actually getting off on this. I was so going to terminate that bitch.

"Let's go," I said to Will. "I don't think I can stomach this anymore." He walked me back to the locker room.

"I'll just get my things," I told him and I slipped inside to retrieve my gym gear from the locker, ignoring the "Cleaning in Progress" floor sign.

The place was a haze of moisture as I maneuvered around the wet patches yet to be mopped up by the janitor. The man shoved his mop here and there as his head bobbed and he hummed to himself beneath long hair and a ball cap, his shoulders hunched. My sense of smell got overwhelmed by perfumes, deodorants and cleaning fluid scents, or maybe I could have avoided what happened next.

My bag was right where I left it on top of the lockers and as I climbed up on a bench to retrieve it, I felt a sharp pain in my ass overlaid right on top of the still-healing scar. Instinctively stepping down, I slipped in soapy water and landed on my back.

I smelled blood and rolled over, reaching down to where the pain had bit me. My hand came away bloody and in my palm was a smashed tranquilizer dart.

Seriously? In the ass again?

Those were my last thoughts before darkness took me.

24

When I awoke, I found myself tied back to back with my sister in a hot, smoky cavern deep in the heart of Knightsbridge Canyon. I'd been here before in wolf form, as I'd explored every bit of the area around town between the Incident and leaving home. A certain set of stalactites that looked like a hanging line of banners made me sure.

My eyes watered and my pulse raced, fighting off the effects of whatever they'd shot me with. I knew my body was trying to drive the drug out of my system. Looking around I saw that Amber and I were flanked by a deep depression like a medieval fire pit, filled with red hot coals and rising heat waves. To the left I saw the climbing flames of a bonfire. Large ancestor rocks ringed it, touching the flames. I recognized them from research I had done on the Cherokees for a travel piece about casino resorts.

Wicker scaffolding arched above us, what I realized was the skeleton of a sweat lodge.

A sweat lodge in a cavern? Okay...

Sean Gottlieb tended the fire, half-naked with his shirt tied around his waist and a handkerchief across his face like a bandit. He had welts and scars crisscrossing his back and shoulders and I wondered what had made them, then winced as I speculated about his and Jeanetta's relationship.

I heard a bark to my right and saw Spanky pawing at the bars of a cage, looking worriedly at me.

"Spanky," I breathed. "Amber, it's Spanky!" I hissed.

Amber didn't answer. Must still be out from whatever they shot her with, I thought. I was a lupine, and in better physical shape than my sister, so naturally I would awaken first.

I felt the heat begin to rise as Sean shoveled some hot ancestor rocks into the depression near my feet. I stared up at him, but he didn't look at me until I spoke.

"Why are you doing this?" I croaked.

Spanky barked and Sean looked away, not saying anything. He went over to pour some water into a bowl and slid it into the cage.

Well, he seemed to like animals. That might be something I could work with.

"Could I get some water over here?" I coughed.

He didn't answer, but brought a water bottle to me and held my chin up as he poured some into my mouth.

"Thank you," I said. "Now give some to Amber."

"She's still out." He looked at me for a moment in apology, and then turned to walk away.

Before I could pursue that thought, Jeanetta Macdonald strode through the cave entrance. She wore a dark bustier and a pair of black chinos, with matching

Doc Martens laced up the ankles, and I had to admit, she looked kind of hot.

For a raving lunatic, that is.

At least Amber would approve of her taste in S&M fashion. Wouldn't want to be murdered by a tacky Vogue reject after all.

"Ah, you're awake. Good. It's just about time to start the ceremony."

"What the hell are you doing, Jeanetta?" I coughed and elbowed Amber in the back. I got a grunt in response, which made me think she was playing possum and buying time, hopefully thinking of a way out of this mess. Mother! I sent out a silent prayer, or plea, or mental message, whatever you do to call ghosts.

What I thought she could accomplish, I had no idea.

"You'll find out soon enough." Jeanetta smirked and turned toward me, taking a burgundy colored velvet bag from her belt and raising it up to the ceiling while she began to chant. The cloth in her hands was threaded with amber strands that caught the light and seemed to spangle symbols across the cavern walls.

Sean proceeded to pull dark cloth over the bamboo and the little light we had dimmed as he affixed blankets to the semicircular poles. Jeanetta approached with a wooden mixing bowl and pulled a hunting knife off her leg harness. "It's probably obvious that this is going to hurt," she said with glee, grinning triumphantly as she sliced a gash in my jeans and thigh, and then held the bowl beneath it.

I clenched my teeth, hissing against the pain as I tried to jerk away, but we were too securely held, not like in the movies where the villain always leaves the bonds too loose, or easy to reach and untie.

Amber wasn't so stoic. "You bitch!" she screamed when Jeanetta cut her.

"Language, Amber." I laughed sardonically.

"Bite me, Ashlee," she snarled. "You got us into this."

"Funny you should say that," I replied, but Jeanetta cut us off.

"Girls," Jeanetta chided us as she took her knife and sliced a few hairs from both our heads and added them to the bowl. She then went to the cage and had Sean pull Spanky out.

Shit.

"Keep her talking Ashlee," Amber muttered and I could feel her manipulating her wrists to try to get her hands free. Good luck with that. I had already tried, and I was stronger and more limber than my sister.

"Hold him still," Jeanetta ordered as Sean lifted the squirming dog. Spanky hated being held by anyone but our family.

"What are you doing?" I demanded as she raised her knife. "I thought you were an animal rights activist? Or was that all bullshit, like the rest of your life?"

Hey, it was all I could think of at the time.

"Oh, don't worry. I like dogs more than I like people." Then she turned to back to Sean, who was frowning at her. "Present company excluded, of course."

Spanky froze in Sean's grip. He seemed to know when danger was coming and he bared his teeth.

"Don't even think about it." She narrowed her eyes at him as Sean held Spanky's mouth shut while he snarled.

"If you hurt my dog..." Amber began, but then I smelled an acrid smell of hair burning, and heard a yelp of surprise and a curse as Spanky went flying out of Sean's arms to hit the ground running. I could hear his barking fading in the distance and I thanked the Lord that at least one of our pack had made it out unscathed.

On the other hand, you would think that he'd show a bit more loyalty.

"I didn't know you were such a witch, Jeanetta," Amber snarled. "A bitch, well, *that* I knew. But blood magic? Are you sure you know what you're doing?"

Interesting. What did Amber know about magic beyond reruns of Charmed and Once Upon a Time? I started to get the feeling she'd been holding out on me again.

"You don't think I came into this unprepared, do you?" Jeanetta mocked.

I looked at her blankly, and sensed Amber doing the same, if perhaps with slightly more comprehension.

"See, I know what you are," Jeanetta continued.

"Oh really." I matched her haughty tone. "And what do you think that is?" I coughed.

"*Yee Naaldlooshii...*" The words came out of her in a hiss, and a malevolent gleam sparked from her eyes. A shiver ran through me. Jeanetta poured more noxious herbs over the fire. "*Ánt'įįhnii!*" Her voice got louder and

I could I feel an ache behind my jaw. "*Adagqsh!*" Her voice took on the cadence of a song as she screamed the last words. "*Azhitee! Nee Yaaldlooshii!*"

"Ashlee!" Amber's voice rose into a different register and I could feel my own anxiety begin to rise with hers as I felt the pads of my fingers tear and claws burst out from my knuckles, straining the tension of the rope that bound us. Blood ran down my wrists and the smell made me woozy.

Holy Shit! I thought. She was doing it. Jeanetta Macdonald was making me shift.

Yee Naaldlooshii. Skinwalker. She'd called me a skinwalker. I'd run into the Navajo legend when I first started researching werewolf mythology back in high school. But I wasn't a skinwalker – I was something else, product of a different magic.

"I don't know how you managed that," Amber whispered. She couldn't see that the sharp things her hands touched were actually a part of me rather than rocks or knives. Who knows what she thought? But I could feel her sliding the hemp fibers across my claws causing them to part, bit by bit, as she sawed at our bonds.

"Me neither," I said.

"Werewolves, shifters, all the same thing," Jeanetta cackled. "I knew it all along!"

But she was wrong. The legend of the skinwalker said that a shapeshifter utilized rituals to assume the form of a beast. In doing so, she would shed her human skin to become the shape of the animal she wanted to change into. But it cost a blood sacrifice to do so. In order to return to human form, a skinwalker had to consume her own human pelt, eyeballs, scalp and all.

Besides being totally gross and nasty, I wasn't a skinwalker. Or a Navajo.

On the other hand, there had to be some kind of overlap, because whatever she had done had affected me.

"After you killed my brother I spent years researching the legends of your kind. In my travels, I found a tribal elder who was willing to share with me the secrets of your people."

"What, Scottish people?" What *my people*? I barely knew what I was.

"He said if I could force the shape of the wolf onto you while the moon was waning, and then burned your skin, you would be bound into your shifted form for the rest of your days."

"You're insane!" I laughed uproariously, which made Jeanetta furious.

"Ashlee," my twin said, "don't antagonize the psycho."

"We'll find out who's insane now, won't we?" Jeanetta said tightly. "Sean, cover them up and then go look for that damn dog. We need it." As she said this I realized that I could still hear Spanky barking from outside the cave. I guess the little furball hadn't run off after all.

Amber whimpered as the cloth concentrated the smoke around us. The heat began to become unbearable as Jeanetta chanted and threw blood and herbs into the fire, causing more choking fumes. My head began to swim and I could hear Amber retching.

"I think I'm going to be sick," she said and then she passed out, her body going slack against me. Jeanetta's annoying noises stopped and it sounded like she moved away, probably to prepare her next round of tortures. I could hear her chanting start up again, farther away.

"Hold on, Amb. I'll think of something." My claws were already out and I could feel my lupine side come out and take on that monochromatic perception where the olfactory senses filled in the visual details.

I wondered if I could continue this partial shift. I never could quite do it before and I ran the risk of hurting Amber badly if I had to go all the way, but if Jeanetta could force me into my wolf form, I couldn't guarantee that I could control it anyway. I didn't think I'd hurt my twin, but I hadn't ever been forced into the change before.

I centered myself and felt the ropes dig deeper into my flesh. My vision began to blur and I got a bad taste in my mouth as my canines began to lengthen.

"Amber, forgive me for getting you into this mess," I said softly as darkness covered us and the muffled sounds of Jeanetta's chant faded away into the background. The sound of pine sap popping and the crackling of the coals around us seemed to get louder in my brain.

Sweat poured down my face and I could feel it drenching my sister's back. She was unusually quiet, and I wondered if she'd passed out again. I kind of hoped she had, just in case...in case..."Amber?"

"I'm here." She coughed. "I've found if you take shallow breaths it's not that bad."

"I have a confession to make..."

"What, that you're a werewolf and spend your full moons running around the hills and munching on forest critters?" she said offhandedly. "Ooh, big secret."

"You knew?" I barked. The sound of betrayal echoed around me in the muffled silence.

"Of course I knew! Why do you think I worry about you all the time? And haven't you noticed that I always call you after a full moon to make sure you're okay? Seriously, Ashlee, you're not a very good liar. Remember, we have the same face and I can read you like a book. Besides: visions, *hellooo!*"

I was floored. All this time, she knew my secret and she never said a thing.

"So, when were you going to tell me that you knew?"

"It wasn't my place." When she said that I could hear echoes of my mom in her words.

"Do you see Mother too?" I asked, and before it was out of my mouth, I knew it was the wrong thing to say.

"What do you mean?"

Crap. I was *so* not good at this.

Finally I felt the rope fibers part and I stood. My mother's face hovered in the darkness and I could see her putting her finger to her lips.

"Nothing. Just visions, *hellooo*," I said with as much snark as I could muster. I tore the restraints off my ankles and proceeded to set Amber free. There wasn't much room to maneuver, but I slid to the ground and lifted the cloth tarp to look out into the cavern. I couldn't be sure that Jeanetta didn't have more tranquilizer darts ready and I wasn't about to waste this opportunity.

I couldn't see much of anything.

"Amber, I need your eyes."

"Sorry, I'm using them, thank you," Amber said as she joined me on the ground. Her voice quavered a little as she stared into my face. "Your eyes are different. Wolfy."

"Yeah, and that means I'm color-blind and can't see worth shit in this smoky mess. So, tell me what you see. Where's Sean? Where's Jeanetta?"

"She's right outside the cave entrance and, um…"

"What?" I asked.

"Well, she's naked…"

"Glad I can't see that."

"Actually…"

"Focus, Amber. No time to go admiring her killer bod."

"That's a bit too apropos. And she's holding some kind of pelt up to the sky."

The sound of chanting rose again and then came a *whoosh*.

I felt my whole body go rigid. "Uh oh," I said.

"What?" Amber whispered.

"What just happened?" I ground out, my tongue getting hung up on my teeth.

"She dropped the pelt into the fire."

I moaned and could feel my bones begin to turn and bend and crack.

"Ashlee!" Amber grabbed my face and looked into my eyes. She must not have liked what she saw there, because she scrabbled back away from me.

"What?" I coughed. My body…I hardly felt human anymore, and I probably wasn't mostly.

"My, what incredibly big teeth you have…"

Yeah, well, humor was one of our strengths. Laughing in the face of danger. That, and, making lemonade out of lemons. Someone should tell Jeanetta to be careful what she conjured, or she might get it.

Or it might get her.

I struggled with my clothes for a moment before I got free of them. With a roar, I leaped from the folds of the sweat lodge and slammed headlong into something. Stars danced in my optic nerves as I stumbled leftward, rubbing up against a barrier I couldn't see or smell.

Looking up, I saw Jeanetta continuing her ritual incantations, and I instinctively tried to rush her again, but I couldn't reach her. I felt as if a wall of glass stopped me, and made my sensitive nose burn as I pushed against it.

On the ground I could see an elaborate symbol drawn, some kind of wheel-shape, like a dream-catcher or magic circle. I tried to scratch at it with my paw but nothing I did could reach it.

Turning, I growled and whined, looking around for some trick or way through. Whatever it was, it kept me out, and suddenly I was wracked with another wave of pain, a convulsion that threatened to drive away my human mind, leaving only the animal. If that happened, Jeanetta would have the perfect revenge, destroying me with no real evidence of what had been done – nothing that would convict her in a court of law, anyway.

"Ashlee!" my sister screamed from inside, and I rushed back into the cave. Amber grabbed the bamboo center-post and brought the fabric down into the coals of the fire like the collapse of a teepee. Smoke poured out of the chamber as the material caught fire, and I leaped in to tug at the ropes still ringing one hand, leading her out into the open air. She collapsed, coughing and helpless.

Another spasm went through me and I screamed, a horrible gut-wrenching sound never meant to proceed from a canine throat. Spanky charged forward out of the darkness to nuzzle me in that way that dogs have, sensing another of its kind in pain. Or maybe he just knew I was family.

Rolling over to stare into his eyes, I tried to make the little Schnauzer to understand. I nudged him with my forehead, pushing him toward Jeanetta as she danced and gestured and spoke words of power. Crawling toward the crazy witch, I tried to tell Spanky what to do.

Somehow, he got it. Maybe it was a dog thing, or maybe that "Speak With Animals" spell I always liked when we used to play D&D really worked, but he turned and began scratching at the design. Formed in the dirt by colored chalk, it only took a few strokes of Spanky's forepaws before he made a gash in its perfection and I was able to press in close to help him. A few seconds more and we had an opening.

I leaped through, and moments later, Jeanetta lay in shock beneath my snarling muzzle.

At that moment, Will charged out of the darkness. Mom must have gotten through to him, or maybe he just decided to search Jeanetta's old stomping grounds and saw the fire. Or both.

Unfortunately he carried an axe, and he lifted it over his head in preparation for cleaving me in half.

I froze with shock, disbelieving that he would ever do such a thing to me, before realizing that all he saw was a big wolf attacking a human woman. A naked human woman. Ew.

"WILL!" Amber screamed as Spanky sank his teeth into Will's calf.

"*What the* —" Will cried as he slapped at Spanky with one hand, forgetting about splitting my skull. The Schnauzer dodged and barked, frantic.

I backed away and then slunk in a circle to where Amber was climbing to her feet, fairly certain Will wouldn't attack her to get through to me. "Will, leave the wolf alone. Jeanetta just tried to kill me and Ashlee."

"Where is Ashlee?" Will asked, looking around, still hefting the axe.

I held my pose and tried to will my sister to do what needed to be done. I guess some of it got through, or we simply thought alike, as she said, "Ashlee's fine. Just tie that bitch up and gag her." It warmed my heart to hear my sister call someone else the b-word.

Confused, Will put the axe down, bound Jeanetta's hands, gagged her, and then threw a blanket over her. Our nemesis didn't protest or resist, seemingly in shock.

"Honey?" Sean stumbled up behind us in the dark after giving up on catching the frantically dodging Spanky. Smoke continued to pour from the cavern as a wind drew it from the chamber. I leaped on him, driving him to the ground, and then Will tied him up too as I stayed out of the way. He kept looking at me, trying to figure it all out, but it was just too bizarre, I was sure. I mean really, if it was you, would you deduce some wolf was your girlfriend without a lot of persuading or proof?

Nearby, Spanky barked joyously around the ghost of my dead mother. She made a shushing motion and he calmed down and sat, staring up at her.

"What's he looking at?" Amber asked me as she tried to brush her clothing clean, a hopeless exercise.

I gave a noncommittal yip as Mother put her finger to her lips. Why I couldn't just tell Amber, I had no idea. Some kind of otherworldly rule, or something, I guessed.

"Fine, be that way," my sister said, as if she understood. Which she probably did. "So much for an honest relationship."

Ouch. That stung, but I wasn't much on defying Mom when she was alive and I sure wasn't going to when she was dead. Then I remembered Shane, and wondered if this all would mean that she would find peace and cross over.

Maybe that was why she didn't want me to tell Amber. Maybe resolving all that would send her away, and I abruptly knew that I did not want that to happen, not at all. I'd rather have some of Mother here than all of her gone.

Maybe that was part of what family is about.

"Who are you talking to, Amber?" Will asked, still completely befuddled. He'd been all ready to rescue me and instead found most of the rescuing all done, and me apparently not around to be saved. That's got to let a guy down for sure.

Suddenly, Spanky tore away and scurried down the hillside toward the trailhead parking lot below. I could see lights from a car, and after baring my teeth at our prisoners one more time, I sat down and leaned into Amber, huddling together for warmth in the chill November breeze. She put her arm around me like I was a dog or a child, and I rolled my shoulder and head into her lap while she ran her hand through my fur. Weird, I know, but it felt right. When in lupine, do as the lupines do, I guess.

"Well, what do you know?" Elle climbed up to the trail to the cavern, her hand on the .357 she carried at her hip. "Looks like the gang's all here," she said as she strode over to look down at the two bound miscreants. She didn't seem at all discomfited by the sight of a hundred-pound wolf laying in her lover's lap.

Lover's lap, Lover's Leap, whatever.

Spanky cavorted around her feet until she told him to calm down, at which point he went over to sit next to the very subdued Sean, as if guarding him. Or maybe he was making some kind of statement about his human captor, that he was just as much a dog as any domestic canine. Jeanetta had certainly treated him like one, I found out later.

My older brother Adam trailed behind Elle, a sword from his collection slung incongruously over his back. "Hey there, girl." He winked at me and ruffled the fur on my head. What, did everyone know what I was, and no one bothered to let me know they knew? I felt like I was left out of my own secret.

I wondered if Dad knew. We kids had kept a lot of secrets from him growing up, or thought we did, but I had to assume one of my siblings or Mom had informed him. In his phlegmatic way, he'd probably just shrugged when he'd gotten the news and said something like, "Oh. That's interesting."

Then I wondered what other things I didn't know that the others were keeping from me. I mean, if I had this werewolf thing going on, and Amber had her visions, and Mom was a ghost, and here my brother was carrying a very real and very sharp sword, ready to smite our enemies…it hardly bore thinking about. Really made my eyes water with that cringey feeling I get when I've been stupid or oblivious for quite a while, and suddenly realize it.

I heard Elle talking to Chief Hernandez on her cell, directing a unit up the canyon to the trailhead. "Yeah. The old Indian cave. Will Stenfield saw the fire up here and called me."

Moments later we saw flashing lights wending their way up the road's switchbacks toward us.

Elle called, "Hey Will. Why don't you meet the Chief down at the trailhead. And look for Ashlee while you're at it. She'd bound to be around here somewhere."

Will obeyed like the beta he was.

As I didn't have human speech just then, Amber filled Elle and Adam in on what our kidnappers had done. They walked over to Jeanetta and Sean, who lay on the ground in their bonds, defeated.

Elle took the woman's gag off. "You've been a very bad girl, Macdonald. You too, Gottlieb."

"She made me do it," Sean said.

"Shut up, Sean," Jeanetta said without heat.

"No, Mi-...no, *Jeanetta*." He spat her name like a curse. "You can't make me do things anymore."

"Oh, Sean," she sighed. "I never made you do anything you didn't already want to."

I thought as I watched, isn't that how life's devils always do it?

The bound woman turned her smarmy smile up toward Elle. "Actually, for the record, I didn't do anything at all. In fact, I tried to rescue these two from this nut here." She jerked her head at Sean.

"Save it," Adam said. "If Sean testifies – and I bet the city attorney here will offer some kind of deal – there will be multiple witnesses telling all about your crimes, not to mention the physical evidence, such as misused tranquilizer darts from the Animal Clinic's inventory."

"But if it goes to trial, I'll tell everyone what *she* is." Jeanetta pointed her chin at me, and I pulled my lips back from my teeth.

"Right," Adam laughed in that superior way he had that I had always hated. Right now, though, I could have kissed him. Or at least licked his face, whatever. He continued, "They'll just cart you off to the nuthouse. Unless that's your strategy? Insanity plea?"

Jeanetta sagged and lowered her eyes. "Just get it over with," she muttered.

When we saw the cops climbing the trail, Will in tow, Amber suddenly shook me. "You gotta go," she whispered, and I realized she was right. "I'll tell them you got away first and must be out there somewhere. That's not even a lie," she grinned.

I chuffed once, nuzzled her neck, and then ran up the hillside. Spanky barked, and I could see my mother waving to me from her position floating above the whole scene like some Christmas angel.

"I guess there really are wolves in Knightsbridge Canyon after all," I heard Adam say as I loped off into the darkness.

25

"Hey," I said to Will as he rolled the rototiller back to his work trailer and up the ramp.

"Hey," he replied as he strapped it into place. Not looking at me. Thoughtful. Pensive. Piccadilly Park was nearly empty on a school day, at least in this corner of the sprawling green space, and the overcast day made everything turn gray, muting the sounds of town around us.

"Lunch?" I asked. I'd jogged over from Amber's where I'd stayed last night, after slinking back in wolf form.

"Sure. Taco truck?" Will took off his battered straw cowboy hat, wiped his head and neck with his bandana, then put the hat back on.

"Sounds good." I climbed into his Chevy, and then buckled in. Didn't look at Will. He didn't look at me. A wall seemed to stand between us, some kind of barrier that could only be torn down by talking about things neither of us seemed to want to talk about.

A few blocks away Will pulled the truck and trailer into a parking lot and looped it around in an open space at the back, away from the people crowding up close to the taco truck at one end. Several of these plied the lunch crowd in town, providing cheap Mexican food to Hispanics and gringos alike. For five bucks you could get a kickass lunch better than most of the restaurants around. The smell of grilled beef, peppers and onions drifting downwind got my mouth watering.

I expected us to sit down at one of the picnic tables there under the awnings after we got our order, but Will took the bag of food and walked back to the truck. Taking down the tailgate, he hopped up on it and patted the spot next to him.

I sat. Woof.

After we'd demolished half a monster burrito each, he turned to me with that look a guy gets when he has to put his hand into the fire, like he's getting ready for pain. "So…"

"So last night," I interrupted. "What can I say? Jeanetta still blamed me for Shane's death, and wanted to take revenge."

"But what was all that Indian stuff?"

"She was just crazy, that's all."

"Ash, she tried to burn you guys alive!"

I shook my head and almost explained to him that the fire was just to provide extra power for the magic, as well as to try to force me into wolf form, but I just couldn't. Not yet. "She's nuts. Look at all the stuff Sean was babbling about – whips and S&M and the occult. Who knows what she believes?"

Will stared at me over the remaining half of his burrito, then wrapped the foil around it and put it down. "You're not telling me everything, Ashlee."

"Nope," I said, surprised at myself for being so blunt. Maybe it was just that kind of day.

"Why not?"

"I tried to tell you that you didn't know me, Will, but you didn't listen. You just pushed what I said aside, as if I was telling you that out of fear or something, like I didn't know what I was talking about and you know best. Guys do that, you know."

"Do what?" I could see him getting annoyed with me lumping him in with other "guys," but I couldn't help it.

"They want what they want so they don't listen. They discount girls' – women's – insights, especially about themselves. Think they know best."

"Maybe it's because the women won't just talk plain to them. Won't tell them what the hell is going on, in words us dumb guys can understand."

My eyes narrowed as I took another bite of burrito, feeling the burn of fresh grilled jalapenos that was nothing like those pickled ones most people are used to. I bought some time to think by pulling out a little clear plastic container of chopped cilantro to add to the juicy goodness in my hands, making a ritual of it.

"How bad do you have to know?" I asked.

"What does that mean?"

"I'm serious. How much would you sacrifice to find out everything, all at once, right now?" See, I was getting sick of the dance, too, and I was tired and still hurting from everything that happened yesterday. I guess what I mean is, I was about ready to say to hell with it and just dump it all on him and damn the consequences. Double or nothing, roll the dice.

"I…I'd do anything for you, Ash."

"But what if the price was me? What if by learning everything you lost me?"

"That's impossible."

"Here we go again." I chucked the rest of the burrito in the bag, suddenly not hungry anymore. "You love me but you dismiss me and what I say. That's not love." I hopped off the tailgate and started walking away.

"Ash! Ash, I'm sorry. I'll stop asking. Really. I love you, and I don't care about your secrets."

I stopped. Turned. "Yes, you do."

"Okay, I do, but not as much as I care about you. I'll wait for you to explain, okay? You're the most important thing in my life, and if that's the price…okay."

"Okay?"

"Whatever it takes."

He looked so forlorn there, twisting his straw field hat in his hands like some kid in a Dickens novel, that my resolve crumbled. "Okay," I said, and came back to him. Once I had returned and we were standing there, I just had to kiss him, right? Kiss him stupid, as Amber used to say, though this time I got kinda stupid too.

We only broke up the clinch when a bunch of boys on BMX bikes started on the wolf-whistles. I smiled in embarrassment while Will winged a dirt clot at the road by their tires, and they took off, hooting.

"Want to take the afternoon off?" I asked with a sidelong grin.

"I think I can arrange that, seeing as I am the boss...just gimme a minute to call Rodrigo."

On the way back to Will's house, my house, I took my shoes off and stuck my feet out the window, rolling off my newly skewered butt cheek and laying across the bench seat to put my head in his lap. He stroked my hair and all was right with the world again, at least for today.

—Epilogue—

It didn't surprise me when Sean confessed to sending me the emails, which actually helped him as they seemed to be warnings, if rather confused ones. In fact, after the shrinks got done with him they convinced the DA to let him plead to a year of inpatient treatment and a suspended sentence, as long as we, the injured parties, agreed.

Amber took some convincing but I knew Sean was under Jeanetta's spell, not innocent but almost as much a victim as we were. That enchantment may have been metaphorical or may have been literal but no matter what, it was true and Amber agreed, and if Amber agreed, eventually Elle would too, I knew.

Jeanetta got eight to ten in the state women's prison down at Chowchilla – I know, funny name, sounds like they should make cheap fur coats there, but look it up – and so for at least that long I don't have to worry about her. The next time I went up to Lover's Leap and waited, Shane didn't appear. I even took Spanky with me, but he didn't seem to see any ghosts.

Mom still haunts me but not Amber as far as I know, but won't tell me why. I want to figure out what she needs to be at peace, but then again, a ghost mom is better than no mom at all. Dad and Adam seem to be cool with me staying with Will, which surprises me a bit, at least in Dad's case. He always was old-fashioned when it came to premarital sex. It would probably surprise him to find out Will and I did it – badly, I have to admit – when we were in high school, and surprise him even more to find out how long we waited to do it again.

But yeah, we're doing it now.

Carefully, with precautions.

Will says he loves me, and I said I love him at least once, but I'm still not at all sure we're speaking the same language. We still haven't talked any more about that night, and what he saw. I think he's afraid to push, so we keep putting off that conversation, but it will come eventually.

Amber says I'm overthinking things, as usual.

So is this happily ever after?

I'm not at all sure. I still have a career, and I'm not going to drag Will around all over the world. He'd just get in the way. Oh, come on, it's true. No matter how much the guy says he'd give up everything, it just doesn't work that way. Guys need their stuff, and their buddies, and more importantly they need something to do, to achieve. Will wouldn't be achieving anything as my take-along boy-toy.

For now, until my editor comes up with an assignment, I guess it's just ever after, happily enough.

THE END of MOONRISE.

Sign up for David VanDyke's Exclusive Insiders Group at:
www.davidvandykeauthor.com